CAT GOT HER TONGUE . . .

The creature Skyla had become turned to Illmuri, who was crouching on the ground with his staff clenched in his hands. She tried to speak, but all that came from her throat was a crooning cat voice, a questioning, humming sound.

"Skyla?" he whispered hoarsely, gazing into her unblinking golden lynx eyes with apprehension and disbelief.

She sniffed him briefly, as if making certain he was all right, then turned to watch intently as another feline figure emerged onto the path. It was a large lynx, as dark as night. It sat down and took a few licks at the blood smearing its silvery breast, then looked at Skyla, uttering a coaxing call.

"Skyla! No!" Illmuri gasped, struggling to his feet. But Skyla bounded away lightly, and the dark and silver-gray figures vanished . . .

By Elizabeth H. Boyer
Published by Ballantine Books:

THE SWORD AND THE SATCHEL

THE ELVES AND THE OTTERSKIN

THE THRALL AND THE DRAGON'S HEART

THE WIZARD AND THE WARLORD

The Wizard's War
THE TROLL'S GRINDSTONE
THE CURSE OF SLAGFID
THE DRAGON'S CARBUNCLE
THE LORD OF CHAOS

THE CLAN OF THE WARLORD
THE BLACK LYNX

THE
BLACK
LYNX

Elizabeth H. Boyer

A Del Rey Book
BALLANTINE BOOKS • NEW YORK

A Del Rey Book
Published by Ballantine Books

Library of Congress Catalog Card Number: 93-90520

ISBN 0-345-37593-9

Manufactured in the United States of America

First Edition: December 1993

PROLOGUE

ILLMURI'S HORSE HAD been limping for the past two days. The tough little creature scarcely slowed her determined pace and made no complaint except to heave a weary sigh each time he halted to look back and let her catch her wind. The mountainous terrain at the top of the world was scaly and treacherous, with sliding rock and ice-filled chasms waiting to swallow the lone traveler. Nothing could grow in the shrieking winds and shifting masses of ice except tufts of moss in sheltered clefts, which the little horse devoured and managed to stay alive upon. Looking at her, Illmuri knew he would be walking soon unless their torturous track descended soon into the green valleys lying below under wreaths of mist.

Perhaps it would be better if he let both their skeletons remain on the spine of the Jarnskard. Six ravens had been following him hopefully for the last three days, perhaps detecting the slight but betraying nod of the pony's head at each painful step. Better to be frozen by the wind and picked to pieces by foxes and crows than to face the wizards of Galdur to tell them that he had failed so utterly.

As his luck would have it, no crevice swallowed him up, and by the end of the day the faintly marked trail was winding steadily downward. The mare stopped frequently to eat, unable to resist the wiry tufts of real grass appearing between the stones. Illmuri got off and let her eat, warming his fingers under her long white mane. Now that it appeared that he was going to survive long enough to reach the wizard stronghold of Galdurshol, he was in no great hurry to confess his stupidity.

Yet somehow nightfall found him and his weary little horse standing at the gates of the hall, being examined by a suspicious and inquisitive porter.

1

"It's Illmuri, and you know me as well as I know you, Hegna, so let me in before I have you boiled for the pigs' dinner," Illmuri said in a fit of exhausted temper. "You should remember. I was the lad who glued feathers all over your cloak so you looked like a great chicken when you put it on. Now open up this wretched door. I need a bath, I'm starving, and I'm almost falling down with weariness, but I must speak to Eyjarr immediately, so send a boy to see if he's gone off somewhere in his fylgja form or gone into a weeklong trance. If he has, I've got to have him back."

"Ah. I suppose it has gone badly for you at Rangfara." Hegna's voice lost its gruff edge, and he commenced shoving back the bars and bolts.

"It couldn't go any worse," Illmuri snapped. "If I'm fortunate, I might be given a job like yours in Galdurshol after the mess I've made. A great many good people are dead, and I could do nothing to help them."

"At least you've returned," said Hegna, clucking his tongue. "Most of the master's other apprentices haven't had the fortune to be quite as long-lived as you."

Illmuri put his reins into the hands of a hostler. "Take care of her and examine her left forefoot. I hope it's only a stone bruise."

The hostler ran his hand down her shoulder to her hoof, lifting it with a grunt. "Aye, we'll see to her. The Jarnskard is no match for a native pony. You were wise to choose her instead of those great, long-legged snorting creatures the Skiplings have been bringing across. Aye, you've pushed her, and her feet are worn thin, but she'll be fine with some rest and fodder."

Illmuri silently thanked the tough little horse that had carried him so far so willingly. She blew a soft warm breath in his face, then the hostler led her away.

Drawing a deep breath, Illmuri turned toward the tangle of roofs and halls and turrets that was the main hall of Galdur. There was no plan to the architecture of Galdur; it grew mysteriously like a crowded clump of odoriferous toadstools quarreling over the possession of a rotted log. Lanes ran through it, often like tunnels, where someone had decided to roof over the lane and build on top of that. Better a small safe place within the walls of Galdurshol than to have all the room in Galdur and fight continuously with the growing chaos outside.

In the center reposed the wizards' school, an ancient structure that predated everything else in Galdurshol except the walls themselves, fifty feet thick and half again as high. Where modern buildings were cobbled together with sticks, stones, bones, mud, and whatever else the industrious builder could lay to hand, the wizards' hall and the wall were composed of enormous blocks of stone, some almost the size of a good-sized hut. No one living was able to say how the ancients had quarried and moved and positioned such mighty blocks of stone. Nor even was the stone like any stone around about Galdurshol, so it had been brought from afar. From the east, claimed those who thought they were learned, and indeed, a long straight road pointed east from Galdurshol, although no one traveled very far upon it. Nothing lay east except warring clans of Dokkalfar, rumors of winged dragons breathing poisonous vapors, and any quantity of trolls and other evil things that routinely dined upon human flesh.

Illmuri rested his forehead a moment upon the stout, scarred door of the school. Then he let the heavy knocking knob fall on the planks.

The doorkeeper was a tall dry stick of a man. The students of Illmuri's age had claimed that old Stinga-stafur had been around when the walls were built, and they had played all manner of vile tricks on him. He had suffered their pranks patiently through how many generations of pupils Illmuri could not guess.

"Stafur, how good to see you again," Illmuri said as the ancient one stood staring at him, one threadlike hand poised in midair.

"Illmuri! My little laddie! You've returned!" he whispered, with a tear suddenly glistening on his ruddy cheek. "All the others are gone, some never to draw breath again. And you— you're here again, truly in the flesh and not just a dream!"

"I am truly alive, Stafur, but not by much," Illmuri said with a sigh.

Stafur plucked at Illmuri's tattered clothing, touched his beard and hair, and anxiously felt his wrist to make certain he was truly of warm flesh and blood and not a walking draug. Satisfied, he crooked one long bony finger and said, "Come. Eyjarr is desperate to see you."

Stafur ushered Illmuri into the wizard's inner hall, where a fire always burned in the old black hearth and all the impedimenta of wizardry were shoved into shelves or were hung from the beams or leaked out of boxes and bottles and barrels.

The long table where the rows of eager young pupils sat to hear the Meistari was still there, and the long backless bench where Illmuri had sat for all of his childhood, in the aromatic darkness of this room, poking at bits of dead things, while the farming lads played outdoors in the sunshine with the living plants and animals and soft breath of the wind.

At the head of the table reposed a tall blackened seat, cheerfully ornamented with carved skulls and bones—designed to remind the young students, Eyjarr had told them merrily, that they didn't have all the time in the world and that everyone was somewhat mortal, so they'd best be about what they were doing before it was too late.

Wearily Illmuri approached the tall black seat where sat the birdlike form of Eyjarr, concentrating upon a dingy page from a book edged with mildew and rot. The old man held up one warning hand for silence, with his finger tracing lightly down the page to the bottom before he would raise his head and speak. His eyes were bright, and his wizened face crinkled into an amazing grin.

"Illmuri. My student. You've returned," he said. "Sit down and shake the journey dust off you. Stafur, how about something to refresh our weary traveler."

Illmuri rested his elbows upon the table, letting his hands cover his face.

"Master, I have failed."

Eyjarr's sunny countenance puckered and clouded. He closed the book softly, first marking the place with a scrap of vellum that was covered with notes.

"How have you failed, my son?"

"They are all dead." The words were so heavy that Illmuri could scarcely force them from his throat. "Jafnar, the wild boys, Otkell and Hakarl, Mistislaus. Skyla is left alone to battle with Alvara or to submit to her spellbinding. Ofarir and Kraftugur are running rampant, and I fear Skyla will not survive long in her quest for vengeance against the Krypplingur—one lynx against the entire clan of those hunchbacked savages. I can do nothing further. It is hopeless."

"Well. And is that sufficient reason to come home?"

"I rather thought so, once the last of the Skyldings was destroyed. I might have dealt with any setback except that one. Now there is no way to find the treasure of the Skyldings and restore a Skylding to the chieftaincy of Rangfara. It can never happen now."

"I fear," Eyjarr said, tenting his fingertips and frowning, "that you've become somewhat of a whiner, Illmuri. I'll have to put a note of that in your record."

"Do as you wish; it won't change anything."

"I must say I'm disappointed in you."

"I knew you would be. But all the odds were stacked against me. I had no chance. I got nowhere."

Stafur returned with a pot of dark and potent ale, a loaf of fresh bread, and a slab of cheese. Illmuri thought he had never seen anything so welcome. He wolfed it down as considerately as he could and felt much better with the ale warming his insides. Eyjarr sat in silence and let him eat, a concerned crease etched deeply in his brow.

"Perhaps I should have stayed and tried to get Skyla to trust me," he said at last, wiping his mouth with the back of his hand. "Perhaps the two of us could have—"

"No. No. The orphan boys were of utmost importance." Eyjarr gazed at Illmuri, yet he seemed preoccupied by vagrant thoughts. Probably he was thinking about the moldy old book under his elbow or whatever he had alchemizing in the pot *plurp*ing over the coals.

"I am sorry," Illmuri went on wearily. "I had such hopes before Mistislaus was killed by that hideous conglomeration of Ofarir and Kraftugur. It was a terrible thing to see how that swine infiltrated Ofarir and tortured him. Not that I have any fondness for Ofarir, but I cannot imagine what it would be like to be overtaken and possessed by a disembodied spirit from the shadow realm."

"It's a hazard," Eyjarr agreed. "You're quite lucky that Skyla brought you back from your own travels in the land of shadow."

"I shouldn't have abandoned her," Illmuri burst out. "She has such talent, such power. I should have brought her back somehow. But after Mistislaus perished, she changed. She was no longer like a light and airy dragonfly; she turned vengeful and embittered. I do not know if she would have listened to me. I do not know if I could have reclaimed her. It was as if she went over the edge from the sunlight into a deep pit of darkness. Could I have saved her, Meistari? You know all things, don't you?"

Eyjarr slipped more deeply into his contemplation. "I fear it would have been difficult, if at all possible. In bright ones such as Skyla the powers of darkness rage the hardest, striving to tear down the walls of their reason and goodness. I don't see Skyla surviving long without Mistislaus to protect her and guide her on the right paths of power. I believe you have done all that could reasonably be expected of you under the circumstances."

Illmuri's ears caught the hesitation in his tone, the reluctance in his nuance. "What do you mean?"

"My son, you are weary and your reason is staggering around like a half-dead horse. Rest yourself and restore your resolve, and then we shall talk some more concerning this matter of the Skyldings."

"I feel that we will not be putting this matter to rest," Illmuri said slowly as the unspoken messages filtered through the interfering curtain of his exhaustion and despair.

"Go and sleep and eat for as long as it takes," Eyjarr said. "I must have you sharp as a sword's cutting edge when next we speak. Don't return until you're ready to continue."

He waved Illmuri away as if he were still a peevish little lad who had gotten himself into another scrape. Illmuri took the bottle and the bread and went out to the kitchen to look for a warm place to sleep. Some cooks and housemaids were slaughtering chickens and feathers were flying everywhere, but he found a bench near the fire and flopped down on it with a long and grateful sigh. How many nights had he dreamed of this cozy, disorderly old kitchen where meals were cooked, eggs were hatched, and new calves and lambs were welcomed in out of the rain? Small homesick students hovered here for a little mothering from the red-faced cooks, who knew it took only feeding up to restore the spirits to a man of any age or stature.

"Are you alright, then?" called out the cheery Katrin. "You wouldn't care for a nice batch of eggs, would you?"

"I care only for some sleep now," Illmuri said. "This ale has taken the edge off all my hurts, and I can almost believe the world is a worthwhile place again. Ask me in the morning what I'd like to eat."

The shelf near the fire had been one of his favorite hiding spots since he was six years old, when he was homesick and sad and lonely, when he was having second thoughts about becoming a wizard. He was still having the second thoughts, and his body was still a mass of aches and pains from his experiences, as was his heart.

Ready to continue . . . Illmuri's heart sank at the words, and a worried little voice in the back of his head wondered if he would ever feel ready to continue. Angrily he denied the voice. Such a voice of fear and doubt would never exist in the mind of a master wizard.

In the morning he awakened to the din of pots and kettles being arrayed for the morning gruel. It was a healthful concoction of grains and powders calculated to put some muscle and substance on the apprentices without the expense of feeding them meat. When one added to it some eggs, all the black bread and cheese a boy could eat, and whatever vegetables and berries came from the garden, no one went hungry. On feast days a portion of goose or hare or mutton might be expected, depending upon what was available or needed killing at the time, and a taste of plumabrot in all its syrupy glory was carefully doled out for dessert. Of course, during their rather scant free time the boys were allowed to hunt birds' eggs and wild berries on the moors for their own picnics.

Illmuri was treated to a marvelous breakfast of meat pastry and cold rhubarb soup, right alongside Eyjarr's current batch of pupils. The younger ones stared at him in awe, the middle-sized ones were too busy misbehaving to be impressed, and the larger ones were very silent, eyeing him slantwise and pretending not to be curious. Finally the subtle elbowing could no longer be ignored, and one of the older ones, who reminded Illmuri of Jafnar, burst out with the question they were all clearly yearning to ask.

"I beg your pardon, comrade," the boy said, "but is it true you are the last of the Meistari's old apprentices?"

"I've never thought of myself as old in particular," Illmuri said, hoisting one eyebrow with a touch of his former hauteur. Once upon a time he had thought very well of himself, indeed. "But I suppose it is true, although we haven't heard the final reports from several of my fellow schoolmates. Only ugly rumors of their destruction, which I won't take as whole cloth until a reputable source tells me it is true."

"Then most of us will die, too?" another lad blurted.

"Wizardry is not a very safe profession," Illmuri said. "If you're worried about dying, it's not the career you want. You'll be quite miserable if you care in the slightest whether you live or die. It's the search for knowledge that's the thing for a wizard, the search for the world's hidden secrets."

"But don't you know for sure if you're the only one left or

not?" queried a very small and anxious lad with huge, worried eyes. "Aren't you frightfully lonely?"

"Yes, I think I am," Illmuri said after a pause, realizing he was answering both questions with one answer.

"Do you think we should go on to become wizards then," another of the larger boys asked, "if it's so dangerous?"

"Some of you will walk away and become farmers or chapmen or wanderers," Illmuri said. "I don't count you at all, because you never truly tried to become wizards. There are many of my mates who did just that—walked away and forgot all they had learned. They're still alive and probably not far from here, happily shoeing horses and digging potatoes. If that's how you wish to spend your time, then do it and be glad. Others of you want to try the lonely road. Very few of you who keep going on that road will live to see its end, like Eyjarr. He is a rare and ancient treasure of knowledge. Most of us will perish, with all that we know picked apart by birds and maggots. It's not for me to say go or stay. You will decide that for yourselves one day."

"But is it worth it?" persisted the first lad who had spoken, his eyes a blaze of intense yearning.

"For you, perhaps yes," Illmuri said. "For most of these others, no. There are some of us whose souls are so tormented by that which we do not know that the terrible and terrifying life of a wizard is the only life that seems fit for someone who is thus made for misery. I am sorry I cannot tell you wonderful tales of gold and treasure and palaces and fabulous creatures. All I have seen is the death of ones who did not deserve to die, and I was incapable of stopping it. Now eat your gruel, you lads, or you'll be late to your forms and Meistari will rage like a mad badger."

They gulped their food and left the table as neatly as was possible for them, clattering away in a great hurry down the passage to the long black table in the main hall. Illmuri felt a peculiar clutch at his throat, watching the last of the small ones racing to keep up. Once he had been the least of Eyjarr's boys, much rapped and thwacked—all with the best of intentions, of course, hoping to prod him along and teach him enough responsibility to hang his cloak on its peg and roll up his eider neatly each day. What a long and harrowing road had taken him from there to where he now stood. He did not wish to begin to add up the costs to judge whether it had been worth it.

On the following day he felt restored enough by the clean,

cold winds of Galdur to contemplate facing his Meistari once again. He sat on the walls for hours, listening to the plovers' and curlews' melodious calls, with the gray roar of the sea only two miles away down the creek. There was nothing like a cold spring day to restore a man's hope that the gray misery of winter could truly melt away into warm and generous spring. It was not quite there yet, but the ground was beginning to thaw. The buds and bark on the barren trees breathed their pungency into the cool air.

"I am much refreshed," he greeted Eyjarr that evening, after the night's chores were finished and the animals and people of the household had settled down to rest.

"Good. I'd hoped as much. Did you see my three newest little fellows? I'm rather worried about them, actually. Lads nowdays don't seem as hearty as you did at that age. They've got fears and nightmares, and a couple of them keep wetting the bed. And some of them cry like little girls. I don't like to think about turning out wizards who are going to be sissies."

"I wish you could have known Skyla. I doubt if she ever cried in her life. Skyla would be more than a match for all of those boys I saw eating breakfast this morning. She had a spark to her, a great defiant spirit—" He halted as his throat closed in rebellion against the words.

"Well. Perhaps I could hire some great dragon of an old woman to chaperone a girls' school. The weaker the male sex becomes, the stronger the women are. It's something worth looking into. However, back to the business at hand." The dancing light of amusement flickered out in his eye, and his brows came down in a brooding scowl.

Illmuri experienced the sinking sensation in the pit of his stomach he had felt so many times when he was about to be chastised. "Yes, to the business at hand. I've made a mess of Rangfara, I fear."

Eyjarr settled back in his chair and clasped his hands, as if ready to embark upon a lengthy lecture. "There is yet another way," he said, again betraying his reluctance.

"Skyla is our last hope? I should go back for her?"

"You will be going back—or so it is my hope. My son, do you know the true nature of time?"

"Time? Years, months, weeks, days, hours, minutes?"

"No, I mean, how does it exist? What form does it take? Where has yesterday's time gone if it is a thing that cannot be created or destroyed? It is nothing you can grasp with your hands. Only with your mind can you truly understand its nature. Only with your spirit can you make the best use of it. Now let your thoughts cease a moment and make a blank void of your mind. Let a picture come into it and tell me what you see."

Illmuri shut his eyes and breathed a deep and relaxing breath. This was a familiar experience. Many times he had banished the clutter of conscious thought to see what his own brain was trying to tell him. In a moment he made out a clear image against the blackness of his inner eye.

"I see a rope," he said. "Twisting around and over itself, and the end is fraying out in threads—countless threads. And at the other end—I can't see it. It's too far away, lost in too many loops."

"Very good. This rope is the thread of all time. One small fragment of the Web of Life. Of course you can't see its end, because it probably hasn't got one. And all these threads you see fraying out, twining around to create the strand of time, these are the lives you are leading all at this moment, determined by the countless choices and consequences that you are endlessly activating by your every movement and decision. At this moment there is an Illmuri somewhere who decided not to become a wizard, an Illmuri who left my school to join a darker school, an Illmuri who chose this path or that, good or evil. It is a vain and presumptuous man who supposes that his life is the single strand of life that all of civilization must live upon. He is in countless other lives, to a greater or lesser extent, a wiser, foolisher, richer, poorer, better, or worse man. All things are possible; have I not told you so? Have you not always wondered how this could be? You are even now living with every one of your decisions—all at once."

"And when I die?"

"It is of no consequence to the rest of the rope or even to the rest of the strands. You continue, a thousand times a thousand. You have in fact died already, more times than you can imagine methods of killing and dying, but you are part of time and thus cannot be destroyed. Destruction is reserved for mortal things like flesh and leaf and stone, but even then, they only change into earth and soil and sand. How can time perish? It cannot, so you go on forever on innumerable strands of time, twisted as closely together as the strands of a rope yet so far apart that you are never aware of yourself on other threads. This is truly what is known as eternity, my lad, where time is neither advancing nor receding like a river, nor blowing like a wind, or like anything else your poor little mortal mind can imagine. It is all things happening all at once, yet so marvelously ordered and orderly that no one ever gets out of place—or at least hardly ever, not without a great deal of effort."

"Hah—I think I'm beginning to see."

"No, I doubt that very much."

"You're trying to tell me that all is not lost, that on another strand things might have turned out much better for the Skyldings and I might have managed to help them find their treasure and become something again. That I should stop brooding about my failure and get along with something else more suited to my abilities. Although I'm a wretched excuse for a wizard on this thread, perhaps on several others I'm a masterpiece of brilliance."

Eyjarr sighed and pressed his fingers to his temple. "What I'm saying is not quite so simple as all that. If there were a way—if only there were a way to get there, imagine how you could affect a particular strand, carrying with you the knowledge of this strand. You see, all you would have to do is arrive at the proper point for your foreknowledge to do you some good."

"Then there would be two of me on one strand," Illmuri said. "That would be confusing for my friends, I should think."

"No, no, you obtuse young bungle brain. How could there be two of you when you have to die before you gain access to the shadow realm, which is the gateway to all the strands of time? All that would remain of you to trouble anyone on a different strand would be a cloud of knowledge, a heightened intelligence, or consciousness of the past and future consequences of certain actions. If only you could be assured of choosing the proper strand, it might just be possible to change history—or the future; it's all the same, since it's all going on at the same time, anyway."

"This is chaos!"

"Chaos it is indeed, which we as mortal creatures have struggled against in a losing battle since we first took notice of ourselves and thought ourselves quite the species. Chaos is far too all-encompassing for us to resolve entirely, so we break it up into neat little segments called centuries, years, months, days—all tiny specks on the threads of time, as I described to you in my story of the rope. Actually, there are no threads or ropes, but I fear your brain cannot fully grasp what I mean unless I use these homely little devices which you can understand. Now—where was I?"

"Transporting yourself from one strand to the other, being quite dead and into the shadow realm," Illmuri said.

"Yes. Exactly so. Once you are dead, you will enter the shadow realm. It is a gathering place of life energies, where all threads and all your lives are spread out before you in a pattern which you will find perfectly understandable, not being hindered by this wretched little sponge you call a brain. All knowledge reposes in the shadow realm, which is the reason for the great interest necromancers have in death. At this point, if you so desired, you could inflict the experiences of this strand upon yourself in another. It would be like choosing one thread upon a massive loom. We know that Skyla is a beacon for all manner of things flying around. Were you to home in on her, you would surely come to rest in the place you are looking for: Rangfara, citadel of the Skyldings, before the decline and destruction of their clan."

"But there would be no orphans present prior to the great destruction," Illmuri said. "No Jafnar, no Thogn, and possibly no Mistislaus. It was the orphan Skyla who caused him to be brought to Rangfara. If she were not orphaned shortly after her birth—"

"Lummox," Eyjarr said. "She will still be there in some capacity. Maybe this time she will be a scullery girl. Maybe she will be an ancient crone. But however she appears, she will be there somewhere, and she is one of the keys to preserving the Skyldings from destruction. You must find a strand where all the key players are in close juxtaposition, as they were in this strand. On other strands you might have been born too soon to be of any assistance to the Skyldings, or you might have been an infant at the time. You must choose one that has everyone we need, at an age that won't be a hindrance."

"You wish to change the strands of time?"

"I believe it can be done, like pulling out the keystone from an archway. That keystone is Kraftugur's curse on the Skyldings. Were we to somehow cause it never to be put into effect or to dissolve it, it would disappear from all the strands, one after the other."

"I confess myself amazed. It seems a reasonable premise. A pity it can't be put to the test until one of us dies."

"I never said it would be easy. There is yet another possibility that will aid you."

"And that is?"

"Jafnar. He is in the realm of shadow now, in the form of all his thoughts and memories of this strand. Were someone to take that cloud of experience and bestow it upon another, more hopeful strand, things might turn out much differently."

"Meistari, are you certain this is possible?"

"My son. How do you think I know so much and have lived so long, without the memories of many strands, past and future? Those of us with wisdom are like men wearing six cloaks, or a dozen, all in layers. You stand here now with two cloaks. If you travel on, you will invest yourself with yet another cloak of knowledge and experience. This is what the necromancers are attempting to do, although in most cases their methods are excessively crude. They've got the right idea that dying and returning from the dead is the way to great power."

"And you have done this, Meistari?" Illmuri whispered.

"I have, and I know that you have, at least once, although you do not seem to remember. With each passing, your memory will improve and you will not be so troubled by memories you do not understand. You chose the wizard's thorny road long ago because of your thirst for knowledge, and now the time is coming when you must decide if you are ready to make the passage yet again."

"Kraftugur is one who has passed many times," Illmuri said. "He is ahead of me in power. If I do not make the passages, then I will never overtake and beat him. How soon must I go?"

"Whenever you wish. We have done this thing before, you and I. Your task is the freeing of Rangfara, and mine is to guide you."

"What do I need for this journey?"

"The protection of the runes." The soft little leather bag of flat stones appeared in Eyjarr's hands. He shook them around and spilled out three before Illmuri, who turned them over, revealing their marks. "Algiz, of course, for protection. Thurisaz, at once the gateway and the barrier. You will not pass through without the proper readiness. And last—Nauthiz, reversed." He scowled and tapped the rune stone with one finger. "This is always a difficult rune. It is the rune of pain and limitation, and you have it here reversed, which puts you on warning that more of the same is going to follow. But don't despair, my son. By your suffering you will learn your own greatness and take lessons from your adversity. You are being sorely tested to see how far you can go, how much you can endure, what scars will be yours to bear. The great ones are not often the prettiest ones to look at, I fear, yet here we are presenting ourselves for yet another battle."

"Will you come with me, Meistari?"

"My time here is almost finished. I shall surely look for you wherever it is you go. You'll never get far away from your old schoolmaster. Besides, I'm most anxious to see Kraftugur get his comeuppance at last. He's destroyed far too many of my prize pupils. Are you ready, then? Is there any sense in waiting and thinking about it?"

"How—shall I go?"

"I have always used certain poisons which are quite painless, I assure you. Put into a drink, they are perfectly undetectable and therefore ideal for poisoning one's enemies if you're not fearful of their abilities to gather knowledge in the shadow realm to their advantage, which will come back to plague you on other strands."

"It will be an extraordinary sensation to know the future," Illmuri said. "Is this how seers do their work? They know because they remember from their past?"

"You must get over the notion of future and past," Eyjarr said. "Such notions are for the little brains of people who do not know that it is all happening together. One does not call one end of a rope one thing and the other something else. So it is with yesterday and today or tomorrow. It is simply a rope. Such is the way of time. A seer merely has seen more of the rope than ordinary folks. You must use your abilities cautiously. Such powers arouse great jealousy and fear sometimes."

"I shall. You're certain I will remember?"

"I would not send you where I would not go myself, nor ask you to do that which I have not already done. Some things you will remember; some things you will forget. Do you wish to take a few days to think about it?"

Illmuri considered. One's own death was a thing much overrated in the present world, Eyjarr had often admonished his pupils. Now Illmuri understood, and he understood also why he was considered the last of the Meistari's students. The others had gone on ahead of him into the realm of shadow, searching for the knowledge and powers he craved.

"I'm ready. I don't wish to be the last any longer. I'll go now. Where is your poison?"

Eyjarr felt for a cord around his neck and drew forth a gold vial, much worn. With a slow and careful hand he poured a cautious measure into Illmuri's cup of ale. With a faint puff of vapor it vanished into the amber depths. Their eyes met over the fatal cup.

"You'll be alright here alone?" Illmuri whispered, not trusting his voice to speak.

Eyjarr nodded his head. "Don't trouble yourself with me; you've got much to do. Farewell—for the moment. We will always be joined by all the threads of time. You'll know me when you see me, of that you have my assurance. Now go. Put an end to the torment of the Skyldings."

CHAPTER ONE

"THE DAUGHTER OF my dead sister is in Rangfara. I am certain she is Reykja's daughter. It is Reykja's face, only she is fair like her Skylding father, Hoggvinn."

"Tall and fair. I have seen her, too." The old woman gazed into the kettle of water, cradling it with her withered fingers.

"You've seen her?" Alvara asked.

"Many times. She comes with her foster father each spring to visit Skjoldur. What do you think a tjaldi woman is good for, if not for seeing things?" the old woman demanded testily. "Do you think it's fun being so old and stiff and continually plagued with visions and premonitions and visiting spirits? Isn't this what a tjaldi woman is kept around for?"

"Yes, of course. I am sorry, my tjaldi, for my impatience and youthful ignorance. The rest of us must be a burden to you in your wisdom and enlightenment."

"You shouldn't be so anxious to wreak havoc until the time is right."

"Then it is time?"

"It is time."

"I have waited long indeed to avenge the death of my sister. The world knows the Viturkonur always get their revenge."

"You are still impatient, Daughter. You would rush off and bury a knife in Hoggvinn's heart, cut the throat of Skjoldur, and rain down ruin upon the head of Mistislaus. You're far too impetuous and hasty, my dear. I have taken nearly twenty years to think of the crime these Skyldings committed against us. And it is true that we are not entirely blameless. Reykja stole the birthright for her daughter from Hoggvinn, against his will and without his knowing, until the spell wore off him and he regained his wits."

16

"But that is not a crime which deserves the death of two people, mother and child. If he had been smart, Hoggvinn ought to have graciously granted Reykja a birth scroll for her daughter and been done with it. No one deliberately provokes the Viturkonur. He had no right to take a girl child. Fathers are entitled to their male offspring, but the females belong to their mothers."

"There is an older law than this which you have not considered, which used to be the only law practiced among the clans of the Alfather. Though it is no longer used, the precedent is terribly ancient. The father had the right to take unwanted female infants and expose them on the mountain to the elements and wild beasts rather than letting their mothers rear them. As time passed, the hearts of the Dokkalfar became indifferent, and the mothers were allowed to keep their female children—as long as the mothers were willing to take them and go far away and rear them however they could and ask nothing of their fathers. It was the beginning of the wandering women's clans, such as we have today. A good plan it is, selling birthrights to the men's clans. It gives us wealth and independence, besides ridding us of the troublesome domination of men."

Alvara shifted restlessly in her seat, perceiving that the ancient little creature's mind had wandered somewhat from her original purpose.

"Yes, my tjaldi. But it has led to a hierarchy among the mother clans in certain cases, such as the refusal of the Skyldings to purchase birthrights from the Viturkonur, which led us to this ugly conflict with Hoggvinn and Reykja. Plenty of grief and anger have resulted from their arrogance and their prejudice against women with magical powers. A pity that ridiculous myth of the wizard warrior ever surfaced to tempt my poor sister. Warfare and wizardry will never mix."

"You are wrong, my child. Warfare and wizardry are a natural combination whose time will come. I think it is time, my child, that the Viturkonur returned to Rangfara and set up a gifting booth there."

"Are you certain this is wise? We've not gone to Rangfara to sell our birthrights since Reykja captured Hoggvinn. And I'm doubtful of our welcome. Hoggvinn and his wife, Logregla, are no more kindly disposed to the Viturkonur than they were when he ordered the baby killed. They refused our birthrights once."

"Do you question my sight, Alvara? Do you think you're the better tjaldi for this tribe?"

"No, my tjaldi," Alvara said. "If you say it, then we will go to Rangfara and tent our booth. I daresay the haughty Skyldings will still disdain to purchase our birthrights from us, though."

"Let them disdain us if they wish. There will be others who don't scorn us. By the time the giftings are over, we will have Reykja's daughter. And we will hold all their fates within the palms of our hands." The tjaldi slowly raised her clenched fist, letting out a fine, sifting stream of sand, opening her hand and letting the last of the sand blow away in a puff of dust. "Hoggvinn will finally pay for his birthright. The day Hoggvinn fathered Reykja's baby, he sealed the doom of every Skylding that walks the streets of Rangfara."

The tjaldi gazed into her reflecting kettle so long and quietly that Alvara feared she had departed on a fylgja journey, leaving her dry little husk of a body sitting in her chair surrounded by magical tokens while her spirit ventured forth in the shadow realm.

"Skjoldur has a son," she said finally. "A fine lad he is, but there is a shadow over him. I can see it gathering as he goes about his business, pretending to study and pretending to learn about warfare and weapons. A pretend warrior is all he ever will be unless—unless—I can't quite see it because of the shadow. I think his life will be greatly changed somehow."

"What has this pretend warrior to do with me, my tjaldi?" Alvara asked with a contemptuous curl of her lip.

"You will see him often, Daughter. His fate is mingled in yours. Skjoldur took pity on the poor baby. He didn't leave her on the fell as his master commanded. He took her to his friend Mistislaus. These three surround her like a triangle, Hoggvinn, Skyjoldur, and Mistislaus. Of the three, Skjoldur is the weakest link. He has other sons, all of them close to gifting age. If we are to destroy Skjoldur, we will destroy him through his sons."

"And if we are to destroy Hoggvinn?"

"We will destroy him through his own daughter. She is his only child, thanks to our curse. His only heir to the vast treasure of the Skyldings."

"And she belongs to us. Or rather, she will."

"Yes, my dear. It will be your responsibility to make certain that the girl belongs to us."

"I can do that, my tjaldi. And what about Mistislaus? How do we destroy a wizard of such power as he's got?"

"Through his own power. And through the child he has raised as his daughter these last nineteen years. Did you think I had not paid my heed to your pleas for revenge? Did you think I had given it no thought whatsoever?"

"There were times when I thought you had forgotten," Alvara said. "Or you didn't think it was important enough."

"No one touches the Viturkonur with impunity," the tjaldi said sharply, her eye kindling. "The murder of a Viturkona and the theft of her child is an insult which the Viturkonur will never forgive. This is vengeance born of nineteen years of thought and planning. No Skylding will escape destruction. Rangfara will be a wasteland of bones and skulls, and we will be rich on Skylding gold."

Her hooded eyes were fixed upon the clear surface of the kettle, as if she were seeing the visions she described. Her dry little tongue darted out like a viper's tongue at the mention of the gold.

Alvara permitted herself to smile. Even an ancient and holy tjaldi was not immune from a secret stab of greed now and then.

"Shall I return to Rangfara, my tjaldi? The wizard Mistislaus is visiting there with his friend Skjoldur, and I don't know how long he will stay. Once he leaves, I shall have no idea where my sister's child will be taken."

"Mistislaus will not leave Rangfara," the tjaldi said in a strong, clear voice. "He will be detained if he tries to go. Tell your sister kin that we will soon strike the tents and move to Rangfara. You, my dear, must go back there immediately and begin your preparations. You have a great deal to do to get ready for our arrival. And I, too, have preparations."

When Alvara was gone, the tjaldi Thordis sat with her hands clasped together, supporting her chin as she concentrated. Her trance deepened until there was no sign of life in her dry little body. Leaving its annoying encumbrance behind, she traveled through the shadow realm, as light and quick as a moonbeam. The body really was getting to be a hindrance, she thought; she had carried it around a terribly long time, and time was taking its toll. The realm of shades and shadows was in fact nothing of the sort, although it had been frightening to her when she was younger. Now she had the wisdom to understand that it was a higher level than the mortal level she lived upon, and she was eager to learn more. As soon as she found a competent replacement, she would leave her mortal shell and not return—but not before the matter of Alvara's revenge was satisfactorily concluded.

She left the shadow realm and arrived at her destination, many miles away from her sisters' encampment. A journey that would have taken days and several good horses was done in a matter of moments.

"Thordis, you are here." The wizard gazed into his skrying sphere more intently.

Thordis could see all around the wizard's dwelling without looking, as one had to do when hampered with eyes. Her host lived in a gloomy hall on the outskirts of the settlement of Rangfara, where he kept the mad and witless ones of the Skylding clan from annoying and embarrassing their kin.

"Greetings, old friend. I have a conundrum for you," she said.

"Indeed? I welcome your conundrums. Let's hear it."

"A clan of women has been wronged by a powerful clan of warriors. For almost twenty years the wrong has gone unrequited. But now the tides of fortune are changing, and the clan of women has an opportunity for revenge. The question is, Should the clan of women seek their vengeance now in one sure, swift stroke by killing the perpetrator of the wrong, which would satisfy justice? The warrior clan won't long regret the loss of their leader, and his killing will look like a simple murder, and the women's clan will have to pay weregild to his kin. On the other hand, the tjaldi of this clan of women has been plotting for twenty years, and she has devised a curse which will follow the warriors for the rest of their days until they are destroyed to the last one of them, and the women's clan will never be suspected of causing their demise."

"It sounds like the most satisfactory plan," the wizard Kraftugur said.

"But no one will know that it was the women's clan who destroyed them," Thordis said. "The first way, the world will know who struck him down, and respect for the women's clan will increase. That is satisfactory. But the other plan is also tempting, to think that the entire clan will be eradicated, even if the women's clan doesn't get the credit for it."

Kraftugur thought for a long moment. "The trouble with the first plan," he said at last, "is that you will always regret not having used the second plan. So the time has come to avenge Reykja's death?"

"Yes. Her daughter is now of gifting age. The Skyldings will think we have forgotten. I'm glad you like the second plan. The Skyldings won't know they've been cursed until it is far too late."

"It must be an elegant and virulent curse of the utmost subtlety," Kraftugur said.

"The curse will actually be upon their favorite gifting clan. They won't suspect their own wives and daughters and sisters."

"The Drottningur? That will be sweet revenge."

"Yes, I've thought of that, too. Their insult to the Viturkonur will be repaid."

"And what is it you wish me to do in your scheme?"

"There's the matter of the Skylding treasure hoard. By using the second plan we ensure that Skyla inherits all her father has, including the chieftain's seat and the treasure."

"Then you can't go wrong."

"Only if there is a suitable husband found for Skyla. That's not something we can leave to her father. We must ensure control of Rangfara when the Skyldings begin to fall apart at the seams. I think you would be an excellent choice to sit on the chieftain's seat as Hoggvinn's heir. When the time comes to divide the treasure, you would have a generous share."

"I? But I'm a humble man, no one but the keeper of a madhouse. I have no such aspirations."

"It would not be difficult to acquire them, my friend. You have a certain amount of respect in Rangfara as a wise man and an arbiter of disputes."

"Yes, I've been negotiating treaties between Skylding and Krypplingur."

"You have no love for the Skylding clan. They refused to allow you to buy a birthright from their precious Drottningur. Now you may yet see sons: wizard warriors, undefeatable, the most powerful race to set foot upon Skarpsey."

"The Skyldingur are too haughty to allow such a one as I to marry into them."

"Remember, Kraftugur, Hoggvinnsdottir is a Viturkona, even though she has been raised by Mistislaus. It is her mother clan that chooses her mate. There lies the beauty of our plan. We will not only destroy the Skylding clan, we will rightfully and honorably obtain the Skylding inheritance. And the

Krypplingur already despise the Skyldings and covet their treasure. They will be easily used in our scheme."

"I don't see how it can fail," Kraftugur said after a moment's thought as he gazed out the narrow window to the Hall of Stars, where Hoggvinn sat as chieftain.

"Good. Then look for the Viturkonur in Rangfara. My daughter Alvara will be arriving soon."

"What other business do we have before us today?" Hoggvinn, chieftain of the Skylding clan and lord of Rangfara, peered down from his high seat on the dais. The Hall of Stars was filled with his retainers, most of them lolling inattentively in their chairs, some napping soundly. The Krypplingur Herrad and his son Ofarir and other assorted Krypplingur looked too similar to differentiate among, except that some were uglier and more warlike-looking than the others.

Several of the retainers smothered groans when Mistislaus stood up.

"You know me well and know what I have to say," he commenced in a pontifical tone, bestowing a baleful look upon them all, lingering in particular over the Krypplingur.

"Mistislaus," Hoggvinn said, darting a rather frightened glance at Herrad and the Krypplingur. "If it's another prophecy, let's discuss it in private. There's no need to blurt it all over Rangfara."

"That's what you're supposed to do with prophecies," Mistislaus said. "People are supposed to hear them and be warned. Otherwise, what's the point?"

"Then I myself shall warn the Skyldings of their impending doom or whatever it is you see," Hoggvinn said. "Skjoldur, have Mistislaus tell you what his prophecy is and see to it that I hear about it before the day's out. I hardly think this is the time or place to discuss something as important as a prophecy."

The chieftain of the Krypplingur stirred after staring at Mistislaus with lizardlike intensity. "I say let the fellow give his prophecy," he said in a growling voice. "I don't know when I've ever listened to a prophet before."

"He's not a prophet," Skjoldur said sharply. "He's a—well, Mistislaus is hard to explain, but this prophet notion is a rather new one to him, and it may not be accurate—"

"I want to hear it," Herrad said, turning to Mistislaus. "Go ahead, wizard; let's hear your prophecy."

"I don't think you're going to like it," Skjoldur said hastily. "Prophets don't care whose toes they tread upon."

"Silence," Herrad said. "Let the man speak, and I shall judge for myself whether my toes are trodden upon."

"Well spoken," Mistislaus said. "But I fear Skjoldur is right. I'm going to insult you terribly."

"Go right ahead," Herrad said with a toadlike wink of one eye. "It won't be the first time, nor the last." His craggy lips curled upward in something that might have been a smile, but it was hard to tell if a Kryppling was smiling or baring his teeth in rage. Generally speaking, they looked like untidy heaps of weapons and armor seated around Hoggvinn's table, short and burly as dwarfs with hereditary hunched shoulders that gave them the epithet Krypplingur and the menacing appearance of surly bulls about to charge. Bits of vanquished foes' persons and habiliments served as their only personal adornment.

"I'm glad you're sporting about it," Mistislaus said. "Otherwise, I don't think you've got many other redeeming characteristics."

"Oh, come now, Mistislaus," a dry voice rasped, and another person in wizardly attire stood up. "I think you're the one who's not being sporting."

"I've heard enough out of you, Kraftugur," Mistislaus said, "and so has everyone else in this hall. You're the one who's deceiving the Skyldings and leading them straight down the path to destruction. You know pretty bloody well these Krypplingur have no interest in making peace with their old enemies. This is a scheme you've cooked up between you to weasel your way into Rangfara somehow and feather your own nest. You're nothing but a robber, a fraud, and the keeper of a madhouse, Kraftugur, and these Krypplingur are murdering thugs. You've all come here on a mission of murder and robbery."

The boredom of the assembly was thus pleasantly relieved. Everyone awakened in the ensuing shouting and arguing as Mistislaus was forcibly taken into hand and ejection proceedings were put into action. This duty fell to two of the least retainers, who each garnered several good thwacks from Mistislaus' staff as they laid hold of him.

The Krypplingur looked on with stoic calm, as if such events were commonplace in their assemblies.

"Wait. We haven't heard the prophecy yet," Herrad said, his

booming voice overpowering the yammering of the Skyldings. They fell silent, looking at Hoggvinn anxiously. He waved his hand and looked resigned.

Mistislaus nodded toward Herrad appreciatively and disengaged himself from the grip of Hoggvinn's retainers. "Thank you. You're the only one with any manners in this hall. A pity, really, that you're planning to kill us all." He patted his clothing into shape again, arranging his hood in its rightful position hanging down his back, after it had gotten wrong way to in the scuffle. "My prophecy as I saw it concerns the destruction of Rangfara and the demise of the Skylding clan. Some of you may have heard this before, so I beg your pardon and your forbearance." He gripped his staff and held it extended, then flung back his head, gazing in the general vicinity of the ceiling. In an oratorical voice he commenced: "Listen to me, all you Skyldings. Your days are numbered, so let my words of wisdom fall upon your heretofore deaf ears and be heard. With the rising in the sky of Fantur the Rogue and Kanina the Rabbit, the Krypplingyur legions will seize the Hall of Stars and hold all there within captive, demanding a ransom be paid for their deliverance. That ransom is the entire Skylding treasure amassed over the centuries by your pillaging ancestors. When the ransom is not paid, the Krypplingur will slay all their hostages and begin a battle that will rage for three days and nights. When it is over, not one Skylding warrior shall survive, save only seven younglings who escape the slaughter. Woe be unto you, Krypplingur, because of these seven who will prove your undoing. Though Rangfara will be laid waste and the streets made red with Skylding blood, you will not obtain the treasure."

"Is that all?" Herrad said when Mistislaus had finished speaking and folded his arms.

"You want more?" Mistislaus demanded. "You wish me to reveal all of your murderous intentions?"

"I think we've had enough," Hoggvinn said, his countenance mottled with rage and pallor. "Mistislaus, I command you to take yourself away. No guest in this hall has ever had to listen to such insults."

"More's the pity, then," Mistislaus said. "If it's any consolation, most of the men who have put legs under this table are little better than the Krypplingur when it comes to honorability. There's something about you, my old friend, that draws the worst of humanity to you like a carcass draws flies. In this hall there are two men who are true to you, who would gladly lay down their lives to defend you—myself and Skjoldur. We three have grown from children together. All the rest of these are as loyal as circling vultures, waiting to stoop upon that cursed treasure. And you, Hoggvinn, attract these predators because you are as blind and stupid a chieftain as ever planted his unworthy rump upon a high seat and presumed to rule his kinfolk."

"Mistislaus!" Skjoldur leapt to his feet to glare across the table at Mistislaus. "As the chief retainer here, I order you to depart!"

"Faugh on you, Skjoldur, and your chief retainer nonsense," Mistislaus said. "You're the foremost dolt of the worst herd of dolts I have ever seen. You gather yourselves together and vest yourselves with a spurious importance for no purpose I can see except making the more humble folk think there's someone important leading them merrily down the road to their slaughter. What a lot of empty sacks you are, spilling out dust and corruption, pretending to ignore each other's crimes because your own crimes present and future are much worse than your neighbor's. If this hall was supposed to be full of honest men, why, I'd be standing here perfectly alone. But what you're going to get at the hands of the Krypplingur, even you don't deserve. Turn them out while you still have time, you fools. There's plenty of time—"

With a roar of fury the retainers shouted him down, picked him up bodily, and carted him out of the hall. In the true spirit of truth and confession, the other retainers fell upon each other with a mighty wrangling and accusing. When order was restored, it was to discover that the Krypplingur had departed from the Hall of Stars.

"Curse that Mistislaus," Hoggvinn said to Skjoldur. "I want him out of Rangfara until this treaty is signed. Find him, Skjoldur. And get rid of him however you can."

"It won't be hard to find him. He's staying at my house. You don't want him killed, do you?"

"Mistislaus is an old friend. See if you can reason with him first."

The lynx knew how to kill silently, swiftly, and with a minimum of blood spilled when necessary. She bounded across a rockfall and crouched behind a thicket, tufted ears twitching at the slightest sound. Even the sensitive pads of her feet felt the approach of the cart and horse, and her nostrils twitched with the scent of horse and human flesh. In a moment the cart plodded into view, the tired horse half-asleep, the driver slumped resignedly in the seat beside an uncomfortable-looking woman struggling with an oversize hood, trying to keep the sun away from her pallid complexion.

"Can't you hurry any faster?" she was exhorting the hapless driver. "You're letting that horse go to sleep. Wake him up or we'll never get to Rangfara. It's going to be dark before we even see it at the rate you're going. I'm going to tell your master you've been the most uncooperative thrall I've ever seen and I hope he thrashes you soundly."

"He'd thrash me all the worse if I bring back his horse in a state of exhaustion," the thrall replied. "I can't run the poor creature's legs off."

"Don't you be rude to me, you beast. I'll have your hide if you get impudent."

"Your mother clan hired this cart and horse and thrall to get you to Rangfara, and I'm getting you there, aren't I? If this horse falls down and dies, you aren't going to get there, are you? I could hurry him up, but it wouldn't be doing any of us a service. I don't know what you're in such a rush for. The giftings will go on for another month yet, if it's yourself you're putting on the market."

"Oh! What audacity! Your master will certainly hear about this!"

"You're just as much a thrall as I am, running to and fro at the beckoning of those Drottning women. And all just for the privilege of walking behind some arrogant young lady and waiting on her like a common slave. Doesn't sound like any kind of life to me."

"When I want your opinions, I'll ask you for them. Being a lady's maid certainly beats mucking out stalls or digging potatoes or whatever you do with most of your time."

"What exact price did your clanswomen get by selling you to the Drottningur as a servant? Sounds to me like I'm not the only thrall riding in this wagon."

"That shows what you know, doesn't it? I'm no thrall, born into servitude, mere property like a cow or a horse, as you are. I've been articled to the Drottningur for ten years. It's not the same thing at all."

Alvara let the cart pass her, as she had done twice before, until the sun was very low and the shadows were long enough to suit her. This time, however, she ran silently ahead and crossed their road, leaving behind an invisible trail of scent.

When the weary horse came to the ribbon of scent, it stopped in its tracks as if it had run into a stone wall, hoisted up its head, and inhaled great gusts of air, exhaling each one with a fearful snort.

"Why is that hateful beast stopping?" the girl demanded. "Don't you have a whip?"

The thrall leapt out of the cart to seize the bridle as the horse began to back away from the scent. The thrall sniffed, too, looking slowly from side to side and feeling his neck hairs start to bristle.

"Something's not right here," he said uneasily.

All attempts to soothe the suspicious horse were in vain; the animal backed quickly and reared when the thrall tried to hold him still. The girl shrieked and leapt off the cart with an agility that told of her rustic background, belied by her overfancy gown and cloak.

From a nearby ravine came a wailing cry, almost like a human child.

"Listen to that!" the girl said. "Did you hear that? Someone's left a baby out!"

"That's no baby. That's a snow lynx!"

"Don't be stupid. I know what I'm hearing. We can't leave the poor little creature to die! Come on; we've got to find it!"

"You're mad! That's no baby! Come back here!" the thrall cried as she slipped past him, intent on the dark ravine. "No, stop! I can't leave this horse or we'll have to walk the rest of the way to Rangfara!"

But she was gone, plunging away heedlessly into the scrub and thickets, leaving him cursing and struggling with a frightened, obstinate horse that intended to turn around and run for the next two days to get back to his familiar stable, where his nostrils were never assailed by the terrifying musk of snow lynxes.

When he had backed himself away far enough, the horse quieted down and stood still, snorting and twitching his ears warily at every slight sound as the twilight deepened.

"Halloa! Young mistress! Can you hear me?" the thrall called out gruffly. His ears also strained at every sound, and he felt as nervous and twitchy as the horse, which hadn't put on such an exhibition of spirit since it was two years old and unbroken.

"I hear you," the girl replied, returning at last through the gloom, fastening her hood more securely around her head. "I guess I was mistaken. It must have been an animal, as you said. But it did sound so much like a baby crying. I can scarcely believe anyone would still practice the old barbaric tradition of exposing babies. You've heard of it, I'm sure."

"It's common enough among the poor people and thralls," he replied. "You're ready, then? It's going to be dead dark when we get to Rangfara."

The once-weary horse could not be dissuaded from trotting all the way to the main gate of Rangfara, where waited the comforting smells of horse and stable and humankind.

"The Hall of Stars is where the Drottningur are," the girl said, pointing down the crowded thoroughfare. "It is the chieftain's hall, the noble and noteworthy Hoggvinn's. You may set me down in front and take your vehicle to the stable. This has been a lucky night for you, if you only knew it."

She dismounted from the cart in the dooryard of the Hall of Stars and accepted her bundle of possessions from the thrall. As she passed by the horse, the jittery beast swung his head around for a sniff of her, startling even himself with an explosive snort and a sidewise scrambling leap.

"Whoa, you fool!" the thrall growled, catching hold of the bridle and trying to stroke and calm the horse. "You've been just about crazy tonight. I'm as glad to get off that road as you are, but nobody is as glad as me to get rid of her." He turned to look back at his passenger of two days, who was just disappearing within the great front doors of the chieftain's hall. A wisp of dark hair escaped from beneath her hood. Strange—he'd thought all along she was fair.

Since the marriage of Hoggvinn to Logregla, the Hall of Stars had been divided, providing two halls, one for Hoggvinn and the men and one for Logregla and her numerous female relatives. When the Drottningur came for the gifting season every spring, they lived with Logregla in high style.

Alvara turned her back on the thrall and proceeded to Logregla's domain, ushered into the women's hall by a tall thrall of mysterious origins, who merely pointed, gestured, and bowed to convey his directions.

Logregla sat on a couch covered in fine fabrics and soft fleeces, surrounded by her favorite acolytes and a dozen overfed cats. Like her cats, Logregla was overfed and completely devoted to a life of indolence, bathing, and mischief. She even looked like a cat, with a round face and tiny pouting features, as she surveyed Alvara from head to toe with obvious disdain.

Alvara sized her up as well—considerably past her prime as far as beauty went but still running strong in putting up a splendid effort to stave off the appearance of age. All Drottningur tended to plumpness, from the adorable stage to the truly massive, as was Logregla. Glancing around at the other Drottningur in the hall, Alvara noted the similarity in form and features.

"Come for a ladies' maid, have you?" Logregla inquired languidly, waving one hand to dismiss the thrall and bestirring herself enough to rise slightly on one elbow. "What do you know about being a ladies' maid, girl? You seem to have come from rather a rustic background."

"These clothes are not my own," Alvara said, raising her chin staunchly. "I lost everything I had at the inn where I stayed. It was stolen in the night, and these strange garments were the best I could muster. As a ladies' maid, I know enough to be always available and never indiscreet. I know how to see and hear everything yet remain as ignorant as a milkmaid. A good maid also knows when to tell what she knows and to whom."

The other ladies lounging around Logregla's throne nodded in agreement, glad for an excuse to ignore the needlework they were pretending to be working on so they could survey Alvara for themselves. Drottningur through and through, they looked down their short noses and simpered behind their plump white hands, rolling their eyes at each other with contemptuous well-bred sneers.

"And do you know how to be amusing?" Logregla leaned back on her couch as if the exertion had totally exhausted her. "We are so easily bored by the trivial and mundane. Do you know lots of tales of adventure and handsome rich young men fighting monsters and dragons or tales with a great moral at the end?"

"No, I'm afraid not," Alvara said. "I'm not one for storytelling."

"Good," Logregla said with an enormous yawn. "I'd have sacked you on the spot if you knew any of those boring, wretched stories of heroes and adventures. And we don't want anything to do with morals, do we?"

All the Drottningur within earshot sniffed or tittered in a

brief display of interest and energy before going back to their languid lolling and sprawling.

"What can you do to entertain us?" one of the other ladies asked. "We've tried almost everything, seen everything, heard everything, so we're not easy to amuse."

"I have a few ideas," Alvara said. "Something which I'm sure you've never done before."

"It can't have anything to do with exercise," said another Drottning, making a disgusted face. "We hate physical exertion."

"And no conundrums, either," another said. "We don't like to think, either."

"This is very easy," Alvara said with a smile. "What I propose is to teach you shape shifting. Doesn't it sound amusing to slip outside in another form, past all your guards and suitors, free from all this nonsense? Think of the fun we could have if no one knew it was us."

The Drottningur's eyes glittered, and they fell into an excited chattering among themselves.

"Yes, I think you'll do quite well," Logregla said with a small feline smile, extending one soft white paw to Alvara to seal their agreement with a limp handshake. "Welcome, my dear. I hope you'll be quite happy among us."

"I'm certain I shall," Alvara said. "It's been the dream of a lifetime to come to Rangfara and join the train of the Drottningur. I can scarcely believe I'm here at last."

"Well, well, don't go on about it," Logregla said. "You'll do well as long as you're interesting. I think this shape shifting sounds quite amusing. Exactly what we've been looking for."

CHAPTER
TWO

"I DO NOT like Rangfara," Skyla said. "I wish I were still at Ulfgarth." Without turning around, she spoke when Mistislaus came to find her beside the old well in the rear courtyard of Athugashol.

Mistislaus stifled a sigh and plucked anxiously at his sparsely whiskered chin. He should not have brought her here. She belonged at Ulfgarth, among the wild birds and windy fells under a pure sky, not moping miserably among the fusty old relics of Rangfara. He disapproved of her sitting there gazing into the silvery surface of the water, no doubt seeing visions and images that would only put more strange ideas into her head. But now that she was nineteen, her pale hair had grown past her shoulders and she refused to cut it. Fortunately, she seemed to have contained the errant powers that had plagued her since she had been an infant, making him think she was cursed or at the very least witless. Still, the piercing gray-green eyes she turned upon him now were disturbing in their clarity. "The city is full of those hulking Krypplingur. They have murder in their hearts, Mistislaus."

Mistislaus concealed a nervous twitch with a feigned sneeze. "Nonsense," he said gruffly, with scant conviction. "They're on the verge of making peace with the Skyldings. We're supposed to trust them and get used to having them around. I daresay Hoggvinn is going to give them half of Rangfara before we're finished. Some say they're very honorable fellows once you get to know them."

"They're murderers," Skyla replied with chilling certainty. "Last night I dreamed again that all the Skyldings were gone, and I was the only one who remained, and Rangfara was a city

31

of ruins and mist people, forever acting out lives gone and forgotten."

"Your dreams have always been a curse to you," Mistislaus said. "Why don't you come in now. It's starting to get dark, and Gunna will soon have the evening meal prepared."

"I wish we had a place of our own," Skyla said, turning a reluctant glance upon the walls of Athugashol, which were bathed in fiery sunset. "I don't like being Skjoldur's guests."

"Why ever not? I've come here for more years than you've been alive. Skjoldur would be monstrously hurt if I didn't come to stay at his house each year. He'd be offended, most likely, that I would so abuse such an ancient and trusted friendship by failing to impose upon it outrageously from time to time. And what about Jafnar? Isn't he a clever and amusing young fellow?"

"He's vain and frivolous," Skyla said. "He never takes a single thought for the future. And he's so obsessed with staring at those Drottningur women."

"Well, who wouldn't stare at Drottningur women? I certainly stare, if only in horror at what the Skylding clan is coming to by marrying into them. Their mother clans used to be good sensible working women—shepherds, horsewomen, warriors, weavers, women with strength and talent—but these empty-headed Drottningur are good for nothing but quarreling and starting feuds. I think I see what your trouble is," he added in a gentler tone. "You're of gifting age, too, and there's no one for you. If you had a name scroll and a pedigree—"

"I care nothing for marrying and bearing children and all that nonsense," Skyla said sharply. "It's nothing but a life of woe and grief. I refuse to earn my way in this life by selling my own sons to some indifferent father and spending the remainder of my days in a women's clan. I'd rather live in a cave all by myself, after you get old and die, and hunt rabbits for food."

"I'm in no danger of turning up my toes just yet, I'm happy to say," Mistislaus retorted. "Unless you persist in keeping me out in the dew and night vapors much longer."

"In a little while. I like sitting here in the dark and imagining I'm back in the garden at Ulfgarth, with the fells beyond the wall, instead of more walls and more people and more lives and troubles than I care to think about, pressing around us like a blanket. So much trouble and scurrying about, like ants after you've disturbed them."

"Many of us and our troubles are not as inconsequential, I'm afraid, as ants scuttling about," Mistislaus huffed.

"You've had another falling-out with Hoggvinn," Skyla said calmly, with aggravating perspicacity.

"That's nothing new," Mistislaus said. "Every year when I come to Rangfara we quarrel over something. But this time he's done something so stupid, I don't know if I can ever forgive it. If Logregla were behind it, I wouldn't be so astonished, but welcoming those Krypplingur within the gates and sitting down with them at his table is suicide."

"Kraftugur," Skyla said with a shudder, casting a sidewise glance at the pool. "He's taking your position beside Hoggvinn as his advising wizard."

"I've talked too much," Mistislaus said. "I've upset you with my paltry squabbles with Hoggvinn. I assure you, my dear Skyla, it is all nothing to worry about."

"But I have seen these things reflected in the water." She glanced toward the reflecting pool, which was now bathed with the fiery red light of the setting sun. "I'm afraid for you, Mistislaus. I've seen your blood spilled on the paving stones, along with the blood of many Skyldings. I wish we could leave here and never come back. I'm afraid of Kraftugur, and I'm afraid of the Krypplingur."

"Skyla, you're trembling. Can't you quit conjuring up these visions of gloom and doom? You're being very morbid. I wish you'd go in where it's warm."

"It's nothing to pass off so lightly, Mistislaus. Don't try to brush me off as if I were a prating child. You know my gifts. I'm telling you that something terrible is going to happen. Just the thoughts of those Krypplingur summon up visions of the future. And Kraftugur is harboring thoughts of greed and murder. I wish you could warn Hoggvinn."

Mistislaus sighed, yearning for a pot of ale to soothe his fears and warm the blood in his veins. It was good, however, to talk to Skyla and say the things that the pigheaded Hoggvinn refused to hear. He hitched up his pantaloons indignantly, thinking of his unceremonious ejection from the Hall of Stars, where he had always been a most welcome guest before Kraftugur had inserted his simpering mug.

"Well, I tried. He's got his head full of airy ideas of peace and prosperity, an era of brotherhood and cooperation, the end to fighting. What balderdash. Kraftugur's talking peace out one side of his face and coveting that cursed treasure out the other.

It was his job, supposedly, to talk peace between Hoggvinn and Herrad, but I haven't seen much done by way of treaties and promises. Just a lot of empty talk and grinning faces and mutual compliments that are nothing but lies. Hoggvinn is an ass. Always has been an ass. If not for me and Skjoldur propping him up, he'd be flat on his face in the mud by now, with everyone using his back for a bridge to get to that treasure. Or murdered, the trusting fool. Drat him. I hate having friends. I'm not coming back here again. Hoggvinn and Skjoldur are on their own from now on. I wash my hands of them entirely."

"Does this mean we're leaving Rangfara?" Skyla asked.

"No, of course not. Hoggvinn may be an ass, but he is also a friend, unfortunately. I should have picked my friends more carefully. Are you coming in now?"

"Not just yet. I want to see the stars and wonder which ones watched over my birth."

"Ah. Yes. I wish I could tell you that myself, but I cannot."

"Cannot or will not?"

"Skyla, don't be a wretched child. I have told you all I can." He turned away from her clear eyes before she saw more than he intended.

"A man or a woman without a name or a clan is little more than a homeless wanderer in Skarpsey. Perhaps one day I shall know who I am."

"You are Skyla. No scrap of vellum can tell you more. It doesn't matter if your parents were shepherds or kings or scavengers. You can take your life in your two hands and determine for yourself what trade you will take, what you will do with your time."

"I have inherited powers and knowledge."

"Yes, and you have learned to use them for good purposes."

"Only the ones I know about. I'm afraid there are others waiting to be discovered which may not be so nice."

"Bah. I know you, my child. You will always choose the side of light and life and love, not the way of destruction and death. I've been able to teach you that much, at least. Are you coming in soon?"

"Go ahead. I like being alone out here."

When he was gone, she gazed into the pool, which now glowed like a pool of blood. Against the fiery red she again saw the figure of a woman in a black cloak.

Her reverie was broken by the huffing and snorting of Guthrum coming around the side of the house, leading Fegurd,

Mistislaus' ancient horse, lovingly brushed and her sides bulging with the best hay and grain Skjoldur's stable had to offer. He lumbered toward the reflecting pool, scowling mightily as he selected the best patch of grass to tether Fegurd on for the night. It happened to be the laundry green for drying clothes on, but nothing was too good for old Fegurd or any horse that fell under Guthrum's care. People he despised, and there was no surer way of offending him than by trying to thank or reward him for his labors. He glanced toward Skyla with an uncivil grunt, which passed for a greeting with the old dwarf. He was one of the landmarks of Skyla's life, standing like a craggy, moss-encrusted boulder in the stream of her memories. Always he grumbled and growled around, doing work for Mistislaus with the persecuted attitude of an unwilling slave, taking offense at the slightest word of gratitude. Yet no fiercer watchdog ever guarded the doorstep of his master, ever willing to expend the last drop of blood in his carcass battling savage minions at hopeless odds at the least provocation. Guthrum lingered a moment, rubbing Fegurd's bony withers as he scanned the surrounding walls and rooftops.

"You'd best go in," he rumbled. "This is the time the lynx appears."

Then he went clumping back toward the stable where he resided, his great boots driving back any possible attackers with their mighty and fearsome treading, the rattle and squeak of his weapons and harness signifying to any listening enemies that a warrior of no inconsequential stature dwelled within the walls of Athugashol. With a last suspicious glower around his surroundings, like the grim and sole survivor of a determined siege, Guthrum disappeared into the stable, where he set his candle in a niche in the stone wall, ate something miserable and dreary for his supper, and made his bed in a cold stone horse trough. Like many people, Guthrum was most content when he was most uncomfortable.

Her concentration broken, Skyla heaved a sigh and went into the house. Watchdogs surrounded her—Mistislaus, Guthrum, and the three loyal old thralls back at Ulfgarth who had helped raise her. The latest one, however, she did not care for in the least. The dark and ill-favored Illmuri escorted her to the Skurdur each day, at Mistislaus' behest, lest something dreadful happen to her the moment she was out of his sight. He was a young wizard, somber and anxious, still studying the various powers available to those who sought them and the

knowledge necessary to survive once the powers were found.
He had chosen Mistislaus as his mentor—a most reluctant
mentor, but he was given no choice in the matter. Illmuri had
appeared at the gate and refused to be discouraged from his
objective of learning from Mistislaus. He took his bed in a disused storage room that smelled of fish, and he was learning to
iterate.

In the morning Illmuri reported to the front step for insults
from Guthrum and his instructions for accompanying Skyla to
the market. He was a grave young man who wore his dark hair
pulled back and tied, and he kept his beard trimmed close.
Mistislaus was always most particular that she speak to no
strangers, and no strangers were allowed to speak to her.

"Keep your hood drawn over your hair," he instructed her.
"No sense in getting sunstroke. And I don't want you bringing
home any more of that junk from the magicians' stalls. If you
want an education in magic, then I shall find you a qualified
instructor—not some pandering quack with a cartload of musty
bottles and crocks of unmentionable bits of dead creatures'
anatomies, which may be powdered dragon's tongue or common house dust for all we know. And don't forget some of that
blueberry tart from old Elva by the bridge."

"The Hangman's Bridge?" Skyla asked absently as another
disturbing image flashed on her inner eye, of a bridge where
criminals were executed in a distant, darker period of time.

"No, no, there is no Hangman's Bridge here," Mistislaus
said with a wary glance toward Illmuri, who listened impas-
sively. "I fear she's wandering a bit today. You'll have to
watch her very closely."

"I'm not wandering," Skyla snapped. "Nor am I a child. I
am perfectly capable of going by myself to the Skurdur to
shop the stalls for your odd dainties, Mistislaus."

"You may be, but I'm not prepared to let you," Mistislaus
said. "I've warned you that there's scant tolerance for anyone
in Rangfara who seems a bit strange or different. You're a wizard's daughter, my dear, and that makes you peculiar to these
people, who have scant use for magic."

"They are the ones who are peculiar," Skyla said with un-
characteristic bad humor. "Come along," she said to Illmuri, as
if he were a recalcitrant child. "I'm going to the market, and
I don't want you slowing me down."

Instead of going to the Skurdur for the tasty trifles

Mistislaus craved for his table, Skyla slowed her quick and irritated pace by the dark street that led to the Kjallari. A stream of scholars pattered by her with rolls of vellum tucked under their arms, chattering earnestly about genealogies of people long ago turned to dust and indifference. A name-day party was emerging from the stone archway bearing the young infant who had just been given a name and a scroll that would accompany and identify it for the rest of its life. Enviously Skyla strained for a glimpse of the lucky infant, who was bawling furiously and waving a puny red fist, totally ignorant of the wonderful blessing it had just been given. A name and a family and a history and a profession, all in one fell swoop.

She halted, watching as the name-day family disappeared down the narrow street. It had always troubled her before that she had no pedigree or any idea of her parentage. The images in the pool had stirred her imagination and curiosity. A woman in black repeatedly appeared, holding up a name scroll, beckoning to her urgently. She even made her way into Skyla's dreams, exhorting her to find her family.

Making her decision, Skyla turned toward the Kjallari street, suddenly filled with an eager spirit of anticipation, as if she were about to meet someone.

"The Skurdur is not that way," Illmuri said in his unfailingly polite tone, which Skyla found most irritating. "Unless you wish to go considerably out of your way."

"I wish to go to the Kjallari today," Skyla said, the words feeling stiff and strange on her lips, as if someone else had said them. "Come now, there's no harm in that, is there?" she added, seeing the wary expression that crossed his face. "One of Skjoldur's own sons is an apprentice there. It can't be such an awful place with so many people coming and going."

"Mistislaus told me to take you to the market, not the Kjallari," Illmuri said cautiously. "I don't wish to do anything to cause him displeasure."

"I can't imagine that he would be displeased because I went to the Kjallari to look around," she replied. "I may be developing an interest in history—after all, I seem to have no history of my own. Mistislaus is not my father, you must know. I'm an orphan, dumped on his doorstep when I was newborn. An unwanted bit of useless offal."

"Tush, that's no way to talk," Illmuri said, venturing to take her arm and guide her out of the way of an approaching wagon. "If some cosmic force did not want you to exist, then you would not have come to be. All this messing about with pedigrees and birthrights is a purely artificial device invented by people for the purposes of excluding other people from their pedigrees for no particularly good reason. These bodies will rot and turn to dust when we perish, but the spiritual entity that animates them will resume its journey toward a goal which our tiny finite minds can hardly comprehend. Our spirits care nothing for these hereditary trades and pedigrees."

Skyla gazed at the young wizard, his normally morose and taciturn manner suddenly warm and eloquent.

"I never thought you were a philosopher," she said when he was done with his speech.

He shrugged with a self-conscious smile. "It's something we're forced to study as young Galdur clansmen."

"But I still wish to see the genealogy scrolls," Skyla said. "When I am dead and turned to dust, it won't seem the least bit important, as you say. But right now I'm alive and very curious."

"Then we will go and satisfy your curiosity if we can. The genealogy scrolls and plates of the Skylding clan are no small undertaking, you must know. Some people spend their lifetimes trying to make sense of it."

They passed under the archway, where a carved cat figure snarled down at them. The family device of the historians, Skyla supposed. Every prominent household in Rangara boasted a device defending its gateways and doorways, featuring some powerful beast—a bull, bear, horse, wolf, or serpent—whose noble attributes might accrete to the dwellers of the house. Mistislaus never had anything over his doorway except the odd wand of hawthorne or holly or some other beneficial plant to ward off the approach of evil while he was mumbling about with his endless and generally unsuccessful experiments.

Resolutely Skyla crossed the Court of Offerings, passing through a dozen little shrines to the deceased where lamps and candles burned as memorials. A faint fetid breath whiffed from the opening of the charnel pit. A wide stairway led downward into the tunnels that led to the crypts and shrines and vaults where the records were stored. As always, it was crowded with scholars and their teachers patiently trying to drill a sense of history into the heads of heedless youth.

"I don't know why it has to be underground," Skyla said

with a sudden shiver as she caught a whiff of the earthy, cool air current wafting up the corridor.

"The records must be kept safe," Illmuri said. "Long ago there was some old prophecy and warning that the Skyldings would prevail only as long as the records were safely kept. The rock under Rangfara is naturally full of tunnels, so they merely busied themselves improving upon nature until the Kjallari was created."

Skyla paused at the conjunction of tunnels, touching the notches carved in the stone.

"The scrolls are this way," she said, and started off immediately down a narrow corridor lit with sconces wedged in the stone.

Skriftur looked up from a scroll he was lettering, his expression pleased and welcoming. His apprentice put down a stack of stone tablets with a sigh of relief, covertly patting his round and flushed countenance with a handkerchief.

"Welcome to the Kjallari," Skriftur said. "Generally we don't get visited much by young ladies. Our gifting scrolls are not the scrolls of active suitors, I'm afraid. In fact, most of them are dead."

"Most but not all?" Skyla questioned.

Skriftur scowled briefly at such a curious question before nodding his head with an amused smile. "Hoary old fellows like me whose gifting days are long gone. No one cares less than we do. Now, if we'd died two hundred years ago, it would be interesting to track us down and make a fascinating family tree of all our descendants. It's tragic to be not quite old enough to be interesting and too old to care about contributing to our genealogies. We'll leave the business of giftings and birthrights and children to stout young fellows like Einka here. He'll be gifting this year, thus ensuring the continuation of the noble Skylding warrior."

Einka turned bright red and scowled at his mentor. "I'm a historian, not a warrior," he said. "Skyldings are not encouraged to be historians, particularly if Skjoldur is your father."

"Show our guests the living scrolls, Einka," Skriftur said, waving his hand toward an adjoining room. "A lady is coming for a name giving, and I've got to come up with a list of suggestions. So far I've got Heilbrigdi the Bright and Fair and Skuljanlegur the Clear Speaker. What do you think?"

"Excellent, of course," Einka said judiciously.

"They don't sound like good Skylding names," Skyla said. "Warriors ought to be named something horrible and gruesome, like Herfang, Hedgun, or Grimmr."

"Skyldings aren't what they used to be," Skriftur said with a chuckle as he turned away to resume his writing of names. "What mother would want to give a child a name like Blood-Axe or Skull-Cleaver or Dread Slaughterer?"

"These are the scrolls," Einka said with dignity, standing aside so Skyla could see the boxes stacked on shelves. "Each one contains copies of the mothers' birthright scrolls and the names of his children. Was there someone in particular you wished to examine?"

"Yes," said Skyla. "I want to see the names of Hoggvinn's children."

"Hoggvinn the chieftain?" Einka asked, his eyes rounding with incredulity. Illmuri made some faint and ineffectual sounds of protest. "But no one is allowed, save the lady Logregla. It's a well-known fact he has no children to come after him. All died as infants."

"There were no giftings outside of Logregla?" Skyla asked.

"None that the clan would recognize," Einka said, reaching for a carved box on a high shelf. "If there were any. Logregla is his permanent and only wife, you know, so outside giftings were forbidden. There's nothing in this box except the scrolls of the infants who died. Was there some reason in particular you wanted to find out about Hoggvinn's bad luck?"

"If there were outside giftings, illegal ones, where would the scrolls be kept?" Skyla asked. "Every child has got to have a birthright scroll. Would it be in this box?" Skyla laid one hand on the carved box.

Einka rolled his eyes nervously toward Skriftur in the adjoining room. "I don't know. I wouldn't think—I don't suppose there are any outside illegal giftings, but there would have to be a scroll somewhere, as the mothers tend to demand such things from the fathers to ensure proper care and instruction for their sons, but—"

"And daughters, too, would have a scroll from their fathers, I would think," Skyla said. "To prove their claims of heredity as well as family name. Why don't you open this box and we'll see what's in it."

"It's our chieftain's box; we've not got the authority," Einka stammered, edging toward Skriftur, whose back was turned to them as he hunched over his scroll. "We have to ask permission—"

"Permission for what?" Skriftur demanded, turning.

"Opening Hoggvinn's scroll box," Einka said. "To see if there are any outside claimants to his name."

"Of course there's not," Skriftur said, snorting with indignation. "I would know about it if anyone did, and that box hasn't been added to since the last of Logregla's children died and we noted it on its scroll. I know exactly what's in that box, and I know there's been no illegal birthrights sold to Hoggvinn. What brings you here on such a useless and, I must say, peculiar quest, my dear young lady?" He removed the box from Skyla's reach, keeping it protectively beneath his hands as he talked.

"There is something in that box which I must see," Skyla said. "I know there's something else than you say inside it. There is an outside birth record in that box."

"Nonsense," Skriftur said. "I am the guardian of the scrolls and have been for a good many years before Hoggvinn inherited the seat from his father, and I know exactly what's inside. What you're suggesting could cause serious problems if Logregla's clan suspected an outside birthright, and Hoggvinn's brothers would be furious at the idea of an outsider inheriting the chieftain's seat. This is the manner in which misunderstandings arise, my lady, and you mustn't breathe a word of such gossip or all of Rangfara will be in an uproar. From what person did you hear of this insane notion of an outside gifting?"

"I saw it in a kettle of water, waiting to boil a pudding," Skyla said calmly. "I also see a woman in a black cloak."

Skriftur stared at Skyla, then turned a baffled look upon Illmuri, who gathered up his thin shoulders in a hopeless shrug. He also managed a faint, sickly smile.

"We must be going now, Skyla," Illmuri said, venturing to speak for the first time after backing himself into a dark corner to hide his mortification. "We're sorry to have troubled you with this interruption to your work."

"The young lady is a seeress?" Skriftur asked, frowning and rolling his eyes sidewise at Skyla.

"We don't know for certain," Illmuri said. "But we think that it may be a hidden talent. We do our best to humor her in case it is a gift that should be developed."

"I see," Skriftur said, shaking his head with a pitying clucking sound. "Well, we must all do our best with what we're given."

Skyla bestowed a furious glare upon Illmuri. She whirled and flew out of the chamber, taking the first corridor that she saw, losing herself in a crowd of other visitors. Illmuri made some faint call behind her, but she never paused to look back. After making five or six more turns, she slowed her pace, satisfied that she had lost him. Slowly a feeling of exhilaration overtook her as she realized she was on her own, completely without supervision, in Rangfara, without anyone hovering over her to protect her from supposed threats. Looking around, she could see no threats to be alarmed at, except possibly five or six ancient Skylding warriors on a stone bench quarreling over which of their ancestors was the most bloodthirsty and audacious. Behind them loomed a massive panel carved into the stone depicting a raging battle, with each noteworthy warrior labeled by name and family device. Lamps flickering on each side gave the stone warriors the semblance of expression and motion.

"A masterful carving," said a woman's voice behind Skyla as she contemplated it.

She turned and faced a woman in a black cloak with her hood tossed back to reveal dark hair smoothly parted, streaked with white from both temples. Immediately Skyla recognized the woman in the black cloak whose image she had been seeing in her reflecting pool, the pudding kettle, her own cup at the table. It was as if she were looking down a long shaft of memory. Strange recollections flew at her like a flock of bats.

"So here you are at last," Skyla said. "Where have you been all this time?"

"Looking for you."

"I never knew it until fairly recently, when I started seeing you in the carp pool. I feel as if I know you."

"You should, because I know you. Better than you can imagine, my child."

CHAPTER
THREE

"ARE YOU A real person or merely a thing I have summoned from the reflecting pool?"

"I am real. Here, touch my hand and you'll know I'm the same flesh as you are. The same flesh indeed, for I am Alvara, your mother's sister."

Alvara extended her hand. Skyla touched her hand with her fingertips. Her heart pounded with excitement and veracity in her ears, but her fingers were too sensitive to be deceived.

"But you are a Dokkalfar, and I am Ljosalfar. I know it by your touch that you favor the dark side of this realm. How can it be that you know my mother is your sister?"

"We grew up together. Of course I know my own sister, and I know my sister's child from your touch. I have watched you and waited for an opportunity to speak to you, but Mistislaus guards you every moment."

"You must have put the idea of Hoggvinn into my thoughts," Skyla said. "I saw Hoggvinn in my reflections also, many times, and a child was with him. A child that I thought was me. Can you tell me why?"

"Yes, I sent you the thoughts of your father. I am pleased that you read my messages. Now I know for certain that you are indeed the daughter of a Viturkona."

"Hoggvinn is truly my father?"

"Yes, but you are not recognized, I'm afraid. Reykja, your mother, wanted a warrior chieftain of Ljosalfar lineage to father her child. It was forbidden, partly because of an old feud between Viturkonur and Logregla's clan, the Drottningur. Reykja decided to pay no heed to this and had Hoggvinn drugged and kidnapped."

"This is why he refuses to recognize me?"

43

"Poor child. It was not your fault. It was well indeed for you that he had no idea of your existence. I fear he is a very coldhearted character. I shudder to think what might have happened. A birthright was bought and the scroll was given, but Hoggvinn decided—probably with Logregla's insistence—that he wanted no surviving child of that union. The infant was stolen from her mother and taken away to be exposed on the fell to die. It was Hoggvinn's first retainer, Skjoldur, that did this, but he must have had a grain of pity in his heart because he gave the baby to some half-wild shepherds to raise. They in turn gave her to Mistislaus when they found out she had magical abilities and became frightened of her. So in secret, Mistislaus raised you from an infant—Mistislaus, who is a friend to Hoggvinn and Skjoldur, who could be relied upon to carry you to Rangfara one day, where you could do the deeds that you were born to do. Skylda is your name, and it means you have a duty to perform for your mother's clan."

"Skylda—Skyla—yes. I have a duty to perform," Skyla repeated. "I have always known it, but I never knew what it was. Can you tell me, Alvara, what it is that I was born to do?"

"That is what I am here for," Alvara said with a smile.

"Skyla!" The call echoed down the corridor. She glimpsed Illmuri surging along by the light of the wicks thrust in the walls at wide intervals, so that he plunged from one pool of light to the next. When she turned back to Alvara, there was no one with her except the old warriors still wrangling on the bench before the carved panel.

"Skyla! You shouldn't have run away," Illmuri said, breathless and exasperated. "You could get lost down here and wander around for days."

"No, I wouldn't," she retorted. "I would ask someone where the door is."

"I shouldn't have brought you here," Illmuri went on. "I never dreamed you could be so troublesome."

"Finding the truth often is a troublesome process," Skyla replied. "There is a birth scroll in Hoggvinn's box. And I met the woman in the black cloak. She was here until you called out. You didn't see her, did you? She told me I was Hoggvinn's daughter from an outside marriage. My mother was a Viturkona. My father wanted to kill me as soon as I was born."

"Skyla, what nonsense. I don't know why you would say such things. I saw no woman in a black cloak, and you can see for yourself there's no way out of this tunnel except the way I came. If anyone was here, I would have seen her. Hoggvinn's daughter—she's lying, Skyla."

"So you think I'm insane, as Mistislaus told you?"

"I've been trained to avoid thinking. It only leads to trouble and misinformation. My feeling is that you are struggling with unknown powers within you. I think you are perhaps a seeress. This woman may be a sending, or she may be a real personage coming to tell you these peculiar things for purposes known only to herself."

"She was real," Skyla said. "I touched her hand, and I saw signs and images, and I had the feeling that I belonged to someone, or something, at last. It was the touch of kin, and I never knew before how lonely I was. I never thought I was kin to Dokkalfar, though. My mother and her sister are Viturkonur, which is a Dokkalfar clan."

"Dokkalfar? Viturkonur? Surely there is some other explanation," Illmuri said. "There is not a particle of darkness in you. It simply can't be."

"I thought so, too, but it is so. Are you going to tell Mistislaus?"

"And what would he do? Lock you in your room in the tower? Refuse to let you out of the house?"

"Very likely. And just when I was not so witless as I used to be."

"I don't believe you're so peculiar. Perhaps Mistislaus is trying to deny to himself that you have powers. The life of a seeker of powers is a perilous one, and he loves you too much to see you follow such a path. I'm a newcomer to that path, and already I've seen the perils. If not for the rewards, I think I'd rather be a sailor or a traveling musician."

"I, too, have seen perils, but no rewards so far. Do you believe I saw the woman in the black cloak?"

"Yes, I believe you saw something, whether a woman or a vision, I can't say. If I were you, I'd say nothing to anyone about being Hoggvinn's daughter until you've got better proof. It would upset many people."

"People are strangers to me. I've lived alone on the fells with Mistislaus all my life, with only three old thralls, an irritable dwarf, and the animals for company. From what I've seen of Rangfara and Skyldings and Krypplingur, I think I'd prefer the fells."

"Not only are you visionary, you're very wise," Illmuri said.

"Wise beyond your years. Are you ready to go to the market now you've had your trip to the Kjallari?"

"Yes. I'm embroidering some linens, and I've run out of red thread. Gunna said I could buy some at the weavers' stalls." She took his arm trustingly and let him lead her out of the tunnel, into the main thoroughfare, and up the stairs into the welcome sunlight above.

"Illmuri," she said, stopping in the street just when he thought he had gotten her safely away. "Will the woman in the black cloak come back?"

"I'd wager my neck on it," he answered grimly. "If she is any decent sort of apparition at all, she'll be back to cause us a great deal more trouble."

Illmuri saw women in black cloaks all the way to the Skurdur and at every tent or booth. Nearly every woman in Rangfara seemed to have decided to wear a black cloak that day. They lurked everywhere, but Skyla seemed to pay them no heed. She seemed to have forgotten about it entirely as she went about making her purchases, including the red thread for embroidering her linens.

"Why do you suppose my father would want to kill me?" she asked suddenly, smoothing some blue cloth with one hand. "Merely because I was not a male child, or is there something else wrong?"

Looking into the clear gray gaze she turned upon him, Illmuri knew there was no refuge in a convenient and soothing lie.

"I think it was because of your mother's clan," he said. "Viturkonur and Skylding are not a healthy mixture of traits. Magic and warfare should be kept separate. Then, too, Logregla might have been jealous."

"I thought he might have known then that I was going to be called a witling—daft—insane." She moved on to the next booth, which had reels of threads in all colors. "In that case he would wish me dead. I think Alvara has come to warn me of my danger."

Illmuri felt a trickle of sweat down his spine. Escorting Mistislaus' daughter to the market had seemed such an easy task a fortnight earlier, even demeaning for a young wizard with so much promise.

"Nothing is going to happen to you," he said firmly.

They proceeded homeward, taking a quiet path that led away from the halls and houses through an area wooded with stunted plum and oak thickets. Illmuri earnestly hoped she wouldn't take up the subject of the woman in black or her father's murderous intentions. She seemed content, walking ahead of him while he carried the basket.

Suddenly she halted as something large and dark loomed in the path. Three Krypplingur with skin bottles of the potent Dokkalfar ale lurched a few more paces until their eyes fell upon Skyla standing and eyeing them as warily as a young doe.

"Well, now, look at this," exclaimed one of the Krypplingur, his ugly features splitting in a wanton grin. "A little lass walking in the woods. Stand aside, you wretched scum, so she can pass."

"Go ahead, Skyla," Illmuri said quietly, moving up to her side. "They won't harm you."

She didn't move, however, and the Krypplingur seemed to scent her fear and hatred, like the biting sort of dog that always knew which person was the most fearful.

"What's the matter with her, can't she speak?" one of the others demanded. "Is she a slave mute or something?"

"Certainly she's not one of the sacred mother clans, or she'd never be out roaming around alone," another said.

"What a pretty little thing," murmured the first, still grinning boozily. Reaching out with one great hand, he caught her hood and pulled it off, taking several hair combs with it so that her hair escaped like a cloud of pale mist. It blew around her like a curtain, though the breeze was scant.

"Leave her alone!" Illmuri commanded, taking a step forward. "Let us pass in peace or Herrad will hear about this. You ought to know better than to touch that Dokkalfar poison. It's got eitur in it which will addict you to it for as long as you live. Now stand aside and let this girl pass by, if you have any decency as warriors."

The three warriors consulted each other with a thoughtful glance. Then the nearest one, without a word, struck out with his fist and flattened Illmuri like a poled ox. Skyla gasped and took a step backward.

"He's a noisy little creature," said the one who had struck Illmuri down. "Much better without him."

"You murderers," Skyla hissed, her heart pounding hard and fast, her ears filled with a menacing roaring.

With one massive paw, a Kryppling reached out and seized her shoulder. Twisting away in horror from such a touch, Skyla stumbled blindly, unable to see through the mist that suddenly rose before her eyes. Not mist; it was smoke, and she was seeing the destruction of Rangfara, women and children murdered in the streets until the ditches ran with blood. She screamed then, the sound filling her ears, mingling with the deadly roaring. Through the smoke the Kryppling loomed over her, his leering grin suddenly dissolving into an expression of terror. The other two Krypplingur fell back and stood staring for a moment.

"Snow lynx!" one gasped, unsheathing his sword.

Skyla hurled herself straight at him with astonishing speed and power, carrying him to the earth. Never had she felt so light and quick. There was no thought in her mind except to rend and tear and claw the life out of this creature, to use her teeth to sink into his hated flesh as he flung his arm up to protect his face.

"Skylda! Skylda!" The call came faintly from the path behind her. She knew that a figure in a black cloak was standing there, beckoning to her even as she bounded at the next Kryppling, razoring his cloak into ribbons with one deadly paw.

Illmuri raised himself on hands and knees, reaching for his staff. The third Kryppling paused in his mad scramble to escape, raising his axe, but Skyla hurtled through the air with a challenging scream and planted all four feet on his chest, driving him backward. Whimpering, gasping, the other two Krypplingur gathered themselves up and scrambled away on rubbery legs, scarcely able to take their eyes off the small gray figure that whirled like a fury between them and Illmuri on the ground. Their mouths formed the shouts of alarm and summons, but no sound except wheezing and whispering came from their lips. Skyla rushed at them for the pleasure of seeing them stagger and fall backward, still whimpering in terror. Sober now indeed, they crashed away through the underbrush, heading toward the familiar busy byways of Rangfara. A low, angry wail made them halt, gripping their weapons in terror.

"Skylda!" the call came again, and this time she turned and looked down the path, seeing the dark figure beckoning to her through the clouds of mist. The figure shimmered, resolving into a lynx with a black coat. It yowled again and vanished into the underbrush.

One of the Krypplingur shrieked, a sound that was immediately strangled into a gurgling gasping, which was soon stilled.

The other two Krypplingur dropped their weapons and ran blindly, like terrified cattle. The small creature brought them down swiftly, without a sound escaping from their throats.

Skyla turned to Illmuri, who was crouching in an untidy bundle on the ground with his staff clenched worriedly in his hands. She tried to speak, but all that came from her throat was a crooning cat voice, a questioning, humming sound.

"Skyla?" he whispered hoarsely, gazing into her unblinking golden lynx eyes with apprehension and disbelief.

She sniffed him briefly, as if making certain he was alright, then turned away to watch intently as the other feline figure returned to the path. It was a large lynx, as dark as night, with tufted ears and large soft paws. It sat down and took a few licks at the blood smearing its silvery breast, then looked at Skyla, uttering a coaxing call.

"Skyla! No!" Illmuri gasped, struggling to his feet. His head ached abominably where the fist of the Kryppling had struck him. Skyla bounded away lightly, and the dark and silver-gray figures vanished.

Illmuri staggered after them, knowing it was hopeless from the way he had seen the creatures moving with such unnatural speed and grace. How was he ever going to explain this to Mistislaus? For a moment he slumped against a rock, trying to gather his wits and his strength. Then he staggered back toward the houses of Rangfara, taking the same direction he had seen her last take.

Skyla easily overtook the black-cloaked figure of Alvara, unable to resist bounding and frisking in her newfound freedom, playing around Alvara's knees like a large pet cat.

"You enjoy it, do you?" Alvara said. "Yes, it's only fitting. The lynx is the fylgja form of the Viturkonur. It is the means of doing some of our finest work. I shall teach you more about the usefulness of the lynx form one day, but for now you must be your old self again."

With a gesture and some low words she banished the spell, and Skyla stood before her in human form again, pale and trembling.

"You're back," she gasped. "Don't leave me again, Alvara. There is so much I need to know. I've had the strangest waking dream. I thought I was an animal of some kind, and the Krypplingur—the Krypplingur were killed."

"Do not trouble yourself about Krypplingur," Alvara said. "They are nothing but fodder in a war they don't understand.

Scarcely anyone understands, but you will soon, my child. You do wish to learn your mission, don't you?"

"Of course I do. I wish to know my sister kin, my mother's clan. I've been without clan for too long."

"Yes, I can imagine how hungry you are. My dear child, I shall take you with me and you will learn."

"But Mistislaus—"

"He will very soon see that you will come to no harm. In fact, you will be very well off when this is all done. You will be with your mother's clan, where you belong, receiving the teaching you have been craving all your life. You may love Mistislaus, but the time has come to take the reins in your own two hands and guide your own life. He cannot take you where you need to go."

"That is true. But I will always remember him and be grateful."

"Hush. It is time we went ahead. You must trust me."

"Will we go to Hoggvinn?"

"Not until I'm sure you'll come to no harm. You must trust me to take care of you and make the right decisions."

Alvara took her straight to Logregla.

"My dear mistress, I don't know what to do," she began. "When I was at the market, I noticed this lovely young creature wandering aimlessly through the stalls. You can see she's well enough dressed so as not to be a scavenger or a wanderer, but she seems to have suffered an accident which has left her confused. I simply couldn't leave her there defenseless, so I brought her straight to you."

Logregla clasped her tiny white hands, lovely soft hands bedizened with rings. She pursed up her lips, scowling slightly at Skyla.

"Does she seem to understand our speech?" she asked.

Alvara looked encouragingly at Skyla, who took it as her cue to nod emphatically, although she was looking askance at Alvara and her surroundings in the women's hall. A curious flock of Drottningur languidly drifted near to stare at her plain clothes with expressions of horror and pity. Their clothes were a dazzlement to Skyla, whose notion of clothing was something designed to be functional under all circumstances and warm and comfortable in all seasons.

"She is a lovely girl," Logregla said. "You did right to bring her here. We can always give her something to do until we discover who she belongs to. Perhaps someone is looking for her this moment."

"I'm almost certain of it," Alvara said.

It was nearly nightfall when Illmuri returned to Athugashol, his scalp still encrusted with dried blood.

"Well?" demanded Mistislaus, who was waiting for him in the courtyard. All day long they had searched. As Illmuri had feared, Mistislaus had not taken the loss of Skyla with much grace. "Bumbling ass" and "nincompoop" were a few of the gentler terms the wizard had applied to him when he had come to tell him of the disaster.

"She's gone," Illmuri said, sinking down wearily on a chair in his dejection. "Simply vanished."

"I can't believe a wizard of the Galdur clan could be so foolish and careless," Mistislaus declared, harrowing his hair with his fingers. "I thought I could trust you to be alert and sensible."

"I never expected to be attacked by Krypplingur," Illmuri said, "even drunken ones. Everyone has always assured me that they're perfectly safe and trustworthy, since they're trying to establish peaceful treaties with the Skyldings."

"You're not a Skylding," Mistislaus said with a weary sigh. "You're a buffoon."

Then he pressed his fingers to his temples. "What could she be thinking of, allowing herself to be tolled away like that? Skyla has never trusted strangers. What hold could this woman have over her? Did she by any chance put a name to this woman in the black cloak?"

"Alvara," Illmuri said, and the name burned in his memory like a forgotten coal. "I think I've heard that name before somewhere."

"Of course you have, you lump, if you only knew," Mistislaus retorted with a blazing eye. "She's been waiting for her chance to steal Skyla away. Where have you been and what have you been doing if you don't know what's going on here? Are you going around as if you were asleep? Don't you know how many times we've gone through this before? How are we ever going to get it right if you've forgotten everything you know?"

Illmuri drew back haughtily from Mistislaus' spewings and sputterings. "I was hired to be a guardian for your fosterling and watch over her excursions to the market. You said she was fey and often couldn't control her powers, but you never once even hinted that I might get crowned on the head and knocked insensible."

Mistislaus didn't appear to be listening. "And three Krypplingur killed by the snow lynx."

"I really don't believe I enjoy being in your employ anymore, and as soon as Skyla is found, I won't be coming around here again. My clan masters sent me here to complete my studies to take my final test in the last standard, and I don't really have time for a lot of strange goings-on if I'm going to pass my test and become a full-fledged wizard."

"Hah!" Mistislaus said. "That's what you think. You're not going to leave me in the midst of all my troubles. I have a dreadful feeling we're just getting started. This couldn't have happened at a more inopportune time. I wonder if that odious Kraftugur didn't have something to do with it. The other day I insulted him badly in front of Hoggvinn and got myself thrown out of the Hall of Stars for my pains." He harrowed his hair again and emitted a gusty sigh. "Well, the only thing we can do is to keep searching."

Mistislaus' method of searching was to assemble every divining and skrying device known to the mind of wizard and man on a long table and contemplate each one with excruciating concentration. No sense, he said, in racing to and fro beleaguering mind and body with a fruitless physical search when they could easily find her with magical powers. He gathered up a bundle of rune sticks. With one hand he motioned Illmuri to follow suit. With a deep sigh, Illmuri picked up a handful of grain and eyed the chicken waiting in its basket to peck out a mystic message as it picked up the kernels.

The chicken, when he turned it loose, ignored the grain completely and went flapping up into the rafters in a flurry of loose feathers and dust. The perverse creature resisted all efforts to cajole it down, merely cocking its head and peering down suspiciously with one reptilian eye at Illmuri to see if he was boiling any water yet. Twice it squatted down and deposited a further contribution on the table of refuse below, unnoticed by Mistislaus, who was riveted to the surface of a pot of water.

"I don't believe this chicken has any skrying proclivities whatsoever," Illmuri grumbled. "And I doubt if you could boil it long enough to extract the least bit of nourishment from such an experienced creature. But I think it might be worthwhile to rid the world of the contrary feathered brute."

Mistislaus made no comment, still riveted, and the chicken looked down coldly and uttered a derisive cackle, as if inviting Illmuri to try it and see where it got him. At such moments Illmuri often wondered what it would have been like to have been born into a peaceful life such as shepherding or stonemasonry. He was also seized by a wave of homesickness for the well-ordered and predictable life of Galdurshol.

"Nothing here." Mistislaus snorted, discarding the pot of water and taking up a handful of fresh goose entrails, a circumstance that elicited a disapproving squawk from the chicken in the rafters. Thoughtfully, Mistislaus slung the entrails against the wall and studied them as they slithered downward. "Have you ever done this one, Illmuri? I've heard of good results with goose guts, but I've never had much luck with them, have you?"

Illmuri was about to open his mouth with some cautious observation when the front door of the hall opened and in strode Skjoldur, with Gunna and a couple of kitchen maids swaggering behind him and casting vile looks at Mistislaus and Illmuri.

"What is going on here?" Skjoldur demanded, his eyes growing larger and more stony as he gazed around the room, particularly at the goose entrails, which were still spelling out cryptic messages as they oozed toward the floor.

"Skyla's gone missing," Mistislaus said. "We're trying to find her, and I can't concentrate if you're going to come storming in here like a brigade of robbers distracting me."

"Mistislaus, we've been friends a great long while," Skjoldur said. "Every year you come and stay with me and eat inordinate amounts of food, and cook up terrible stenches with your spells and experiments, and offend the neighbors with your endless iterating from the rooftop. All this I have cheerfully tolerated in exchange for your delightful conversation and interesting company and fascinating adventures, most of which I am sure are glaring lies, but I've enjoyed them nonetheless."

"Thank you, but really, it isn't necessary to thank me," Mistislaus said. "If I didn't come here, I'd have nowhere else to stay except an inn, which I probably couldn't afford, anyway. You're a dear friend, and I shall always be pleased to come and dwell in your house."

Skjoldur drew a deep breath and clenched his fists. "That's

exactly the problem. You are such an old friend that you're beginning to reek to high heaven. Look at this hideous mess
here. The womenservants are all terrified of your experimenting and skrying and alchemizing and iterating; they're
threatening to pack up and leave the household without benefit
of female supervision. In short, my dear old friend, I'm throwing you out, and I don't ever want to see you coming back
here again. You're nothing but trouble in my life, and the trouble seems to be getting a great deal worse."

"Hah," Mistislaus said, putting down a skrying sphere and
looking closely at Skjoldur. "You mean that set-to I had with
Hoggvinn and Kraftugur."

"I'm Hoggvinn's chief retainer," Skjoldur said. "It doesn't
look good for me to be harboring you in my own house. A
dozen of my so-called friends are rubbing their hands with delight, plotting my demise because of you. All of them are coveting the seat I sit upon at the right hand of Hoggvinn, and all
of them are anticipating my forthcoming ejection because of
your big mouth spreading heresies in the Hall of Stars."

"I see. So it's not really so much that the womenfolk are
throwing me out, it's the fact that I insulted Hoggvinn and
Kraftugur?"

"Exactly, you oaf. Your magic is harmless nonsense, but
when you start messing about in the political matters of
Rangfara, you're going too far. You're going to ruin me unless
I get rid of you for once and for all. So pack up this rubbish
and take yourself out of my house before my life is entirely in
a shambles."

"Well, you've made it pretty plain you no longer want me
around here," Mistislaus said. "So I shall depart forthwith,
thanking you nonetheless for your hospitality, such as it was.
I shall never trouble your threshold again by crossing it, I can
assure you. Now that our friendship is at an end, I'd like to inform you of a few of your own faults. You're a toady,
Skjoldur, and when you're not licking Hoggvinn's boots,
you're lying in the mud so he can use you for a footbridge.
You're not so much a man as you are a pudding, taking any
shape Hoggvinn shoves you into, a great spongy mass of
spineless, quivering slop with no mind of its own. If he told
you to drink poison, you'd do it gladly. If I hadn't known
Hoggvinn before he was a chieftain, and you before you were
his chief retainer, I wouldn't care to know either of you at all."

"You're hardly worth knowing yourself. A failed wizard, a

breather of paltry spells, an overstuffed glutton. I daresay you've never worked a decent spell in your entire life, have you?"

"Dogsbody. Toady."

"Charlatan. Trickster."

"Shall I see you next year?"

"Certainly. Who else could I insult so freely? I'll have the women help you pack. Besides all this, I've just received word that Solveig is on her way to visit Jafnar."

"Great Hod. I'm well away from here, then. I have no intention of sharing a house with your wife."

"Me neither. I've got friends I intend to stay with until she's gone. It's not me she wants to see, anyway. I detest these yearly visits of hers to her son. Nothing comes of them except trouble."

"If Skyla should come back here, tell her I've gone to old Mira's house."

"She's just gone off like that, without a word?"

"Our young Galdur genius here lost her. Attacked by three of your precious Krypplingur in a ravening mood. Have you seen a woman who calls herself Alvara?"

"There is a new ladies' maid with Logregla's Drottning nieces who calls herself that name. A common name, though the woman herself does look quite remarkable."

"Tell the dear Drottningur they are cherishing a viper in their fair and precious bosoms. The Alvara I know is a Viturkona, a clan which despises the Drottningur with the last vengeful ounce of its blood. They're a witchy clan besides. Since I won't be around to deliver any warnings, you'd better caution them. A Viturkona is always up to no good, and they've got plentiful cause for grievance against the Drottningur. I predict—no, prophesy—that there's going to be a wagonload of trouble resulting from this."

Skjoldur heaved a weary sigh. "Mistislaus, take your prophecies and go. I have enough to deal with right now without worrying about these women's feuds and broils. It is a wretched man indeed who gets ensnared in women's battles with each other."

"How well we know, and Hoggvinn knows best of all," Mistislaus agreed with another sigh and a shake of his head. "But all the Skyldings will come to rue the day Logregla quarreled with the Viturkonur."

By unspoken consent Illmuri commenced helping Mistislaus

pack up his belongings. Guthrum brought Fegurd and the cart around to the door.

"Skyldingur," he grunted. "No idea of hospitality. Ought to just cut his throat and stay as long as we like. I've been expecting something like this."

"Well, I can see his point," Mistislaus said. "He knows I can't do him any good, but Hoggvinn has put butter on his bread for many years. He's not about to let mere friendship interfere with his prosperity."

Illmuri left the goose guts to the end. With a shudder of revulsion, he turned to the mess at last, when the cart was heaped with Mistislaus' belongings. Mistislaus and Guthrum were out in the courtyard shouting at each other. To his horror and disgust, the slimy mess still oozed and writhed on the wall. Wretchedly he thought about Skyla, cursing himself for his weakness and stupidity in letting something happen to her. It was justice, he thought, and these goose guts were scarcely punishment enough for his failure. Suddenly his eyes widened, and he took a step back.

"Mistislaus," he called faintly, his voice quivering with astonishment. He did not dare take his eyes off the goose entrails for an instant. "Mistislaus!"

"What are you bellowing about?" Mistislaus demanded, barging into the room in a tumult like a portly tornado, shedding small objects out of the baskets and boxes he was carrying in his arms. "Guthrum says there's no more room and we'll have to make two trips, and I say nonsense, we can always shove small things into the cracks. He's afraid that rack of bones he calls a horse can't pull the load."

"Mistislaus," Illmuri whispered. "The goose guts. It worked, it really worked. I read the goose guts."

"It did? Well, did you find out anything about Skyla?"

"Yes. She's in the Hall of Stars, with the Drottningur."

"What? Impossible! What would she be doing there? Was her woman in black a Viturkona?"

"I don't know," Illmuri began.

"Of course it makes sense. We'd find her anyplace else Alvara chose to hide her, and she knows it. Nobody can get near the Drottningur except their own servants. It would be easy to lose her among all those women. For every Drottning, there are four or five maids to bathe her, dress her, comb her hair, fetch, carry, and do practically everything but breathe for her. That's Alvara alright, cold and clever and calculating. Did you get any idea what her intentions are?"

Illmuri squinted at the goose guts, which were now nothing but uncommunicative offal smeared on the wall. "I think I saw cats," he said.

"Of course you saw cats. Logregla keeps a hundred of them. Is that the only impression you received?"

"As near as I can remember right now. Something may come back to me later."

"When we get settled again, I'll see if I've got something to jog your memory," Mistislaus said, uncorking a vial and sniffing its contents warily. "These things often come back to you suddenly. Your physical eyes may see things you can't remember easily. But with a little judicious digging about, we can uncover something."

"I don't think I want anyone digging about in my brains," Illmuri said in alarm, as if Mistislaus were a sheepdog digging for bones among the cabbages.

"Never mind," Mistislaus said soothingly. "Now finish up with that mess and let's be off."

CHAPTER
FOUR

IT WAS A dream, somehow. Jafnar opened his eyes and shook his head to clear it of the roaring and ringing of pain. Gingerly he lifted his hand and felt the stickiness of drying blood on the side of his head where the Kryppling sword had caught him. Too late he had realized that Ofarir, guided by his interior master, Kraftugur, had been waiting in the shadows with half a dozen experienced Krypplingur. They had made short work of Otkell and the last of the Skyldings. Visions of the horror and the broken walls and heaps of fallen masonry still shimmered before his eyes. Blinking, he gazed around in stupefaction as the visions slowly dissolved into neat trim walls and the velvety green turf he was lying upon.

Surrounding him was a crowd of unfamiliar people carrying weapons. His wild-boy instincts for flight and self-preservation surged to the fore, and he gathered himself for a mighty surge to escape. He got his legs under him despite the shouts and protests of the strangers, but he felt strangely tremulous, and they brought him down again after he had staggered only a few steps.

"Let me go! I didn't steal anything!" he blurted.

"Now, then! Of course not! Be still!" a rough voice commanded. "Let's look at that knot on your head!"

Jafnar blinked and squinted, trying to clear his vision so he could better see the countenance peering into his own. He expected a Kryppling face, but it was not, although it was scarred and ugly enough to have compared well.

"Who are you?" Jafnar demanded.

"How could you forget this face? It's Engi, of course, your fighting instructor," came the answer from the stranger who was bent over him with his ugly features contorted even further by consternation.

"I've been fighting all my life," Jafnar said with a faint snort. "I've never needed an instructor."

"That was a wicked whack you took, my lord. A right dastardly trick, Modga. You could have killed him. Are you feeling alright?" Engi demanded, giving Jafnar's arms a shaking and pummeling to see if they were broken.

"Modga? He's alive? Where's Modga?" Jafnar turned his head painfully to look at the circle of unfamiliar faces surrounding him where he lay sprawled on the grass. Jafnar looked at the walls again; they were neatly chinked with tuffets of green moss and grass. "How did the walls get put together again? At least Otkell the Slaver won't trouble us anymore, with his guts strewn around. What have you done with all the bodies of my brothers?"

"He's talking nonsense," one of the strangers said. "What did you want to hit him that hard for, Modga? It wasn't very sportsmanlike, with his back turned that way."

"He should pay better attention if he fancies himself such a great warrior," another replied with a scowl.

Jafnar looked at the speakers, two tall fair Alfar he had never seen before. Yet recognition was stirring faintly in the back of his fragile consciousness. Some faint voice told him that these strapping youths leaning on swords and lances were his Skylding brothers. They were all nearly man-grown and tall, and their hair and young beards were all white as newly washed wool or shades of pale silver and gold.

"Modga," he said, peering into their faces. "And Ordvar. Lofa, Lampi. All of you look different. You've gotten older. And you're much better fed."

The rest of them laughed in relief and jostled each other good-naturedly. Modga still scowled as much as ever, which gave him a menacing appearance. Jafnar felt his own limbs, looking at the size of them in astonishment. Instead of the hungry, stringy wild boy, he, too, was grown tall and strong, as if he had never missed a meal in his life or foraged for something remotely edible on the fringes of the Skurdur.

"How long have I been gone?" he asked.

Engi chuckled and shook his grizzled head, as did the other warriors clustering around him and leaning upon their swords and lances.

"You were away quite a while," Engi said. "For a while we

thought you'd been killed. Caught you right alongside the noggin, Modga did. Unintentionally, I hope."

"Modga. How you've changed since I saw you last." Jafnar frowned, struggling with a parade of confusing memories as the tall young man with a dark scowl reached out his hand to help him briskly to his feet none too gently. He dropped his hand immediately afterward.

"No hard feelings, I hope," Modga said, his voice deep and unfamiliar, his stature far more lofty and powerful now. Jafnar stared at him as if he had never seen him before yet perfectly knowing his piercing, angry gaze and his lean and scowling features.

"Why are you still angry?" Jafnar asked.

"You should know that better than anyone," Modga muttered impatiently. He scowled and flushed even more darkly, looking away across the green practice field to the surrounding fells. In the distance stood the black and forbidding walls of Rangfara.

"Rangfara!" Jafnar gasped. "And look at it! It's beautiful! It's not crumbling away! The Krypplingur haven't destroyed it yet—" The words stuck in his throat as his thoughts raced ahead. Or was it backward? He had no idea where he stood in time. The very ground under his feet seemed to swell and heave, and he rocked unsteadily and would have fallen if Lofa and Lampi hadn't caught him and lowered him gently to the soft green sward.

"He's not ready for standing up yet," Lofa said.

"There's a lump like a hen's egg on his head," Lampi said. "Better let him rest awhile."

"We'll have to fetch a cart," Engi exclaimed. "He's in no shape to be up walking about. Ordvar, run and fetch a cart from the Skurdur."

"Skurdur!" Jafnar murmured, struggling halfheartedly against the hands that laid him down. "Where's Ordvar? Wait, I want to see him. Ordvar! Is that you?"

Of course he knew it was Ordvar, half recognizing the young man who quickly returned from his horse and came to kneel beside him. He knew the young ragged wild boy behind the steady blue eyes and the generous mouth that wanted to smile but was now drawn up firmly with manly concern.

"We've had some good times in the Skurdur," Jafnar said. "Don't you remember the time we stole an entire joint of meat from old Sveppur's baking stall? And how the Krypplingur chased us?"

Ordvar raised his eyes appealingly to Engi. "Lie still and be calm, Jafnar. I'll go fetch a cart and we'll have you home in no time."

"He's out of his head," someone murmured anxiously. "You'd better fetch his father from the Hall of Stars."

"The Hall of Stars!" Jafnar's hearing seemed unnaturally acute. "My father? What's he doing there? Is old Fegurd still grazing there? And Mistislaus—Mistislaus is dead, killed by the Krypplingur! Where's Skyla? Is she here? You must tell me!" He clutched at Engi's sleeve.

"He's raving! Maybe we'd better fetch a physician!"

"Go, then, and quickly!" Engi said in an undertone.

Ordvar hurled himself onto his horse and rode away at a gallop.

"Where's my father?" Jafnar demanded. "He's here? He's alive? I want to see him! Where is he?"

"In the Hall of Stars with the other chieftains," Engi said in a patient tone.

"You're sure he's alive? He's not dead? He's here?"

"What does he mean?" the surrounding warriors murmured, exchanging concerned glances and shrugging their shoulders.

"This can't be Rangfara." He struggled to rise enough to catch a glimpse of the familiar rugged black walls, where airy towers and spires rose up in graceful entreaty toward the heavens. "Look, the sky is blue! Since the Krypplingur took over, the sky is almost never blue. Remember what they did to the climate with their sorcery?"

"You'd better fetch Skjoldur from the Hall of Stars," someone murmured. "Let him know Jafnar's been hurt."

"Skjoldur!" The name sent a shudder through Jafnar's frame from one end to the other as he recognized his father's name. He could have wept, knowing at last that he had a name— Skjoldursson. "Where is my father?"

"At the Hall of Stars," Engi said again.

"But why is he there? The roof's gone. But Utsala's pool is still there and the sacred carp—" His head commenced a furious buzzing, as if warning him away from such thoughts and words.

"Just rest easy until the cart gets here," Engi said gently, tucking his own cloak under Jafnar's head as a cushion. "Things always seemed a little confused to me, too, when I got a knock on the head. I remember one time it took me nearly a fortnight to get my thoughts straight again."

"But I've been here before," Jafnar said as clearly as possible. Still his brother and cousin Skyldings didn't seem to understand. "I've seen Rangfara before. Or maybe it was after—" Even as he was speaking, his conviction faded into uncertainty.

"Of course you have," Engi said. "You were born here. When I got rapped on the skull at Vegnafjord, I couldn't even remember my own name for three days. The brain plays odd tricks when it's rattled around. You recollect your own name, don't you?"

"Jafnar," he said, slowly adding, "Skjoldursson. Jafnar Skjoldursson, of the clan Skylding of Rangfara. I know Modga and Ordvar, Lofa and Lampi—"

"And Engi. You must remember old Engi, who has been like a second father to you ever since you were old enough to drag a broadsword along the ground after you." Engi grinned broadly, showing an assortment of broken teeth, but his eyes were veiled with anxiety.

"Engi? I don't think I remember. You seem a nice enough old chap, though." His eyes traveled slowly around the circle of unfamiliar faces, struggling between waves of uncertainty and faint recognition. They were all Skyldings, and they had come to the practice field to polish their skills at fighting and weaponry. "But where's Einka? He should be here. He was one of us."

"Einka?" Lofa and Lampi still talked in turns, as if they had one brain between them. "He's Skriftur's apprentice now. A fat little fellow who squints has no business training as a warrior. He spends most of his time writing on scrolls down in the Kjallari with Skriftur."

"Kjallari!" Jafnar gasped, reaching out and grasping Lofa's arm with a death grip. "You don't know what's down there? You don't know what's going on with the dead bodies? There's horrible creatures down there, created from the flesh of dead things thrown down the charnel pit and lost spirits conjured by Kraftugur, and they want nothing more than to get hold of living souls. And the Kellarman—"

"Now, then, don't get so excited," Engi said soothingly. "You'll do yourself a damage. Those are old tales told to frighten small children into behaving themselves."

"But I've seen things down there," Jafnar said. "Kjallari-folk, made all wrong and evil. It's Kraftugur, and he must be stopped. He doesn't understand how to manipulate the powers of creation. You've got to tell them to make him stop, or one day those creatures will rule the Kjallari from end to end and creep into the streets at night—"

"No, no, hush, it's alright," Engi murmured, trying to soothe him as he babbled on.

The cart came rattling over the velvety sward, drawn by a pair of sleek fat ponies with flaxen manes, with Ordvar standing up, urging them on.

"You'll never get to the top of the Street of a Thousand Steps with that," Jafnar murmured as they lifted him into the cart, which was well padded with cloaks and tunics. "You'll have to go the long way around."

Ordvar drove, and Engi cradled his head against the bumps. The rocking motion lulled him half to sleep. Suddenly a jolt in the road awakened him, and in an instant he was riding in the cart with Alvara, his foot afire with the deadly bite of one of the Kjallari creatures. He gripped the sides of the cart, galvanized by the memory.

"Kjallari fever!" he gasped. "I'm going to die! Tell Mistislaus I've got to have more than useless iterations! I saw him walking in the shadow realm, coming to look for me. Where is Mistislaus? Is he dead yet? Is he still alive?"

"Hush now!" Engi said gently. "We're almost there."

The gates and buildings, bridges and archways of Rangfara were familiar yet strange in their unbattered condition. All was new and holding together with a living, vital force reflected in the brisk and prosperous appearance of the passersby and merchants hawking their wares. No slinking skulkers and scavengers, no lurking Krypplingur menacing with their armor and weapons, no cartloads of shrieking, enslaved Slaemur women. An orderly queue of young children trotted obediently at the heels of their gowned instructor, who was leading them on some educational expedition through the city. An enormously laden wagon drawn by six great horses halted to let the children trip past the noses of the foremost horses. In the Rangfara, Jafnar knew, such an event would have resulted in terrible shouts and imprecations and whip crackings from the carters perched aloft on their towering load, not halting the clashing thunder of their horses' huge metal-shod hooves for an instant. More than once Jafnar had seen cripples, blind beggars, and careless children ground to jelly beneath the hooves and wheels of uncaring carters.

The cart turned into a narrow dark street. Jafnar sat bolt upright again. The stench of fear seemed to exude from the tall archway, gripping him by the throat and heart as they rolled past the lynx gate. The terror was there, unsuspected as yet by those who casually traversed the narrow street, gazing curiously after the cart carrying the raving madman.

"No, not the Kjallari street!" he yelled before falling back in a fit of dizziness. "They know I'm here! The Kellarman and all his legions crave to devour my vitals! He'll string my soul on a cord like fish in the market!"

"Hush, Jafnar," Engi whispered anxiously.

Jafnar struggled to sit up, seeing a knot of Krypplingur strolling casually along the pavement.

"Swine!" Jafnar shouted furiously as they rattled by. "Get out of Rangfara or we'll gut you like rabbits! This is our city, not yours!"

"Jafnar! Quiet! I beg of you!" Engi squeaked. "You mustn't insult the Krypplingur! We've got to make them feel welcome here!"

"If you've got any sense at all, you'll drag Herrad into the street and kill him now!" Jafnar said, gripping Engi's forearm with desperate strength, dragging him nearer.

"Hush, you have no idea what you're saying," Engi said.

"I've never been more clear in my life," Jafnar said, almost weeping. "I know what I've seen. Rangfara in ruins, murders in the streets, ghouls in every shadow, and the Krypplingur shall put the sword to every Skylding. Herrad has murder in his heart, and he has come here for the treasure of Rangfara!"

"Now, now!" Engi said soothingly, as if he were speaking to a frightened horse. "It's not so bad as that!"

Jafnar scarcely heard him. He peered over the side of the cart at a different Rangfara. He even recognized old Hofud the seer, respectably cloaked and gowned, standing on the doorstep of a comfortable turf house with three steep roof gables. He was apparently forecasting the future success of a client with a string of pack ponies, laden and outward bound.

"If Hofud were any kind of seer at all, he'd see what's going to happen to Rangfara," Jafnar said with a shudder. "And to himself. Engi, where's Skyla?"

"Who is Skyla?" Engi asked.

"Mistilsaus' girl," Ordvar said. "He brought her with him this time. Our father threw Mistislaus out of his house after that last disruption of the council. Mistislaus left, and I suppose Skyla went with him."

Jafnar's burst of energy left him drained, and he fell back and shut his eyes, feeling as if he were trying to communicate with blocks of wood.

"How long ago did Mistislaus leave?" Jafnar asked weakly. "Is he still in Rangfara?"

"I don't know," Ordvar said. "You're the one who lives at Athugashol with our dear father, not me. You should know more about it than I do."

Jafnar suddenly caught a glimpse of the Hall of Stars, where the wild boys had lodged, homeless and carefree as brown sparrows. It now stood intact, roofed and turreted and resplendent in full sunshine. Flags of all colors and devices flew from every pinnacle, window, and gate arch, announcing the presence of the great ladies of noble birth within.

"Oh, just look at it!" Jafnar breathed. "It was worth getting a cracked skull to see it as it used to be. I never dreamed it was anything quite so grand."

He pointed as they rolled past the entrance, guarded by a pair of Skylding warriors on horseback. He saw a pure white pennant with a black figure when the wind unfurled the device on the white flag.

"Look! The black lynx!" he whispered.

"Oh, aye, the lady Logregla's new colors," Engi said with a sage nod and a wry grimace. "She still fancies herself quite a killer."

"The black lynx—is it here?" Jafnar demanded, his skin rippling with waves of gooseflesh. "Have the killings started?"

"Hush! No talk about that!" Engi hissed in fright.

"Three Krypplingur with their throats torn to shreds is nothing to hush about," Ordvar retorted in a low voice. "Three others with their hearts and livers gone, torn out by something with claws—"

"I don't want to talk about it!" Engi sputtered.

"You'll do more than talk about it in days to come," Jafnar whispered, trembling in the grip of his knowledge of the future. "Rangfara will arm itself against the lynx. Everyone will dread the fall of night, fearing the cry of the lynx. It will be a city of fear and death."

"Hush now!" Engi commanded, adding in an undertone to Ordvar, rolling up his yellowed eyeballs, "Oh, this is worse than anything we thought. He's totally lost his wits! This is a fine thing to happen when his mother is here visiting!"

"My mother is here, too?" Jafnar gasped, his head reeling in shock as he struggled to rise.

When they came to Athugashol, Ordvar leapt down and rang at the bell furiously until the gate opened. The cart bumped through the narrow dark courtyard and halted at the doorstep. A tall woman opened the door and stood poised a moment on the top step. She must have been washing her hair. It flowed loose around her in a billowing cloud as she swooped down the steps like a harrier on its prey.

"What's happened?" she demanded, touching the side of Jafnar's head and examining the lump and the blood with professional fingers.

"He's taken a bit of a knock on the skull, that's all," Engi said soothingly, dismounting from the cart. "We were practicing, and I think he took his eyes off Modga for just an instant, and before we knew it he was flat on the ground, as senseless as a stun-poled ox. This is a fine way to conclude your visit. But I think your son will recover quickly. I've seen this sort of injury before. He doesn't seem to remember or recognize anything. When I was wounded at Svipaford—"

"Mother?" Jafnar reached out his hand tentatively and touched her on the cheek with just the back of one knuckle. Only barely did he remember her. He didn't remember her face at all.

She smiled and kissed his hand. "He remembers me. You always were hurting yourself when you were a little lad in my house, falling off walls, ponies, anything that would raise a bump or make a scratch. Your father hasn't taken much care of you, it seems."

"I remember your house. But I was born in Rangfara."

"Yes. You belong to your father."

His heart seemed to be fluttering and dying in the cage of his chest, alternately beating itself to death with joyousness and throbbing with terrible anguish. She was more beautiful than any twenty-year-old bride, tall and golden-skinned from being outdoors, with blue steady eyes and firm lines of character giving strength and substance to the transitory veil of beauty. And her hair hung loose and damp down her back to her waist in a flowing curtain of rich deep gold, the hair she had plucked to braid into bowstrings for Skjoldur in the fatal, final battle of Rangfara.

Taking a handful of the strong, silky strands, he marveled that each was as fine as a cobweb but that together they formed a strong cord.

"Never cut it, Mother," he said, looking into the concern in her eyes, wanting to cast himself into that deep and irretrievable well of security and love. "Someday you'll use it to save my father."

"Your father!" she repeated, hoisting one eyebrow. "He's never in need of saving, except from himself."

"There will be a battle, and you will braid your hair for a bowstring," Jafnar said, his voice choking.

"You see what I mean," Engi said, his tone slightly disgusted. "He's been in a strange humor ever since he woke up. A death journey will do that to a man, and when he comes back, he is forever changed. We must take care of him, Solveig, and watch him closely."

"I shall be fine," Jafnar said, struggling to light down from the cart by himself to prove it. His knees wobbled pitifully at just the wrong moment, spoiling the dignity of his descent. He would have fallen if Ordvar hadn't caught him.

"We'll put him in the little room downstairs," Solveig directed as they bore him inside, half stumbling and shuffling his feet as his attention wandered elsewhere.

The hearths were still as he remembered them, where Mistislaus had sat in his tall chair, smoking his pipe and shedding ashes everywhere or tenderly nibbling some toothsome dainty while dispensing his impenetrable wisdom. There was the narrow door to the stairway that went up to the little room where Skyla had nested high in the rooftops, near the wind and stars. The broad stairs led above to the rooftop observatory and more rooms that had been mostly roofless when he had seen them last. Walls were plastered, the beams were painted with designs in red and blue, and everything was much neater than he dreamed was possible.

"We'll have to fetch a healing physician to look at this," Solveig said, blotting at the still-oozing wound on the side of his head after they had placed him on the sleeping shelf, hoisting up his wobbling legs like so much lumber.

"I'll do it," Ordvar said, suddenly uncomfortable and awkward in the presence of their fallen companion now that womankind had taken over. "I'll go to the Tower of Horses and fetch one of the healers, quick as a hare."

"Ahaldr is my favorite," Solveig called after him.

"What about Mistislaus?" Jafnar demanded. "I want to see Mistislaus. Where is he? Wasn't this his house?"

They all exchanged a wary glance, freezing a moment.

"This is your father's house," Solveig said. "Mistislaus was only a guest. He's gone now. Ahaldr will come in an instant."

"I can't believe you're here," Jafnar said after Engi had gone to return the cart and horses to their owner.

"Well, I've come to visit you every year since your father took you away," she said. "And you're going to be gifted soon, so I thought I should be here."

"Gifted? I am? I never thought much about marriage," Jafnar replied with a frown of consternation.

"I expect your father has got one of those Drottningur picked out for you," Solveig continued with some asperity in her tone. "I can't see it, myself. The most expensive birthright to buy in all of Skarpsey, and what does a Skylding get from marrying into that clan? No fighting ability, no intelligence—"

Jafnar interrupted. "Mother, have you never felt as if you had been in two places at once, at different times?"

"Let Ahaldr explain that to you," Solveig said. "I'm sure he knows all about damaged skulls and wandering wits."

"But it is possible, Mother. I was here once before, only it was all ruined and different. Rangfara was a place of ghosts, and the Skyldings were all dead, except for eight of us, and we were young orphans, living like scavengers. I didn't even know the names of my parents."

"Hush, hush. Mistislaus has put strange ideas into your head. A good thing he's gone. Don't even try to remember such disturbing dreams."

"They weren't dreams. I was a different person—yet the same in many ways—and now I am here. I feel like a prophet of doom, knowing the future and seeing what is going to lead us straight into it."

"No one knows the future except those wizards who are trained to study it," Solveig said. "You are an ordinary Skylding warrior, not a prophet, and you may count yourself blessed on that account. You've none of the wizard in your pedigree to taint your blood, I'm proud to say."

"And the pedigrees and records are all down in the Kjallari with Skriftur and the catacombs," Jafnar said.

"Certainly. Whatever happens, the records will be safe."

"But something does happen, and the records are not safe. A great many were destroyed by the Krypplingur."

"The Krypplingur! You're being preposterous. They may be ugly fellows and fierce fighters, but they are honorable down to their toes and completely loyal to the Skylding clan. They would never do such a thing."

"They would and they will," Jafnar said.

"How can you say they such a thing about men who have eaten at your father's table and shared your father's ale? You certainly seemed admiring enough of Herrad, and you were ready enough to accept his gifts for someone who is so distrustful now."

"I wasn't distrustful before because I didn't know the future," Jafnar muttered, closing his eyes in sudden weariness of the burden of knowledge he was carrying.

"Rest now," she commanded gently. "All this raving and nonsense has worn you out, I should think."

When he opened his eyes from the trough of sleep he had fallen helplessly into, he looked straight into the pale and narrow face of Illmuri, who was contemplating him as if he were a cat carcass posing as a hare on offer at the butcher's stall.

"What are you doing here?" Jafnar hissed furiously, struggling to get his elbows under him so he could glower from a more upright position.

"Ahaldr was suffering from a badly inflamed toe," Illmuri said calmly, "brought about by eating too large a dose of plumabrot. I just happened to be passing by when I heard the news of the accident."

"Lucky for me," Jafnar said, striving to swing his wooden, uncooperative legs onto the floor. "It will make it so much the easier for me to kill you, since I'll be spared the difficulty of looking you up. What did you do with the gold you got for selling us to Kraftugur?"

"Dear me, he's gone raving again," Solveig said, clucking her tongue and shaking her head. "Pay no attention. I warned you that his wits were awandering."

"Yes, indeed you did," Illmuri said, pushing Jafnar back into his cot with scarcely any effort. "Now the questions is, Where did his wits go awandering to? Would you fetch me a cup of ale. I came in such a hurry that I've worked up a terrible thirst."

"Oh! I've forgotten my manners! Of course you shall have a drink." Solveig hurried out of the room.

"You know what you did," Jafnar accused, seizing a handful of Illmuri's gown. "What are you doing here? Did you come

to finish off the job you started then? I think you'll have a little more difficulty now. An orphan wild boy is a paltry target
compared to what I am now."

Illmuri extricated himself. "Don't waste any more of my
time with your nonsense than you have to."

Jafnar stared at him intently as he rummaged around in his
satchel and came up with a powder to stop the bleeding.

"You don't know me, do you?" he asked slowly.

"Of course I do," Illmuri retorted. "You're the son of one of
Hoggvinn's chief retainers. You're a lazy, useless fellow who
has been pampered and spoiled all his life and educated very
little and allowed to do whatever he pleases. A fine example of
what the Skylding clan is coming to since it became so
wealthy."

Solveig returned with a tray laden with bread and cheese
and pickled trotters as well as ale.

"It doesn't do to put ale down on an empty stomach," she
said, "and I thought you had a hollow look about you."

"Thank you, kind wife," Illmuri said, sitting down to his
small feast. "It was a lucky day for me that Ahaldr's toe became inflamed."

"And probably no accident," Jafnar muttered.

"And a lucky day for us as well," Solveig said, giving her
son a reprimanding stare.

"Actually, I'm new to Rangfara," Illmuri said in his best
smooth and oily tones. "I'd heard of Rangfara and yearned to
see what a city was like and whether there was an opportunity
for a young wizard like me to find a mentor among the wizards of Rangfara to further my expertise."

"Well, I wish you good fortune," Solveig said. "If you require a recommendation, I'm sure I can supply one. My son
seems much more calm now."

"Yes, I think it was just temporary excitement brought about
by the blow to the head," Illmuri said, his deep-set eyes boring
warnings into Jafnar. "Time will heal the imbalance he's feeling right now. I would advise strict quiet and rest. No visitors
and no going out. I shall return twice a day to make certain
he's not doing anything he shouldn't in this excitable condition. I urge you not to greatly heed anything he says for a
while until he gets both feet planted firmly on the ground
again."

"What a lot of rot!" Jafnar exclaimed. "There's nothing
wrong with me, and you know it, you charlatan!"

"You see what I mean?" Illmuri said. "He has no idea of what he's saying or doing, so he must be watched very closely. Let him eat anything he wants except very rich treats such as plumabrot."

"Yes, plumabrot has never agreed with him," Solveig said. "As a small boy it made him sick once when we got a batch that was either spoiled or a little too strong with age. How about some nice hot broth and stale toast? I've never known broth and toast to go down wrong with anybody."

"Sounds perfectly admirable," Illmuri said. "And a poultice on this head wound would be helpful. One of the strong-smelling ones, and leave it bound on for as long as possible."

"Very well," Solveig said. "I know several very strong and smelly poultices that have worked well in the past."

"And don't forget to keep him in," Illmuri added.

"Don't worry, Meistari Illmuri; he's not going anywhere with a bag of steaming fjallagross lashed to his head."

"I want to see Mistislaus," Jafnar said, suddenly convinced that the fat old wizard's circumlocutions were exactly what he needed to hear just then. Mistislaus often seemed batty, but under all his words was a layer of truth.

Illmuri shook his head, his eyes meeting Solveig's. "You see what I mean. We can only hope this accident doesn't lead to a brain fever."

"Where's Mistislaus?" Jafnar demanded, struggling to prop himself up on one elbow and making threatening movements to get his feet onto the floor. "I want to see him. I need to talk to him. I know he must be here somewhere, so don't tell me a bunch of lies about him."

"Hush, don't fret yourself," Solveig said hastily. "We'll do what we can to fetch him if only you'll lie still and rest. You don't want to get a brain fever, do you? Then you'd better stop thrashing around. If you want to speak to Mistislaus, then we'll see if he'll come. Are you certain it's Mistislaus you want to see? He's fallen somewhat under question of late."

"Yes, I want to see Mistislaus," Jafnar insisted. "I don't care if he's fallen out of favor. It's all the doing of Kraftugur. But Kraftugur is the one who loses."

"So now you've taken up with wizards and foreseers," a new voice said. "It's much as I might have expected. Now what's all this uproar about Jafnar being half-killed?"

CHAPTER
FIVE

SKJOLDUR STEPPED INTO the room. His height and stature were only average, though he carried himself with the dignity of a man who had earned respect. He was well dressed in a fur-trimmed cloak, and there was not much of the seasoned warrior about him, except for a slight limp as he moved forward and a wary scowl that had entrenched itself in his brow.

"He's nearly had his brains knocked out," Solveig said with a sudden protective fierceness in her gentle voice. "He looks well enough now, but you should hear the nonsense he's been talking."

Skjoldur stalked forward and inspected the knot on Jafnar's head. "Looks like nothing to me. How will he ever become a decent warrior if he faints away at every small scratch?"

"This is no small scratch!" Solveig spit. "He's been raving like a lunatic! It could develop into a brain fever!"

"If you weren't here to coddle him, he'd scarcely notice it," Skjoldur retorted, glaring at Jafnar. "There's a lot of blood and nothing more. If he wants to be a Skylding warrior, he'll have to get used to fighting, not just practicing with old Engi. His half brothers aren't so minching and squeamish about being knocked around a bit. I warrant it would take more than this to put Modga down flat on his back. Now, there's a good lad for you."

"Modga is a murdering fiend," Solveig said. "And he's always been jealous of Jafnar. You'll have nothing but more trouble with that one. A fine son indeed, clobbering his brother at the first opportunity."

"Modga always hated me," Jafnar blurted with a convulsive twitch that made his head ache afresh. "If I were out of the way, then he would stand in my place as firstborn."

"Oh! I knew your precious Modga clouted him deliberately!" Solveig declared. "Is this the way you teach your sons to behave? Smashing in skulls and giving people brain fevers? I've turned Jafnar over to you to make a beast of?"

Illmuri coughed discreetly and vanished.

"My sons are proper Skylding warriors," Skjoldur said. "Raised and taught by men, not their mothers. If he's got brain fevers, it's because a woman has put the wrong notions into his head. I wish you would go back to your clan and your sisters and leave him to me. I think you've visited here long enough."

"I shall leave when I please and not before," Solveig said. "From this moment you are no longer any husband of mine. But Jafnar will always be my son."

"No, he is mine. I paid for a birthright twenty years ago with the expectation that you would bear me a Skylding son. Your part of the bargain was finished when he was six. Now you keep troubling us with your visits. We don't need any women nattering around here about the way we chew our food and how we drink and who our friends are and where we're going and when we'll be back. Skyldings are warriors, true men true to each other."

"And truly stupid most of the time," Solveig added. "You won't see me again, Skjoldur. I wash my hands of you forever."

"You've said that before," Skjoldur said. "Many times. I hope you mean it this time."

"Fool!" Jafnar said, surprising himself with the bile of fury he felt rising in him. The words poured out from some well of knowledge that he desperately wanted to put a lid on, but he couldn't stop the flow. "You'll regret her leaving one day, a day when the battle is gathered thick around you and your bowstring breaks. She would have been at your side, braiding a bowstring from her own hair for you, which no other woman would have done, nor even any of your other sons, your closest battle companions, or their mothers. Without her you will perish alone and unregarded."

The prophetic flow abandoned him suddenly, leaving him as winded as if he had been running a footrace. Jafnar fell back on his cot, closing his eyes.

"What talk is this?" Skjoldur demanded in astonishment.

"You see, it's as I said," Solveig said in exasperation. "He's been going on like that. He thinks he can see the future. You're the one who brought a wizard into your household. I shouldn't wonder if Mistislaus has stolen his wits away with some sort of sorcery. Wizards are at the very least a bad example for impressionable youngsters. They oughtn't to be brought into the house and encouraged. But of course you never listened to me. I knew being thick with that Mistislaus would end badly."

Skjoldur whacked his forehead with his palm, turning to Jafnar. "Hah! This explains it! You've been corrupted by that hoary old relic of a wizard! How dare he imperil what little knowledge you've got by trying to add wizardry to it?"

"And to think," Solveig continued, "how you've invited that old gasbag into my son's home every year, spouting his strange ideas and mumbling who knows what over that knotted string. If you're going to be a Skylding warrior, Jafnar, you can't have anything to do with useless old superstitions. Or useless old wizards trying to stir up trouble."

"Mistislaus is a decent enough fellow for all his peculiarities," Skjoldur declared staunchly. "I was always proud to call him my friend."

"Until he fell out of favor with Kraftugur and Hoggvinn," Solveig said. "What was it all about? Something to do with old troubles in the past, perhaps?"

"Well, he kept on harping about the Krypplingur long after everyone else decided to accept them," Skjoldur said. "He should have learned to keep his mouth shut even if he didn't like them."

"Not Mistislaus," Jafnar said. "He knows the truth. You've all grown fat and satisfied here in Rangfara. You've forgotten how to fight for survival. You should be smashing the skulls of these slinking, grinning Krypplingur instead of figuring out ways to marry them."

"There's no harm in the Krypplingur," Skjoldur said. "Good hearty fellows, every one of them, as honest as the day is long. I'd trust my back to any Kryppling almost before my own relatives."

"I've seen Krypplingur split the skulls of Skylding infants and put the sword to women and children," Jafnar hissed, trembling in every muscle with the force of old memories that came churning unbidden to his mind, things he had seen as a child and buried like the horrors they were. "They slashed off the hands of their captives, then taunted them far into the night, by the light of heaped-up bodies burning. Old people were run down by horses and trodden in the streets. The Skurdur ran with a torrent of Skylding blood, and when it was all finished, not one remained alive. The Krypplingur gorged themselves on our blood, then began to search for our treasure. For our treasure the Skyldings all died. It would have been better that Rangfara was never built and the Skyldings had stayed in their tents and huts, roaming the wastelands like the wild people, than to have turned into a clan of fat and prosperous city dwellers. Where are your warrior ways? Where went the instincts that warn you when your enemies are present? All the wildness has gone out of you!"

Jafnar shook his clenched fist, his face drawn into a terrible rictus of rage and despair.

Skjoldur retreated several cautious steps until his back pressed against the cool stone walls, a sheen of sweat bursting into beads upon his brow.

"You see what it's like?" Solveig said, her voice tremulous with tears. "I think we should get Mistislaus in here and force him to account for this. I know he's at fault. Our son is a raving madman."

"Nonsense, he's not mad," Skjoldur said, offering her a clumsy and heavy-handed patting on the back for comfort. "Jafnar, how could you know all those things? Mistislaus has put strange ideas into your head. You've been nowhere except Rangfara all your life."

"But which life?" Jafnar demanded, struggling to sit up unsteadily on the edge of the sleeping platform. "The Web has many lives, all going at the same time together. Haven't you ever seen someone you're certain you know from somewhere? Sometimes we remember bits and pieces. Though I was just a child, I was here and I did see the bodies and the bonfires, and I'm warning you: Turn out Herrad and Ofarir and all the others and lock the gates of the settlement or your bones and flesh will burn with the rest of the Skyldings."

He swayed then, and the grip of the prophetic force suddenly released him. His eyes rolled upward, and he would have fallen on his face on the floor if his father hadn't steadied him and guided him back down onto his bed.

"Help! Halloa! Is anybody there to help me with this madman?" Skjoldur called.

A small and elderly maidservant crept in warily, her eyes wide and fearful.

"Fetch Mistislaus instantly," Skjoldur said. "Tell him he can't go away and leave me with this lunatic. And don't say a word to anyone or I'll have you whipped." To Solveig he added, "I don't know what those barbarian Hestur brothers of yours will do if you come home carrying tales of lunacy in Rangfara. Probably come galloping in here on their horses and cut my throat and make water bottles out of my hide or whatever it is they do to their enemies. Whatever this misery is, it didn't come from my side. For all we know, this is Hestur craziness coming to the fore after generations of lurking just beneath the surface."

"The Skyldings are the weak ones," Jafnar said faintly.

"A fine way to speak of your own kin and clan," Skjoldur said with a deepening of the scowl that Jafnar had no difficulty recognizing as the same one Modga had inherited. "Even a madman ought to have the sense to show a little loyalty and gratitude. Now lie down and be quiet. I don't want to hear any more of this nonsense."

Closing his eyes, Jafnar gratefully anticipated deep and oblivious sleep. Perhaps when he awakened, he would be a wild boy again, scavenging the streets of Rangfara, stealing and hiding from the Krypplingur in the way he knew and loved.

"He looks peaceful enough for now," Skjoldur said in a low voice to Solveig. "Keep an eye on him, and if he awakens, keep him indoors. I hope this fit will pass. In my position, I don't relish the idea of having a mad prophet for a son."

Solveig replied with a disdainful sniff. "Sometimes you and your exalted position are totally insufferable."

Jafnar awoke much later, when it was dark in the room. For a long moment he struggled to remember where he was, but gradually the familiar feel and smells of the room reassured him that he was indeed at Athugashol, his father's house. Burrowing down under a thick eider coverlet, he thought it would be easy to pass off his strange memories and prophecies as side effects of his fractured skull. Easy to dismiss that alien knowledge in his head which told him that in another time the room he was in had smelled of mice and spoiled grain and fishy barrels and that it was here that he had left his body behind and walked in the shadow realm. In the room adjoining he had experienced dreadful visions brought on by ingesting plumabrot, while the lynx stalked her prey in the streets outside.

Sweating, he sat up and listened, straining his ears. His eyes traveled to the narrow window for ventilation, high in the opposite wall. He heard a soft thud and a grunt as if something had leapt off the roof onto the wall outside. It sniffed between the bars, then made the low crooning call of a lone cat on the prowl. Listening rigidly until his muscles quivered, he heard nothing further, so he lay down again and waited for dawn, alternately sleepless as an owl or half dozing to the accompaniment of bizarre dreams and half-forgotten recollections from both realms, blending together until he wasn't certain where the old Jafnar left off and the new Jafnar began.

When he could stand inaction no longer, he wrapped his eider around him, got out of bed, and crept into the main hall, where a fresh fire crackled with much cheer and, as yet, little heat. Gazing into the twisting flames, he sensed that even as a well-attended young lordling, there were still dangers about to unfold around him that he did not yet comprehend. He hoped he had retained enough of his wild-boy instincts to protect him now.

When he had warmed himself adequately, he moved to the narrow slit window and gazed out into the courtyard, which was still veiled in shadow and mist. Beyond a green pasture stood the high wall barring access to the Hall of Stars. A cold shiver ran up his spine as he recalled the white pennant with the black lynx device hanging over the doorway. Was the curse of the lynx within? How could such a thing be? His head ached with fierce persistence as he thought about Skyla and her bag of forbidden spells and the lynx curse.

"Whatever do you think you're doing out of bed?" Solveig's voice demanded behind him. "Get back in there at once before you fall and crack your skull again! Who knows what would come out this time?"

"I must see Mistislaus," Jafnar said, allowing himself to be propelled back to his cot. Barely in time; his legs were beginning to tremble. "He'll be at his morning iterations as soon as the sky is light."

"I shall send the girl for him again," Solveig said. "He couldn't be found yesterday. As soon as your father is out from underfoot. We can't have him interfering with a lot of blathering and fretting about his reputation."

"Where is Mistislaus? Is it far?"

"You'd like another look at that daughter of his, wouldn't you? I swear I don't know what the fascination is, when I would be more than delighted to help you pick out a suitable wife from a good clan in good standing."

"Mother, I don't care about that. Skyla—"

"Well, you should care about it or there's going to be too

many mixed-up people in the world who don't know what it is they're supposed to do with their lives. How would it be if a poet was born in the Skylding clan, or a warrior to a peaceful clan of scribes? Or someone who didn't have a strong vocation in anything? You wouldn't be what you are today if your ancestors hadn't chosen their mates very carefully indeed, to avoid confusion. A good thing you're going to be properly gifted. In a few years you'll be in charge of your own small sons, and you'll know then how important it is to—"

"Mother, I meant to say that Skyla needs help."

"Yes, indeed. The girl is very strange, Jafnar. Very nearly a witling, I'd say. It's very peculiar that she lives with her father instead of her mother's clan—whatever that may be. I suppose they didn't want her. A good thing you'll soon have a good wife so you'll stop thinking about inconsequential things."

With a disdainful little sniff she went out of the room. Jafnar gladly pulled up the eider and went back to sleep. It was not a deep sleep, however, and he alternated between troubling dreams and listening to the noises of the household awakening around him. Skjoldur grumbled around the house, dispensing orders to Solveig and the servants and generally infusing a spirit of chaos and gloom into everyone, before finally taking himself off to the Hall of Stars to seek out Hoggvinn's advice on something or other.

"And no more wizards," he said in parting to Solveig. "If you want a physician, I shall send for one."

After a period of quiet the maidservant came back with the news that Mistislaus did not deem it politic to be seen at the house of one of Hoggvinn's retainers after his recent decline in fortune.

Quietly Jafnar got up and pulled on his boots, sweating and trembling at the effort it took. While Solveig was busy in the bathhouse lighting fires and heating rocks and water for the troublesome process of bathing, he let himself out into the narrow front courtyard, where he heard the maidservant and the porter arguing over the firewood.

"You may tell my mother I have gone to visit Mistislaus," he said to his father's little old maidservant.

"You're supposed to be terribly sick," the maid said with a frown, peering up at him with professional womanly concern. She was of indeterminate age, a wiry little creature of extreme durability. "I don't think your father would approve of you leaping out of bed and running around looking for wizards."

"Perhaps not," Jafnar said with utmost civility. "So I think it would be a good idea if you came along with me in case I fall headfirst into a ditch and start to drown."

"Mistislaus did not seem much interested in talking to you when I was there," she continued, propping one fist on her skinny hip.

"He won't turn me away if he sees my face at the door," Jafnar said in mounting exasperation. Who were these women to tell him what to do or not do? Was that their chief interest in life, telling men not to do something?

She continued, "Now, I've belonged to this household nigh onto thirty years and raised you from a sprat that could hardly keep your pants dry, and I've never yet gone behind the master's back against his orders for anything or anybody. I'm not about to start now."

"Not even in exchange for a glimpse of your future?" Jafnar asked, as if by afterthought.

Her nutlike face changed at once. "You really think you can do that?" she demanded with a crafty glint in her eye. Warily she glanced around to see if anyone was eavesdropping.

"Only if I'm given the chance," he replied. "Ask me a question and I shall answer it."

"Alright. Tell me if my daughter will marry well."

"Your daughter will marry well and live a long and prosperous life only if she gets as far away from Rangfara as possible."

"Ah! There's a seafaring man, a whaler she fancies, though I don't think much of him myself. He's not got any money and couldn't set her up in her own house. She would have to live with his parents. She ought to marry him and go away, then?"

"Far, far away. And you'd do well to go with them. I'm sure they'd be glad to have you. When they die, they're going to leave you a great pot of money. Now, are you ready to accompany me? I shall go whether or not you do, and if I'm found upside down in a sewer, dead, it's going to be blamed upon you, Gunna." Gunna. He remembered calling her that when he was just a little boy and frightened of living in a new house with a stranger who was his father. She had cared for him, taught him how to catch toads so they wouldn't pee on his hands, and fixed the bumps and scrapes he got from falling off his pony.

"Well, you're a man grown," Gunna admitted reluctantly,

without much conviction. "I guess you're entitled to your own mind by now, aren't you?"

"Certainly. Come along. I've got to get away from here before my mother decides to forcibly hold me captive."

Gunna kept up a pleasant grumbling and nattering all the while they walked, traversing the city from the noble edifices surrounding the Hall of Stars to a less-desirable area where the houses were small and leaning against one another, built on top of each other like crowded chicken coops.

"This is it," Gunna said with a sharp sigh. "This is as much walking back and forth as I care to do in one day. Shall I wait for you or shall I go home?"

"Go home," Jafnar said. "I don't know how long this will take."

He rapped on the door planks and stepped back to look up at the windows. Built on a scrap of ground between two other houses, it was a tall tower house, true to Mistislaus' predilection for rising above the common crowd to be as near the sky as possible. Moss grew between the stones, and ivy nearly smothered the small windows.

High above, a contented bumblebee droning came to an abrupt end. The dim light shining within was obliterated momentarily as Mistislaus thrust his head out to peer down through the ivy to the doorstep below.

"Who's down there?" he roared. "What do you want? Don't you know it's infernally early?"

"Mistislaus! It's Jafnar!" came the reply. "I want to talk to you."

"Jafnar? What do you want here? I was bodily thrown out of your father's house, you recall. I thought I was done with you."

"You're no more done with me than you don't love pickled svid and those meat pastries from the old woman with the baking stall by the Hangman's Bridge."

"Hangman's Bridge? What Hangman's Bridge?"

Suddenly Jafnar realized that there was no Hangman's Bridge in this Rangfara, where the favorite public spectacle was certainly not eight or ten hangings of wretched scavengers who had stolen from shabby merchant carts or stalls.

"And I know you've been feeding wild boys," Jafnar added, feeling a little desperate at the notion that perhaps Mistislaus in this strand of time was not aware of Mistislaus in the other strand. "Mistislaus, I think you're playing games with me. You know who I am; now let me in so I can talk to you without shouting all over Rangfara."

"Come up, then, and get yourself out of sight. As you know, I've suffered some disfavor of late in the Hall of Stars. It wouldn't do for the son of Skjoldur to be seen talking to one such as I."

Jafnar pushed at the door and found it locked.

"Hold your water! I'm coming!" growled an irascible voice like the grumbling of subterranean boulders.

"Guthrum!" Jafnar exclaimed the instant the door had opened a crack. A hooded dark eye peered warily out at him, assessing the advisability of his admission into the tower.

"Aye. Guthrum." The dwarf pulled the door open all the way. He glowered a moment at Jafnar with his most ferocious glower. "Come in and don't be slow about it. I can't hold this door open forever, letting in the flies and smells."

CHAPTER SIX

MISTISLAUS WAS PUTTERING around a great sooty hearth with a vile pot of something that burbled and muttered nastily as if he were cooking a pot of troll pups. He snatched his hand away, sucked on a burned finger, and warily edged the vessel nearer the bed of coals that made the room like a furnace.

"I think I'm going to get it this time," he greeted Jafnar with a pleased grin, rubbing his blackened palms upon his ragged old yellow gown. "What are you doing here, by the way? I thought you were at death's door."

"I don't see how you can think about alchemy at a time like this," Jafnar retorted.

"I don't know why not," Mistislaus said with a shrug of his shoulders. "Care to share a pastry? Sit down and stop looking so worried."

He left off his stirring and pulled a pot off the scorching coals. Lifting the lid, he filled the room with the delicious smell of a large meat pastry.

"Mistislaus, I don't know who I am," Jafnar said, trying to keep his tone even and calm. "I mean, since that crack on the head, I think I'm somebody else."

"Indeed," Mistislaus said, setting the pastry on the table and gently prodding it with his knife.

"I asked a boon of you for doing your work at Athugashol, and you promised to help me find the Skylding treasure." Jafnar saw Mistislaus' eyebrow quirk upward skeptically, but he plunged onward. "I was a wild boy, and you were here to cure Herrad of Kjallari fever. Skyla shifted into the shape of a snow lynx, and she kept going down into the Kjallari and getting away from us. You were killed by Kraftugar, and Illmuri sold us to Otkell the Slaver. Don't tell me you don't remember. I can see by your eyes that you do."

"What we really need is some cheese, don't you think?"

"Why—why—" Jafnar's head began to throb warningly, and he sank down onto a stool, teetering precariously.

"Because the cheese makes it good, you fool. You do like cheese, don't you?"

"Mistislaus! I came to you for help, and you're offering me cheese on my pastry? You were there. You knew me, and I knew you. And you recognize me now. You do, don't you? We have the same memories, don't we? We were both there, and we remember. Don't try to lie to me, Mistislaus. I know too much about you."

Mistislaus sucked his scorched thumb for a moment, scowling with increasing gloom in his expression. "Only prophets and madmen talk about past lives, Jafnar. Do you want to get us both thrown into a pit somewhere and chained up with the lunatics?"

"Well, then! You admit you know me and know about my other life? That's progress! It's such a relief to know I'm not just insane! Now the question is, How did I do it? And why am I doing this again?"

Mistislaus sighed wearily and pushed away his pastry as if he had momentarily lost interest in it. "Because you never got it right. Most people shift over nicely without a bump, without any troubling memories from their old lives. It's going to be difficult putting the two Jafnars together. Many people simply go mad."

"How did it happen that I remember?"

"Messing about with that plumabrot, I would guess. You are violently allergic to the stuff. That means it doesn't agree with you," he added, seeing Jafnar scowl in puzzlement.

"I'm going to stop it," Jafnar said. "This time Rangfara won't be destroyed. This is the reason I keep returning. I'm going to warn them, Mistislaus. This time it will be different."

"As your friend," Mistislaus proceeded ponderously, "I advise you to keep all your warnings to yourself. Prophets have a way of coming to evil ends sometimes by prophesying too much of the truth."

"Knowing what you do about the future of Rangfara, are you going to stand idly by and watch certain dreadful circumstances occur, or are you going to do something about it?"

"Precisely the question I should ask you," Mistislaus said. "Perhaps you're the one I've been looking for all these hollow centuries. Perhaps you're the one that will put a halt to this endless destruction of Rangfara. You can give this place a future, Jafnar. If Rangfara is not destroyed by the Krypplingur, it has a new history waiting ahead."

The thought gave Jafnar a stab of pure pain from temple to temple, as if his brain were rebelling at the introduction of such an idea. "I hate this pain!" Jafnar rubbed his temples in anguish. "I thought my life was like a journey. I begin here, go along this way, do this and that, and eventually I shall die and that is the end of it. Or it should be."

"Like this, you mean?" Mistislaus held up his hands, gripping a length of string between forefingers and thumbs and holding it out, stretched straight. "You believe that your life is a finite thing with an end and a beginning."

"Yes, or so I thought," Jafnar answered.

"A common mistake in the mortal experience, for the first time or two." Mistislaus wagged an admonitory finger in the air. His eyes roved upward fondly, and he commenced pacing around the room in his favorite expositional manner. "But now you are beginning to realize that the experience of life is not a thing with one end and another, and when you're at the far end, poof and you're gone. It is a thing that goes on forever, because it always was and always will be, like this." He rolled the string into a ball between his palms and spread his hands apart. The string had vanished. Suddenly a complex spiderweb hung glimmering between his hands, a sphere of silky threads composed of endless facets all joined one to another, instead of the two-dimension webs Jafnar had always encountered in fences and bushes and corners. He gasped at the intricate loveliness of the image, dazzled by the complexity as well as the miracle of the vision.

"The Web of Life," Mistislaus whispered.

Jafnar gaped at it, speechless, seeing himself lost in a maze of complex interlocking strands.

"This was only a small demonstration. The true possibilities are almost countless," Mistislaus said, banishing the illusion with a flick of his hands and once more turning his attention to the pastry steaming upon the table. "And they are continually evolving. Is it any wonder most people feel confused most of the time, pulled about as they are by the subtle threads of lives imperfectly remembered, clumsily lived, rudely terminated, repeatedly suffering the unknown consequences of undone or forgotten deeds devolving upon them?"

"It sounds like the way to madness."

"Your limited brain is your curse as well as your protection," Mistislaus said. "Only wizards, prophets, and madmen are permitted to hear the voices and grasp the knowledge of the other strands."

"Then it seems I am cursed to be a prophet," Jafnar said. "I intend to warn them, Mistislaus."

"Wretched fool. Do you think they will thank you for it, when they have no recollection of their past lives and past mistakes?"

"Why are we stuck doing the same life over and over?" Jafnar demanded. "What is the point of endlessly repeating the same stupid mistakes and ending up in the same disasters and tragedies?"

Mistislaus gazed at him a moment with a mixture of amusement and weary sorrow. "The answer to that question has eluded every wizard who has spent his life in the search for the meaning of the Web. Either the meaning is something too large for us to understand or the Web simply *is*, we *are*, we do our best, and that's that. Others believe that we repeat the past because we keep making the same mistakes. Some wise men think that once someone figures out the meaning, the entire Web will disintegrate into chaos and oblivion, since the quest is the purpose. Some think it will put an end to the endless lives and strands for that man who finds out, and he will rest sweetly in the bosom of all knowledge and serenity. There are those who think that every step we take upon any plane is foredestined by the great and inscrutable weavers of the Web and there is nothing we can do to change what happens around us, or to us, and the best course is just to accept whatever happens. Others believe they will gain more and more power until all the Web and its people are under their control. Still others are convinced that the Web is an evil thing, a form of bondage, and that it should be destroyed. These are the forces of chaos."

Jafnar shuddered and got up from his stool, still a bit unsteady. "We are doomed to keep repeating the past because we keep making the same mistakes," he said.

"It's a good theory," Mistislaus said. "Unfortunately, few people remember the past once it's over. Particularly if they have died in the process."

"Now I am haunted by scores of terrible memories," Jafnar said. "Even though this seems so pleasant now, I can't look at anyone without knowing or feeling something terrible is going to happen."

Mistislaus turned to face him. His eyes lost their lively sparkle, the light and enjoyment dying to a lusterless stare. His voice fell to a flat monotone. "Yes, I remember. So do you. The destruction of Rangfara and the Skylding clan again approaches."

Jafnar could not speak, his throat choking, his heart pounding with unspeakable horror, his body perhaps reliving the memory of its final stilling on that other strand. After a great struggle he whispered, "Skyla—what happened to her? Did Alvara take control of her? The black lynx—does she do it again? What about the treasure and the Krypplingur?"

Mistislaus shook his head from side to side like a dying ox under a barrage of blows from the slaughterer's hammer. Then he sprang away with astonishing agility, shaking off the grip of the warring forces that wracked him.

"No more questions," he said smartly, wiping the beads of sweat from his brow, using a convenient ragged sleeve already blackened from much service. "I can't abide giving the answers, and you may not be able to abide the answers. You are not strong yet, Jafnar. You see the toll that knowledge of the strands can take on a mortal man. Never forget, though we may be Alfar and possess a great many of the answers to the ills of mortality, eventually, one day, we cannot escape the inevitable exit from this strand, to embark upon yet another life span, naked and squalling and fouling our own garments and needing to be fed and cleaned by someone who ignorantly thinks it unkind to leave us on the fell to freeze to death. Love, my young fellow, is the source of all our difficulties. Love no one or nothing, and you will soon come to the end of all your strands and chaos will rule. I have said so a thousand times a year, but unfortunately, though it is the best advice I can give anyone, I can't put it into practice, and I know very few others who are able to, either. Luckily for us all, it is a very small acquaintanceship. Now, that's enough talk. Let's eat this pastry while the temperature is exactly right.

"I have little appetite for food," Jafnar said, "when my entire brain and body are in such a turmoil."

"Food is the only cure I know of for distress of mind or body," Mistislaus said, demonstrating his principle with healthy energy by shoveling in a generous mouthful of the pastry, assisted along with a thick slab of black bread swabbed with drippings. A cheery slosh of ale, and Mistislaus was well on his way to perfect health.

"I always secretly wondered," Jafnar said, "about the meat the old woman at the Hangman's Bridge used; whether it was scraps from the butchers' stalls, as she said, or was it something far less savory? You always ate her pastries willingly enough then, not knowing what—or who—you might have been eating. Bodies were plentiful on that strand."

Mistislaus shook his head. "One of the worst Rangfaras I have ever seen. You had better eat something soon," he admonished Jafnar. "You are going to need all your strength. Perhaps this time all the people and events will work in harmony. I have arrived before the destruction of Rangfara. You are neither too old nor too young to be of assistance. Kraftugur has been my nemesis in every other strand I have pursued. But this time— perhaps this time we've got him, Jafnar. You're certain you can't eat anything? Some bread and drippings, perhaps? Ale?"

Jafnar sat down with a sigh and touched the side of his head gingerly. "I don't want anything, Mistislaus—except answers to my questions."

"They will come soon enough." Mistislaus wiped his fingers on his sleeve and leaned across the table to gently probe the wound on Jafnar's temple. "A nasty thing. It looks like it could go septic if something's not done for it. We live in unclean times, Jafnar. A tiny scratch from a thorn can kill a man just as easily as a great gaping hole made by a lance. It's not the size of the wound that will kill you, it's the germs that get into it and multiply until your body is overwhelmed. In days to come people will do all manner of miracles to combat the germs, forgetting that the simplest method of healing is to first treat the mind and then the body; the mind will take care of the body. You do remember when you had Kjallari fever and I had you say iterations? You healed yourself. Just as now, you will heal this wound in your skull yourself by clearing the pathway of healing. The Second Path, as it is called by those who have studied it."

As he talked, Mistislaus plucked a bit of earth from the turf walls, spit upon it, and rolled it into a small ball of mud. It tumbled about on his hand, taking the form of a tiny person with a blob for a head and tiny waving arms and legs like a beetle. Mistislaus spit upon it again, reducing it to a small mud plaster, which he adhered to Jafnar's skull over the wounded place before Jafnar could gather his wits to make a protest.

"Those are the forbidden powers," he said. "You yourself forbade Skyla to practice them!"

"I was afraid she would destroy herself, or others, when she got to the Fourth Path, which is death. I was wrong not to teach her when I had the chance. There is no regret like the regret for the good I might have done then and didn't do. Are you feeling much better now?"

Jafnar touched the mud plaster reluctantly with his fingertips. "Yes. Yes, I am."

"You needn't sound so astonished. It isn't the least bit complimentary. These are the powers you are heir to and should rightfully possess. But are you studying magical powers? No, you get useful subjects such as skull bashing and weazand slitting. And not nearly enough of that."

"Are you a Skylding, Mistislaus?"

"Goodness, no."

"Then what is your clan?"

"A very small one thought by most to be extinct, and it very nearly is. Perhaps because so many of them have found the way to end their cycle of strands. I am one of the stupid ones. I keep coming back, endlessly drawn to the destruction of Rangfara."

"And what about me, Mistislaus? What keeps drawing me back? Is it Skyla?"

Mistislaus sighed, the desolate sigh of a solitary reasonable man in a wilderness of howling maniacs. "So it would appear, you poor creature."

"Where is she now?"

Mistislaus sighed and shoved away his food. "She got away from me again. You know how she is in that lynx form. She's in the Hall of Stars with Alvara."

"Why? For her powers?"

"I wish it were that simple. Something is unfolding over which I have very little control."

"What? Why not? You're a wizard, aren't you?"

"It has to do with the past and its consequences for the present. Things that simply cannot be undone."

"Like what?"

Mistislaus sighed and rolled his eyes around impatiently, as if searching for a weapon. "I can't explain it to you now. There are plots within plots in Rangfara just now. It's a configuration of events and people I haven't seen before. All I do know for certain is that the combinations will be disastrous for the

Skyldings yet again. Kraftugar has a great deal of power, and Alvara has captured Skyla. Perhaps this is the end this time. So many things are converging."

"I don't care about Kraftugar or Alvara. I want to save Skyla."

"All in good time. We can't just attack the Hall of Stars and demand her release."

"Why not? She's your daughter, isn't she? What's to lose besides our lives again?"

"You're sure you can't eat anything before you go?"

"I'm not leaving without you," Jafnar said, rising to his feet. "If we return everything to the way it was before, perhaps we'll defeat the Krypplingur this time. There is power in repetition."

"You don't need to tell me that," Mistislaus retorted testily. "And I won't go back to Athugashol. Skjoldur has insulted me for the last time."

Jafnar returned to the stairway and treaded heavily downward, where Guthrum still waited morosely to let him out. He trudged back up the hill to the Hall of Stars, where he slipped in through the gates with a crowd of visitors to do some prowling around to compare his memories of the old Hall of Stars with the present edifice. Thralls' huts, barns and paddocks, pathways, all the small buildings that had fallen into rubble now stood neat and trim. As he admired it, he heard a babble of female voices as the Drottningur and their servants came trooping out of the main hall. Though he knew it was strictly forbidden to spy upon them, he dived into a woodshed and peered out through a crack as they passed by, chattering and cackling like a flock of birds. It was a calculated display, he soon realized, as they trooped across the washing green in clouds of filmy garments, their loose hair catching the morning sun.

Jafnar rubbed his eyes, which had gone blurry on him for no reason. Probably from squinting through the cracks in the woodshed door. Looking back at the parade still progressing leisurely across the green, he suddenly recognized Skyla among them, carrying herself like a queen among her subjects, her long white cloak sweeping the ground behind her. Her silvery hair was longer than Mistislaus had ever allowed it to grow, standing out in an unruly mane like brushed wool that reached halfway down to her waist. Behind her walked Alvara, dark and severe in her long black cloak.

"Beware the women!" a voice suddenly whispered beside him. Scarcely daring to turn his head, he cut his eyes sharply to see who was there and perceived a transparent figure leaning upon a peat-cutting tool: old Utar the firebuilder, whose huge sooty hands had terrified Jafnar when he had been a very young child in his father's house and the thrall had come clumping in to start a new fire.

"Speak your doom, prophet!"

For an instant a vision flashed into Jafnar's inner eye, and he saw Skyla's face smeared with blood, her hands and forearms red to the elbows.

"They come to wash away the blood!" Utar declared.

Jafnar closed his eyes involuntarily and shuddered, not liking visions. Warily he looked around for more mist people, but old Utar was gone. Nor was there any sign of Skyla among the Drottningur, although he did glimpse a black-cloaked and hooded figure that might have been Alvara. He waited until they were gone, then hied homeward to Athugashol, still a bit shaky from seeing the vision of old Utar. It was not a pleasant thing being a prophet, never knowing when one was going to see something disquieting.

"There you are!" Solveig greeted him with considerable indignation when he put in his appearance in the house. "How do you expect to get better if you're constantly running around acting as if nothing is wrong with you? Don't you realize what an injury such as this means?"

"I feel fine," Jafnar said unconvincingly, still shaken from his encounter with the mist form of Utar and what he feared was a prophetic vision of Skyla.

"I suppose you're going to take your weapons and go right back out there today to prove it was nothing," she went on. "Those barbaric half brothers of yours were already here looking for you. I told them you'd be spending the day resting in bed."

"I'll bet they were glad to hear that," Jafnar muttered, wincing at the embarrassment of it and wondering if any of their mothers ever came for protracted visits.

"Beastly creatures, all of them," she continued. "You have me to thank for all of your finer sensibilities, Jafnar. Obviously the Skylding side of your heritage has little to recommend it except the ability for warfare. At least it makes Rangfara the most secure settlement in Skarpsey. We shall never have to worry about being attacked by our enemies."

"Our enemies are the Krypplingur," Jafnar said grimly. "And we have welcomed them with open arms. When the attack comes, the Skyldings will die before they even get their hands upon their weapons."

"Such talk. Why, the Krypplingur are the most benevolent and gentle of creatures, in spite of their looks. Their loyalty to the Skylding clan and all its mother clans is totally without question."

"It will be the question of birthrights that brings down Rangfara," Jafnar said. "Are the Krypplingur allowed to buy birthrights from the Drottningur and other women's clans who carry the Skylding blood?"

"Of course not," Solveig said primly. "They may be loyal and fierce fighters, but after all—they are deformed, with those humped shoulders. We certainly wouldn't want to pass it on to our children, would we?"

"And Kraftugur won't miss a chance to pass on that information to the Krypplingur," Jafnar said.

"You've been talking too much with Mistislaus," Solveig said. "His opinions did not meet with much popularity in the Hall of Stars. It wouldn't do for you to go on with his line of reasoning where other people can hear you, unless you want to damage your father's standing with Hoggvinn. It was mean and foolish of you to go chasing off to visit that wizard so early this morning without telling me where you'd gone. Imagine how I felt when I looked in and you were gone. I thought you were wandering the streets like a witling, about to fall into some Kjallari hole somewhere."

Jafnar shuddered at the mention of the Kjallari. "Where are my weapons? I've got to talk to my brothers."

She fumed and grumbled, but he went anyway, heading straight for the practice green, trying to formulate a plan as he walked.

Engi's only students of murder and warfare on the field that day were Jafnar, Ordvar, Modga, and the hulking giants Lofa and Lampi, mysteriously grown from small boys to truly menacing proportions. Jafnar decided to accord them a greater degree of respect. He thought he comported himself rather well on the practice field, knocking down anyone who came against him and taking especial pleasure in soundly thrashing Modga for his presumption of the day previous.

Wrestling and gripping were particular wild-boy skills, developed from an early age when much tussling was essential for grabbing enough food from other boys to survive. Jafnar discovered that his half brothers seemed to have forgotten all the lessons they had learned early in life, choosing instead to adhere to a ridiculous set of rules and rather ineffective artificial maneuvers.

"Where did you learn to do that?" Lofa demanded, his voice muffled by the moss where Jafnar had promptly thrown him down. Modga had suffered a similar humiliation and was sulking about it.

"It's cheating," Modga growled.

"If it works in a fight, then it's fair," Jafnar said. "Right, Engi?"

Engi's expression of absolute amazement and confusion cleared for a moment. He nodded energetically. "Exactly as I have always said. I always thought you'd be a fast learner, when you decided to learn. When did I teach you that maneuver? You've certainly been practicing. The rest of you would do well to follow your brother's example."

"How did you do it?" Lampi inquired interestedly.

"You don't remember?" Jafnar asked in a low tone, and they all looked at him blankly. "Alright, never mind where I learned it, as long as I can teach it to you. The thing to remember is that your enemy will never expect you to drop down to your knee. Then you simply lunge forward between his knees, grab him by an arm and a leg, and hoist him onto your shoulders and toss him where you want him. Size is no obstacle, since you are simply acting as a wedge in a butt of firewood."

Demonstrating, he neatly tossed Lampi off his feet and onto his back with a crash like a falling horse. Amazed, Lampi shoved his thick mane of hair out of his eyes and grinned amiably when Jafnar unsheathed his sword and pressed it to his throat.

"That's good, Jafnar," he said. "Show us."

They spent most of the day on the practice green until everyone had it down perfectly. Jafnar also demonstrated other wild-boy techniques of fighting that might not have been elegant but had proved functional many times in Jafnar's life. With satisfaction, Jafnar repeatedly used Modga as a demonstration dummy until Modga began strenuously objecting.

"I think we've all had enough for one day," Engi said in considerable alarm after Jafnar had dealt Modga a particularly hard fall. "I shall see you here first thing in the morning. I've got my position to watch on the wall."

Dutifully and with dignity, he marched away with a slight limp toward one of the wall watchers' huts, a rather neglected position in the present Rangfara. On his way to the green Jafnar had observed other watchmen's huts abandoned and fallen down completely. It made no difference, he told himself; the enemy was already within the gates.

"Stop a moment," he called when Modga shouldered his lance and prepared to leave. "We've got something to talk about."

"Oh?" Modga said with a characteristic sneer on his face, one that Jafnar yearned to rub off in the dirt. "I suppose you haven't gotten revenge enough for that crack on the head I gave you yesterday? Maybe you think your favored son status with our father entitles you to order us around, just because you get to live in his house while the rest of his sons are barracked with old Engi, like minor retainers."

"Get over it, Modga," Ordvar growled. "It's not an intended slight, although I'm sure if Skjoldur got acquainted with your true character, he would send you out on the next boat. Just be glad he doesn't."

"Perhaps that is something that ought to be changed," Jafnar said. "We are all Skylding brothers, are we not? We have the same father, which unites us in a brotherhood which cannot be broken. Either you will live at Athugashol or I will join you with Engi. There is something that we must do, and only the seven of us will be able to do it."

"Seven?" queried Modga, ever the critic. "I count only five, depending upon whatever it is you want us to do."

"Where's Einka?" Jafnar asked. "He's our brother, too, is he not?"

"We wish he weren't," Modga said.

"Shut up, Modga," Ordvar said. "Einka's not such a bad fellow. It's just that he turned out a little wrong for a Skylding."

"What do you mean?" Jafnar demanded. "What's wrong with Einka?"

"Jafnar, my esteemed elder brother," Modga said, "it is not alright for a Skylding to want to be a scribe. Einka doesn't know one end of a sword from the other. All he wants to do is bury himself like a maggot in the Kjallari with old Skriftur, inhaling the dust of dead Skyldings and writing down histories. Our father is so ashamed of him that he doesn't even want to see him. Two out of seven attempts gone bad is enough to make any man discouraged."

Ordvar gave Modga a shove. "And if Jafnar should ever be killed, it will be your turn. You're just panting to see the day, aren't you? You've already started out by trying to kill Jafnar yesterday."

"If I'd wanted to kill him, he'd be in the Kjallari now instead of running around acting half as crazy as Thogn," Modga said. "Insanity seems to run in this family. I wish I'd been born elsewhere."

"So do we," Lofa said with a grin, nudging Lampi.

"You two can shut up," Modga said with a scowl. "I'm older than you, and I can make your lives very miserable."

"But we're bigger than you," Lampi said. "We younger sons are all in the same boat, Modga."

"And we've wanted to throw you overboard for a good many years," Lofa added.

"Well, don't do it yet," Jafnar said. "We've got to get Einka and Thogn, and then the brotherhood will be complete."

"Thogn! You are mad!" Modga said. "Nobody is ever going to see him with me. I don't want my name or my pedigree smirched with any connection to Thogn. If word leaks out that I've got a half brother who is crazy, I'll never get a decent gifting. I'll be doomed to marry scrubwomen and sheepherders, and my sons will be great dumb clots who forget to come in out of the rain."

"I'm going to see him," Jafnar said. "You're coming, too, whether you want to or not. There's a matter of family concern that I wish to take up with all of you."

"There is?" Ordvar said curiously. "You've never cared about the family before, Jafnar. Not until that clout on the head yesterday. What do you want to see Thogn for? He's been at Kraftugur's for months now, and you've never gone."

"What are we going to do with a crazy person?" Modga demanded. "Or two crazy people, if we count you."

"You can watch him, Modga," Jafnar said.

"What, me watch him? Not I!" Modga declared fiercely, gathering up his weapons to beat a hasty retreat, adding over his shoulder as he walked away, "I happen to know that the Drottning matchmaker is considering me for Borgildr. If she ever saw Thogn, she'd throw my genealogy scroll right in the fire and strike me off every list of eligible bachelors in all of Skarpsey and see to it I ended up eating fish heads with the pony herders for the rest of my life."

"Sit on him, everyone," Jafnar commanded, "until he begs to be let up and promises to listen to what I've got to say—and to mind his tongue!"

CHAPTER
SEVEN

WITH GLEEFUL YELLS reminiscent of their boyhood days, they chased Modga down and sat on him, with much shouting and laughing—swearing from Modga—until Modga gruffly allowed that he would mend his manners and at least listen to what Jafnar had to say.

Looking at their faces, which were still flushed and grinning from their recent clobbering of Modga, Jafnar regretted the necessity of destroying their peace of mind.

"Since Modga so kindly cracked my skull yesterday," he began, "I've come to the realization of many things. Strange things, some of them, which you would probably not believe if I told you. I've had ... visions of the future, which seems like the past to me now, as if I'd lived another life and so now I've seen what is coming next. Don't think that I'm insane because I can see more clearly than I did before. We all know there are prophets and seers, like old Hofud."

"But not in a good family like ours," Modga said, his expression astonished and grieved, like a man who had found half a worm in his apple. "Oh, Jafnar, Jafnar. If I'd only known what I was doing when I hit you. I'd rather have you dead than wandering in your wits this way."

"Shut up," Jafnar said. "Do you want Lofa and Lampi to sit on you again?"

"No," Modga said, eyeing his hulking, grinning twin brothers. "Do go on and share some of your prophecies with us, O Wise One."

Jafnar glared at him and decided to let it pass. "The Krypplingur are going to destroy the Skylding clan," he said in a low voice. "Every Skylding will be killed, except for eight."

"Nonsense," Ordvar said after a shocked silence wherein the

brothers all covertly exchanged wondering glances. "The Krypplingur are now our allies."

"The Krypplingur will destroy us," Jafnar said. "It's the treasure they've come for, and Kraftugur brought them. Long ago he was refused a Skylding birthright, and he has burned for revenge ever since. He's got a vision of a race of wizard warriors that will rule the world one day, and he thought he was the one who would engender it."

"And he has no taste for the Kryppling mother clans," Modga said with an evil snicker. "I can imagine what they must look like to produce such ugly offspring. The worst-looking ones probably get the highest marks."

Without being told, Lofa and Lampi sat on Modga and commenced stuffing his mouth with moss for such disrespect to anyone's mother clans.

"Where did he learn to be so rude?" Ordvar marveled, shaking his head. "It's almost as worrisome as having a lunatic in the family. And now a prophet. Are you quite certain you saw all this and it wasn't just an ordinary nightmare? Did you eat something that was spoiled?"

"Only plumabrot," Jafnar said wryly. "Nothing is more deliberately spoiled than that."

"Plumabrot! Don't ever eat that stuff!" Modga exclaimed in horror, spitting out some moss. "It gives me spots and chills and convulsions. It made us all terribly sick last midwinter feast day, remember? Old Engi thought it would be a fine treat, and he nearly killed us. But we didn't have any visions, Jafnar."

"You wouldn't, anyway," Lofa said with a grin. "The only vision you care to see is Borgildr or your own face in a looking glass."

"This is no joking matter," Ordvar said. "Have you told anyone else about this, Jafnar?"

"Only Mistislaus, and he agrees that I'm speaking the truth. He and I have had many of the same visions about the destruction of Rangfara."

"Mistislaus?" Modga murmured with a scowl. "Hoggvinn kicked him out in favor of Kraftugur. I wouldn't take his word for anything."

"Mistislaus is an honorable man," Jafnar flared. "Kraftugur has evil alliances with the Kellarman, and he's performing bizarre experiments with the Four Powers. There are hideous creatures down there, or there will be—" His voice choked, remembering. His brothers stared at him in startled silence.

"You are our eldest brother," Ordvar said. "We are bound to do as you tell us. In the past you've been a very decent and fair brother, as much as possible, so I'm willing to listen to your ideas, even though I've never heard of a Skylding prophet before. We've always hired our prophets from the very best prophetic clans instead of creating our own. I don't suggest you make it common knowledge yet—until maybe you've proved yourself and your claims."

"By then Rangfara will be destroyed," Jafnar said.

"Isn't there a smaller prophecy you could prove to us?" Lofa asked. "Something easy, such as Modga and Borgildr, maybe?"

Jafnar glared at him. "I don't see inconsequential things such as Modga and Borgildr. Either you believe what I'm saying or you can turn your back and leave right now. But if you do, I'm warning you that you're putting Rangfara in greater danger of being destroyed. This time could be different, according to Mistislaus."

"What must we do?" Modga asked. "We can't single-handedly chase all the Krypplingur out of Rangfara. We're good but not that good. If we oppose this treaty, we'll be a disgrace. We'll be outlawed, hunted down like rats, and strung up on the walls."

"If you don't do it, you'll be dead, along with everybody else in the clan," Jafnar said.

"But it does seem a bit strange to me," Modga said thoughtfully, "that the Krypplingur have been so obliging during the negotiations. For such fierce fighters, they've seemed more than willing to compromise on every issue. Thinking perhaps of the treasure hidden somewhere in Rangfara, which they intend to have one day."

"You're always suspicious of everyone," Ordvar said. "Nothing is going to turn out well, according to you."

"Maybe that's true. But I'm right about half the time," Modga said, "and I don't have any nasty surprises. If I believe that Jafnar is totally crazy and that the Krypplingur are going to destroy us, I won't be shocked if it turns out to be true."

"I think we should go and talk to Einka," Lampi said. "He's a levelheaded fellow in spite of being buried in books and records and dust. We used to have some good times before Skjoldur apprenticed him to Skriftur."

"Let's go see Einka, then, and force him to come out and learn to be a man instead of a mole," Modga declared.

With much the same brotherly merriment Jafnar remembered from the wild-boy times, the half brothers trooped back to Rangfara and through the winding streets. The farther they went, the deeper grew Jafnar's forebodings. By the time they turned into the Kjallari street, he was sweating from every pore and trying not to tremble. Under the archway with the snarling stone lynx, his feet stopped moving of their own accord and he stood still, breathing deeply and feeling like a fool.

"Why, you're as white as a drowned corpse," Modga said. "Look at him, Brothers. If he was a horse, I'd say he was on his last legs."

"Just a little overexertion," he explained, trying to get his breath. "You must remember, you nearly killed me yesterday. Worse luck for you, Modga."

"I'd make a much better eldest son for Skjoldur, that's all," Modga said with an innocent shrug. "He says you're too much like your mother's side and not enough Skylding. Well, are we going to stand here until a charnel cart runs us over or are we going down to bother Einka?"

The Kjallari was no longer a temple of death and terror. A long queue of young boys in scholars' gowns trailed obediently at the heels of their instructor, who was lecturing them on the relevance of the memorials engraved upon the plaques on the walls. The remains of a great many famous and heroic Skyplings lay disintegrating in the tombs beneath the streets of Rangfara, and the elders evidently believed that the younglings ought to take an interest in their achievements. Historians pottered about with their pens and vellums, turning over stacks of stone tablets and recording their writings on more suitable materials. Genealogists pored over the birth and death records, quarreling among themselves vociferously over the gifting scrolls of forgotten generations. Sheaves of rolled scrolls were bundled up and stacked about, and apprentices scurried around worriedly, trying to oblige everyone.

Seeing how many people were going about such mundane affairs, Jafnar bucked up his courage and did not falter again until they passed the central courtyard, which was crowded now with a naming party for a new infant. Recognizing the genealogy shrine where he had nearly lost a foot to a ravening Kjallari creature, he stopped and steadied himself against a pillar, shaking his head and willing the image to leave him. Like the mist people, his memories of what had once happened crowded around him until he could smell the horrid stink of their bodies and the dust of disturbed graves burned with reproach in his nostrils.

"Come on, don't get sentimental on us," Ordvar said, giving him a poke for encouragement. "We know the Kjallari is a reverential place for Skyldings, but don't exaggerate."

"I'm not reverencing or exaggerating," Jafnar snapped. "I'm seeing what it looked like—or will look like."

"That's the trouble with prophets," Modga growled. "They have a better view of the future than the present."

Jafnar gazed around at the multitudes of people trooping about cheerfully on their business, raising the echoes in the lofty arches, lit from above by air and light shafts. "What about the Kellarman? Don't these people know what is lurking in these tunnels?"

His Skylding brothers burst out with muffled laughter, then quailed under the stern gaze of a cloaked historian, who glowered at them beakily over the top of a stack of stone tablets.

"You must be more respectful of your ancestors," the historian advised them, and went back to his deciphering and lettering.

"Kellarman," Lampi muttered, elbowing Lofa, who snickered, elbowed Jafnar, and slung a large arm around his shoulders. The force almost made Jafnar stagger. "It was only a story told by our old nannies to frighten us into behaving. He doesn't really exist, big brodir, with his great teeth and claws and horns. Now that we are practically grown men, we don't need to be afraid of the Kellarman to make us behave. Look at Modga, for instance. Nothing frightens him except the thought that Borgildr might choose someone else for her first gifting. We all live in fear because of young Drottningur lasses who would as soon wipe their feet on your livers as look at you." He rubbed Modga's hair all around, as a big brother would do to infuriate a younger and smaller sibling. "I don't know what she'd want with such a puny little scrub as you, anyway."

Modga uttered a wrathful howl, which garnered them more deadly looks from the naming party. He glowered and flushed, but with Lofa and Lampi towering genially above him now, prime examples of what gifting well could produce, he didn't want to be quarrelsome about it.

When they finished their winding route through the Kjallari and reached the historian's hall, Einka was not pleased to see them. He looked up and scowled, but the effect was not very

fierce with such a round and good-natured countenance where-
upon hardly a whisker had consented to sprout yet. Jafnar
stared at him, amused to see he was still as rotund and untidy
as ever. Though considerably larger and taller, Einka was easily recognizable as the same old little brother.

"What do you want?" he greeted them in as surly a tone as
he could manage.

Modga rubbed the top of his head with his knuckles and sat
down upon the table where Einka was working at a beautiful
manuscript, copying the old work in a neat, authoritative hand
on a vellum.

"We haven't seen you out on the practice field for too long,"
Modga said. "We miss having a live target to strike at. It was
such fun chasing you."

Einka darted Modga a savage look. "I've got far too many
important things to do to waste my time learning how to chop
off the arms and legs and heads of people far more stupid than
I am, whose ultimate death on the battlefield is a most de-
served one for ever thinking to attain glory by such an idiotic
means. The only advantage I can see to warfare is that it gives
the genealogists something to do. It also eliminates a lot of stupid people and provides the ravens so much fodder to peck at.
So leave them to it and me out of it, I say."

"He hasn't a fighting bone in his body," Modga said to
Jafnar. "He's such an old hen and absolutely stuffed with white
feathers. I can't think where he got it from. Another unfortunate gifting for our poor father."

"Yours was the least fortunate of all," Jafnar agreed, giving
Modga the same rough knuckle rub across the crown of his
pate. "All you got was the looks, while Einka got the brains
and Lofa and Lampi got the size."

"And Ordvar got the disposition," Einka said, nodding in
vigorous agreement. "Everyone likes Ordvar. He's got a sense
of justice."

"And Jafnar got the craziness," Modga added with a wicked
grin, sliding off his seat on the table in case Jafnar decided to
come after him. "No, wait; Thogn's crazier. They have to keep
him chained to a wall. I wonder if he's a prophet, too."

"Shut your yapping mouth, Modga!" Einka snapped. "Leave
Thogn alone! What did you want down here? Was there something you intended besides making a nuisance of yourselves?"

Modga opened his mouth, his eyes waggishly alight, but

Jafnar treaded heavily on his foot. "It's a serious matter, Einka," he said, "something that concerns our family."

"I'm not going anywhere until I'm done with this," Einka said, resuming his careful lettering. "Skriftur's got me doing this historical manuscript, and I can't leave it."

"Skriftur won't mind," Jafnar said, watching the tall thin scribe as he appeared in a doorway and came toward them. "He thinks you're becoming far too dull and pale from all these subterranean labors. An outing for the rest of the day with your brothers would do you good."

Skriftur nodded in a pleased way to Jafnar and smiled.

"Exactly my thinking, Jafnar," Skriftur said, grinning with his long narrow teeth, much like a benevolent horse. "I said as much to your kind mother the other night at dinner, as you recall. You used my exact words. You young lads need to get away from the dullness of Rangfara life. Every morning when you wake up you can be relatively certain that a pleasant day will pass and you will survive to see the night. That is an unhealthy state of affairs for young men. Uncertainty is what they thrive on, or they become fat and complacent old men before they're two score and five. Time is growing short, my lads. What will you do with your lives before it is too late?"

"I'm going to marry well and become very wealthy," Modga said. "I haven't got the time for risking my life. Besides, what a great waste it would be if I were to die doing something stupid and reckless."

"Hah!" Skriftur cried. "This is one of the walking dead already! He moves, he speaks, but there is no spark of manly virtue or ambition within him!"

"I'm all for adventuring," Lofa said, and Lampi added solemnly, "The sooner the better. That's why we've been training with Engi."

"All we need is the opportunity," Lofa continued. "Have you heard of any good wars nearby we could go join up with?"

"I have other things to do besides killing myself," Modga said virtuously.

"Skarpsey is regrettably peaceful just now," Skriftur said.

"But not for long," Jafnar said. At once his brothers eyed him nervously, as if wondering what he would say in front of Skriftur. "Everyone is too complacent. Now the enemy is among us."

"Oh, no!" Modga exclaimed in exasperation. "He's talking crazy again! Should I give him another knock on the head?"

Skriftur raised his hand to silence their sudden outburst of arguing and chattering. He looked at Jafnar with a gleam in his eyes.

"You'd all better be still and listen to him," he warned. "Everyone has visions, but most of us are too stupid to recognize them. History is not a thing that happens unexpectedly. A great many strands go into its weaving."

Jafnar's heart thudded at the mention of the word "strands."

"Like a bowstring," he hinted, not taking his eyes off Skriftur's face, and he was rewarded with a sudden covert gleam of recognition. He breathed a sigh of relief. Skriftur, too, had memories of other strands.

"What bowstring?" Modga demanded.

"I know the story of the bowstring," Skriftur said. "It's difficult, is it not, seeing and knowing what others cannot and being unable to do anything about it."

"Perhaps I can, this time," Jafnar said excitedly. "Mistislaus thinks so."

"A visionary man is Mistislaus," Skriftur agreed. "I wish him luck. Perhaps there will come an end to all this one day, one lifetime, and the book of Skylding history will be correctly written at last."

"And when it is, what then?" Jafnar demanded.

Skriftur waved one long hand and sighed. "Don't ask me. I'm a historian, not a futurist. I leave to others the chore of looking ahead and figuring out what to do about it. Now, then, away with you, Einka, and take the rest of the day with your brothers. Get some fresh air inside that skull, instead of Kjallari dust."

Grumbling, Einka cleaned his pen and sanded his wet letters. "A waste of time," he muttered, casting his eyes in his brothers' direction. "I've got important work to do here, and my brothers are nothing but roistering gadabouts, looking for trouble to get into."

Modga dropped an arm around Einka's round shoulders and gave him a rough hug. "On our way out Jafnar wants to see where you keep the Kellarman. He was almost too frightened to come down here until I assured him that you had the Kellarman all locked up where he couldn't get out."

"There is no Kellarman!" Einka exploded, shaking off Modga's arm with a great fling. "If you've come down here just to make fun of me, you can leave now before I lose my temper. Or better yet—" He glanced around to make sure Skriftur had padded away out of hearing range. "—I'll lose you in the secret tunnels. That would do the world a favor." He grinned and preened arrogantly.

"Secret tunnels?" Jafnar prompted. "You know about the secret tunnel?"

"Of course I do," Einka said, monstrously disdainful. "I know every inch of the Kjallari, better than almost anyone, except maybe Kraftugur."

Jafnar lifted his head warily. "Kraftugur comes down here?"

"Yes, endlessly prowling all the forgotten tunnels and snooping over the old scrolls and histories as if he could make something of them," said Einka. "He says there is someone he's looking for by tracing certain events in the stars, earthly disasters, wars, and whatnot. The perfect pedigree for greatness, he calls it, but I don't think such a thing exists. As if certain celestial conditions could affect the destiny of a child born under them."

"I've had enough of tunnels and darkness," Modga declared suddenly. "I'm not a mole like Einka. If I don't see some sunlight and blue sky, I fear I'm going to go mad." He began to puff and gasp and roll his eyes around. "I could never abide close, dark places! I've got to get out of here before I suffocate!"

"Very well, coward, follow me," Einka said, and in short order they were churning around and around in a spiral stair that spewed them into a narrow courtyard down the street from the lynx gate.

"Skriftur's gate," Einka said in a casual but pleased tone. He hitched up his long scholarly gown to get at the breeches he wore underneath, wherefrom he extracted a large rusty key. "He doesn't like to come in at the main gate. People always want to talk to him there, to show how important they are. He gave me a key, too, so I can get to work as quickly as possible." He darted them all a quick sideways glance to see if they were impressed. "One day I shall be chief scribe of the Skylding clan. No one needs to feel sorry for poor old fat Einka anymore. Now, would someone like to tell me where we're going?"

"For one thing, to get Thogn back," Jafnar said.

Einka's round face puckered up in concern. "But Kraftugur's

got him. Besides, are you sure we want him back? He's not the most cooperative person I've ever met."

"Things are going to happen in Rangfara," Jafnar said. "I want us all together under the same roof from now on."

Einka shivered suddenly, twitching his shoulders. "You're giving me a most unpleasant premonition, Jafnar. But I think there's some truth in what you're saying. From what I know of history, a warlike clan like the Krypplingur does not deliberately seek to put itself into servitude, particularly to another warlike clan such as the Skyldings. Historically, the Krypplingur and the Skyldings were the bitterest of rivals. And now they suddenly want to form a peaceful alliance? The lessons of history—"

"Oh, bother the lessons of history," Modga interrupted. "We've got one brother with hundreds of years of hindsight and one brother who thinks he's a prophet. I don't know which one is the most annoying."

Einka rolled his eyes in Jafnar's direction in sudden alarm. "I heard about Modga practically scattering your brains all over the practice field," he said. "And it was feared you'd lost your wits. I had no idea how near the truth washerwomen's gossip was."

"Historically speaking, great prophets are made, not born," Jafnar said. "You should know that, being such a scholar of history."

"That may be true," Einka said, squeezing out the words with great reluctance and thought. "But I still don't see what this has to do with getting Thogn."

"Things have to be as similar to certain events in the future as I can make them here," Jafnar said. "The seven of us brothers have to be reunited."

"Yes, that's the principle of similarity," Einka observed with a scholarly squint. "Like produces like. Are there other people involved in this hideous scheme of yours?" Einka eyed Modga with extreme distaste. "There are certain people I don't wish to be associated with for more than the briefest of encounters."

"Yes, there are others," Jafnar said in relief, gratified that Einka had grasped and accepted his changed status with so little objection. "Herrad and his son Ofarir. Illmuri. Kraftugur. The wizard Mistislaus and Skyla, his daughter."

His brothers stared at him in shock, except for Einka, who raised one forefinger in mild protest. "It is a common mistake to assume that anyone who practices any of the magical arts is a wizard. Wizardry is actually the art of summoning demons and elementals to work one's will—or for allowing demons and elementals to work through one. From what I know of Mistislaus, I tend to believe he is more of a sorcerer than a wizard, although he practices certain ritualistic magic from a most ancient school of power simply known as magic, for lack of a more understandable term—"

"Silence!" Modga roared suddenly, causing a dozen people in the street to turn around and stare at the source of such a rude outburst. "Einka, you're stuffed to the ears with information, like a pudding bag with too much suet in it, constantly spewing forth your contents on the least provocation. We really don't want to know all of this. Why do you have to talk so much?"

Einka retorted, "Well, I thought you would appreciate being relieved of your thundering ignorance in at least one small particle of your vast fund of stupidity, misinformation, and downright malice. It appears, however, that you would rather bungle along under the load of your minuscule intellect, like an ant carrying a dead beetle."

"You are a self-righteous vermin," Modga said. "Good for no earthly purpose, unlike the rest of us, who defend the safety of our mother clans and preserve the peace of the landholders. You lurk about in the dust of dead men's entrails, trying to figure out what happened two thousand years ago, as if anybody living really cared."

"Those who don't study the past tend to repeat the mistakes of their ancestors," Einka said.

"Endlessly repeating their same mistakes," Jafnar said. "That is why we're together. This is our chance to correct their mistakes."

"I don't know how we can," Ordvar murmured, shaking his head. "We're just ordinary people, not wizards or sorcerers," he added quickly, darting a stern look at Einka. "How do you know? How can you be so sure, Jafnar?"

"I know what I've seen," Jafnar said. "I wish you had the same sight. You were all there and played your roles, although I fear they were cut short by Kraftugur before I could see exactly what it was you did. Mistislaus will be our guide—if we can keep him alive long enough to tell us."

Modga's glum expression brightened. "Someone's trying to kill him?"

"Yes. Kraftugur."

"Kraftugur? The peacemaker between the tribes?" Einka demanded incredulously. "I can't believe it! Him? Kill Mistislaus?"

"He'll succeed, too, unless we do something to stop him," Jafnar replied.

"Like kill him?" Lofa asked with a professional frown.

"We've never killed anybody before," Lampi said, "but being Skyldings, that's what we're supposed to do. I guess we've got to get started somewhere."

"Don't be too hasty," Jafnar said. "We've got to get the pieces and the players together first."

An uneasy foreboding seized hold of Jafnar the moment he saw the building where Thogn was kept. His half brothers fell silent, even Modga, who had been complaining the entire way. It was an old hall with three steep turf roofs with ornaments like dragons' heads at the peaks of the gables. The madhouse stood apart from the rest of the halls of Rangfara, dark and forbidding. A high wall surrounded it, letting in very little light, and the windows had been blocked with stone and mortar, too small to even stuff a cat through.

"Thogn is here?" Jafnar said. "It looks like a foul place."

"Kraftugur makes it one," Lofa said. "It seems a strange thing that a man would collect the weak-witted ones gladly and keep them in his house."

"I've heard he doesn't do it for entirely charitable reasons," Lampi said.

"Oh, aye, that's true," Einka said in a whisper. "I've seen the charnel cart going off to his house many times and coming back with as many as six bodies. And nobody cares, because it's only the witlings and crazy people he's experimenting upon. No one is going to defend them."

"If he's found a use for them, good on him, I say," Modga said.

"This is no place for Thogn!" Jafnar sputtered. "He likes the sunlight and green growing things and the feel of the earth under his feet. Being locked away in a pigsty would drive anyone mad. What's our father thinking of, leaving him in a place like this?"

"Kraftugur promised to keep him out of trouble," Ordvar said, "and out of sight. A great many things changed quickly when the Krypplingur showed up wanting to negotiate a truce instead of fighting. Kraftugur thought it best to rid Rangfara of the witlings—the weakest of the flock, he called them."

"At first he promised cures," Einka said. "Then he just kept them out of sight. Nobody really knows or cares much what goes on in that place."

A chorus of desolate voices rose from the madhouse, murmuring like the sea, punctuated at intervals by a wail or a wild cackle of mirthless laughter. A stout guard in a long ragged cloak opened the gate for them and quickly locked it at their backs.

"Welcome," he said in an unwelcoming tone, lowering at them suspiciously with one good eye. "What is it you want in this place of sorrow?"

CHAPTER EIGHT

"WE'VE COME FOR our brother, Thogn," Jafnar said, his voice sounding high and strange to his ears. "To take him home again."

"I shall have to ask the master." He rang a glum little bell, and presently Kraftugur shuffled into the courtyard. A pair of narrow eyes the color of peat peered out at them incuriously from the interior of a plain hood made of fine material. It was a face Jafnar could not take his eyes from, the face of the entity that had sought and destroyed him once before. His brothers were struck dumb by that face or by the repelling atmosphere that surrounded Kraftugur, reminding some hidden part of them that this had been their destroyer.

"They wish to see Thogn," the porter said.

"I am very busy just now," Kraftugur said, starting to turn away indifferently, a shade impatient with a disturbance so inconsequential in nature. "Perhaps you could come back tomorrow."

"No!" Jafnar said, wishing he could quiet the thudding of his heart. "We will not come back tomorrow. We wish to take our brother home today, right now. Our father pays you well enough for his keep and troubles you very seldom with his presence. We shall not trouble you any longer with his upkeep if you will just bring Thogn to us."

"Thogn is one of my worst," Kraftugur said, his narrow face tightening even further with disapproval. His eyes bored into Jafnar intently. "You won't be pleased with what you see. I have to use measures that would offend many people just to contain him. He has not responded to my cures. I suspect there is a demon possessing him which is highly resistant to being removed. It would be very foolish on your part to attempt to take your brother home."

The only demon possessing him, Jafnar wanted to say, is you. But he held his tongue. "Take us to him," Jafnar said. "We'll decide for ourselves how bad Thogn is."

"Very well. You can always bring him back. If you survive." Kraftugur opened a door and beckoned them through into a dark hall that smelled like the warren of beasts. At intervals a sconce burned smokily, a grass wick thrust into a shallow dish of oil, illuminating doors securely chained shut. Jafnar had no idea there were that many crazy people in Rangfara. All the rooms contained numerous people, muttering, weeping quietly, or shouting pointlessly at one another.

"Very well. Don't say I didn't warn you. It was your father's wish that he be kept and fed in a safe place where he is out of sight and out of trouble. People with affected brains are not well tolerated in Rangfara. Particularly when the Drottningur come to visit."

"We are fortunate that you are so willing to attend to these hapless creatures," Jafnar said, speaking to the narrow shoulder blades of Kraftugur in front of him. His courage was returning fast. "What is it, exactly, that you do with them?"

Kraftugur swung around for a brief glower at him. "Do? What is there that anyone could possibly do with them? I keep them here as prisoners, more or less, so they won't harm anyone or come to harm themselves. But mostly it is to keep them away from their families, who are ashamed of them and too foolishly softhearted to allow them to be killed or frozen to death on the fell like poor beggars. You and others like you are not doing them any kindness by extending their miserable lives. And I am weak enough that I like the money that I earn by keeping them hidden. So there you have it. We are nothing but a house of parasites."

"I thought you tried casting out possessing demons," Jafnar said, "and other interesting experiments."

"If the situation seems to warrant it," Kraftugur snapped, "I look for possession by unembodied entities."

They found Thogn by himself, in a room scarcely as big as a stall for a cow, illuminated only by a narrow grate high overhead. He sat in a pile of dirty straw with a collar about his neck, which was chained to the wall.

"He causes too much disturbance among the other captives," Kraftugur said. "So we keep him here alone."

"Thogn!" Jafnar said, his voice choking. He dropped down on his knees to look into Thogn's face which was dulled by dirt and lack of interest. "There's no need to keep him like this. He's the most gentle and reasonable of creatures when he's treated with a little kindness."

"So you say," Kraftugur said. "You've probably never seen him when a fit comes on him. Like a terrified beast, he is, if you mention certain words."

"Thogn! You know me, don't you? Look at me, Thogn." Jafnar tried to look into his eyes, which were like uninhabited pools on a gray day. He dropped his voice to a whisper. "It's Jafnar, and I know where you've been. I know about the other strands, Thogn. I know how these things can addle your wits. I've come back, Thogn. I know about the Krypplingur, the Kjallari-folk—and the Kellarman."

Thogn struggled to his feet, uttering a wailing cry. A light of terrible intelligence burned in his eyes. The vacancy was gone, replaced by a blaze of urgency. He seized hold of Jafnar as if he would never let go.

"Jafnar! You're back? You've seen them? The teeth, the claws, their great hairy bodies, all coming at you, and you can't get away from them?" He spoke in a croaking voice, as if his throat were sore from screaming.

"Get back, you!" Kraftugur shouted, stepping forward to attempt to use a stout stick to thrust Thogn away from Jafnar. "You'd better leave now; you've got him worked up into a state where he's not safe to be around. He'd as soon smash your skull into that wall as look at you!"

"Knowing you and what you have done, I don't blame him for that," Jafnar said furiously, shoving Kraftugur backward and bracing himself between him and Thogn. "I know who you are and what you and that filthy Kellarman have done. You're nothing but a murderer and a soul snatcher and a conjurer of unclean creatures. I've been into the Kjallari and seen your creations. That was your best work of all, wasn't it? Creatures after your own heart, made on the same pattern as their creator. You're not going to pull the life out of Thogn to make your creatures. Your powers are perversions, and the intention in your heart is murder."

Kraftugur took a step backward, shifting his eyes to Ordvar. "I see this unfortunate strain runs consistently through your family. A great pity. I've always thought Skjoldur's sons were well favored in all things, except for this one I have here, which I considered to be an accident of nature. How long has this one been spouting such nonsense? Has there been an injury to his head?"

"Yes, he was hit at sword practice yesterday," Ordvar said. "And he hasn't been the same since."

"Don't talk about me as if I were a post or a horse," Jafnar said furiously. "I'm more sane than all of you put together. At least I know where I am, which you don't. Kraftugur does, though, and he knows we've met before under very different circumstances. I was a wild boy, and he was a disembodied spirit possessing the form of Ofarir—it wasn't a fair match then, but now perhaps it will be a more equal battle. We're not the lone and helpless lads we were then."

Kraftugur regarded him with rocklike immobility, nothing moving about him to betray any emotion except for a certain flickering of his eyes.

"As you say," he replied in a noncommittal tone.

"Jafnar!" Modga said, gripping his arm and shaking it. "You lunatic! Why are you talking like this? Do you want us to leave you here with Thogn?"

"Not in the least," Jafnar said. "We're taking Thogn with us when we go."

"What will we do with him?" Modga demanded. "He's got to be watched at every moment or he'll do something stupid, like eating bugs or playing with mud."

"Then we'll watch him," Jafnar said.

"But he's dangerous!" Modga protested furiously. "Look how they've had to chain him up!"

"He's not dangerous," Jafnar retorted. He swung around and glared at his other brothers, who were struck dumb with alarm and dismay. "You've known him all your lives. Did you ever see him do anything that would have harmed anyone? Does Thogn deserve to be put in such a place? Don't you know his life is in more danger here than if he were loose on the streets? Don't you realize that Kraftugur is creating monsters down in the Kjallari, using these poor witless creatures who can't defend themselves? Is that the fate you want for your eldest brother?"

Jafnar halted to consider his last words. Thogn had always seemed such a child when they were wild boys that his status had automatically been relegated to the last position, without thought or plan, although he had always been considerably larger than any of them. As the eldest brother, he ought to have been their leader, second only to their father, Skjoldur.

"Unfasten that collar," Jafnar commanded with scarcely a perceptible pause. "We're taking him home, where he belongs."

"You're going to regret it. You'll bring him back soon. If you're alive to do so." Kraftugur took a step toward Thogn, who cowered back with a frightened wail.

"Here, you great booby, let me do it," Modga snapped, stepping forward and giving Thogn a halfhearted clout on the side of his head. "No one could ever manage Thogn except me. The rest of you treat him like a spoiled child, when what he needs is a firm hand and some discipline." He unfastened the collar and let it fall to the ground. "Now come along, Thogn, and let's not have any nonsense. We're going home now."

"Home?" Thogn inquired with such an illumination of his grimy countenance that no one save Kraftugur could have failed to be shot to the heart. "Home? Home?"

"Yes, home, you great ninny," Jafnar said, putting his arms around Thogn and hugging him close, unresisting, like a young child.

"You've been gone, Jafnar," Thogn said accusingly.

"Yes. But I'm here now, and I'm not leaving again," Jafnar said.

Thogn's eyes darted secretively under his mane of pale hair. He eyed Kraftugur in alarm and whispered, "Skyla, Jafnar! She's in a bad place!"

"I know, Thogn. We'll have to help her, and we need your help most of all."

Thogn nodded his head and mumbled something as the gray curtain descended once again and he stood passively awaiting whatever would befall him next.

Kraftugur made no move to hinder them further from taking Thogn away. He even returned the ragged bundle of sticks and bits of useless substances that Thogn always carried around.

Instead of bidding them farewell at the gate, Kraftugur only remarked, "I'll be seeing you soon," and shut the portal with a heavy crash of chains and bolts.

"We did it!" Einka declared, shaking and pounding at Thogn in delight. His normal rosy color was returning to his cheeks. He had cowered behind Lofa and Lampi the whole time, moaning softly like a trapped rabbit. "We got him out, and we're taking him home! Did you see how that old beak glared at us? He knew he couldn't stop us, though, didn't he? He wasn't half-mad about it, was he?"

"Pabbi is going to be more than half-mad," Modga said. "What's he going to say when you come dragging Thogn home, Jafnar? Have you thought about that? And you can't keep him with us at the warriors' hall, so where are you going to keep him?"

"At Athugashol, of course," Jafnar said. "Since there's plenty of room, the lot of you are going to move into it and share it with our father."

"Now, that will be a lark," Modga said, grinning wickedly at Ordvar. "I wonder how Pabbi is going to like it."

Thogn lost no time proving what a nuisance he could be. It was an arduous journey through the back streets. Thogn cowered at the approach of everyone they met or attempted to scuttle into nearly every dark alleyway, whimpering and cringing as if Rangfara were a dangerous and hideous place.

"Thogn, why don't you know how to act?" Modga demanded, digging in his heels and arresting yet another mad dash for shelter from some imagined threat.

"He remembers a time when it wasn't safe to walk down the streets this way," Jafnar said.

"What time was that?" Einka demanded, breathless and red-faced from his struggles to restrain Thogn, whose strength when he was frightened was almost too much for all of the rest of them put together.

"A time you don't remember," Jafnar said, puffing and sweating. "A time that is coming yet is no more."

"Two crazy people." Modga groaned, clinging to Thogn's arm like a dragging anchor. "It isn't fair. I think we should tie something over his head, like blindfolding a horse."

Desperate, Jafnar tied his cloak over Thogn's head. It was an idea that garnered them some strange looks from passersby, but it worked. Breathing sighs of relief, they led Thogn to Athugashol. Mercifully, Solveig had gone visiting some distant cousin of hers who had come to Rangfara for a gifting, so no one was there except the porter and Gunna, who stared and sputtered as they carefully closed the doors behind him before taking off the cloak.

Thogn crouched down and peered around wildly like a frightened cat in strange surroundings, then with unerring certainty shot up the narrow stair to the little attic room that had been Skyla's. When his brothers came puffing and pounding up the stairs, they found him sitting contentedly by the little window, gazing out at the sky, which was changing into sundown colors. In one hand he was kneading a small blob of earth.

"I think he'll be happy here," Jafnar said, breathing a sigh of relief. "And it's got a door we can close on him when we have to. He's going to like it up here, close to the sky and the stars."

"Our own house," Einka chortled after they had trooped back downstairs and stoked up the fire. "No more of Engi's snoring—or cooking. I'm starving. We should have something to eat in celebration."

"I'm supposed to feed this herd?" Gunna demanded, propping one fist on a bony hip, raising her elbow like a sharp weapon. "Does your father know about this?"

"He will shortly," Jafnar said.

In short order Skjoldur's larder was cleaned out and strewn on the table. Gunna was in despair.

"Don't worry, Gunna," Modga said, sinking his teeth into a large slice of bread and cheese. "It's our father's duty to keep us fed until we've found our own places in the world. We'll have someone trot around to the Skurdur for some supplies once we get settled here."

"And you intend to do nothing to earn your own keep?" Jafnar demanded with an incredulous scowl.

"What's there to earn?" Modga replied. "Skjoldur is one of Hoggvinn's chief retainers. He has plenty to share. You least of all have anything to worry about, as eldest son. Everything our father has is yours. I suppose one day we'll be living on your charity, like thralls." He bestowed upon Jafnar a cheesy grin and reached for the ale bottle.

The day was spent when Solveig returned to the scene of carnage and destruction. Einka was still picking around, finding small edible bits, and the others were sated and lounging around the hearth with the last of the ale.

"These are my half brothers," Jafnar explained.

"Which doesn't make them my half sons," Solveig said, eyeing Modga suspiciously. "And just when I've finally gotten this house cleaned! How long are they going to be visiting, Jafnar?"

"Until the destruction of Rangfara," Einka answered in a proper doomful voice. "He's a prophet now, you know, and sees these things."

Solveig took umbrage at his tone and his high-pitched giggle. She glared at him and the others sprawled about the hearth in various indolent positions. "If he says it, then he means it, and I raised him to be a truthful person, so if a destruction is coming, I suggest you prepare for it rather than lolling in your father's chair as if you belonged there, you wretched lump, and with your boots on besides. And you there—" She poked fearlessly at Lofa and Lampi. "—when was the last time those clothes were washed? Didn't your mothers raise you up with any proper house manners, or did you grow up wild, like a litter of wildcats?"

Einka squirmed and flushed beet-red, casting a yearning look toward the door.

"Actually," Ordvar said in a humble, piteous tone, "none of us have seen much of our mothers since we were six years old. We weren't as lucky as Jafnar."

"Oh! Well! You poor things!" Solveig exclaimed. "What a pity! But I expect it's too late to teach you anything now. It's what comes of barracks life, I guess. But say—I have a splendid idea. Why don't you all move in here with Skjoldur and Jafnar? There's plenty of room for twice as many of you. It will greatly improve your manners to have closer supervision by your father. Isn't that a splendid idea, Jafnar?"

"Certainly, Mother," he said with a grin.

"Sons being with their father," Solveig said firmly. "I never approved of keeping them in herds like uncivilized little animals. I do wish I were going to be around to see how it all turns out, but I've got to get back to my sisters before they move camp for the summer. I've a dozen more relatives to visit. It seems you'll be well taken care of here, Jafnar. I'll be leaving in the morning."

"I hope you're not leaving on our account," Modga said earnestly around the end of half a loaf of bread, with a flask of ale cradled in one arm.

Solveig curled her lip slightly, changing distaste at the last instant into a winning smile. "Certainly not," she replied. "It's just that my relatives pester me so to come and visit this time every year. Family ties are so important to maintain. It gives me no end of gratification to think of the lot of you moving in here and sharing your father's roof. It will do him so much good. You may tell him I told you to stay. As long as you wish, of course."

As he looked around at his brothers, Jafnar wasn't so certain of their welcome. Their manners were execrable, eating and drinking like pigs, belching and scattering the scraps with joyous abandon. Too much ale was running down their throats, with the accompanying increase in exuberance and irresponsibility. Einka commenced weeping on everybody's neck, and Modga leapt across the table trying to seize Lampi by the throat for some imagined insult. Lofa assumed it was his duty to take Modga apart for attacking his brother.

A thundering at the outside gate put a halt to this interesting procedure. Jafnar leapt up in consternation, suspecting it was Skjoldur at last.

"Hallooa, open up in there!" a gruff voice commanded.

"It's time I was going, anyway," Einka said, rising up briskly and looking for the back door.

"Stay, you fool! It's your own father's house, you great nit," Modga hissed, grabbing him by the back of his breeches and setting him down again. "You've every right to be here."

"Not really," Einka said worriedly. "I belong with Skriftur, remember? Skjoldur sold me off as an apprentice."

"Maybe it's old Engi, coming to fetch us back to prune porridge and hard beds," Ordvar suggested. Lofa and Lampi groaned and rolled their eyes.

"Prune porridge!" Jafnar gasped and shuddered. Many times as wild boys they had subsisted for days on nothing more than a weak gruel with a few withered prunes thrown in. "I hope to never eat that stuff again."

"As if you ever did, in this house," Modga snorted, rolling his eyes. "Porridge is for younger sons. You probably had fresh meat every day. Old Engi thought prune porridge was good for us."

"Come on, let's go see who it is at the gate," Jafnar said impatiently. "What's there to be afraid of? No one's going to throw us out. This is our father's house, and we're his sons, are we not?"

Nevertheless, he drew several deep breaths when he stepped out onto the porch and listened to the heavy pounding at the gate, which had not ceased. The porter added his imprecations to the din, and people across the street were beginning to take an interest.

"Open up in there at once!" came the growling shout. It was not Skjoldur.

"What should I do?" the porter squeaked. "There's a great

lumbering fellow out there with a box on his back, demanding to get in!"

"Who's there?" Jafnar replied, his voice sounding rather more shrill than he'd hoped. "What do you want? This is a private house you're attacking."

"Shut up and open the gate. We're not attacking anybody. My master wants to talk to you."

"And who is your master?"

"Mistislaus, you fool! Now open up!"

"It's Guthrum!" Jafnar said, hastening to open the gate despite the frantic expostulations of his brothers.

"Mistislaus! Welcome!" he said as Guthrum thrust him aside and strode into the house with a trunk nearly his own size and a bundle perched on top, the whole burden balanced on his wide shoulders.

"Where shall I put this?" the dwarf rumbled, flinging down the chest with a crash and glaring around with his sinister hooded eye. "These young vermin seem to be inhabiting the lower floor."

"Up the stairs," Mistislaus said, striding in and flinging his dusty satchel. The dark and silent Illmuri shadowed Guthrum up the stairs. "I prefer a view of my surroundings, and the air is fresher up there above the street level. Oh, yes, by the way, Jafnar, I've been thrown out of my accommodations for making stenches and setting the place on fire. I thought you'd have room here on the upper story, but I didn't have time to wait for an invitation. Skjoldur and I have an understanding—in spite of some recent unfortunate circumstances."

"My father's house is yours for as long as you care to stay," Jafnar said. "You took me in once and tried to make something of a wretched wild boy. I did learn to eat with something other than my bare hands. Make yourself at home. It's the least I can do to return your favor."

"Yes, my thoughts exactly," Mistislaus said, settling himself in the best chair with a weary sigh. He peered around brightly at the five half brothers. "This is almost like old times, is it not? Except your brothers were living in the Hall of Stars and Skyla had the little room in the eaves. I saw a candle. Who's got it now?"

"Thogn," Jafnar said.

"Ah, yes, Thogn. The firstborn. You went and took him from Kraftugur? I don't imagine that tightfisted old vulture was very willing to part with him."

"He was almost decent about it," Jafnar said.

"Yes. He knows he must be careful. You're a traveler, the same as he is," Mistislaus said, picking through the remains of the celebratory feast and finding one last pig's trotter and a piece of pastry. "He's biding his time. It was his doing that got me discredited with Hoggvinn—this time, last time, every time. I don't suppose there's any pickled cabbage or mustard left, is there?"

"In that crock there," Jafnar said. "Don't you think it wasn't very smart to offend Hoggvinn by criticizing his treaty with the Krypplingur?"

"Hoggvinn and I are old friends, too old to stand upon mere convention. We offend each other all the time. Isn't that what friends are for? He has plenty of far more offensive guests than I."

"Kraftugur," Jafnar said.

"Kraftugur. My onetime friend." Mistislaus helped himself to a generous cup of ale. "Until he got into trouble with sorcery. I warned him, but he would keep calling up those hideous creatures until one of them got the best of him. Well, don't trouble yourselves about me. I shan't bother you in the least, and I'll put my share in for the cooking pot. If anyone's going to the market in the morning, fetch me two of those meat pastries from the old woman by the bridge, more trotters, some sausages with spice, and a loaf of plumabrot. I shall pay you back when my fortunes permit it."

"There's no need. My father is feeding us," Jafnar said, preoccupied. His mouth burned and watered at the mention of plumabrot. He shook his head fiercely to forget the tantalizing taste and the sensations that accompanied it. "And you are our guest. It will be our pleasure to provide you with whatever you wish from the market stalls."

"How long exactly do you plan to stay here with us?" Einka demanded worriedly, watching Mistislaus shoveling down several boiled eggs.

"Didn't our father kick you out once already?" Modga added. "Will he be glad to see you back?"

"I shall stay only as long as I find necessary," Mistislaus said. "Or until my presence becomes dangerous for you. Failed wizards and old fish have a way of becoming exceedingly tiresome very quickly."

"Mistislaus can stay here as long as he wishes," Jafnar said.

"Lovely manners," Mistislaus said around a mouthful of

kraut, bread, and mustard. "Your mother must have taught you your lessons well. But they won't get you where you need to go." He leaned forward suddenly, gripped Jafnar by the back of the neck, and drew him forward to hiss rather boozily into his ear, darting suspicious glances all around.

"Good manners aren't worth a gnat's ass in the Kjallari," he hissed. "You know what Kraftugur's going to do down there. He's got to be stopped. There's still time before he puts a knife to Hoggvinn's throat."

The other brothers stared at him in alarm.

"I'll show you the rooms upstairs," Jafnar said. "There's a good view of the sunrise and a private place for your iterations."

"I can find my own way," Mistislaus said. "I've stayed here every year since Hoggvinn gave this house to Skjoldur. Don't let me pull you away from your warm fire and your companions. Now that Hoggvinn has given me the kiss of death, I'm not worth anyone's bother."

"Except mine," Jafnar said, taking up a lighted lamp. "Now follow me. Mind your head on that beam. I've become well acquainted with it lately. I'm not used to ducking through doorways."

Chuckling, Mistislaus followed him up the stairway to the attic rooms. Jafnar glowered at Illmuri, who promptly excused himself.

"Must he be here, Mistislaus?"

"Of course. He is my apprentice. This is very kind of you, Jafnar," Mistislaus said, looking around the room by the light of the flickering whale oil. "The Jafnar who was here before would have thrown me out in the street rather than besmirch his father's name with my presence."

"Then he was a fool. Where is he now, Mistislaus?"

"Having a miserable time somewhere, I expect. I recommend you get some sleep if you can get those young ruffians downstairs bedded down for the night."

"How long has Skyla been missing?" Jafnar asked in a low voice. He had been burning to ask about her, but not with his brothers listening.

"A fortnight," Mistislaus said with a sigh, sobering instantly. "And what an ominous fortnight it's been. Three Krypplingur killed the day she disappeared, then two others. I was thrown out by Hoggvinn and Skjoldur both the same day."

"I know where she is," Jafnar said. "I had a sort of vision.

I saw her with Alvara and the Drottningur—with blood on her hands and face."

Mistislaus turned toward a window that faced the Hall of Stars. "Yes. Illmuri saw the same vision. Curse those Drottningur," he muttered. "And curse Alvara in particular."

"We can get her back, Mistislaus."

"Yes, and we'd better be quick about it," Mistislaus said, unpacking a few possessions from his satchel—the brainpan of a skull for an oil lamp, a frazzled old book that was worn and blackened by much use, a crystal sphere as cloudless as a raindrop. "I've tried to shield her from Alvara and Kraftugur and Ofarir many times, Jafnar. Every time I fail her."

"What happens to her, Mistislaus?"

"It doesn't help to brood about other pasts, Jafnar."

"Just tell me what happens."

"She dies. Kraftugur destroys her."

"Does she remember?"

"Of course. It's why she seems daft, according to present standards. The nightmares, the shape shifting—she wants to find the way off this endless circle. Always she finds her way to me for help, and always I fail."

"Don't despair. There may be hope for her. And I always come across your path, too, don't I?"

"Of course. We're helpless, like blobs of mud on a revolving wheel fastened to a wagon bound for some unknown destination."

"I wish you'd take her away from Rangfara," Jafnar said. "Why is it that you always end up bringing her here, when you know she's going to be killed? And yourself, too, for that matter."

Mistislaus shrugged. "It can't be helped. We could go to the far side of the earth, but something would always draw us back to this place. And if you took her and went, it would be the same, so stop thinking what you're thinking."

"You're her father," Jafnar said. "It's up to you to determine her gifting and birthright selling, since she seems to have no mother."

"Silence! It's a waste of time to even think about it!" Mistislaus snapped. "This child is of a very strange mixture of heredities. And I am not the sole proprietor of Skyla's future, by any means. There are many others who are terribly interested in what becomes of her—and would be even more so if they knew the complete truth about her. I advise you to be as silent about Skyla as possible Don't entertain any fond notions about her. Perhaps one day—no, we should know by now we cannot greatly alter what fate has in store for us."

"We can," Jafnar said. "We change our fate whenever we make a decision."

"Don't complicate my life even further, Jafnar," Mistislaus retorted. He flung his cloak on the makeshift bed and sat down to tug at his boots, a difficult enough maneuver for a much thinner person. Jafnar obligingly stooped and drew off the boots. "Leave Skyla out of your pleasant daydreams. I can guarantee you she'll bring you nothing but misery."

CHAPTER
NINE

A FURIOUS POUNDING on the street door awakened them in the morning. Skjoldur's voice, upraised in a protesting shout, brought Jafnar out of the house and into the courtyard, where Guthrum was snorting and fanning his axe around and bawling threats to Skjoldur on the other side of the gate. The gate porter was nowhere to be seen, except for a frightening eye peering out a crack in the door of the gatekeeper's hut.

"Guthrum!" Jafnar exclaimed. "Open the gate! It's Skjoldur!"

"How was I supposed to know who he was?" Guthrum growled perversely, commencing the unbarring of the gate. "He said he was Skjoldur, and he sounded like Skjoldur, but I didn't believe him. You know how people are nowadays."

"Jafnar! What is this fellow doing here?" Skjoldur demanded with a smoldering glare at Guthrum. "This must mean that Mistislaus is back again. You, dwarf, tell your master that I can't have him here. If he values our friendship, he'll make himself exceedingly scarce."

Guthrum grounded his halberd with a clunk and turned his small and furious eyes upon Skjoldur and Jafnar, radiating insult. "A dwarf knows no master," he rumbled. "I serve Mistislaus because I choose to and he needs someone to look out for him. I don't belong to anyone except myself. As to valuing your friendship—" He eyed Skjoldur up and down like a bad bargain at the horse market and spit eloquently upon the ground.

At that moment the hall door opened, and the other brothers peered out to investigate the uproar.

"Oh, is it a celebration?" Skjoldur asked on a note of

pleased revelation. He rubbed his hands together. "Has Solveig finally gone home?"

"No indeed!" Solveig replied, shoving her way to the front. "Skjoldur, you created these creatures. It's your responsibility to feed them!"

"Good morning, Pabbi," Modga said. "Won't you come in for breakfast? I think there's something left from yesterday. Some old bread, perhaps. A pitiful lump of cheese."

"Is that how you plan to feed young warriors?" Solveig demanded. "Isn't your mighty position next to Hoggvinn worth any more than that? Give them your token and send them to the Skurdur for something to eat."

"Engi's fed them well enough," Skjoldur growled, scowling like a cornered badger. "I certainly pay him plenty. If they're hungry, let them go back to him."

"That tightfisted old curmudgeon?" Solveig said. "Is he still alive? Can he still lift a sword? Why on earth is he teaching your sons their battle arts instead of you?"

Skjoldur grimaced in fury. "He's a great veteran of a great many battles. One of the best instructors at arms, and believe me, it was no easy thing to hire him to come here and train these untried youths when he was in such demand elsewhere."

"As a scarecrow in the fields, perhaps?" Solveig inquired. "I wondered what barrow you unearthed him from. Why don't you teach your sons yourself?"

"Because I've trained extensively, but I've never really fought in any battles," Skjoldur said with great dignity. "All the good fighting was done with by the time I got there. Now, if you're quite finished embarrassing me in front of my sons, I'll come in for some breakfast, if you don't mind."

"There's nothing to eat," Einka announced. "But I'd be happy to run to the Skurdur. Then I've got to be off to the Kjallari. I've got a great deal of work to do to catch up on what I was doing yesterday when I was so rudely interrupted."

At that moment Thogn chose to glide down the steps, intent upon a mud puddle near the paving stones. Stooping down, he scooped up a handful of mud and began crooning as he shaped it into a little human figure. Overhead, on a walkway, Mistislaus intoned a greeting to the newly risen sun in a booming voice that carried well into the street. He commenced his morning iterations: "Let this day bring peace, joy, health, and serenity. Keep away chaos and oblivion." He always droned out the last word, resonating the final sound with great relish, like some huge bee buzzing. Years of practice had improved his technique until it was truly remarkable, particularly repeated a hundred times at top volume.

Skjoldur uttered a despairing moan and hurried inside, making frantic signals for someone to collar Thogn and bring him in quietly.

"Jafnar!" he said once they were inside. "What's the meaning of all this?"

"I'm calling together my kin before it's too late," Jafnar said. "I know what's coming. Maybe this time it can be prevented. At least we're going to try."

Skjoldur shook his head and sighed. "I don't know what you think you're doing here with dwarfs and wizards and your unfortunate half-wit brother. You were a peaceful lad before that knock on the head."

"I was a fool from what I can gather," Jafnar said. "But I am that person no longer, Father."

"Yes, and I miss that person considerably. Now you're going about making prophecies and foreseeing doom and destruction on all sides. It won't do, Jafnar, it just won't do. Hoggvinn is going to get wind of all this, and he'll have my head on a platter."

"Nonsense," the voice of Mistislaus said before Jafnar could form an answer. Mistislaus came down the stairs, stuffing his iteration string into his pocket. Only the most dire of circumstances permitted an interruption of his morning iterations. "You and Hoggvinn won't let something as minor as a lunatic and a prophet come between you. There are far worse secrets between the three of us. We've known each other for a long time, Skjoldur."

"Mistislaus." Skjoldur darted a quick glance toward Jafnar and the other brothers still lingering in the courtyard as Einka was trying to depart for the Skurdur. "Jafnar, take this ring and present it to any of the stall merchants in the Skurdur and bring home whatever you wish. Someone sensible needs to be in charge of that lot of young savages." To Mistislaus he added in a jocular manner, "It keeps me destitute just feeding them. In the old days there were wars and feuds to keep men occupied. I can see why some people despise peaceful times, particularly fathers of young bachelors."

"They are a fine, spirited group," Mistislaus said when they were gone. "You should be proud."

"You should leave," said Skjoldur. "Thank you very much

for putting these strange notions into Jafnar's head. He's not the same person he was before getting his skull cracked."

"And that gives me great hope for our future," Mistislaus said. "In case I should be found in one of Rangfara's unsavory alleyways with my throat cut from ear to ear, there's something you must do."

"What is there I could possibly do for you?" Skjoldur asked in a voice edged with misgivings.

"Remember the child you took from its mother twenty years ago?" Mistislaus said in a low, rapid whisper. "The child of the Viturkona?"

"No! Stop!" Skjoldur rasped, his features suddenly haggard and colorless.

"The newborn child you stole on Hoggvinn's orders from her mother's breast and left to die on the fell," Mistislaus went on remorselessly. "His own daughter, to be torn by wolves and eagles, and her tiny bones scattered like seashells."

"No!" Skjoldur whispered. "Hoggvinn did no such thing. He took pity on it and changed his mind. The child was sickly. It died on its own. The Viturkona infant was not normal at birth. We didn't have to kill it."

"Try convincing the Viturkonur of that," Mistislaus said. "The child dying was far too convenient. Luckily, only you and Hoggvinn and I know it died. Luckily we bought that scraeling infant."

"They must never find out or they'll be at our throats like weasels. You said that one infant looks much like another, so all we needed was a baby of some sort. You told Hoggvinn you'd keep the child. We should never have tried to fool the Viturkonur."

"It was either fool them or fight them," Mistislaus said. "Unfortunately, it seems they are no longer fooled. If they ever were."

"Mistislaus, are you trying to tell me in your usual blathering way that they have found out?"

"I don't know. All I know for certain is that one of them is here, posing as Logregla's ladies' maid, and she's got Skyla with her."

"Then they must suspect something, coming back this way to spy around," Skjoldur said. "I am doomed. I am the one who stole the child—and caused the mother's death when she fell from her horse chasing after us. Mistislaus, what are we going to do? Have they done anything yet?"

Mistislaus rubbed his chin. "Since the arrival of Alvara five Krypplingur have had their throats torn out and their hearts and livers eaten," he said with reluctance.

"If this Viturkona has done five unspeakable murders, we'll go into the Hall of Stars and drag her out and sink her in a bog!" Skjoldur said, his eye kindling with a sudden combative flare. "She can't get away with this sort of thing in Rangfara!"

"Yes, and wouldn't that delight the Viturkonur?" Mistislaus said. "No one ever wants to make a Viturkona angry. Revenge is rather a speciality of theirs. Utter destruction and endless revenge in exchange for the smallest offense."

Skjoldur drew himself up indignantly and opened his mouth, ready to bluster on, but suddenly the wind went out of him and he slumped in his chair, too dispirited to continue the charade of righteous innocence any longer.

"What shall we do?" he asked.

"Guard Hoggvinn with your life. He is the one I think is in the greatest danger."

"Hoggi? They want to kill Hoggi?" Skjoldur gasped, his face blanching. "Then they'll have to kill me first. And you, too. We swore a blood oath to protect him all our lives when we were twelve years old, remember? We pricked our fingers and signed in blood that we would stand together forever. What shall we do, Mistislaus?"

"Nothing immediately. Just go on as usual. But you must swear to me you'll never tell Hoggvinn or anyone that Skyla is not the Viturkona infant. Skyla herself could be in great danger if they know she is an impostor."

"But this Alvara woman is under Hoggvinn's own roof," Skjoldur said. "She could kill him almost at her own choosing. Five Krypplingur have met horrible deaths since she arrived in Rangfara, mauled and eaten by the snow lynx. We can't just let her kill Hoggvinn. Skyla herself may be a tool in Alvara's hands. Or a weapon."

"It is my worst fear that Alvara will use Skyla to kill Hoggvinn," Mistislaus said. "We must move slowly and carefully."

"A strange thing for a man to say who has just rammed his head straight into a hornets' nest," Skjoldur said.

Mistislaus went back to his interrupted iterations, and Skjoldur went back to the Hall of Stars, leaving directions for the establishment of bachelors' quarters for his six sons. Solveig and her baggage departed with brisk haste and much feigned reluctance to visit her insistent relatives, leaving Athugashol to Jafnar and his brothers.

"I shall be back to check on you," she said briskly. "Perhaps next spring."

"Don't come back to Rangfara, Mother," Jafnar said impulsively. "Not until I'm sure it's safe."

"Another prophecy," she said with an impatient sigh. "I hope you get over this before I return."

After an impossible breakfast consisting of every rich, heavy thing available in the Skurdur cooking stalls, the brothers lugged themselves to the practice field, where they all felt too full and lazy to do much profitable practicing. Modga sneaked away and was discovered atop a wall, sound asleep in the sunshine, like a gorged snake sunning itself on a rock.

"Prune porridge," Engi snapped. "This is why young warriors eat simple food, sleep on hard beds, and live lives of sparsity and self-denial. You'll never amount to anything with a soft mattress and rich food!"

"I agree," Jafnar said in disgust. "From now on I'm in charge of the food and drink in Athugashol."

By the end of the day he and Engi had flogged the others into shape, including a most reluctant Einka.

"Remember, now," Engi said at sundown when they were finished. "Eat a pauper's supper. Drink very little ale. Go to bed before the stars are completely out. Get up at the first cockcrow. Eat your prune porridge. This is the way you make yourself a warrior."

"I am not a warrior," Einka said bitterly, still simmering at having been dragged away from the Kjallari. For him the day had been a totally miserable experience. He was too short, too rotund, and too breathless. "I will never be a warrior. No one can ever make me into a warrior!"

"We'll need every warrior we can get to drive them out of Rangfara," Jafnar said grimly, noting a group of Krypplingur swaggering past the practice field. "They always carry their weapons, a peculiar habit in a friendly camp. Engi, how many other young Skyldings are learning warfare and weaponry?"

"Maybe fifty," Engi said grudgingly, casting his one good eye upward as he mentally inventoried Rangfara's prospective warriors. "But some of them are scarcely twelve years old. The older they get, the more likely they are to go off somewhere visiting or adventuring. It's been so long since Rangfara had need of protection, everyone has forgotten what sort of place this world really is. Seeing these Krypplingur makes me remember. We fought them when I was a young man. Terrible opponents they are. It seems to take a lot more effort to kill one of them."

Jafnar ignored the complaints of his brothers that night and ordered them to fix a simple man's meal for supper. Skjoldur suddenly remembered someone he had to go visit—and probably eat a decent supper with—and promptly vanished.

In the middle of the night, when everything was silent, Jafnar awakened suddenly, intent and listening. As a wild boy, he knew that such an awakening always meant that he had heard something important in his sleep. He got up and went to an arrow slit to listen, his neck hairs bristling, his subconscious quivering with the memory of a cry. He contemplated going back to bed as a test for his interior warning mechanism that had served him well as a wild boy, but the warning clamored too furiously for him to ignore it. He let himself out the back door and stood listening.

Beyond the mossy walls of Athugashol rose the spires of the Hall of Stars, glowing pale against the dark sky. Age and smoke and misery had not darkened the stones of Rangfara yet; they still gleamed white and silvery even by moonlight. Looking at those spires, he thought of Skyla hidden away among the Drottningur, with Alvara. He stepped off the threshold purposefully, knowing what he had to do.

Guthrum grumbled suspiciously but let him out.

"If it's trouble you're looking for, who am I to stop you?" Guthrum growled. "Trouble has followed me all the days of my life as a constant companion. No one else has been so faithful, except possibly Mistislaus."

"Do you remember me, Guthrum? Were you always here with Mistislaus every time?" Jafnar whispered.

"Dvergar forget nothing," Guthrum grunted. "Now get on with you and leave me to my watching."

"I'll be back soon," Jafnar said.

"Maybe," Guthrum added. "I suggest you try the wall there in that corner by the trees. It's where you used to go over all the time as a small lad."

Jafnar's old wild-boy memories guided him unerringly, except for a slight mishap with a shallow pool that shouldn't have been there. The Hall of Stars courtyard, once a jumble of rock and scrubby brush, was now a garden, laid out in intricate walking paths. His eyes strained upward, wondering which of the dark windows under the eaves was Skyla's. He knew she would be as high as possible and alone instead of sharing the common hall downstairs, where all the visitors tended to pile onto the sleeping platforms in happy confusion. This would not be Skyla's way, he reasoned.

As he padded silently along, he became conscious of a sound rising and falling, murmuring like the whisper of wind. Curious, he followed the sound. Presently he came into view of a clump of trees, a shrinelike place where several small fires were burning. The damp breeze carried to him the unmistakable stench of burning flesh, and he halted in his tracks with his neck hair bristling like hackles. Creeping closer, he saw a group of cloaked figures gathered in a circle around a fire where the charred remains of a creature of some sort were being burned to ashes. Jafnar's heart thumped with superstitious dread as he edged nearer, trying to see the faces of the people around the fire. Not a beard in the group—the cloaked figures were women. Their voices chanted softly, almost hypnotizing him. His chest constricted. Every fiber of his being remembered the horror of the Kjallari and urged him to turn and run, but he lingered, frightened and fascinated.

Suddenly something struck him in the back between the shoulder blades, knocking him breathless, and an irresistible weight flattened him to the ground. Rolling over, he instinctively threw his arms up to protect his face and throat, and his assailant jumped on his chest before he could draw enough of a breath to utter a squeak, let alone a shout for help. Inches from his face, the gleaming eyes of an animal blazed with fury as the creature drew its lips back in a deadly hiss, revealing sharp white teeth. The moonlight also revealed a furry face, long whiskers, and tufted ears backswept in rage. On his chest he could feel the prickle of claws digging into his flesh. A piercing lynx call shattered the night, ringing in his ears with the sound of incipient doom. The fetid breath of the lynx warmed his cheeks like a deadly kiss, freezing his heartbeat and glazing his unblinking eyes. Distantly, he heard a soft clamor of women's voices.

"It's nothing but Jafnar Skjoldursson. Let him go, Logregla," said a clear voice, which broke the grip of the golden lynx eyes. The weight vanished from his chest instantly, and he leapt to his feet to confront the creature. Instead, he confronted Alvara, standing stately and composed in a long dark cloak, with a smile as cold and cruel as the moonlight, and beside her stood the queenly figure of Logregla, gazing at him with utmost contempt.

"We must finish him off!" Logregla demanded, her eyes glinting with hatred.

"No," Alvara said. "This is not his time, nor the way. He has to wait for his appointed moment on the Web of Life, when the weavers see fit to cut his life thread."

"But he has seen all," Logregla said. "He's going to talk. What if he tells my husband?"

"No one is going to believe him," Alvara said. "No one will ever believe a man who gets a rap on the head and believes he is a prophet." Her laughter tinkled like a frozen stream.

"You don't know the danger he presents," Logregla said, her eyes venomous. "As Skjoldur's son, he is far too close to Hoggvinn to know our secret and live."

"Danger? From Jafnar?" Alvara tossed her head and laughed again, a sound that chilled Jafnar's blood. "What could he do? Tell his father? Would Skjoldur dare breathe a word against the Drottningur? Skjoldur knows where the butter is on his bread. If Jafnar goes about saying that your clanswomen are lynxes, he's likely to find himself hanged in the nearest archway. No one speaks ill of the Drottningur—if they are sane."

"Lynxes! You are all lynxes!" Jafnar gasped, tearing his eyes off Alvara long enough to scan the circle of women gathering around him. "Where's Skyla? What have you done to her?"

"She is here with us," Alvara said, nodding toward the shrine and the circle of women. "Skyla, come and tell this fool he must never breathe a word of this to anyone."

Skyla came forward, robed in black from head to toe. All he could see of her was the pale oval of her face.

"Come home, Skyla," Jafnar said. "Come back to Mistislaus."

"I cannot," Skyla said. "Alvara is my own flesh and blood. I belong with her, and she with me. I was born to perform a duty, and I must fulfill my destiny. Go away, Jafnar. Leave Rangfara. There will be terrible things to come."

"I cannot and will not leave my clan," Jafnar said. "Skyla's destiny is not to destroy Rangfara. This time it is you who will perish, Alvara."

Thrusting her face closer, Logregla glared into Jafnar's eyes. "If you so much as utter a single word concerning what you have seen here tonight, yours will be the next carcass they find with its heart and vitals torn out. You see that fire pit, those charring guts there? Those will be yours one day, unless you keep your mouth closed. Bad things also could happen to your dear little Skyla if you begin interfering."

"Now go away, Jafnar," Alvara commanded. "Go back to your bed and pull your eider over your head. Tomorrow this will all be nothing but a bad dream. You will tell no one of it. You won't have the courage. Overimagination in a supposed warrior is often regarded as cowardice."

The other women tittered scornfully as Jafnar backed away. Terror and shame raged in his chest, mingled with a strong and growing dose of defiance and outrage. Swinging around, he faced Alvara, who eyed him with suspicion and contempt in her haughty face.

"You remember the other Rangfara, the other Skyla," he whispered rapidly. "You know me and I know you, or you wouldn't realize what a danger I am to you and your bloodthirsty cult of cats. You may have Skyla in this life, but before it is done, I shall have her and you shall be dead, Alvara."

"Be on your guard, then, Skylding," she hissed. "Know that I cannot allow you to live in this life. You fancy yourself as quite a Web traveler now, I suppose. But I am a Viturkona, and we have the gift of manipulating the future as well as the past. There are other lives, other strands to the Web, and I have seen the ends of many a one, including this one. I win, Jafnar. I'm going to kill you. I can carry you forward and show you." She lifted one finger and pointed to his temple.

CHAPTER TEN

WITH A DAZZLING crack like a bolt of pure lightning, Jafnar caught a glimpse of himself, or what was left of him after being ravaged and shredded by a dozen lynxes, while his heart blackened on the coals of a fire. He clutched his temples and doubled over, stifling a cry of pain.

"You see, your tiny finite mind can scarcely tolerate a glimpse of the truth." Alvara sneered. "Some prophet you would make. It would be better for you if you had died tonight, knowing as I do what torments you are going to embark upon. And so utterly useless. I have your Skyla now, daughter of Hoggvinn, chieftain of the Skyldings. Her mother was the young tjaldi of the Viturkonur, Reykja, who was killed by Hoggvinn and Skjoldur. Skyla is destined to rule clan Skylding. And the Viturkonur rule her."

"I shall stop you," Jafnar said, his voice thick with fury. "You are using her for Viturkonur revenge."

"Of course. And so sweet it will be to see the pious Skyldings reduced to dust and ashes. Think how the clan of the lynx is going to spread across Skarpsey and even to lands beyond the seas. Everyone may despise the Viturkonur, but everyone knows how desirable and prosperous is a Drottning wife."

"You've taught the Viturkona curse to the Drottningur?"

"Yes, and one day soon the curse, as you call it, will return to Rangfara to exact its full price. Think of spiders, how the female nourishes her eggs on the blood of her spouse. So it will be when Skylding marries Drottning." She tossed back her head and laughed. "The dear old Krypplingur will have scarcely anything to do when we get finished with the Skyldings, merely to clean out the remaining survivors to

132

make way for the new chieftain of Rangfara and his new Viturkona wife."

"Skyla!" Jafnar turned to her. "How can you allow such a thing to happen? I can't believe you'd turn your back on Mistislaus to follow this creature!"

"This creature, as you call her, is my dead mother's sister," Skyla said with an angry flash of her eyes, "my kinswoman and clan sister. Hoggvinn intended that I should be exposed to die, and my mother died attempting to save me."

"No. Hoggvinn would do no such thing," Jafnar said.

"But he did once upon a time," Alvara said. "He so disdained the Skylding-Viturkonur birthright that he preferred to see his daughter perish. He did, however, change his mind at the last moment. Skjoldur and Mistislaus arranged to have the child kept and raised."

"Yes, Mistislaus kept her himself," Jafnar said. "Though he always said she was given to him by scraelings."

"Skjoldur had no right to steal me away from them," Skyla said. "And then for Mistislaus never to breathe a word of my true heritage is the same as stealing my clan from me. I shall never forgive him for lying to me for nearly twenty years."

"Mistislaus wanted to protect you," Jafnar said.

"This is the purpose for which I was born," Skyla said. "To help my clan destroy the Skyldings. There is nothing more interesting or important that I can do with my life. Hoggvinn and Mistislaus certainly had no interest in my future except to attempt to destroy it."

"But you were saved by a Skylding," Jafnar said. "My father, Skjoldur, couldn't bear to see you die. Are you going to conveniently forget that?"

Skyla stared at him a moment, then turned her back. "I don't wish to argue about it any longer," she said. "I know what I must do. It makes no difference."

"Well, prophet of Rangfara, are you quite finished with your interview?" Alvara asked with a cold smile. "Are you ready to go back and tell everyone how doomed they are, how helpless they are to avert their fate?"

"We are not helpless," Jafnar retorted with a cold trickle of sweat starting down his spine. "We can beat you. A women's quarrel will not be the destruction of Rangfara and the Skylding clan!"

"It always has been," Alvara whispered with a taunting grin. "A hundred times, a hundred times a hundred, it makes no difference what you do. All the circumstances are turned against you. It is like two mirrors facing each other, endlessly reflecting the same image. The image is the total destruction of Rangfara. It is eternal and inevitable."

Alvara turned her back, gesturing to her followers. They drifted away swiftly, back to their fire. On trembling legs, Jafnar returned to the wall. With a mighty effort he climbed back up the wall, tottered along its length, and almost fell as he climbed down on the side of Athugashol. He wasn't certain how he found his way inside and back to his bed in the small room, but that was where he awakened much later, when the sun was fairly well up and shining in through the bars of the small high window. A rooster crowed indignantly, and from everywhere came the sounds of bustling, cheery life.

Jafnar shivered, unable to shake the chill he had acquired in the night. He wrapped his eider around him, wondering if it had been a nightmare or another prophetic vision. Certainly it had been far more detailed than his brief glimpse of the old firemaker and Skyla walking with the Drottningur with blood on her gown. It might even have been one of his memories from yet another strand.

Pressing his hand to his aching brow, he cursed the accidental gift that had made him a seer of the future. His hand came away wet with cold sweat. A brain fever. Perhaps his mother was right, he thought gloomily, unable to stop the shivering that wracked his tremulous body. Weakly he rose from his sleeping shelf and shuffled into the main room, where a fire was burning.

With a light tread from his soft boots, Skjoldur came into the room, whistling softly and rubbing his hands before the flames.

"At last," he said, "a house without women. I always thought it a comfortable house as long as your esteemed mother was not in residence. Perhaps it won't be so bad, the lot of us living under one roof. It reminds me of my younger days, when I was a youth in training to be a Skylding warrior."

"Have you done any practicing lately?" Jafnar glanced at Skjoldur's bow hanging on the wall, its string frazzled by nibbling mice.

"With weapons, you mean? The need simply does not exist anymore. We have reached a pinnacle of civilization in Rangfara that has removed us from the sphere of the common clans and from the necessity of making war upon each other and the Dokkalfar."

"That may have been true enough before," Jafnar said, "but no longer. The Krypplingur and the Viturkonur have not reached that pinnacle yet. They still like to make war to get their business done. Skyldings still have to protect themselves."

"You sound like Mistislaus, all fire and gloom. It must be a trait of prophets to see only the worst possibilities. Don't you ever see anything pleasant?"

"Where are all the warriors now, Pabbi?"

"Still here—many of them. Some have gone traveling around to visit friends and kin, but if ever the call went out, they would come flocking back to defend Rangfara. As if it needed much defending. It's a natural fortress, and if the enemy got inside the gates, we would retreat to the Hall of Stars in case of dire extremity."

"And you will find the Krypplingur already in possession of the Hall of Stars," Jafnar said.

Skjoldur sighed and massaged his temples. "Curse Mistislaus and his bad news. Webs and murders and massacres."

Jafnar felt the wound on the side of his head. "All this feuding started long before you and I came to this place, a hundred times over with the Skyldings and the Viturkonur. We are just players in an entertainment that repeats over and over. How can I get into the Hall of Stars to see Hoggvinn?"

"Hoggvinn? Why do you want to see him?"

"That woman Logregla took in is a Viturkona. She's responsible for those horrible murders among the Krypplingur."

Skjoldur squinted apprehensively. "I don't think there's any need to alarm Hoggvinn unnecessarily. I really don't see what damage one Viturkona can do, if indeed Alvara is here. Perhaps it's not as bad as Mistislaus thinks. He's always one to look on the gloomy side of every issue."

"You can get us in to see Hoggvinn?"

"Of course, we're old friends, but—"

"Good. We'll go now," Jafnar said, and started up the stairs. "We must have Mistislaus with us. We'll have to get him at once, before he starts his morning iterations. He eats his breakfast first thing so he can concentrate on something besides his hollow stomach."

"Jafnar, Hoggvinn isn't going to be pleased to see Mistislaus any time, let alone first thing in the morning, with his gloomy prognosticating and direful warnings. He's not the most amusing company, the old gloom monger."

"Am I indeed?" Mistislaus's voice demanded from the room above. "The food around here is enough—or little enough—to make anyone gloomy. Are any of those useless sons of yours going to the Skurdur any time soon?" He brushed past Jafnar on the stairs and commenced rummaging in the detritus left over from the previous evening's feeding.

"Mistislaus, we've got to talk to Hoggvinn," Jafnar said.

"I already did that," Mistislaus said, "and he threatened to have me outlawed. I was hauled out bodily by two of his thugs. I've got nothing to say to Hoggvinn."

"Things are worse in Rangfara than you know." Jafnar came close so he could speak in a low voice. "Alvara is here, and she's festering with vengeance. Skyla is part of a tremendous plot against the Skyldings."

"Aha!" Mistislaus said on a triumphant note of discovery, and speared a small scrap of food out of a clay jar. "Smoked sausage. My favorite."

Skjoldur slumped into a chair, suddenly abandoning his confident bluster. "Why does this have to happen now? Just when I've finally gotten my life in order and everything is looking so well, you come along and ruin it by telling me there's going to be another cursed war."

"And worse, we're not even going to win, yet again," Mistislaus said, sniffing warily at the contents of a crock. "Let's discuss something more interesting, Jafnar, such as the purpose for this meeting this morning, which is cutting severely into my iterations."

Jafnar drew a deep breath to steady himself as he recalled the scenes of the previous evening. "I saw something last night. I'm not quite sure whether I was actually there or if it was a vision of something that had happened on another strand. I saw the Drottningur and Alvara and Skyla. They had a fire, and they had killed someone. When they discovered me, a lynx knocked me down and would have ripped my throat out. It was Logregla, Mistislaus. It's the same curse, only there's more of them this time. A dozen, at least. Maybe the entire Drottning clan has been converted."

Mistislaus rubbed his eyes a moment. "No one has raised the alarm yet for a lynx killing."

Skjoldur scowled incredulously at Jafnar. "And you say it

was Alvara and the Drottningur? Holding some strange ritual by moonlight?"

"Yes, Drottning women. About twelve of them, including Skyla. They were roasting the heart over the coals."

"A worse bunch of vain, arrogant, blind-sighted, coldhearted creatures I never saw," Skjöldur said with a shudder. "But I doubt they would be guilty of anything so dreadful as this. And no one has reported anyone missing. You've been ill. It sounds like a nightmare."

"I assure you, I saw it with my own eyes," Jafnar said. "If not here, then on another strand of the Web. I was knocked down and nearly killed. I was a hairsbreadth from having my throat ripped out."

"But you can't ever breathe a word against the Drottningur on the basis of a prophetic dream," Skjoldur said. "They've been our sister and mother clan for years. No one will ever lift a hand against a Drottning."

"Then they will go on with their killing? We aren't going to say anything to warn Hoggvinn?" Jafnar demanded. "He's in terrible danger, with the lynxes right under his own roof."

"We don't have any real proof," Skjoldur said. "Hoggvinn doesn't hold much by dreams or prophets. A warrior relies upon his own arm and sharp steel."

"If I could get Skyla away from them, bring her here, perhaps—"

"The last fellow I ever heard of who tried to kidnap a Drottning was gibbeted outside the main gate," Skjoldur said, shaking his head vigorously. "The Drottning matchmakers do not look tolerantly upon such breaches of etiquette."

"How did she seem when you saw her, Jafnar?" Mistislaus asked rather wistfully. "Did she look well? Are they feeding her properly, did you think?"

"I assume she was feeding quite well, if she has any taste for seared meat."

"I feared as much," Mistislaus said. "Alvara has done an excellent job of turning her against me. Perhaps if you see her again, you could put in a good word or two for me."

"I think the two of you have a conspiracy of lunacy," Skjoldur said, "designed to humiliate me before my chieftain and the other retainers."

"Unfortunately," Mistislaus said, "there is a certain ring of truth to Jafnar's words, and if I have one fault, it's my outstanding honesty. Dream or not, Hoggvinn must be told. The clan must be protected even at the cost of infuriating the Drottningur."

"Hoggvinn will want proof," Skjoldur said.

"Then I shall get proof, if it exists," Jafnar said.

Skjoldur and Mistislaus were well known to the gate guards outside the massive arched entrance to the Hall of Stars. Nor did they glance twice at Jafnar treading impatiently at their heels.

Once inside, they passed through a courtyard and stable yard where the sounds and smells of many horses warmed the air with the sweet perfume of hay and stable. A few half-awake thralls stirred about with buckets and hay forks, their movements eliciting hopeful nickers from the hungry horses as well as some impatient kicking.

A formidable thrall posted upon the doorstep of the main hall informed them that no one in the house was awake just yet, and they would have to wait, and it was doubtful if Hoggvinn would consent to see anyone—let alone Skjoldur, Mistislaus, and Jafnar, his cold and suspicious eye seemed to say. He was a strange creature of towering stature and alien origins, with coal-black hair drawn back tightly in a long pigtail and small slitted eyes in a rubicund face.

"You're Logregla's, I presume," Skjoldur said in a pompous tone.

"Yes, and I've been ordered to keep everyone out of the hall until my lady is awake," the thrall said, still scowling.

"This is a matter of utmost urgency," Skjoldur said, tossing back his cloak in a calculated gesture to clear the sword at his side. It looked as if it had scarcely ever been out of its elaborate sheath, let alone for the mundane purpose of shedding messy blood. "I don't really care if Logregla is awake or not. The safety of Rangfara rests upon our speaking with Hoggvinn. Don't you know who I am, you lowly dog?"

"But when the lady Logregla is in the hall, she leaves strict orders not to be awakened," the thrall said in a much distressed tone. "By anyone. She'll cut off my ears, she said, if anyone awakens her. And she would, too. Perhaps what you could do, if you wish to speak to Hoggvinn, is to go around to the back of the hall and speak to him in the bathhouse. He takes his breakfast there early. You'll have to go around the visitors' hall, past the laundry green and the kitchens, and beyond the old stable—"

"I know the way," Skjoldur interrupted impatiently. "Do you

think I'm not acquainted with the habits of my own chieftain? I shall inform him of your insolence, and he will speak to Logregla about it. Where did she find you, by the way? You're one of the uglier thralls I've ever seen. She's always bringing home these terrible curiosities from her travels," he added by way of explanation to Jafnar and Mistislaus. "Once she brought home a tiger, but it caught cold and died. But only after tearing up a dozen cages and quite a few thralls and dogs. Good hunting dogs, too."

Skjoldur led the way toward the back of the hall, where resided the thralls and servants in a warren of huts and byres and walls and pens. Everything was different now, roofed in and not collapsed, but Jafnar knew the turnings and twistings of the Hall of Stars and its history of additions and changes quite as well as he knew the streets of Rangfara and all its escape holes.

"This seems an out-of-the-way place for a chieftain of such importance," Skjoldur said as they tiptoed over the laundry green, listening to the cooks in the kitchen arguing and slapping the young kitchen help around. "But when the women are in residence, he makes himself as scarce as possible. Close to the kitchen and a long way from the main hall. Come this way. I know a shortcut to the old bathhouse. There's where Logregla roosts." He pointed to a corner tower. "Like an eagle, so she can see everything that goes on."

It used to be their lookout point in the old wild-boy days—the old days, or was it a catastrophic future?

Jafnar shook his head impatiently to clear it of the old memories, which caused a stab of pain that made him stagger. Skjoldur caught his arm in his strong grip to steady him.

"Are you feeling alright?" he demanded, a note of concern in his voice.

"Yes, I'm fine," Jafnar said.

Jafnar thought of the lynx women and started to sweat.

Hoggvinn was done with his steaming and birch flogging and was wrapped in a long gown like a wizard's, looking as pink and cheery as a freshly washed baby.

"Halloa! Come in! Sit down!" he shouted, hearing the door open. He did not look up from the breakfast he was enjoying in the cozy warmth of the bathhouse. Great drafty halls were suitable for large gatherings of people, but a solitary breakfast in such cavernous surroundings was no one's idea of comfort. A fire always burned in the bathhouse, particularly with a houseful of female relatives, who thrived upon bathing and steaming. The walls and floors were luxuriously draped with fleeces and tapestries to stop the slightest draft.

"Oh, so it's you again," he said, his eye falling upon Mistislaus first, then Skjoldur and Jafnar, with deepening suspicion. "I thought I told you I'd have you hanged if I ever caught sight of you again."

"I didn't believe you," Mistislaus said. "You've thrown me out and threatened me before, and nothing came of it. Too much has passed between us for threatening, my old friend. Either you kill me now or offer us breakfast."

"Well, at least we ought to eat first," Hoggvinn admitted, glaring at Mistislaus and Skjoldur through his thick and beetling brows. "Sit down, all of you, and let's get started. I have a feeling this isn't just a social call to exchange meaningless pleasantries."

Jafnar obediently seated himself on the other side of the small table and looked expectantly at Hoggvinn. A tall, spare individual with a mane of white hair and a twinkling, lively eye, Hoggvinn did not look the part that his name suggested— Hoggvinn, which had to do with battle and bloodshed and mayhem. His countenance was ruddy from years of exposure to the sun, and his shoulders were broadened by hard labor, perhaps practice with a sword.

"Here, relieve me of some of these sausages," he commanded, pushing a trencher at Jafnar and shoveling some sausages onto it. "If I eat all these, I shall get too fat to see my feet, like Logregla. A fine-looking lad you've got here, Skjoldur. All your crop are fine lads." A dim shadow passed over his bright gaze for an instant. "Why haven't you come for breakfast before? You're getting to be man enough to take your place in the Hall of Stars, if you've got the courage to face Logregla." His tone was bantering, but his eyes were flicking over Jafnar observantly.

"You're surrounded by enough fools already," Skjoldur said. "I thought you didn't need one more."

"Is this the one who got clouted on the head?" Hoggvinn demanded, pointing his knife at Jafnar, who nodded. "They say you've lost at least part of your wits, if not all. That you've been seeing visions and things."

Jafnar paused a moment to glance at Skjoldur, who was averting his eyes and wincing as if waiting for an axe to drop on his head. He nodded slightly. "Yes, I've seen lots of things."

"Good. I'm a visionary man myself. Tell me what you've seen." Hoggvinn fixed his piercing blue gaze upon Jafnar like a gaff fixing a salmon.

Jafnar stared back at him, unblinking, feeling a rush of heat starting in his brain and spreading down his spine. His voice when he spoke was hoarse and unfamiliar. "Rangfara destroyed. Blood on the hands of the Krypplingur. The Drottningur are lynxes who prey upon Rangfara. They killed last night, and they will kill again, many times."

"Ah, yes. I recognize Mistislaus behind your prophecies. All except that curious bit about the Drottningur. I've known all my life they're bloodsucking leeches, but I'm shocked to hear them called lynxes."

"You'll come to dread the sound of the word 'lynx;' " Jafnar said. "You'll find their victims' torn bodies, with hearts and livers ripped out, throats slashed—"

"Prophecy is a gruesome business, it seems. What else have you seen?"

The words came out as if drawn by tongs. "The Viturkona girl child you fathered and ordered my father to destroy will be the weapon of your destruction." The words seemed to burn in Jafnar's throat. "Mistislaus! It's Skyla, isn't it?" he gasped.

Mistislaus' gaze slid away, around the bathhouse walls, and he whistled soundlessly a few moments, his attention finally diverted from the elusive bit of sausage he was trying to spear with his knife.

"So it would appear," he said reluctantly.

Hoggvinn set down his knife and looked at Mistislaus and Skjoldur smolderingly. "How did this come about? I gave you specific orders to tell no one about that child. I thought it died."

Skjoldur and Mistislaus each waited for the other to speak.

"No one needed to tell me," Jafnar snapped. "No wonder the destruction of Rangfara is endless. The murder of a child by its own father is an unforgivable crime."

"There was no murder. A child is the father's property," Hoggvinn said. "He can do with it what he thinks best. I have since bitterly regretted ordering the murder of that child since none of Logregla's survived. Fortunately, I had an attack of remorse and pity for the wretched little thing and told Mistislaus to have it raised by some decent person. Then I was told it was dead. But if Jafnar truly is a prophet, everything I feared would happen if the infant survived is going to happen now since she is truly alive."

"He's not a prophet," Skjoldur said, shaking his head.

"How did that child get to Rangfara?" Hoggvinn demanded, shoving away his plate.

"I raised her as my own daughter," Mistislaus said, wiping the grease off his chin. "And now the Viturkona has kidnapped her. The question is, what are you going to do about it?"

"It's true about the Drottningur being lynxes," Jafnar said fiercely. "And I saw Skyla among them. All we have to do is get her away from the Drottningur and nothing will happen."

Hoggvinn gazed at Mistislaus. "I can hardly believe you've done such a thing and kept it from me for nearly twenty years. You told me she was dead."

"We lied," said Mistislaus shortly.

"That's not the deed of sworn friends. And I suppose you knew all about it?" He turned fiercely upon Skjoldur, like an eagle striking.

"We couldn't—the Viturkonur—we thought—"

Mistislaus put down his eating knife, briskly chewing a bite of sausage. "I didn't want to entrust anyone else with the task of raising your daughter, so I kept her myself and passed her off as a foundling."

"Your girl is my daughter?" Hoggvinn's gaze traveled away for a long moment, seeing inner visions. "Then I have a child. After all these cold and barren years, I have got a child to inherit when I am gone."

"Yes, but she's a Viturkona," Skjoldur said. "The clan your excellent wife Logregla insulted and rejected and inspired to a deadly hatred of anything Skylding, who have vowed revenge and utter destruction for all of us. No one hates us as the Viturkonur hate us. For years they have plotted their vengeance, and now they have got Skyla, they will bring all of this crashing down on our heads."

"That's no matter," Hoggvinn said with a flap of one hand. "I have a child, when I thought there was no hope. Bring her to me, Mistislaus, and I will make a reconciliation."

"I can't," Mistislaus said. "She's in your women's hall with Logregla and that Viturkona woman, and no one can get near her."

"It's the Viturkonur!" Jafnar blurted suddenly, his head roar-

ing with pain and visions. "Viturkonur and Drottningur together will destroy the clan Skylding!"

"You will deal with these Viturkonur, Skjoldur," Hoggvinn
said. "Invite them to Rangfara. Shower them with honors until
they forget this gifting insult."

"No, it's not the insult!" Jafnar said. "You don't understand.
It's the treasure. Skyla is only a pawn in their scheme to get
the Skylding gold."

Hoggvinn replied, "Pay them whatever they require to cool
their desire for revenge for this insult."

"What they desire are our vitals cooked up for their dinner,"
Skjoldur said. "With Viturkonur there's no forgiveness, Hoggi.
Some things you just can't buy."

"That hasn't been my experience," Hoggvinn said with a
cold glint in his eye and a slight sneer. "If you have riches
enough, principles and causes tend to get prices put upon them.
I can buy any cause, any principle. We'll have the Viturkonur
fawning at our feet, adoring us as if we were old and valued
relatives."

"That's not something I'd care to see," Mistislaus said.
"Friendship is never a thing to be bought. Like an excess of
fresh fruit, it can go bad very quickly and unexpectedly. Look
at us, Hoggi. We're your true friends. You've never offered to
buy us, and we wouldn't take your gold if you offered it.
Countless times we've quarreled and hated each other, but here
we are again across a table from each other and sharing food
and drink."

"If you can't make sense when you talk," Hoggvinn replied,
"I wish you'd just shut up."

"I'm getting to the point," Mistislaus said, hissing between
his teeth. "Which is, you can't trust the Viturkonur no matter
how much you give them."

"I said nothing about trusting them," Hoggvinn said virtuously. "I make it a rule never to trust anyone, especially females."

"Good," Jafnar said. "Then you won't feel at all badly about
getting rid of the Drottningur. The Viturkonur are turning them
all into lynxes. Any Skylding who marries a Drottningur is going to be killed, and his heart and liver eaten."

"The Drottningur have got nothing to do with this old quarrel," Hoggvinn said.

"They do now, since the arrival of Alvara," Mistislaus said.

"Alvara," Hoggvinn repeated in a whisper. "I remember an Alvara. She was the one who drugged me."

"Yes," Mistislaus said. "Sister to Skyla's mother, who died when her infant was kidnapped by Skyldings. Through all the strands and threads of the Web, Alvara uses Skyla as the instrument of the Skylding's final destruction. Even when only seven remained."

"I must see Skyla," Hoggvinn said. "To think, my own daughter was under my nose all these years when you came to Rangfara, and you never breathed a word of it to me, you old traitor."

"How was I to know you wouldn't want to kill her?" Mistislaus demanded. "I've grown very fond of the girl, as if she were my own child. I wasn't about to trust you with the knowledge of her—until now, when all our lives seem to be in peril."

As they quarreled, neither of them noticed a slight sifting of dust coming down the smoke hole in the roof. Jafnar glanced up and saw a pair of eyes glowing for a moment in the light of the fire and lamps.

"I can't wait to see her," Hoggvinn said. "As a man ages, he thinks about what will be when he is no more. Now I know I have a daughter who will marry, and her husband will be chieftain of the Skylding clan. A suitable man must be found. If she is nearly twenty, then she is of gifting age. We'd better take care of it quickly. If we wait until I die, then I won't have any say in who is chosen to be my successor." He chuckled at his own joke and speared another sausage with his knife.

Mistislaus glowered at Hoggvinn with increasing wrath until he could contain himself no longer. "A daughter is not a piece of property to be bartered around for the best political advantage," he snapped. "I don't think Skyla would appreciate being sold off to the highest bidder as if she were a slave at an auction!"

The eyes vanished, and Jafnar wondered if he had imagined it.

"Ho," Hoggvinn said, amused. "As if any of us had a great deal of choice in the lot we're dealt in life. Skyla will be glad to do as she is told. It's not every day a little ragamuffin wizard's girl discovers she is the daughter of the chieftain of the most powerful clan in Skarpsey. She'll be quite humbled by the honor of it, I should think."

Skjoldur cleared his throat. "Then I wouldn't tell her how you wanted to kill her when she was born."

Hoggvinn scarcely heard. "I want to see her. As soon as possible, I want to see my daughter. I want to tell her of my splendid plans for her. And as for this accusation against the Drottningur, don't speak a word of it until you have ironclad proof. I don't want to arouse their suspicions or their wrath."

"But in the meantime people are going to be killed," Jafnar said indignantly.

"We must go about this matter with circumspection and utmost caution," Hoggvinn said. "Perhaps if we work it right, we won't have to sacrifice our treaties with the Drottningur. They have enormous power among the other clans."

"What if we get proof the Drottningur are lynxes?" Jafnar asked, glancing at the smoke hole and wondering if Alvara was listening.

"Enough of this nonsense. I wish to see my daughter at once," Hoggvinn said with an impatient flap of one hand.

CHAPTER
ELEVEN

"THERE WILL BE no seeing of any of the fair female creatures until after they've bathed," Skjoldur said. "You'll be lucky to get an audience around noonday if they are trying to hurry. Are you certain it's quite . . . wise? I'm sure Alvara has told Skyla of her history by now. She might not be exactly pleased to learn who her father is and what his first idea was after she was born. Putting one's child in a sack and drowning her like a kitten is not generally a very fatherly attitude to take."

"That was a long time ago," Hoggvinn said. "Everything has changed now. She will understand that. She must realize that in her position, attending to the needs of the chieftaincy is of utmost importance."

Jafnar slowly shook his head as he thought of the Skyla he had known. A chieftaincy was the last thing she would consider of utmost importance.

"Skjoldur, you will arrange the meeting," Hoggvinn continued. "Today, as quickly as you can manage it."

"I shall be glad to, but don't you think it would be better to break the news to her that you would like to see her, then let her think about it for a while before you meet with her?" Skjoldur suggested hopefully.

"Don't be absurd," Hoggvinn said with a flash of ire. "She's my daughter, is she not? I have every right to see her when I wish."

"But Hoggi, my dear friend." Skjoldur's voice dropped to a whisper. "If what Jafnar and Mistislaus say is true, then Skyla may be one of the lynx creatures stalking Rangfara. If she is, it could be dangerous for you."

Skjoldur quailed before the look of dawning fury on Hoggvinn's face.

"Silence! I refuse to contemplate such a thing!" Hoggvinn snapped.

"Skyla is a Viturkona," Mistislaus said. "It may be their plan to have her tear your throat out. A nice plan, don't you think? That's the beauty of revenge. The best sort is so dreadfully ugly."

Hoggvinn's angry flushed countenance gradually drained away to a mottled mask of dire hatred. "If either of you ever breathes this suspicion to anyone in Rangfara concerning the Drottningur," he seethed in a low and deadly voice, "I shall personally cut your throats, my dear old friends. On that you can rely. And that includes you, too, you young meddler," he added, turning his wrath upon Jafnar. "Your prophecies are going to cause you nothing but grief!"

At that moment someone knocked heavily upon the door.

"Who's there and what do you want?" Hoggvinn replied impatiently, blinking his red-rimmed eyes like a bear disturbed during his breakfast.

"It's the washerwomen," came the reply in a no-nonsense voice. "We want to get in and start the laundry if you're done with breakfast, as you should be by now. We have so much extra work now, with the Drottningur and all. We've got to get started earlier than ever."

"I'm done, I'm done," Hoggvinn retorted, bundling up in his fur-lined cloak and reaching for his boots. "Come along; we can't get in their way when there's important work to be done, like washing the clothes of the Drottningur. These spring gifting visits put the laundrywomen in such a state of rage that I don't know if it's worth it. All the female creatures from the least scullery maids on up get so worked up when they think someone's standing in their way . . ."

Still growling, he opened the door, beckoning Skjoldur and Jafnar to follow whether they were done with their breakfasts or not. Skjoldur and Hoggvinn went off together while Jafnar hesitated, looking at the laundresses with their bundles of clothing, tubs, and wash poles and the red arms and put-upon expressions that washerwomen always wore. Jafnar let Hoggvinn and his father go on without him.

"Do these things belong to the Drottningur?" Jafnar inquired, prodding the nearest bundle with his toe.

"So they do," the largest and stoutest and reddest representative of the clothes-washing clan answered. "It's unusual for a man to be interested in laundry."

They all snickered at the impudence of their leader.

"Are they very fine clothes?" Jafnar asked. "It must take a lot of skill and care to wash some of the things they wear. Those veils you can see right through, that float in the air like scraps of clouds. I expect those would be difficult to wash, wouldn't they?"

The laundress braced one beefy fist on her hip. "Not at all," she replied with a grin and wink to her companions. "The filmy things just wad up into a tiny ball when they get wet. I expect you'd like to see some of those things, wouldn't you? Most men would." She snickered meanly, rolling her eyes, echoed by her straggly, snaggletoothed cohorts.

"Well, then, let's have a look and see what's in here." Jafnar gave the bundle another prod. The laundress folded her arms across her huge bosom, clutching her wash pole.

"Never, not in a million years," she declared. "Laundry is a very private business. We been trusted to do it, and that's how we do our work, with no outside interference. Now I suggest you run along, my laddie, and stop being so curious about things that don't concern you. I know who you are and what a nuisance you've always made of yourself, spying over that wall at the noble ladies and getting chased away by dogs and thralls. It seems you've got your father's eye when it comes to womenkind, don't you think?"

The other laundresses all uttered muffled shrieks at such audacity. Jafnar shrugged and grinned good-naturedly.

"Yes, well, I guess you've found me out," he confessed. "You see, there's one of the fairest Drottningur that I'm so smitten with that I can scarcely eat or sleep. If I could just possess a handkerchief of hers or one of those filmy scarf things, I could die quite happily, I think."

"And which of the fair Drottningur is it?" the laundress demanded. "Borgildr, the most beautiful? Svana? Or is it Spana?"

"Her name is Skyla," Jafnar said. "One of the youngest and, I think, the most beautiful."

"Hah!" the laundress grunted with an incredulous scowl. "Her? Why, she's nothing but a tiring maid! Well, one man's meat is another man's poison. She's a scrawny little creature, truth be told, and she has none of the fine manners of the true Drottningur. Perhaps she's only young and timid, this being her first gifting season, but it seems to me you could do much better with Skjoldur for your father."

"Perhaps," one of the lesser laundresses made bold to add, "it has something to do with that whack he got on the head the other day. I heard he was a raving lunatic on the way home in the cart."

"And he thinks he's a great prophet now," added yet another with a feral smile. "Tell us what our fates will be, O Wise One. Will I be rich one day? Or just more beautiful?" She showed a mouthful of crooked yellow teeth, and the other washerwomen shrieked with laughter.

"Will I marry a chieftain?" another demanded.

"Tell me my future!"

"I predict," he said, "that all of you will be going on an unexpected journey very shortly. There's a snow lynx on the roof of the bathhouse."

The laundresses goggled upward a moment, and one of them held up her lantern. Eyes gleamed in its glow, blinking down at them balefully from the rooftop. Dropping the lantern, they gathered up their skirts and ran toward the gate, pushing and crowding with the manners of a herd of startled cows. Being sensible working women, they didn't waste any time screaming and fainting.

The eyes regarded Jafnar coldly for a moment, then disappeared. He stood his ground, holding his breath a moment, then he quickly untied the bundles and sorted through them until he found what he was looking for—not a little silken remembrance but gowns liberally smeared with blood and soot and dirt and cloaks likewise soiled with blood that was still fresh. Making his own smaller bundle, Jafnar looked around warily to his own defenses before making his retreat. He saw no sign of the lynx in the thinning darkness. The washerwomen, however, were waiting for him around the corner of the stable wall with their wash poles and sticks in their hands.

"There he is!" their fierce red-armed leader crowed, pointing in triumph. "The clothes snatcher! It's our duty to defend the laundry of the Drottningur! Give back those gowns or we'll crown you again, you thief!"

"Wait," Jafnar said. "First I have a riddle for you. What sort of creature kills in the streets by night and wears women's gowns and cloaks and a pious face by day?"

The washerwomen exchanged somber glances, lowering their wash poles and laundry sticks suddenly.

"Yes, you know about it, then!" Jafnar whispered. He came forward a few steps, and the laundresses retreated hastily, making signs to ward off evil. "And so do I, and now I've got the proof. You know their guilt, don't you? You know, and you're afraid to say it even among yourselves! Why punish me for my crime when others are allowed to go free for no reason except their birth? If it were you, you'd be hung up in gibbets and you know it, but were it the Drottningur, not a word of accusation must pass."

"You're mad!" the laundress declared, her broad face pallid in the dawn light. "How dare you accuse the great ladies? You'll come to grief soon enough unless you close your mouth. And we will come to grief, too, because we let you steal their clothes! Do you wish our blood to be on your hands?"

"You're a traveling clan," Jafnar said. "I suggest you suddenly conceive a strong desire to leave Rangfara for distant places if you want to survive much longer."

"That we will," the laundress huffed. "Indeed we will, and you would, too, if you had any sense at all. If I could tell you how many times we had to wash blood from their clothes, you would be frightened for all your clan and not your own neck alone. I'll give you a prophecy, my young seer. Those Drottningur will be the doom of Rangfara!"

So saying, she and the other laundresses bundled themselves away in high dudgeon, darting nervous glances behind them as they went.

"And he used to be such a nice, timid little fellow," one of them complained plaintively. "That thump on the head has done him a world of harm."

"Not nearly as much harm as the Drottningur would like to do," another one said darkly.

"Hst! Mustn't talk!" the others whispered. In a very short while they were gone, their absence not discovered until Logregla's handmaidens were berated for the missing laundry and a scandal ensued over the missing cloaks and gowns, which were by no means cheaply made or easily missed.

In the hall of women, when the messenger from Hoggvinn arrived summoning Alvara and Skyla to the main hall, there was a flurry of speculation as to what crimes they had committed. Skyla looked at Alvara in wide-eyed alarm, unable to speak a word.

"This will not be tolerated," Logregla huffed, throwing five or six dozing cats off her lap and rising to her feet. "Come along. We'll see what ridiculous scheme Hoggvinn thinks he is about to pull on us."

"You don't think he knows?" Alvara murmured in her ear as she adjusted Logregla's wimple. "There was a terrible fuss about that Kryppling killed last night. It seems he was somehow important."

"Hoggvinn's always the last to know everything that goes on around here," Logregla sniffed. "I don't see how that could be it. What could he possibly want with that little waif of a girl? If he thinks he's going to throw her out, I'm going to fill his head with something besides new ideas. I'll knock his brains out, if he's got any."

Hoggvinn sat upon his chieftain's seat, leaning slightly forward and waiting intently for Skyla to be ushered into the hall. Mistislaus, Skjoldur, and Jafnar stood on one side, with Illmuri lurking a step behind. Mistislaus had insisted upon bringing him in case another fight broke out, so he would have someone else on his side.

Kraftugur stood alone upon the right-hand side, a circumstance that caused Mistislaus' hackles to bristle. The two wizards glared at each other across the chieftain's chair.

"I don't know what you want this vulture in here for," Mistislaus grumbled. "He's here only to pick the bones of Rangfara once we're all dead."

"Hush!" Hoggvinn commanded. "I won't hear any of your doom and gloom today, you old warmonger. This is a happy day for Rangfara and for me, and I won't have it spoiled by a lot of quarreling and prophesying."

"A happy day, indeed," Kraftugur said, a thin smile lightly brushing his narrow features. "And many more are to follow now that your daughter has been found."

"Liar." Mistislaus snorted. "What's your part in this scheme, Kraftugur? I know you've been cozy with the Krypplingur a long time, and I've heard you're pretty tight-knit with Thordis of the Viturkonur, too. Was it just a coincidence you happened to volunteer to arbitrate the new treaty between Kryppling and Skylding? I think not. I think you're being paid by one of them."

"Jealous, aren't you?" Kraftugur returned. "A pity no one any longer considers your services worth paying for. You used to amount to something, however, I'll give you that much. It could have been you as easily as I standing in this position."

"What, the traitor's position?" Mistislaus demanded. "The goat who leads the sheep to slaughter? I think not!"

"Silence!" Hoggvinn roared. "There she comes! Show my daughter due respect or I'll hang the two of you!"

Skyla trembled as she was ushered into the great hall, a vast echoing place with a huge hearth at either end and rows of weapons and shields and banners hung on the walls. Near the center stood the dais and the chieftain's high seat, overlooking the rows of tables and benches where visitors were fed and bedded. Hoggvinn sat gazing at her sternly, an impressive figure of a man long seasoned by life yet unbowed by infirmity. His white hair and beard were neatly groomed, parted and braided, and he wore a gown and cloak of sumptuous blue material trimmed with gold thread. Gold ornaments hung upon his chest, denoting honorable events in his past.

Alvara made a slight bow to Hoggvinn and turned to exchange a nod with Kraftugur. He returned her faint acknowledgment with the barest hint of a smile.

"Come forward, child; don't dawdle," Hoggvinn said when Skyla hung back, taking refuge behind Alvara's black cloak.

"Don't be frightened, my dear. He wouldn't harm a hair of your head." Mistislaus took a step forward, but Alvara's grip tightened warningly upon Skyla's arm.

"Don't allow yourself to be swayed by mere sentiment," she whispered. "Your destiny is no longer with Mistislaus. This is the moment we have awaited for a great many years."

Skyla looked at Mistislaus coldly, having realized that he was the one responsible for keeping her from her clan and heritage all her life.

Logregla advanced ahead of them, her eyes sweeping over Kraftugur and Mistislaus with contempt to fasten upon her husband.

"Hoggvinn, what's this nonsense?" she demanded. "You have nothing to do with my sister kin and their business. No woman should concern you except me." Imperiously she pointed to a chair, and Jafnar scuttled to fetch it for her to sit down upon.

"Yes, you concern me greatly at a constant rate," Hoggvinn returned on a note of exasperation. "This is some old, old trouble just come to light, my dear, and you needn't worry about it in the least."

"I've grown extremely fond of Alvara and Skyla," Logregla said. "I don't intend for you to do anything that will cause them distress. It's my right to choose my own servants, as I have always done in the past."

Hoggvinn's eyes darted from Logregla to Skyla. "My excellent wife, if you could just listen a moment—"

"I'll listen when I'm ready to, but first you listen to me," Logregla said. "I've tolerated a lot of nonsense from you in my lifetime. My patience with your foolishness is very fragile. I don't want my maids troubled with your interference."

"This maid, as you persist in calling her," Hoggvinn interrupted, pointing to Skyla, "is my daughter."

"Daughter?" Logregla gasped, her features turning a pasty gray color. "Skyla your daughter? What nonsense!"

"It is true," Hoggvinn said, trying to restrain his glee at the maddened expression contorting her features. "She is my only surviving child."

Logregla's eyes darted as she thought. "From that wretched Viturkona witch that seduced you? I thought she was dead. You promised me that the child was dead! What's she doing alive, you fool? Didn't I tell you—and you!" She turned suddenly upon Alvara, blazing with wrath. "I've nourished a viper in my bosom all this time! You must have known! That story about finding her wandering in the market seemed a little too convenient at the time!"

"What's to be done about it now, my lady?" Alvara replied with perfect aplomb. "All this was fated to happen."

"Come here, my child," Hoggvinn said, beckoning to Skyla. "You've nothing to fear from me now. I'm getting to be no more dangerous than a toothless old dog. I wish to make up for the past. I was foolish and frightened then, but now I realized what a precious gift a child is. I am getting old and weary of all this trouble and toil. All I have is yours, my dear. You need only stand by my side and see me to the end of my days. Can you forget the past and what a coward I was then?"

Skyla advanced toward Hoggvinn, ignoring Logregla, who turned away with a strangled, wrathful snarling sound. She stopped at arm's length and gazed at him with her clear-eyed, considering gaze.

"I forgive you," she said. "I shall be your daughter. It was a lucky day that Alvara found me and told me of my duty. At last I know who I am." She darted Mistislaus a reproving look that struck him like a lash.

"I sent that wretched Illmuri to protect her," Mistislaus said. "He was attacked by Krypplingur, and Skyla was snatched away by this Alvara woman. Who is, I might add, living here under false pretenses. If I had been approached reasonably—"

"You wouldn't recognize reason if you saw it," Kraftugur said, "having lost your reason many years ago. It's a good thing the girl was rescued when she was."

"But not for such a purpose as this," Mistislaus retorted.

"Silence, or I'll have you all tossed out!" Hoggvinn roared. "Now, then, I wish to speak to my daughter. Come closer, child. I won't harm you."

Alvara stepped forward. "As her dead mother's sister, I will speak for her. She is, after all, a Viturkona first and your daughter second."

"Viturkonur!" Logregla spit, but she subsided into civility when Alvara turned her gaze upon her. "It's an old feud and best forgotten," she hastened to add, but the smoldering sparks in her eyes belied her insincere smile.

"She's as much Skylding as she is Viturkona," Hoggvinn said. "And she is my only surviving child. All the others perished as infants and children."

"Was that my fault?" Logregla demanded, her eyes suddenly swimming with tears. "I employed the best physicians to keep them alive, the poor sickly little things. They kept them full of all sorts of medicine and elixirs and potions and emetics, but they still sickened and died. I often thought it must be a curse put upon us." She leveled a brief but deadly glower at Alvara. "The Viturkonur were furious because I refused to allow them to sell birthrights to the Skyldings, and we all know how they dote upon revenge."

"It's a hard thing to be judged inferior," Alvara said with a thin smile. "But all that is past now and easily forgiven. We have a common bond now, don't we?"

Logregla looked at Alvara warily an instant, then she smiled brightly. "Of course we do. You mean Skyla. Why, this practically makes us kinfolk, doesn't it?"

"We are truly sisters in many ways," Alvara said. "What matters now is Skyla's happiness in her new life. It must be a dreadful strain to go from a humble wizard's girl to the daughter of a powerful chieftain."

"If you women wish to continue your chatter," Hoggvinn said, "you can go outside in the courtyard. Either be still or depart. I wish to speak to my daughter and get acquainted."

He held out his hand, and Skyla put hers into it.

"What luck that I have two such friends as Skjoldur and

Mistislaus to guard me from my foolish impulses," he continued gruffly, a trickle of moisture slipping from his eye. "I shall be proud to call you daughter. I only hope you will be as proud to call me your father."

"Yes, of course I will."

Skyla sat down beside him on the seat where Logregla sat during occasions of importance. Her back stiff, her head high, she surveyed the others with a queenly smile. Her gaze lingered a moment on Mistislaus, whose eyes were watering with emotion.

"I guess she'll be better off here than with me," he said with a crusty shrug. "Now you'll discover what an everlasting nuisance a female child is. Skyla, I bid you farewell from my care and house, and I wish you well in your new endeavors. I hope you realize someday that I did what I did for your own good and not because I wished to deprive you of your parentage. It's not as if we'll never see each other. I shall always come to Rangfara in the spring—as long as there is a Rangfara to come to." Catching Jafnar's eye, he added, "I think it's best I go now. We'll meet again before I leave, I think. Your father is going to hold some fabulous feast in your honor. I'm still in disgrace, so I'm not invited, but I'm going to come anyway."

"I'll have you hanged if you do," Hoggvinn retorted. "I don't know if I've forgiven you yet for keeping my daughter away from me so long." He gazed at her fondly, still holding her hand protectively in his own. "What a joy, what a radiance she is in this gloomy old hall."

"You said that about me, once," Logregla said.

"And it was true, for a while," Hoggvinn said. "Now all of you go away so I can talk to my daughter. Leave Alvara here. My dear wife, you don't mind giving up Alvara as your dressing maid, do you? Now that we know she is my daughter's kin, she'll be requiring a maid of her own. She is now our esteemed guest, and I shall do everything to make her as comfortable as possible in the women's hall."

"Do you think I know nothing of the laws of hospitality?" Logregla said. "I thought of all that already. I'm just going now to see to everything."

Logregla departed with a glare at Hoggvinn that would have withered solid rock, but the glance she threw back at Alvara did not appear so much angry as fearful.

"We'll have a grand feast," Hoggvinn said gleefully. "Three days of eating, drinking, dancing, music, horse fighting, games, and whatever else we can think of. Skjoldur, my oldest and best of friends, I'm putting you in charge of it. I want everyone I know invited and all those scurvy half brothers of mine who used to think they had a chance for this seat. Now we'll show them. The line of Hoggvinn Shield-breaker will continue forever. Start spreading the word. I can't wait for all of Rangfara to know I have a daughter."

Outside in the courtyard, Jafnar seized Mistislaus' sleeve before he could escape, drawing him away from Illmuri, who stopped and looked back at them curiously.

"Mistislaus!" he hissed. "You must protect Hoggvinn! He's alone in there with his worst enemy! I saw murder in Alvara's eyes, not reconciliation!"

Mistislaus shook off his grip with a preoccupied scowl. "I raised Skyla as my own child, and he takes her away with not so much as a thank you. Poor Skyla—how did such a wretched mess happen? How could I have brought her into such a den of snakes? And now I've lost her completely. If Hoggvinn's put himself in danger, that's his lookout, but Skyla is only a child in many ways, so trusting, so unworldly. So like her to have blindly followed this Alvara woman who claims to be her mother's sister. She's in terrible danger."

"Nonsense," Jafnar said gloomily. "Hoggvinn will guard her like an eagle with a single chick."

"If you want to see murder in someone's eyes," Mistislaus continued, "look at Logregla. Deposed and despised."

"We'll get Skyla back, Mistislaus," Jafnar said. "The sworn duty of the orphan Skyldings is to protect Skyla."

"No, you won't," Mistislaus said sharply. "She is his daughter. He is entitled to her, and she is where she belongs."

"No! Skyla doesn't belong with all those Drottningur. All they think about is clothing and gossip and causing trouble! She isn't like that!"

"Come along," Skjoldur called impatiently, overtaking them at the gateway, bustling importantly with a preoccupied gleam in his eye. "Don't dawdle about. We've got a thousand things to do for Hoggvinn's grand feast."

"I'll have nothing to do with this travesty," Mistislaus flared, rapping his staff on the ground with a puff of smoke.

"Then you'll be leaving," Skjoldur said. "Good. I'm sick of having you cluttering up my house, and you'll be nothing but a drag on the festivities."

"Leaving? Me? Don't get your hopes up," Mistislaus

snapped. "If you had any idea of the trouble that's coming, you'd be glad to have me around, you bag of self-conceited offal."

Skjoldur drew himself up, his features mottling with rage. Then he turned his back on Mistislaus and addressed Jafnar. "As long as you insist upon harboring this reprobate and his unspeakable assistant under my roof, I shall take myself elsewhere. I wash my hands of the lot of you as long as you have anything to do with Mistislaus. That includes supplying you and your brothers' insatiable appetites. You'll not get so much as a crumb or a particle from me until he is gone!"

Skjoldur's indignation was scant impediment, however. Einka merely told the merchants and cooks that Skjoldur would pay if they sent a lad around to find him.

Skyla was settled in the most comfortable quarters the women's hall had to offer, which was Logregla's own tower room overlooking the yard and grounds below. Logregla was moved out without ceremony and with very little complaint. Stoically she settled herself in a smaller room off the main hall with a wall bed and its own little hearth.

"I'm afraid this isn't very fair to you," Alvara said while Logregla sat at the window of her new quarters, alternately sighing and dabbing at her eyes with a handkerchief.

"I don't mind," Logregla said a trifle sulkily. "I've gotten used to abuse since I married Hoggvinn. If my brothers knew about this outrage, they'd make Hoggvinn suffer for it. But I'm hardly one to go crying to my brothers to avenge every insult. I'm far too noble and decent for that. I'll just hold my head up and smile bravely while my husband elevates a total stranger to his inheritance. If all my babies hadn't died, this never would have happened. The poor little darlings. I guess I just didn't try hard enough to save them." She wiped her eyes and looked at Alvara with barely concealed malevolence. "I always wondered if it mightn't have been a Viturkonur curse."

"Yes, my dear, it was," Alvara said, smiling slightly at Logregla's startled gasp and frightened stare. "You see, it upset us when you interfered in the sale of our birthrights to the Skyldings. At first our tjaldi women thought it was enough to steal a birthright from Hoggvinn and punish you with the loss of your children. Then Hoggvinn caused the death of Reykja and tried to murder her child. So the Viturkonur decided upon revenge. You know how the Viturkonur dote upon revenge."

"Yes, of course," Logregla said faintly, clasping her delicate hands to conceal their trembling. "But when will you be done with your revenge? Skyla has her rightful position now."

"Yes, that is true. I hope you don't take this all too personally. I really do hold you in the highest esteem. But as long as Hoggvinn and the Skyldings live, the vengeance will continue until not one Skylding is left and the treasure is in our hands."

"And the Drottningur are sworn to help you," Logregla said. "I was wondering, my dear, if your sudden change in station is going to affect our new pastime."

"Is that what you wish?" Alvara asked.

"No, no, I merely meant it could be risky for you now that you're a person of considerable importance around here. It wouldn't do for you to be caught out at night under questionable circumstances. Herrad has lost six Krypplingur so far, and he's beginning to be annoyed about it."

"Dear me. Are we afraid of Herrad?"

"Certainly not. We need fear nothing. We are death itself, and nothing is more fearsome than that."

"Good. For a moment I was afraid you wanted out of our little agreement."

"Oh, of course not. I merely feared we were losing our leader."

"The clan of the lynx will keep increasing. With every gifting scroll, I wish to see an initiate into the sisterhood, particularly if the bridegroom's clan is Skylding."

"Won't that mean the death of many Skyldings? If the bride is a lynx and the groom a Skylding—"

"And I was told you were not clever, Logregla."

"Ah, yes. I have many detractors." She heaved a sigh, turning her petulant scowl out the window, where news of Hoggvinn's daughter was still filling the courtyard and the streets beyond with an excited bustle and buzzing. "I shan't miss them when they're gone. I yearn to sink my teeth into Skylding flesh and tear them all from limb to limb."

"Good. You shall have your chance. Poor Logregla, I expect you'll be very much cast aside now that Hoggvinn has got his heir."

Logregla would have gnashed her teeth if it weren't so ill bred, so she merely smiled as prettily as she could, her heart seething in a fiery broth of hatred, fear, grief, and overwhelming rage.

CHAPTER TWELVE

THE DAY OF the feast arrived, and everyone who knew or remotely feared Hoggvinn of the Skyldings had tented a booth on the green surrounding Rangfara. Flags, banners, and ribbons flew from the tent poles, denoting the clan of the owners thereof, and scores of shaggy ponies and horses were picketed on the lush grazing surrounding the walls.

At a reserved distance from all the others stood the smoke-blackened tent of the Viturkonur. The only evidence of festivity was a red banner emblazoned with a black lynx that hung from a pole over the doorway. Daily the Viturkonur made a solemn procession to the Hall of Stars, or Hoggvinn and Skyla were escorted to the black tent by a contingent of his retainers dressed in their finest garb flanked by an honor guard of Krypplingur. No one else was allowed to attend those meetings. Jafnar shadowed them jealously, hoping for some scrap of information, but his curiosity was only piqued further by the absolute silence the participants maintained and by their vigor in guarding their secrecy.

Jafnar and his brothers took turns attending Hoggvinn's public courts at the Hall of Stars to defend Skyla every moment she was publicly displayed, like a bone dangling just out of the reach of the leaping, caracoling suitors. It was a welcome diversion from their lessons and instructions. Distractions were legion. Throngs of acquaintances crowded into the Hall of Stars to curry all the favor they possibly could, relatives of the most distant variety made themselves at home, and hordes of hopeful suitors amassed themselves in the hall, ridiculously dressed and boasting inordinately about their wealth and accomplishments. The birthright to the future chieftancy of the Skyldings suddenly became a topic of lively speculation, until incredible amounts of gold, horses, weapons, and cloth were being bandied about the Hall of Stars. Rumors flew thick and strong that a gifting announcement was in the offing, a rumor that filled Jafnar with gloom and despair. The gaming booths offered odds on the favorites, as if it were a horse race.

Jafnar lay in wait for Skjoldur in the Hall of Stars, knowing his father was bound to appear each day to sit beside Hoggvinn to interview new suitors, welcome old friends, settle disputes, and greet distant acquaintances, impoverished relatives, and rivals with as much diplomacy as possible.

"I should think, as Hoggvinn's chief retainer," Jafnar suggested, trying to squelch some of his jealousy, "that you should at least make an offer for the birthright. It is expected of you, you know."

Skjoldur waved one hand, indicating the crowded hall. "Look at them. I can't offer half of what the least of them will make as a preliminary offer for Skyla's birthright. If I didn't have so many voracious sons to feed, I would be a far wealthier man. I'm sorry," he added, "it's just that she's suddenly gone a lot higher than we can climb. I'm only a chief retainer, not a chieftain. I have Athugashol and a parcel of land with five tenant farmers, and my fealty is sworn to Hoggvinn. I'm little better than a high-class thrall myself. These are all chieftains' eldest sons, the pick of the litter, or chieftains themselves with bags of gold and herds of horses. I wish there was something I could do for you, Jafnar, but this is a high-stakes game. You're better off not to even play. The Viturkonur have their say in the matter, too, which must be considered."

"I'd love to know what is said in those meetings with Hoggvinn and Thordis," Jafnar growled bitterly. "I'll warrant the Krypplingur know more about it than I do."

"Well," Skjoldur said, glancing about in the guilty anticipatory manner of all gossips. "I can tell you what I know. The Viturkonur have a husband all picked for Skyla, but Hoggvinn is having nothing of it. They've settled on Kraftugur for past services rendered."

"What! That horrid old stick?" Jafnar exploded, leaping up and whirling around as if someone were menacing him with a sword. "I'll slit his weazand first! I'll crush his wretched little skull beneath my boots! Those old hags! What are they thinking of?"

"Don't torment yourself. Kraftugur has been voted down, and there's someone else you won't like."

"Who? Tell me!"

"Ofarir of the Krypplingur."

Jafnar's steam and fury deserted him as if he had been punctured. His shoulders sagged, and he stared unseeingly at the busy scene around him. Horses, carts, people, all merged into one indistinguishable blur of misery. He felt as if a horse had kicked him.

"Ofarir!" he repeated woodenly.

As if the speaking of his name had summoned him, Ofarir and a swaggering entourage of Krypplingur warlords came strutting into the courtyard. Ofarir was a mean, narrow, dark creature, sparely built for a Krypplingur. His hair hung long and lank, and he had a habit of grinning unexpectedly, showing a set of long yellow teeth, like a weasel.

Jafnar stood his ground as the Krypplingur approached, refusing to budge an inch until Skjoldur dragged him out of the way. Ofarir grinned and halted, making a halfhearted salute with one hand, which ended in a suitable location for picking at his nose.

"Thank you for standing aside," he said. "One of the Skjoldurssons, aren't you? I've seen you around the Hall of Stars quite a lot lately. One of the suitors for Hoggvinn's new daughter, I presume."

"Jafnar is my name. You've heard of me, I'm sure."

"Ah, yes, the prophet who hates Krypplingur." He and his cohorts chuckled and snorted with the disdainful confidence of men securely armed and armored.

Jafnar eyed the Krypplingur with such loathing that his limbs almost trembled with the force of it. "You would be wise to leave Rangfara, but being Krypplingur, you won't, I don't suppose."

"No, indeed," Ofarir said. "There are rumors of great things to come. I can't tell you any of it, of course. A pity your powers of prophecy don't reveal it to you. I suppose all prophets have their limits, however."

"Yes, I have my limitations," Jafnar said. "I miss things like births and giftings and other happy events. All I seem to be able to see is the way people die."

"Indeed," Ofarir said, squinting and losing his wolfish grin. "Tell me, have you seen how and when I will die?"

"Yes, but I won't tell you," Jafnar replied.

"Come now, let's share a friendly drink," Ofarir said, taking hold of Jafnar's arm and propelling him invitingly along in his iron grip toward the nearest ale booth. They left the Hall of Stars behind and descended into the Skurdur, jostling everyone off the path as they went. At the booth, most of the other customers eased themselves out of the tent, making room for the Krypplingur and their armor and weapons.

"Now, then, drink up," Ofarir commanded when horns of ale had been handed around. The ale went down six hairy Kryppling throats as if it were no more than water. Ofarir wiped his mouth without so much as blinking an eye and swiftly downed another horn. "What we need is some Dokkalfar ale," he said. "It takes a barrel of this watery stuff to slake a man's thirst."

Jafnar thought it was potent enough as he sipped at his rather nervously, wondering how he was going to extricate himself from Ofarir's clutches.

"How is it you're able to tolerate the sun when you're of Dokkalfar heritage?" he asked by way of diversion to steady his nerves.

The Krypplingur glowered at him threateningly from under their jutting brows, as if he had asked a very personal question.

"Dokkalfar heritage, yes," Ofarir said. "But the stock has been improved upon by carefully chosen giftings until we have the advantages of both Ljosalfar and Dokkalfar."

Jafnar looked at their countenances, which resembled leather baked in the sun, almost as tough as the leather armor they always wore. Their faces were more like masks, frozen into perpetual expressions of suspicion and downright ugly meanness.

"Enough chat," Ofarir said. "Tell me how I will die."

Jafnar downed the horn of ale in a few inspired gulps and suddenly felt courageous. He raised one hand significantly and brought it to bear, pointing at Ofarir. "Are you certain you're strong enough to know the future?" he demanded in a low and menacing tone that further piqued the interest of the Krypplingur. The others put down their drinking horns and stared at him in anticipation.

"Of course I am," Ofarir said. "Now tell me."

"You are going to die at the hands of your own wife," Jafnar said, leaning forward to hiss the words into Ofarir's face. "With your throat ripped out as if by teeth and claws. It won't be a pretty death; you'll struggle and foam and flounder for a long while, while she dabbles her fingers in your blood, singing to herself. And then your spirit will be wrenched away by force and an evil entity will inhabit your body, tormenting you and goading you like a vicious rider on an unwilling horse. The evil you do then will make your present life look like child's play."

Ofarir reared back, his eyes round and startled and the leathery color of his face blanching almost gray.

"As to the when," Jafnar continued, "it shall be when Kanina the Rabbit and Fantur the Rogue are married in the sky. When the stars conjoin, you will die."

"What rot," Ofarir said after too long an interval, and reached for his horn, but his hand betrayed a slight tremble.

Jafnar stifled an elated grin, knowing he had struck the buried vein of truth that ran deep in all mortal mankind, hidden but undeniable when brought to the light.

"I don't even have a gifting scroll, let alone a wife," Ofarir snarled, his rage beginning to simmer. There was nothing like a fright to make a Kryppling angry.

"You will have one very soon," Jafnar said, rising to his feet. "Thank you for the drink; it was ample payment for my gift to you. And by the way, I have a warning for the rest of you Krypplingur. Beware the lynx; she's not done feasting yet."

Jafnar scampered out of the ale tent while Ofarir was still trying to sort out his experience. Swiftly he lost himself in the maze of carts and booths that crowded the Skurdur. Glancing back, he saw the Krypplingur lurching out of the ale booth, glaring up and down as if they were looking for him.

In the following days, whenever Jafnar glimpsed Ofarir—taking care to keep himself well out of sight—he observed the Kryppling wearing a worried scowl, like a doomed man who knew his hanging was nigh.

The time came to announce the gifting on the third day of the feast, at noonday. Hoggvinn made his short announcement to his crowded hall of friends, relatives, and enemies before the meal was brought in. Skyla sat beside him, looking pale and impassive in her black Viturkonur garb, as if it were someone else's gifting being chosen and declared.

"We have settled upon Ofarir," Hoggvinn announced tersely, "son of Herrad, chieftain of clan Kryppling. One year from today the gifting will take place in Rangfara."

Waves of shock and disapproval roared around the Hall of Stars, while the Krypplingur sat in the middle of it like immobile rocks. Also impassive were the Viturkonur, seated on

Hoggvinn's left on the dais of honor. Somehow, in the crowded, noisy hall, Jafnar felt that Skyla's eyes were fixed upon him in mute appeal. He leapt up from his place at the table, resolved upon action of some indefinite sort to help her escape from the web in which she was becoming more securely entangled. The stuffy atmosphere of unwashed guests, food, and spilled drink was suddenly too much to tolerate. Unnoticed in the uproar, he shoved his way outside to breathe fresh air in great, choking gulps. A boisterous crowd chivied around the doorway, striving to catch rumors of what was said, passing on their own versions to those behind. He pushed through the crowd and found a quiet dark spot around the corner.

In a moment someone else came out of the hall and around to the side where Jafnar was lurking, not noticing him leaning in the shadows of a pillar. In the silvery light of the pale night sky Jafnar recognized Kraftugur and automatically crouched a little farther into his shadow instead of strolling casually away. The wizard stood still, looking back as if expecting someone to follow.

Very shortly another figure joined Kraftugur.

"Well, I suppose you're going to take this badly," the voice of Alvara said.

"Why should I not? I was promised the chieftain's seat by none other than Thordis. She has gone back on her word."

"She is a Viturkona. She did not give you her word, because a Viturkona has no word to give. She merely used you, and you did a good job of bringing the Skyldings and Krypplingur together so well. But we decided it would be a more advantageous match if we took the Kryppling alliance rather than an obscure wizard of a small clan. We are prepared to make you a suitable recompense."

"You want to pay me off, in other words."

"Most certainly. We prefer not to kill you to get you out of the way, but it can be arranged if you don't take what we offer. We bear you no malice, you understand. Viturkonur are not maliciously inclined. It's just that we have found a better way to get what we want."

"And I was not helping you to get what it was you wanted?"

"Yes, but the Krypplingur will be so much better to marry into. I do hope you're not going to be difficult."

"Difficult? Now that you seem to be riding high on the wheel, the rest of us are nothing but difficulties to you. Well, we shall see how long you're flying high. Nature has a way of creating equality sooner or later. Just remember that one day you may be back down here with the rest of us in the pit, so be careful who you step upon climbing out. That young girl of yours is a very slender stalk for the weight of the scheme you're putting upon her. Without her you have no chance. I would hate to see something happen to bring all of you crashing down."

"Don't be angry, you fool. We haven't cast you aside. There is a great deal for you to do. The treaty with the Skyldings is not complete. We need your help in making it as favorable as possible for the Viturkonur."

"Then you can do it without me," Kraftugur snarled. "I advise you to be on your lookout for all your lovely plans. Things are apt to go drastically wrong."

With that, Kraftugur strode away, smiting the ground with each step as he walked. Alvara shrugged her shoulders, glancing around at the dozen or so curious eavesdroppers, who suddenly commenced looking as if they had business elsewhere.

"Well, then," a new voice said from the shadows, and Illmuri stepped into Alvara's path. "Again we meet. Thanks to you, I lost my job walking Skyla to and from the market. You must have known early on that she is Hoggvinn's daughter. Just watching for your chance, were you?"

"Yes. Luckily there are buffoons like you around to make life easier for the rest of us," Alvara replied. "I can't think of anything you and I need to talk about."

"You've had quite an elevation in station, it's true. But it's only due to Skyla being Hoggvinn's daughter. Nothing else has changed. The Viturkonur have not forgotten their vow of vengeance for Reykja."

Alvara moved to detour around him and caught sight of Jafnar's face in the shadows.

"Who's that?" she demanded. "Is this some murderous plot between you?"

"Hardly," Jafnar said, stepping forward a little sheepishly. "I was just standing there in the shadows for a little privacy, when I saw this fellow accost you and try to start up a conversation. I have no great respect for him, besides having several grievous causes for dispute. If you wish, I'll send him on his way and escort you back to the hall." He put his hand upon his sword hilt, and he and Illmuri exchanged a threatening scowl.

"Fool," Illmuri said quietly. "You don't know what game you're playing at." Then he was gone.

"Thank you. I accept your offer," Alvara said. "You're Skjoldur's eldest son, are you not?"

"Yes. We've met before. I would like to beg a boon of you," Jafnar said in a low voice.

"What is it?"

"I want to talk to Skyla. You can get me in to see her. Alone, I can't get anywhere near her."

"No, you cannot. Even I have limited influence."

"More than most. It was the night of the first full moon when we met, wasn't it? Just over there in the clearing behind the Hall of Stars. I believe you and the Drottningur were having a little late-night cookout."

"I couldn't say, really, except that from what I hear, you're regarded in Rangfara as more than a little addled."

"Addled talk is still talk, and I don't think anyone can afford to be suspected of being a lynx."

"Perhaps we met and perhaps we didn't. You're an old friend of Skyla's, this much I know, so maybe I should have a little compassion for you. It might cheer her up to see a familiar face for a while. Come to the tjaldi tomorrow and I'll let you see her."

"No, not there. Here, in the Hall of Stars, with no Viturkonur around."

"Distrustful? That's a good sign. Very well, tomorrow, then. It makes no difference, you know. It is all settled, and there is nothing that you can do about it. About anything, for that matter. You say you are a prophet?"

"Yes, I am."

"Then why haven't you realized that the doom you see is your own?" With that she was gone, vanished into the crowd waiting to shove into the Hall of Stars the moment there was space at the table. Jafnar plowed into the throng, determined to get back within eyesight of Skyla.

"Stupid ass, I ought to cut your ear off!" a voice said at his elbow as he trod heavily on someone's foot.

"Modga, halloa," Jafnar said without a trace of regret or apology. "Where are the others?"

"I don't know. Here somewhere. I suppose you've been in and eaten already, as the exalted eldest son."

"Watch things carefully tonight, Modga. I don't think this is a very healthy climate for Skyla. There are people here who wish her harm."

"Is this another prophecy?"

"Not one that comes true, I hope. I intend to see to it that it doesn't. Come on; let's go find our brothers."

"I was hoping for some food," Modga said.

"You can eat later."

"Are we going to eat?"

"We're going to protect Skyla."

"With all those Kryplingur around her? What does she need us for?"

"We're her own kin and clan."

"Not if she's a Viturkona, we're not."

"But she's half-Skylding. I just heard Kraftugur threatening her. The Viturkonur had promised her to him if he would help them get into Rangfara for their revenge."

"Kraftugur? That old scarecrow?" Modga snorted.

"The Viturkonur are going to start the Skyldings and Krypplingur fighting when they kill Ofarir."

"Kill Ofarir? Did you get another knock on the head? They just got Skyla and Ofarir promised to be married, and they're going to murder him? I don't think that's very likely. I think you'd better go and lie down and rest. Maybe your brain fever is coming back."

"Ordvar!" Jafnar dragged him away from the table, protesting. Einka also was forcibly separated from his dinner.

"It's such fun having an insane brother," Modga said bitterly. "At least Thogn was kept locked up."

"Look at them, look at them all, come to do her honor," Logregla said, clenching her fists under her shawl. She sat behind Skyla on the dais, half-hidden and very much ignored by all except her littlest tiring maid, who always stood solemnly beside her chair in case she wanted to stand up. Then she held Logregla's raiment so it wouldn't drag on the ground or get stepped on or caught on something. When Logregla sat down again, she arranged the cloak and gown and skirts in an orderly fashion around her mistress' feet. It was also her job to listen earnestly to the rantings and ravings of her mistress, nodding and clucking in sympathy.

"And those hideous women," Logregla continued, turning her eyes upon Alvara and Thordis and the clan genealogist and matchmaker seated behind Skyla. "To think they have the

nerve to show their brazen faces in Rangfara again, after I sent
them packing once before. To think they would return and my
own husband would shame me by inviting them to tent their
booth in the gifting fair. Oh, but they will regret it one day. I
was the one who told Skjoldur he must kill that child or destruction would break over his head one day. Mark my words,
havoc and destruction will claim him for their own. And that
little slinking cat who wormed her way in like a harmless
stray. Skyla, the one who stole my place. Her neck I'd like to
wring like a chicken's. Pick up my dress, girl; I'm going to my
room. Not that anyone would notice or care," she added bitterly.

The little maid clucked sympathetically. "I'm sure, my lady,
that your husband will miss you."

"Husband! I want him dead!" Logregla said venomously. "I
hate him for what he's done to me! Every instant that creature
lives beside him is a century of shame for me! I want him
dead, dead, dead!"

The next morning, early, Jafnar presented himself at the gate
of the Hall of Stars, doubting if Alvara would keep her word
to let him in to see Skyla. But to his gratification, the guards
let him pass without question. He went around to the bathhouse, where Skyla would be sharing breakfast with Hoggvinn.
After a short wait he saw two dark forms coming from the hall
to the bathhouse.

"I kept my word," Alvara said. "Here she is. You may talk
to her, but only on one condition. From now on you'll abandon
this ridiculous scheme of yours to snatch her back from us.
She is a Viturkona, and Hoggvinnsdottir, and she is where she
belongs."

"Alright, I'll cease to make a nuisance of myself," Jafnar
said. "Now go away so we can talk."

"I don't know why you're doing this," Skyla said when
Alvara had retreated. "You're a stranger to me."

"Skyla, am I truly a stranger? You have no recollection of
me, of other times? Jafnar, the wild boy? Remember when
Rangfara was nothing but ruins and we eight were the only
Skylding survivors? Remember the lynx and the creatures from
the Kjallari stalking the streets at night?"

"I remember many things," Skyla said with a shiver.

"Then you must know that we can stop it this time," Jafnar
whispered urgently. "This gifting cannot happen. The

Krypplingur only want to destroy us and take the gold. Alvara is not your friend. You are nothing but a tool of destruction in her hands."

Skyla drew back. "She is my mother's kin, my own family. I cannot hear you speak that way."

"Be warned, Skyla. I'm speaking the truth."

"Jafnar, you're not a prophet! You're nothing but a wild boy, a scavenger, and a thief!"

"You see, you know me."

She stared at him a moment. "Perhaps I do—or did. I have searched all my life—or lives—for my name and my family, and now I know who I am. I won't give that up, not for all the dire prophetic visions in the Prophets' Guild, of which I'm sure you're not a member. I have found the place where I belong, and I shall stay here. It will be different this time."

"I can't believe you relish the idea of marrying a Kryppling," Jafnar said.

"If it brings peace to Rangfara, then it must be," she replied. "Go away now, Jafnar. My mind is made up. It's good to see you again, but don't trouble me further with your face from the past. Now is the time we have to worry about."

"You're going through with this?"

"I am a Skylding, am I not? It's my duty to protect Rangfara, is it not? Then I shall do whatever I can as Hoggvinnsdottir to defend my home and my kin. Good-bye, Jafnar. Don't trouble me again with your old memories."

"Skyla! We want to help. We need your help."

"It is better to tame the Krypplingur than to try to fight them," Skyla said. "We know what happens if a battle breaks out. This time there will be no battle, Jafnar."

"Only a great many lynx killings," Jafnar said. "Skyla, it's the Skyldings the lynxes will be killing. Every Drottning gifting will be a curse of death. Alvara has turned them into lynxes just for that purpose."

"I don't believe my kinswoman would do such a thing. She was right when she said you would talk nonsense."

"Skyla, I think she wants to kill Hoggvinn."

"And I think you're insane."

Skyla turned away and stalked toward the bathhouse, with Alvara promptly shadowing her heels. The door opened, emitting a slice of yellow light and the welcoming rumble of Hoggvinn's voice. Then the door closed and the light vanished, taking most of Jafnar's hopes with it.

CHAPTER
THIRTEEN

"WELL, BRODIR, YOU'VE certainly set the world on its ear this time." Red-haired and glowering, Vigulf bleakly contemplated the throng of celebrants disporting themselves riotously at his brother's cost. A vain lot of greedy parasites—if it had been his hall, he wouldn't have allowed half of them to set foot over his threshold. But Hoggvinn was trusting; he was generous; he was well liked. Vigulf was none of those, he was proud to say. He eased himself into Skjoldur's vacant seat beside Hoggvinn, casting a long look at Skyla seated on the dais behind them, drooping like a pale flower in the smoke and heat and noise of the crowded hall. "What a charming creature your daughter is. A pity we didn't have the pleasure of watching her growing up in our midst." He ground his teeth a little, involuntarily, and reached for his ale horn.

"Yes, she's so lovely. I can scarcely believe an old rogue like Mistislaus could raise such a fine child. Just look at her—you can tell she's a Skylding."

"There is a birth scroll hidden away somewhere, I suppose. You'll be called upon to prove her claim beyond a shadow of a doubt when the chieftancy of the clan Skylding is at stake."

"There is," Hoggvinn said. "In my scroll box in the archives."

"And how do we know that the infant Skjoldur stole and gave to the scraelings was the same one the scraelings gave back to Mistislaus?" Vigulf pursued. "I would hate to think of a lowborn scraeling ascending to the chieftain's seat of Rangfara."

"Just look at her, you oaf," Hoggvinn said. "Did you ever see a scraeling with such a face? Such grace?"

"No, she looks very like the Viturkonur, though—like a

hunted fox with those great eyes and pointed chin. She doesn't look at all like you, or I expect she'd be rather fat and red in the face. Certainly she is well favored, but the fact of the matter is it all boils down to absolute proof when you're talking about five hundred marks in gold for a birthright. It will be expected, Hoggi."

Hoggvinn waved his hand impatiently. "It's there, I tell you, in my scroll box in the Kjallari. I saved it along with the birth scrolls of the other infants who died. It wasn't something I wanted to look at ever again, so I buried them all in the catacombs. Now, will you quit trying to worry me about inconsequential things at a time like this? All Rangfara is celebrating with us, and you're niggling about a birth scroll."

"Someone's got to worry about the details around here," Vigulf retorted. "That's what you keep the rest of us younger brothers around for, isn't it? We're not worth anything else except to kick around like dogsbodies, are we?"

"I know what you're getting at," Hoggvinn growled, his eye lighting up with wrath. "Your treasured dreams of putting yourself and your sniveling son on this seat are now all completely dead and without hope, aren't they? For years you've been hoping I'd die childless so your fame and fortune would be made. Well, my dear brodir, now you know what disappointment tastes like. This is what I've been tasting all these years, but now I've got a child of my own. A pity I have to disappoint you and your brood, but somehow I can't feel much sorrow for you. Not with Skyla sitting there before my eyes."

"And a Kryppling for a son-in-law," Vigulf added. "That's what I can't forgive. Are you really that frightened of them? Was it your idea, or was it that little scab of a woman Thordis?"

"It wasn't my idea," Hoggvinn said, "but it's a good one. We'll put an end to the Krypplingur threat and the Viturkona feud, all at one stroke."

"You're giving Rangfara away to our worst enemies," Vigulf hissed. "It would be better to keep a Skylding on the chieftain's seat and to fight them rather than to give it up this way. I think you're losing your courage, Brodir. Our enemies are snapping at our throats, and you're falling down like a stag too old and tired for the chase. What kind of a leader succumbs to the enemy without a single drop of blood shed? There are others who are talking, too."

"Faugh! And you're the one that started it. All your life

you've been just yearning for a chance to plant yourself on this seat. It won't happen, you fool. There's still enough fight left in me to dispose of the likes of you! Now take yourself away and don't trouble me any more about this! It's no concern of yours!"

"Very well," Vigulf said in a reasonable tone, and he took himself away to a table where his younger brother Mord Fidla sat, supposedly drinking himself insensible in honor of Skyla's gifting. Vigulf's eldest son, Asi, scowled at his father, seething with impatience.

"He's standing fast beside her," Vigulf said in a low voice, filling his horn and lifting it up, staring over its rim at Skyla beyond on the dais, in the place of honor.

"He'd be hard put to prove her claim, if not for Skjoldur and Mistislaus," said Mord Fidla, the darkest-haired of the pair, too dark to look much like a Skylding.

"And if not for her birth scroll, locked away in Hoggi's scroll box in the Kjallari," Vigulf said.

"Well, we've got to start cleaning house somewhere if Asi is to be the next chieftain of the clan," Mord Fidla said, draining the last of his horn and tucking it away in his pouch. "Mistislaus and Skjoldur won't be any problem. Tomorrow we'll go pay a call on old Skriftur. We'll have a look at this scroll before anyone has a chance to change it or hide it. Do you think old Skriftur will come up long enough to watch the horse fighting?"

"If he does, he'll leave someone behind to guard the records," Vigulf said. "He never leaves them alone for an instant."

"He's got a new apprentice. A large fellow."

"But fat," Asi said. He had the tall, rangy, red-haired looks of his father, Vigulf. "And not a fighter. I know Einka. One glimpse of steel and he'll take to his heels."

"I think he'd be interested in the horse fighting," Vigulf said. "Skriftur will be alone, perhaps."

Skyla in her new status was required to attend all the outdoor games, also. The aggressive Krypplingur war-horses outran the soft and pampered Skylding horses, which were mostly grieved and astonished at being taken out of their peaceful stalls and paddocks and expected to race or fight for the honor of their clan.

The first horse fight resulted in a spectacular rout. The

Skylding stallion took to his heels across the fell with the Krypplingur opponent in hot pursuit, snapping his teeth and squealing unspeakable stallion epithets.

Amid the barking and snorting that passed for Kryppling laughter, Kraftugur discreetly made his way to Herrad's side and hemmed politely.

"I came to offer my congratulations to your son," Kraftugur said. He had chosen to approach the Krypplingur chieftain when no Skyldings were around, after the amusing diversion of the two stallions bolting away.

"Thank you, but I hate to glory in your misfortune," Herrad said. "It was a low thing for the Viturkonur to promise you the gifting, then to change their minds. I thought you would be far more angry than you seem to be."

Kraftugur shrugged his shoulders. "It is of small consequence when you consider the grand scheme of the Web of Life. Perhaps on some other strand I shall be the successful inheritor and the father of the race of wizard warriors which I have for so long envisioned. Something was not quite right on this strand, so I shall be content to wait until fate chooses to deal me a more fortuitous thread. It is not wise to break yourself upon unavoidable circumstances. The things that missed you in this life could not possibly have hit you, and the things that hit you could not possibly have missed you. So it is with fortune and misfortune, but there may always be another chance."

"You are a very wise man," Herrad said. "You have the wisdom and patience of a great prophet. Which brings me to a point of some concern on my part. The Skylding prophet Jafnar has made a dire prophecy about my son Ofarir."

"I wouldn't give much weight to the prophecies of one so young and untried," Kraftugur said. "The world has seen no Skylding prophets before. Their skills are not of the mind and the finer senses. What was it he said?"

Ofarir stirred uneasily. "That I would perish at the hands of my wife, my throat torn to shreds, while she sings and dabbles her fingers in my blood. I can't imagine it myself, her being such a small and fragile creature. Now, the Kryppling mother clans are a different matter. You wouldn't want to turn your back on any of them if they had an axe nearby."

"I wondered if it might not be some Skylding plot," Herrad muttered.

Kraftugur pursed his lips thoughtfully, a frown corrugating

his forehead. "I would hate to think that of the Skyldings. They have always been such an honorable clan. Hoggvinn would never stoop to such a devious deed ordinarily. He is aging, however, and perhaps the fears of the cold and dark years of infirmity and the loss of his powers are making him strange. He can't fail to realize that the strength of the Skylding clan is waning with their rise in prosperity. The Skyldings are no longer as dragons sitting on their hoard of gold. It is beginning to worry him that he can no longer defend the treasure of his ancestors in the way he knows it must be defended."

Herrad nodded slowly, crossing glances with Ofarir like twin rapiers. "A pity that a strong warrior must fall into decline. But he has plenty of young warriors around him to defend the treasure."

"Not that I have noticed," Ofarir replied with a wolfish grin. "Unless they're keeping them hidden from sight. And I don't think they are."

"The Skylding clan is weak," Herrad said. "They could be easily destroyed. But then the treasure would never be found. I have heard that this entire mountain where Rangfara sits is riddled with tunnels and tombs and vaults where the Skyldings have hidden centuries of loot from their plunderings."

"It is true," Kraftugur said. "I have tried to explore as much as I could. In my trusted capacity in Rangfara, I was able to do what I wished, and no one questioned me."

"Did you find the treasure?" Ofarir demanded, his eyes shining with a feral gleam.

"Not quite, but I believe I have found certain clues that lead the way to it," Kraftugur said, lowering his voice but not managing to conceal the excitement in his tone. "You know Hoggvinn would not reveal its hiding place even to his daughter's bridegroom. It would be many years before you ascended to that degree of trust. Marrying Hoggvinn's daughter is not going to get you what you want. At least, not immediately." His glance was veiled, but no fisherman could have thrown out bait more industriously.

"Krypplingur are not the type who wait around much," Herrad said, licking his lips.

"I thought not. The Krypplingur are a clan of action. They take what is on offer." Kraftugur smiled his thin and faintly taunting smile. "And weakness is surely an offer. It would only be a kindness to restore the protection this treasure once had, when the Skyldings were at their prime. As near relatives of the Skylding clan, you might look upon it as your duty."

Herrad closed his eyes for a pious moment. "I wouldn't dream of doing anything that would damage my friends the Skyldings in any way."

"How fortunate that the Skyldings have chosen you for their protection," Kraftugur said. "Fate certainly smiles kindly upon this new friendship. May it endure until the end of Rangfara."

"I hope we won't have to wait that long," Ofarir muttered in an aside to himself.

"In this new light of mutual trust and friendship," Kraftugur said, "I think you should go into the Kjallari and study the history of the Skylding clan. Since you are to have a Skylding wife, you truly ought to know who their great men were and where they are buried, and where their scrolls are kept. In one year from today the Skylding clan will be as much your clan as the Kryppling clan you were born to."

"True and noble words, my friend," Herrad said.

Kraftugur continued. "I would deem it an honor to escort you to the Kjallari and show you what I know. Others, I'm sure, will take you further into the secrets of the Kjallari. We shall first visit Skriftur, keeper of the genealogy scrolls and historian of the Skylding clan."

"Will this take long?" Ofarir inquired. "I'd hate to miss the horse fighting. Not that the Skylding stallions have a chance. Nice and fat for the stew pot, though."

"Quiet," Herrad said. "If Kraftugur thinks it wise to visit the keeper of the scrolls, then we will do it."

"Another thing concerns me greatly," Kraftugur said with reluctance. "Perhaps I'm an overcautious fool when it comes to things that might happen in the future."

"You're a prophet," Herrad said. "I'd stake my sword that you're not a fool."

"I've hesitated to mention it before for fear of offending my Skylding hosts. I've been concerned about the safety of Skyla's scroll. The Skyldings are so trusting that nothing is done to protect any of the scrolls. There are people in Rangfara who are not happy about Skyla inheriting the chieftain's seat. They would do anything to obstruct her path, and yours. If you were to put that scroll in safekeeping, it might avoid trouble with certain people whom Hoggvinn wouldn't dream of distrusting."

"I agree," Herrad said. "Although I don't put any value on

a scroll of sheepskin, I know that other clans do. Wars have been caused by words on vellum. If this scroll is going to cause trouble, then we will put it in a safe place."

"Why should I have to miss the horse fights?" Modga demanded. "You're the one who thought it was such a good idea to fetch Thogn out of Kraftugur's place. You should be the one to watch him at least part of the time."

"What's wrong with taking him with you?" Jafnar asked.

Modga snorted. "And be seen with a person who talks to mud? No thanks. I'm just going to stay home where nobody can see me. I hope you enjoy the horse fights. I know I always did. It's my favorite entertainment, and I look forward to it tremendously. And they say it's going to be even more exciting because of the Krypplingur stallions. But I don't mind missing it, not at all, even though Borgildr will be there, probably wondering where I am."

"I doubt it," Lofa said.

"She'll have plenty of company," Lampi added encouragingly. "Lots of young blades hang around her all the time. She won't even miss you."

"Mistislaus isn't going," Modga said. "Why can't he keep an eye on Thogn?"

"You don't just keep an eye on Thogn, and you know it," Jafnar said. "Besides, Mistislaus would forget all about him, mumbling around with his iterations or something. Just take Thogn out in the courtyard by the carp pool and let him do what he wants. I'll watch him next time. It's just that I want to see if I can get close enough to Skyla to talk to her again."

"Exactly what I'd like to do with Borgildr," Modga muttered. With a martyred sigh, he touched Thogn on the shoulder to get his attention. Thogn looked up from his contemplation of the dust motes dancing in the sunlight and smiled in bright recognition.

"Modga, where have you been?" he asked.

"The question is, Where have you been?" Modga replied. "Why don't you ever stay here with us?"

"Because of them," Thogn said, gesturing with his hand as if he were in the center of the crowd. "The mist people. They want me with them. You should come with us, Modga."

Then the veil dropped over his expression. He gazed at Modga vacantly, as if he had gone away and left himself standing there. Modga shivered and darted Jafnar an outraged look as he herded Thogn out the door and into the courtyard.

Jafnar had no luck getting near enough to speak to Skyla. A platform of wagons had been built for the highborn to watch the horse fighting from, and Skyla sat with Hoggvinn on one side of her and Skjoldur on the other. Behind them sat the Viturkonur, including Alvara, and there was an empty seat where Logregla was supposed to sit. At least Jafnar had the pretext of joining his father, which gave him ample opportunity for gazing at Skyla helplessly, a circumstance that was not particularly appealing to him. She looked pale, and her back was stiff with determination.

"I don't know where the Krypplinger are," Hoggvinn said, craning his neck around. "I didn't think they'd want to miss this. I daresay a lot of money will change hands today."

"Yes, and most of it ours, more's the pity," Skjoldur replied gloomily as he scanned the Skylding fighting horses, which were fat, pampered fellows, little suspecting what a shock awaited them when they encountered the muscular Krypplingur stallions.

"And Logregla is missing, also," Hoggvinn went on with a scowl. "I wonder what she could be up to."

"She's probably placing bets on all the Krypplingur stallions," Skjoldur said. "I wish I had."

The next fight was a complete rout and was over almost instantly. After the horses had turned their rumps to each other for a short flurry of kicking and squealing, the Skylding stallion conceded the battle and raced away at a dead run in the direction of his home pasture. The watching Krypplingur raised a derisive roar of mirth.

"Blast! I lost money on my own horse!" Hoggvinn fumed. "The lazy clot! Not an ounce of fighting spirit! Where's Herrad and Ofarir? They said they'd be here. I've got to go find them. Skjoldur, come with me. I'm sorry to leave you, my dear," he said to Skyla, "but I've got some important errands to attend to. I'll be back very shortly."

Jafnar could scarcely believe his luck. If he didn't move, if nobody noticed him, perhaps he could catch Skyla's eye.

"Skyla!" he hissed, and he felt a thrill of immediate recognition from her. He also felt the monumental cold wall of her dismay and grief. Her eyes were as dull as the gray sea on a dark winter day.

"Don't worry," he whispered. "I'm going to help you."

She shook her head warningly, and he felt the hopelessness that turned her heart to heavy lead. There was no deliverance, no hope that anything would turn out well.

"No, it's going to be alright," he said.

"Here now," snapped the harsh voice of the ancient tjaldi behind him, and he felt a sharp poke between his shoulder blades. "There's no talking to her now she's gifted. Take yourself away from here, you young rogue!"

Jafnar turned in time to duck a good whack from the old tjaldi's walking staff. Her eyes glared at him furiously from behind the mask and wrapping she wore, looking like the eyes of a maddened badger in a dark hole.

"I'm not a rogue, I'm an old friend of hers," Jafnar said. "I knew her when she was with Mistislaus."

"That's exactly what she's got to forget," Thordis snapped, leaning forward to snarl at him in a low voice. "If you want to do her a favor, just keep your face out of her sight. She's a chieftain's daughter now, not a little wild thing running about the fells."

"Skyla will always be wild!" Jafnar retorted. "You can't change her like this!"

"Who are you to say what can or can't be?" Alvara demanded contemptuously. "You fancy yourself a prophet, so you should know the inevitable end. Now begone before I call a Kryppling and have you thrown out." She glanced toward a knot of the dark and loathsome brutes who looked more than ready to do violence to someone.

Jafnar withdrew to a safer distance, simmering inwardly with rage and frustration. He scarcely saw the next horse fight ending in an undignified retreat by the Skylding defender. Suddenly someone grabbed him from behind. With a startled leap, he whirled around to confront his attacker. It wasn't a Kryppling; it was only Einka, blinking at him apprehensively.

"I'm sorry. I didn't mean to startle you," he said. "But it's Thogn. He's disappeared. Modga turned his back on him for just a moment—"

"How long of a moment?" Jafnar demanded furiously.

"Only long enough for us to watch over the wall as the Drottningur were leaving for the horse fights," Einka said unhappily. "You wouldn't think Thogn could move so fast. He seems half-asleep most of the time. We just climbed the wall and watched while they left the hall and went down to the horse pasture—"

"You searched the house? The barns?"

"We searched the house. Guthrum searched the barn and pigsty and hen coop."

Jafnar glanced around, half hoping to see Thogn wandering through the clustering tents, booths, carts, and throngs of merrymakers.

"Where could he have gone?" Jafnar demanded.

Einka gathered up his thick shoulders in an enormous shrug. "How should I know? He's crazy. He'll do anything, go anywhere."

"Thogn's not crazy!" Jafnar flared. "I hate how everybody thinks he's crazy! Just because he's traveling on different strands—never mind, you wouldn't understand." He glowered furiously at Einka, who was looking more confused than ever.

"It's alright, Jafnar," Einka said, venturing to pat him heavily on the back. "I know you must feel terrible about Skyla. We all know you were enthralled by her from the moment you first clapped eyes on her. But all's not lost, Jafnar. It never is completely, is it?"

Jafnar gave him a long dark look. "Yes, Einka, there is an end to everything, sooner or later."

"But you don't have to go dwelling upon it, do you?" Einka demanded, pausing at a pastry booth to dwell upon the dainty wares displayed there. "You've got to live for the pleasures of every day or you'll miss them."

"I think you've had enough of everyday pleasures," Jafnar said, grabbing him by the arm and propelling him onward. "Now, where do you think Thogn might have gone?"

"I don't know. The Kjallari, maybe," Einka said.

"What? He wouldn't go there. He's terrified of the Kjallari. He sees what's down there, or will be down there. I know Thogn. He won't go into the Kjallari."

"But he likes dead things," Einka said. "It's disgusting how he kills everything he gets his hands on. I think maybe Kraftugur's place affected him."

"Of course it did," Jafnar snapped. "Kraftugur probably did strange experiments on him. Well, we can go and ask if anybody saw him go down there. I'm glad you came and found me. I guess we can't expect any help from Modga."

"Of course not. Modga made his escape, rejoicing."

They hurried smartly to the Kjallari, with Jafnar silently resolving not to disgrace himself this time. But the sight of the archway with its carved lynxes brought on the prophetic rage, and he began to gasp and tremble. He froze and clutched Einka's arm, his eyes seeing the misty images of what had happened in his other life.

"Bodies by the cartload will be dumped down the great shaft," he whispered. "Endless pollutions and corruptions of earth, atmosphere, water, and spirit. The Kellarman is real, and he is here, stealing people's souls and creating monstrosities."

"Jafnar! Not here! Not now!" Einka cried in an agony of embarrassment. "People are watching! Come on!"

They went down the broad stairs into the Kjallari rather more hastily than Jafnar's wobbling knees would have preferred. He flinched away from stench that assailed his nostrils, earth tainted with ancient carrion.

"It's foul, foul," Jafnar whispered. "Don't you smell it? The scent of death?"

Einka inhaled deeply and sighed impatiently. "No, I don't smell it. I swear, you're just as bad as Thogn. Oh, bother, here comes somebody. Don't do anything prophetic while I talk to them, please."

They stopped and let the footsteps approaching behind them grow louder and closer. As they passed through the light of a sconce thrust in the wall, Jafnar recognized the squat forms of two Krypplingur and a slight lean figure in a gown and hood.

"Oh, no, it's Herrad!" Einka whispered. "And Ofarir! Let's keep walking!"

"No, I'll talk to them," Jafnar said, stepping forward into the light of the lamp before Einka could grab him. "Halloa there; stop a moment."

"Who's there?" demanded a non-Kryppling voice that Jafnar instantly recognized as Kraftugur's. "What do you mean, accosting us this way?"

CHAPTER
FOURTEEN

"I MEAN TO have some talk with the chieftain of the Krypplingur," Jafnar said, addressing Herrad's shadowy form. "I think you know who I am."

"It's the young prophet of Rangfara," Kraftugur said with a withered sneer. "A title I use with considerable reservations."

"At least I have a title besides murderer, traitor, and madman," Jafnar said.

"Madman?" Kraftugur sniffed. "I?"

"Yes. You'll go mad. You were promised the Skylding birthright, and just as you had it, someone snatched it away. Enough to make any greedy pirate maddened with rage. So mad that you won't even enjoy a quiet grave."

"You're making quite a specialty of dire prophecies, it seems," Kraftugur said in an amused tone. "A common fault among beginners."

"Yes," Ofarir said with a menacing rumble as he glanced at Jafnar. "He said I was to die at my own wife's hand."

Kraftugur flapped one hand impatiently. "I wouldn't give it too much credence. I've learned from years of experience that the future is seldom as black as it appears at first glance. So many mitigating factors can come into play between now and then. A few subtle changes will alter the future drastically."

"Then I won't be killed?" Ofarir asked.

"I know what I've seen," Jafnar said in a low voice to Kraftugur. "I was there, and so were you. I'm sure you remember as well as I do what you do to Ofarir."

"Oh? What?" Ofarir asked warily.

"This is absurd," Kraftugur said, shaking his head and starting away. "There's no sense in wasting any more time here. We'll go down to the main genealogy vault and start our tour there. Skriftur can give us some advice, I'm sure. He knows the history of the Skylding clan as if it were his own name scroll."

"You're taking Herrad into the Kjallari?" Jafnar queried, making so bold as to follow. "Herrad, chieftain of the Krypplingur, listen to me. Don't you want to know what's in store for you in the Kjallari?"

"I know well enough what's in the Kjallari," Herrad said. "Dust, bones, history, and other nuisances." He turned and gazed upon Jafnar in growing astonishment and displeasure.

"All you're thinking about is that treasure," Jafnar said. "I can see it in your eyes. That's the only thing that brought you to Rangfara, not any ridiculous hopes of peace between Skylding and Kryppling. I've seen you destroy the Skyldings to the last man, filling the streets of Rangfara with blood, Skylding blood. And you, Herrad, your fate is worse yet, worse than dying of wounds in battle. I've seen you shrunken and raddled by poison, withered to nothing but a skeleton with skin, except for one leg, bloated with vile humors, rotting slowly while inevitable death creeps nearer each day. No cure for Kjallari fever unless it's madness. And while you weaken, your son begins to covet the chieftain's seat he will one day claim, as soon as you die and get out of his way."

"That's a lie!" Ofarir snarled.

"What heresies come spewing from your lips!" Kraftugur cried, swinging around with blazing eyes, certainly looking like a madman. "I would take those lips and sew them shut with your own entrails!"

"Because it's the truth and you know it's the truth," Jafnar replied, emboldened beyond all common sense by the strength of his vision. He turned to Herrad and continued. "If you want to preserve your life as well as your leg, get out of the Kjallari now and don't ever come back down here. You will lose many good men to the creatures of the Kjallari. If you want to save them and yourself, leave Rangfara now, before anything else happens."

"Leave Rangfara?" Herrad rumbled with a glint of bared teeth. "Leave Skyla and the treasure?"

"Yes," Jafnar said. "Leave Skyla and the treasure."

Kraftugur chuckled then, shaking his head. "Now I know what lies beneath all this. You have here a disappointed suitor for Hoggvinn's daughter. He has looked into his own future and realized that he can never climb so high as to attain the chieftain's daughter."

"I have warned you," Jafnar said to Herrad. "So make your decision, Kryppling. Consider that if I am a disappointed suitor, what do you call Kraftugur, who had the birthright in the hollow of his hand, only to have it snatched rudely away? Listen and be warned, Herrad."

"Tell me, prophet," Herrad said, swaggering forward a step or two to ram his face closer to Jafnar's, breathing the stinking meat-eater's breath in his face and exuding the strong animal smell of Kryppling. "Will I ever possess the Skylding treasure?"

"No, never," Jafnar said without flinching. "You're going to rot like a piece of carrion."

"Be off," Kraftugur said, stalking away disdainfully. "We've got no time for your ravings."

Einka crept out of the niche he had taken refuge in. His face looked pale even in the ruddy glow of the nearby rush light.

"Thank you very much for casting such a questionable light upon our family name that it probably will never recover," he said to Jafnar. "I don't understand you prophets. Why can't you just keep all your bad news to yourselves? Nobody wants to hear it. Do you really think very many people are going to believe you? What proof have you got for anything? What's the point of being a prophet if nobody is going to believe you?"

"I don't know," Jafnar said, suddenly deserted by the warming fire and courage of the prophetic gift. "I wouldn't wish this curse on my worst enemy."

"Come on, we'll go see Skriftur," Einka said. "He'll have something to eat. You'll feel better soon. Maybe he's seen Thogn. Seems like everyone else is in the Kjallari today." He shrugged one shoulder down a tunnel they were passing, where they heard the soft tramp of boots echoing not far away.

"We're not alone," Jafnar said in a whisper. They stopped to listen and did indeed hear the whisper of footsteps ahead of them.

"Skriftur never has this much company," Einka said. "He's not going to get any of his work done."

"Look, who's that?" Jafnar whispered, pointing at the dark form of a woman in a long cloak gliding through the distant pool of light from a whale oil lamp.

"I don't know," Einka said, starting away. "I don't understand why so many people want to miss the horse fighting."

"Kraftugur's going that way to Skriftur," Jafnar said.

"I know a shortcut," Einka said, sticking out his chin stubbornly and leading the way down a dark tunnel. "If I know anything at all, I know the Kjallari."

Quite promptly they were lost in the maze of tunnels and catacombs.

"Don't worry," Einka said several times. "I know perfectly well how to get out of this."

When they reached Skriftur's court, they found the old historian working and Mistislaus seated at the long table studying a pile of curling scrolls that were blackened by age around the frayed edges. At his feet sat Thogn, peacefully crooning to a small army of mud people.

"There you are!" Einka declared.

"There you are, yourselves," Mistislaus retorted, running an irate eye over them. "Can't I trust you to watch Thogn for a moment? You've scarcely taken your eyes off Skyla for almost a fortnight, but the instant I leave you in charge of Thogn, he wanders off and I find him in the Kjallari. If he ever got into the charnel pit, we'd never see him again."

Jafnar squatted down beside Thogn, who darted him a single pleased glance, then went back into his own dark world.

"Thogn, Thogn, what are we going to do?" he whispered.

"Thogn, Thogn, what are we going to do?" Thogn repeated in the same whisper.

"Take him home," Mistislaus said. "If your father knew he was out wandering around alone, he'd have a fit."

"Skjoldur was here not long ago," Skriftur said, looking up briefly from a stack of old dusty vellums that smelled as if they had come out of a barrow. "Came with Hoggvinn to look at the scroll box. What an appalling mess this is. Rats have eaten the ends of the scrolls. Some very important dates have gone down the throats of a pack of wretched rats."

Thogn commenced smashing his mud army with the appropriate sounds of battle. Mistislaus rolled his eyes upward and started shoving the scrolls and weights into his satchel. "I can't work in a madhouse," he declared. "Jafnar, take Thogn home. And if you see Modga, tell him I wish to speak to him. Severely."

"Come on, Thogn," Jafnar said, urging his brother to his

feet. "Einka, you're not staying, are you? I can't find my way out of this rabbit warren alone."

Einka sighed with elaborate impatience and cast a yearning eye upon Skriftur's scrolls. "It's perfectly simple," he said.

"You brought me on a shortcut. I can't remember a thing. And it's dark besides. I get all turned around."

"Go on, go with your brother," Skriftur urged. "Young men should be out enjoying the horse fights and races and the company of living creatures, not moldering about with old scribes and dead histories. Go on and enjoy yourselves." He ignored Einka's sputters of protest and shooed them out, while Mistislaus cleaned up his clutter and prepared to take his leave.

For a while Thogn proceeded peacefully along the corridor, then suddenly he darted ahead and turned down a side tunnel. Cursing and puffing, Einka lumbered at Jafnar's heels in pursuit.

"Charnel pit!" Einka huffed, trying to point, run, and talk all at once and not doing well at any of them. "Crumbling—not safe—old well—"

They overtook Thogn as he paused under a crumbling carved arch, waiting for them. He turned, seized Jafnar by the arm, and dragged him forward, whispering, "Kellarman! Kellarman!"

"No, Thogn, there's no Kellarman," Einka gasped.

"Where is he, Thogn?" Jafnar demanded.

"Down—things in the water." Thogn tugged at Jafnar, dragging him toward the blackness of the unlit tunnel beyond the archway.

"What must I do, Thogn?" Jafnar whispered rapidly.

"Clean the water!" Thogn replied fiercely. "It's all blocked up with dead things! Kellarman—evil things—"

Then the fit passed from him, and he relaxed his grip on Jafnar, coming to a halt and staring around vacantly.

"Thogn, you great ox," Einka muttered, grabbing him and pushing him back through the archway into the main tunnel. "I think he lives just to madden us."

Jafnar stood still a moment, his heart pounding. He recognized this place by its feel and smell—different from the close warm tunnels of the Kjallari. A breath of air stirred there in the vast darkness of the pit, carrying up faint scents of water and ancient decay.

"Jafnar!" called a distant voice, exactly as it had happened before. It sounded like Skyla's voice, so convincing that he took a step forward.

"Jafnar, help me!" the voice pleaded, faint yet piercing.

"I won't be fooled again," he said to the darkness. Grimly Jafnar turned his back and hurried after Einka and Thogn.

The horse fighting was still going badly for the Skyldings. A great deal of money and property was changing hands, and most of it was going into Krypplingur pockets.

"I can't understand all this feasting, dancing, and horse fighting," the old tjaldi muttered to Alvara the moment Hoggvinn was gone. She was half-stifled under the mask and wrappings that protected her face against the perils of the sunlight. "As if one week wasn't enough to celebrate finding his daughter, now Hoggvinn's got to celebrate another week because she's going to be married. What a lot of bother. And expense, considering the way his relatives eat."

"Skyldings are an extravagant lot," Alvara said, her tone bored as she scanned yet another pair of snorting stallions. "Are you certain you don't want to go back to the tent? It's getting hot out here. I could take your excuses to Hoggvinn when he gets back."

"When he gets back?" Thordis demanded with a withered scowl. "Go after him and watch him. Who knows what he might be up to? We've got to keep our eyes upon him, my daughter."

"Yes, of course, my tjaldi," Alvara said with a glance toward Skyla. "You'll watch her?"

"Just go. I have my sisters to watch her. Even if she is Hoggvinn's daughter, she belongs to our clan."

"I've made sure she knows it."

Thordis' hand shot out and fastened upon Alvara's arm like a claw. "What we need is to be rid of Kraftugur," she whispered. "I don't care for the look on his face anymore."

"If you wish him gone, tjaldi—"

"I wish him dead. He knows about the Drottningur and the lynxes. We can't have our enemies holding valued information. You'll take care of it?"

"Yes, my tjaldi."

Logregla had begged off attending the horse fights this day, not finding the courage within herself to sit upon a wagon surrounded by Skyla and her Viturkonur relatives. At first she had thought to stay in bed all day, but her restless dissatisfaction wouldn't permit such indulgence. She dressed and paced about her small chamber, stopping to look out the window at frequent intervals to exacerbate her irritation by looking down on the scenes of revelry below.

Never had her condition seemed so utterly desolate to her. She had always taken advantage of Hoggvinn's wealth to purchase any form of entertainment or travel she wished. When she brooded upon the deaths of her unfortunate infants, she sent to the Skurdur for the most tempting dainties to keep her company in her solitary grieving. When her ire rose against Hoggvinn for some callous slight or hint of complaint, she sent for veils, cloaks, gowns, slippers, anything to cover herself like armor against her own doubts.

Now, however, mere food and entertainment and clothing were paltry sops in the vast ocean of her misery and rage. While the horse fighting proceeded with much mirth and jeering and insulting, she paced to and fro in her small room, bosom heaving with indignation, eyes burning with dry, searing passion. No one was near; everyone was outside celebrating the existence of a creature she had wished destroyed twenty years earlier. She still wished Skyla destroyed, more fervently than ever. She would far rather see Vigulf's redheaded son on the chieftain's seat than a hulking Kryppling.

There was no way she could get to Skyla for quite some time. Hoggvinn she was willing to bide her time for, plotting the perfect death for the traitor. For the present—she pursed her lips and thought deeply, wondering what she could possibly do immediately to hinder the process of being supplanted by Hoggvinn's usurping daughter.

It was an easy matter to throw on a dark cloak and slip out of the hall. Nervously she hastened along the familiar street toward the Kjallari, unaccustomed to going anywhere without an entourage of dressers and maids and sister kin to keep her company. Being alone made her feel so unimportant and ordinary, especially when everyone else was in his favorite company to celebrate the gifting of Hoggvinn's daughter.

She passed under the archway of the the Kjallari, glancing up at the stone lynxes carved there as guardians over the dead and their treasures. She knew every step of the way to Skriftur's court. When her grief was most dire and unbearable, she came here with one attendant, who was sent away, and Logregla took the box containing the scrolls of her dead children and sat with them, studying each one as if it were the lost child. She had never regarded the other scrolls in Hoggvinn's box, only the six that represented the children the Viturkonur curse had taken from her. The other scrolls never seemed important, just something of Hoggvinn's. Now she burned to get her hands on those scrolls, particularly the one that had brought her all her present agony.

"Ah, my lady, you're here again," Skriftur greeted her. "It seems I see you only in the bad times."

"Times are very bad just now," Logregla replied. She seated herself at her customary place at Skriftur's table. "There is no joy for me in all this celebrating. Bring me the box, Skriftur."

He made a slight bow and returned to the room where the boxes were kept. In a moment he was back with Hoggvinn's carved scroll box. With a discreet muttering about seeing to something important, he took himself out of the room, leaving Logregla alone. She looked at her soft, white trembling hands resting upon the lid and suddenly despised them for their dainty weakness. Never in all her life had she done one useful, determined thing with her hands except to haul out a handkerchief and weep until she got her way or to slap a lazy serving girl.

Slowly she opened the lid and took out the six birth scrolls of her dead infants, one by one, lining them up steadily in a row. Then, with her heart thumping sickly, she reached back in for the other scrolls. Hoggvinn's marriage scroll, his birth scroll. There was nothing else. She stared dumbfounded, then her heart surged exultantly. Skyla had no scroll to prove she had the slightest relationship to Hoggvinn. She uttered a shriek, stifling it in a nervous cackle.

"Oh, Skriftur! Come here at once!" she cried.

"Is everything alright, my lady?" he replied courteously.

"No! Yes! Well, look!" she gasped, spreading out the scrolls. "See here, six for my poor dead little ones, Hoggvinn's birth scroll, and our gifting scroll. There's nothing for Skyla—unless it's been stolen."

"Stolen! Certainly not!" Skriftur huffed, his hands fluttering through the scrolls. "You're right; it's gone. It was here just moments ago, and I haven't left my post once. It's been stolen. I know it was here. I've known it was here for twenty years, and now it's gone."

"She has no claim," Logregla crowed. "She's nothing but a stray cat without that scroll."

"Hardly, my dear lady," Skriftur said, his face puckered up

in a rage of puzzlement and indignation. "We know it was here. Someone has stolen it. Someone took it for reasons of his own—right beneath my very nose."

"So here you are," a voice said suddenly behind them. Logregla gasped and gave a guilty start, turning pale. "Is there something wrong?"

"The scroll is gone," Logregla hissed in thinly masked triumph. "I came to mourn my poor babies and discovered that some thief had taken it. Poor Skyla!"

"How could that have happened?" Alvara's eyes flicked to Skriftur, sharp as daggers. "This is supposed to be a safe place for matters such as this."

"I've no idea," Skriftur said. "I couldn't have left it unattended. I never once left. If Hoggvinn had taken it, he would have told me."

"There are those in Rangfara who would like to dispute Skyla's claim," Alvara said, "those who stand to lose a great deal which they were counting upon."

"I can't imagine a dear little thing like Skyla having enemies," Logregla said righteously.

"Who else has been down here, asking to see the scroll?" Alvara asked.

"Oh, a lot of people you'd never guess had an interest in genealogy—" Skriftur began.

"Genealogy had nothing to do with it!" Alvara interrupted. "This has to do with fortunes and power! And possibly your head being cut off for dereliction of duty. Quick, now, who was it?"

"There was Vigulf and Mord Fidla," Skriftur began slowly, anxious to get everyone in proper chronological order.

"Yes, of course," Logregla said. "Vigulf wants his son to be Hoggvinn's heir."

"And then there was Herrad and Ofarir. Hoggvinn himself with Skjoldur. Mistislaus, the lad Jafnar with his brothers Thogn and Einka, who is my apprentice—no, it was Thogn who appeared first. The one who is wandering. Oh, yes, and Kraftugur was with Herrad and Ofarir, and we had a lovely chat about Skylding history. Really, it's quite gratifying to see Krypplingur so interested in knowing our past, which is a good thing, considering they will be our kinsmen this time next year—"

"Kraftugur was here?" Alvara interrupted.

"Lots of people were here. I can't imagine how you failed to see any of them as you came in just now."

"Unless they didn't want to be seen," Alvara said. "The Kjallari is an excellent place for hiding. And did you show the scroll to all of them?"

"No, indeed," Skriftur said haughtily. "Such things are private. I told them all the scroll would be shown tomorrow at the scroll ceremony. Dear me, what shall we do for the scroll ceremony tomorrow, when we read the gifting scroll? I'm sure Hoggvinn will want to show the birth scroll to everyone present."

"You'll have to tell him you're working on it or some such," Alvara said.

"You could make a false one," Logregla said, her elation suddenly departing from her. Narrowly she eyed Skriftur, not daring to add that the first one might have been a false one, also. Or maybe there had never really been a scroll, if one discounted what old Skriftur said. Unfortunately, he had a reputation for perfect honesty.

"No, no, I would never create a false birth scroll under any circumstances," Skriftur said. "Such a thing might be made under the best of intentions, but consider the confusion in years to come when men have forgotten what we do here today. No, I believe the scroll will turn up somewhere, in honest hands."

"We should be going, my lady," Alvara said to Logregla, taking her arm firmly in hand to help her to her feet. "It's very late, and you're going to be missed soon from the celebration."

"I doubt that," Logregla muttered. "No one has given me a thought for more than a week."

"It will all be over soon," Alvara said. "All this fuss is just because there's something new to think about for a little while. Skyla is just a novelty, and we all know how the world loves a novelty—very briefly."

"But because of this novelty, we are losing Rangfara to the Krypplingur!" Logregla snapped furiously. "Can't anyone see what a terrible mistake this is?"

"Shh! Come along; you're exhausted," Alvara said, hurrying Logregla out of Skriftur's hall. "You shouldn't have walked all this way, and alone besides. I wonder what you were thinking of."

"Just my poor innocent children," Logregla retorted, "who died because of a Viturkonur curse. It's something that I can't seem to quit thinking of, somehow."

"It seems to me that you and I had the same idea," Alvara said. "That the scroll was in some sort of danger."

"I come here often," Logregla said. "To look at the scrolls of my children that might have been. Nobody knows I do this—except Skriftur. It's foolish, I know, but I come to grieve." Hastily she pulled out a handkerchief, hoping to hide her eyes in case they were blazing with wicked triumph and rage.

"I'm sorry for your children," Alvara said. "But you are not entirely innocent in this dispute, so you must expect to suffer some consequences."

"What are you doing here? Did you follow me?" Logregla tried to summon her old lofty pride, but she was trembling.

"I had a strange feeling that Skyla's birthright scroll might be in some kind of danger. It seems we think very much alike now that we are sisters under the skin."

"Under the skin of the lynx, you mean," Logregla said in a low voice, darting a nervous glance around for passersby. "We are bound together closer than family. I think I'm done with my grieving now."

"Good," Alvara said. "It isn't wise for you to go on about your children. You have other responsibilities now. Soon you'll find no time for looking back. Come, I'll take you back to your rooms and see to it you're comfortable, like I used to do."

"You're very kind for an old enemy," Logregla said.

"We are enemies no longer," Alvara said. "We have formed a sisterhood that will outlast Rangfara and the Skylding clan. You will need no children or family or clan with the sisterhood of the lynx."

They walked down the echoing tunnel, passing from one pool of light to the next. Suddenly Alvara halted, raising one hand in a listening attitude. Distantly, a restless rustling faintly disturbed the stony silence of the tunnels.

"There's something strange in the Kjallari," she whispered. "Do you hear that noise?"

"I hear it," Logregla said with a shiver. "There's never been anything like that down here before. What do you think it could be?"

"I don't know," Alvara said, "but I have my fears. Can't you walk any faster?"

"These shoes aren't made for walking," Logregla said. "I need to sit down and rest a moment on this bench." She sat down with a sigh and stuck out her feet, which were ridiculously small and clad in something scarcely as substantial as a baby's slipper. For effect, she took out her scrap of handkerchief with a sigh and dabbed at her eyes.

"Only for a moment." Alvara remained on her feet, listening intently to the faint undercurrent of sound. Testing the air for traces of essences, she detected misty vapors of the restless sort that lingered around unquiet graves. Certainly none of the self-satisfied Skyldings moldering to dust would do anything so disreputable as wandering about in a disembodied state. Certainly she had never detected haunting spirits in the Kjallari before. But then, she had always visited when the tunnels were crowded with eager dayfaring visitors.

"Who could have stolen that scroll?" Logregla commenced chattering nervously, glancing right and left and drawing up her cloak as if she, too, felt the clammy touch of the spirits. "I can't imagine who might have done it. There were so many people here, and every one of them had a good excuse for taking it. Vigulf and Mord Fidla, Kraftugur, Mistislaus—"

"Hush! We must keep moving!" Alvara hissed sharply. "There are rampant spirits loose in the Kjallari. Come along; get to your feet!"

"I can't move!" Logregla moaned in terror.

"My dear, I can't leave you here alone," Alvara said. "Unless, of course, you're going to go spread the word to the world that Skyla's scroll is missing. Then I shall have to leave you."

"No! No! I won't breathe a word of it to anyone!" Logregla gasped. "If you think it's best, then I'll just forget what I saw—or didn't see. I promise I won't tell anyone. It doesn't matter, anyway, does it? The Krypplingur and the Skyldings will all be gone, won't they?"

"Of course, of course. But until they are, you'll have to be very quiet and good, Logregla. Listen to me and I'll tell you what you must do. Or mustn't do."

"I'll tell no one about the missing scroll."

"Yes, that's right. Now come along. Let's get out of here. Nothing will happen to you as long as I'm here."

Logregla got to her feet, whimpering under her breath. Alvara pushed her along, piloting her toward the main stairs, then up to the courtyard and out into the street. The reassuring sight of clumps of drunken celebrants weaving from house to house and the sounds of singing upraised by joyous throats from many quarters immediately erased the cold feeling of dread inspired by the Kjallari.

"Well, now, we survived that, whatever it was," Logregla said, drawing a deep breath and patting at her hood to make sure it covered her head neatly. Already she was beginning to forget the experience. "What on earth was it, do you suppose? The Kjallari is getting very strange. I think there's something different about all of Rangfara since this daughter business began. Now, who do you suppose has got that scroll? I wonder—"

"Mistislaus was in the Kjallari?" Alvara interrupted, suddenly remembering this one gem in the midst of the dross of Logregla's chatter.

"Yes, Mistislaus. He and Skriftur are old friends. And that apprentice of Skriftur's is living in the same house with Mistislaus. Skjoldur's house, and all his sons moved in with him, but he moved out. The apprentice, in fact, is a son of Skjoldur's, but not one of the better ones, if you know what I mean."

"And Kraftugur."

"He's certainly lost his popularity, hasn't he? Since the Viturkonur rejected him as Skyla's suitor—"

"My dear. Sometimes I wish you were as quiet as the grave."

CHAPTER
FIFTEEN

JAFNAR HAD THE extreme good fortune to attach himself to the scroll-reading party the next day. By dint of lurking around the steps of the Kjallari from the earliest hint of daylight, he was able to waylay Skjoldur and hurry inside on his heels.

Walking sedately at Alvara's side, Skyla wore a beaded Viturkonur headdress with tassels of ermine tails and a long white cloak. Jafnar could get nowhere near her, thanks to the black-cloaked Viturkonur surrounding her, treading along in a solemn procession, as if it were an execution instead of a happy, triumphant occasion. Their mood suited Jafnar's mood exactly whenever he looked at Ofarir slinking along and grinning self-consciously at the crowd.

In honor of the occasion, the Kjallari was closed to general traffic. Crowds of well-wishers lined the way, interspersed with clots of stone-faced Krypplingur, like bits of stagnant detritus caught in a bright stream.

When they descended into the Kjallari, the way narrowed so that the scroll party could no longer go thronging along, so they proceeded by threes and fours in order of least important first. That way the principal players would arrive last, when everyone else was gathered along the walls. The last ones in would have the best view. As a happy result of this arrangement, Jafnar and Mistislaus were shoved ahead first into Skriftur's court.

"The flaming arrogance!" Mistislaus sputtered. "As if I wasn't her father for nearly twenty years! Now I'm shoved under the rug and forgotten! Disregarded! Unwelcome! I wouldn't even be here today if I'd waited for an invitation. This time I've had enough of their insults. I'm going—"

Mistislaus forgot where he was going. He paused, coming to a halt. Skriftur was seated at the table ahead of them, hunched over a pile of manuscripts with his back to them. A rush light burned low beside him, the grass wick nearly gone.

"What is it?" Jafnar hissed, suddenly sensing a powerful tension still crackling in the atmosphere of the underground chamber.

In three swift strides Mistislaus approached Skriftur, his face drained of any hue except a grayish sick color. Skriftur did not move to greet him. Jafnar joined Mistislaus, seeing then the pool of blood congealed upon the table and floor. Skriftur lay with his head against a stack of stone records, one hand still clutching the gilded handle of a dagger that was buried to its hilt in his chest. The other hand reached out helplessly toward a scroll box spilling its scrolls across the table. It was Hoggvinn's box, which should have contained Skyla's birth scroll.

In a moment more people came swarming into the room, and the murder was discovered. Pandemonium erupted. The Viturkonur gabbled about the missing scroll, the Skyldings argued about the murder, and the Krypplingur looked on in stoic silence. A few of Skriftur's closest friends gathered around him to grieve, including Mistislaus. Jafnar tugged at his cloak urgently, dragging him away almost by main force.

"Does this mean the wedding is off?" he hissed.

"I don't know!" Mistislaus snapped. "You'll have to ask Hoggvinn and the Viturkonur. Can't you leave me alone for just a few moments?"

"Is anyone going to step forward?" Hoggvinn demanded, scouring the crowded hall with a blazing eye. "Is anyone going to announce this killing?"

The room went dead still, but no one stepped forward.

"A secret murder, then," Hoggvinn said grimly, and the room buzzed with excited chatter. Straightforward killing was frowned upon, but the weregild tended to soothe the hurt feelings of the survivors. Secret murder, however, was always an entirely dishonorable way of attending to one's differences of opinion.

"Then a court of inquiry will be held," Hoggvinn announced, his voice booming around the room. "Now clear out, everyone, and we'll deal with this problem."

"But is there any sign of the scroll?" the old tjaldi demanded, clearing the way before her with her walking stick.

"No, it seems to be gone," Hoggvinn said heavily. "But it can't have gone far. It's still within Rangfara, I'm sure. We'll start a search immediately."

"Too late for that," Alvara said. "Skriftur has been dead quite some time. Whoever took that scroll could be miles from here by now. If they chose to leave Rangfara, that is. I believe the thief and murderer is still here, perhaps in this very room."

That caused a ripple through the audience. Everyone peered around warily at his neighbor, wondering if he was standing beside a murderer.

"All this will come to light," Hoggvinn said. "I don't intend to rest until Skriftur's killer has been brought to light, and punishment exacted. If no one steps forward by dusk, I shall send for a judge from the Skynsamur clan. Now let's clear out so we can deal with the body of our old friend."

The day passed in muted shock, and at dusk a messenger on a fast horse was sent out the gates of Rangfara. By the time he returned in two days with the judge from the Skynsamur clan, the mystery of Skriftur's death was no nearer a solution for all the talking and arguing that had gone on about it. The case was presented to the wise and gentle Eadgils from many different people. He listened to all their opinions without saying much, except to ask questions, then retired to the quiet rooms that were provided to him and commenced to think. It took him a day and a half of isolation before he summoned Hoggvinn to say he was ready to appear in the council hall.

"As I ponder this problem, it seems to me that more questions than answers come into light the more I think. Central to the question of who murdered Skriftur is the question of who wishes this gifting stopped and who wishes it to proceed."

"Then the killer is someone who wishes to stop the gifting of Skyla and Ofarir," Hoggvinn said, running his eye suspiciously over his audience of friends and retainers.

"There are people who believe Skyla is not truly your daughter," Eadgils went on. "Are they people who oppose the gifting, or are they in favor of it? And the matter of the scroll complicates this case as well. If you can find out why the scroll was stolen, you may discover your killer. Is there something in that scroll which would prevent the gifting? Or is it the loss of the scroll that will stop the gifting? Without a birth scroll, a gifting of this importance cannot take place."

"If we can find the scroll and whoever stole it, then will we have the killer?" Hoggvinn asked. Since the death of Skriftur and the loss of the scroll, he had been drinking late into the night with Skjoldur and other trusted retainers, lashing himself into a fury at the injustices being heaped upon his head. Red-eyed and grim, he crouched in his chair like a lion about to spring.

"Is the killer the same one who stole the scroll?" Eadgils asked, and he shook his head in answer to his own question. "I doubt it very much. If Skriftur knew what was in the scroll that was so dangerous, he was killed to ensure his silence."

"Perhaps he was killed because he refused to relinquish the scroll to the thief," Hoggvinn said.

"A killer thief is a desperate man," Eadgils said. "I don't believe that sort of desperation is involved here. If Skriftur refused to surrender the scroll, the ordinary thief would have gone away and plotted a more devious way to get it."

"Perhaps our thief is not ordinary," Hoggvinn said.

"Maybe he was hired for the job," Skjoldur added. "To steal the scroll and kill Skriftur."

"Indeed, I don't believe our thief is an ordinary man," Eadgils said. "Nor do I believe he is a killer. No one has seen any hired killers in Rangfara since the beginning of the celebrating. Therefore, it is my opinion that we are searching for at least two different people." He took a small scrap of vellum from his pocket. "When we consider who wants to stop this gifting, there is a list of natural suspects for stealing the scroll. First and foremost is the jilted suitor, who was once promised the hand of Hoggvinnsdottir in exchange for negotiating peace between Skylding and Kryppling—the wizard Kraftugur."

All eyes turned upon Kraftugur, who calmly acknowledged this scrutiny with a small shrug of his shoulders. The ripple of whispering passed out the door and down the steps to the people listening outside via word of mouth.

"Kraftugur has been the peacemaker between Skylding and Krypplingur," Hoggvinn said with a note of incredulous protest in his voice. "He has never expressed any resentment about being passed over. I'd stake my life on Kraftugur's innocence."

"And along with Kraftugur were Herrad and Ofarir."

"Rubbish!" Hoggvinn flared with a worried glance toward Herrad and Ofarir. "Our honored guests and future kinfolk? What possible reason would they have to kill Skriftur? Besides, it's well known that Krypplingur have no use for the written word."

"Next is the honorable lady Logregla."

"Come, now! That's preposterous!" Hoggvinn sputtered.

Eadgils eyed him in mild reproof, not appreciating Hoggvinn's commentary. He elevated his tone somewhat and continued sternly. "Not only has she lost her own children because of this irregular alliance between Skylding and Viturkonur, but she is supplanted by the offspring of that alliance as the heir to Rangfara. Her own position is in jeopardy."

Logregla hoisted her chin and dealt Eadgils a deadly glare. "I am not a thief or a murderer," she snapped. "I assure you, I have no need to stoop so low."

"I make no accusations," Eadgils said. "I only wish to bring all sides of the issue to light. And to continue in this vein, I also call attention to the brothers of your chieftain Hoggvinn, Vigulf and Mord Fidla. As long as Hoggvinn was without an heir, Vigulf's son Asi stood in position to inherit Rangfara. Now Vigulf's hopes are dashed."

When the crowd studied Vigulf and Mord Fidla, they fell perfectly silent. The fiery temper of Vigulf was well known in Rangfara, and the dark and brooding Mord Fidla was no one's idea of a jocose drinking partner.

"And then there is Skyla's foster father, who raised her for twenty years as his own daughter, never suspecting that she would be taken from him. Mistislaus, wizard, itinerant traveler, and longtime friend of Hoggvinn, who has done little to contribute to the friendship except to take advantage. After Skyla was taken from him, Mistislaus was thrown bodily out of this hall and told to leave Rangfara or he would be hanged."

"All that is meaningless bluster," Mistislaus said. "Hoggvinn doesn't mean a word of it, so I ignore him. We're old friends, so we can fight all the time without any harm. Is there anyone else you wish to incriminate in your rather bumbling search for the killer?"

"Only one other comes to light," Eadgils said. "A young man, young but still perfectly capable of stealing a scroll or killing an elderly scribe. The eldest son of Skjoldur, Jafnar. He, too, was in the Kjallari, in Skriftur's chambers during the horse fights. Perhaps he had his ambitions frustrated when Skyla was betrothed to Ofarir."

"Then I would be more likely to kill Ofarir than poor old Skriftur," Jafnar said. "And nobody has made any attempts on Ofarir's life yet."

The audience chuckled appreciatively but was quickly stifled by a glare from Hoggvinn. Herrad and Ofarir stared back at everyone without the least hint of a smile.

"To continue," Eadgils said, clearing his throat warningly. "Strange how such a crowd of people chose the same moment to disappear into the Kjallari. I'd say all of them had the same thought in their minds."

"You're forgetting someone from your list," Jafnar said. "Perhaps you were coming to her, but I saw a woman in the Kjallari, also. It was Alvara of the Viturkonur."

That caused an excited murmur in the crowd, and even Eadgils was so astonished as to hike up one eyebrow a quarter of an inch.

"Well. That is a surprise," he confessed. "You're certain it wasn't Logregla? She was easily recognized going through the Kjallari gate."

"The lady Logregla is also easily distinguished from Alvara," Jafnar said as respectfully as possible, but the crowd snickered anyway. No one could mistake Logregla's grandiose dimensions for the diminutive Alvara.

"And why was I not apprised of the fact of her presence?" Eadgils demanded, glaring in the direction of the Viturkonur, who were sitting in a row like blackbirds on a fence.

"You never asked me where I was during the horse fights," Alvara said. "I thought it would look quite strange to volunteer myself as an automatic suspect by announcing to everyone where I was. Yes, I'll freely admit I was there, with the lady Logregla, who was going through the scrolls of her dead children when I got there. Skriftur was very much alive and somewhat put out at the great number of visitors who had interfered with him that day."

"Have you reached any conclusions you'd like to share with us?" Hoggvinn inquired. His countenance had undergone changes from boiling red to marble white, cold and grim.

"Yes," Eadgils said. "I have concluded that if there are any more killings or attempted killings, I suspect they will be among the people I just mentioned—those who are opposed to the wedding of Ofarir and Skyla. Our killer is a man who is afraid of something becoming known. What better way to protect a secret than to kill the ones who may be privy to it?"

"Will there be more attempts?" Hoggvinn asked.

"It is my opinion that there most certainly will."

The crowd buzzed furiously for a moment, then hissed itself

into silence. Everyone craned his neck, straining to hear what Eadgils would say next.

"Now, then. It is exceedingly difficult to say who is doing the killing. We are inside a fortress with two clans of fierce warriors who make killing their livelihood—a point of honor, even. We also have the Viturkonur, a clan of sorcerous women who are also known to be relentless when it comes to a question of revenge. There was the ancient matter of Skyla's birth and Hoggvinn's attempt to put her to death. The theft of the baby resulted in the death of Reykja, the mother of the infant. At that time no revenge was taken or attempted by the Viturkonur, a circumstance which I find most peculiar, considering their reputation."

The old tjaldi struggled to her feet, leaning on her stick for support. "Revenge does not always mean bloodshed," she said. "Along with our vengeful disposition, we have a strong sense of justice. We wronged Hoggvinn in forcing a birthright upon him which his clan did not sanction. He tried and failed to kill the child, and the mother was killed when she fell from her horse in pursuit of her stolen child. A wrong for a wrong. If anything, the Viturkonur have come out ahead because the child is still alive and she is heir to the chieftain's seat of the Skylding clan. Her children will be the inheritors of the chieftain's seat. This is a great honor for the Viturkonur, and we are satisfied that our claim to justice in the death of Reykja has been more than fulfilled. We no longer are seeking revenge."

Everyone nodded in approval and fastened his eyes upon Eadgils once more.

"But even without the scroll, the gifting can still continue," Eadgils said, raising a ripple of astonishment. "At the time of the infant Skyla's birth—or Skylda, as her Viturkonur relations actually named her, which means 'duty,' as you are aware—at the time when she was born and her scroll made, there were two others present with Hoggvinn who can testify to the truthfulness of her claim. If those two were to step forward, their word would be bond enough for the gifting to continue. Skjoldur, chief of retainers to Hoggvinn, and the wizard Mistislaus, who was given the child to raise. Skriftur died in vain, whether he was trying to hide the information in the scroll or simply trying to protect the scroll from disappearing. Whatever the information might be in the scroll, that information is well known by the people who were present when the scroll was made. Hoggvinn, father of the child, Skjoldur and

Mistislaus, the tjaldi Thordis, and Alvara, sister to the deceased mother of Skyla."

In the electric silence of the Hall of Stars every eye was turned to Hoggvinn and the Viturkonur seated on the dais. Hoggvinn gripped the arms of the chieftain's chair and slowly rose to his feet.

"I assure all of you," he began in a low voice, "that there is nothing in Skyla's scroll which is sufficient to prevent her from marrying Ofarir of the Krypplingur or any other man in Skarpsey. There is no hidden defect, no hidden terms of gifting, nothing which need stand in her way. At the time of her birth and scroll making there were hard feelings between those of us making the scroll. It was a gifting of deception and sorcerous trickery, one I wanted no part of, in my youthful arrogance. Now I see that it has turned to a good thing. Nothing should stand in the way of this gifting because I was being stubborn then. I am immeasurably grateful that I have a daughter now who will be the keystone in building a bridge of trust between Skylding and Kryppling."

That speech warranted a cheer, so everyone cheered and stamped his feet, even out into the courtyard. The Viturkonur nodded their heads and smiled faintly, which was as pleased as Jafnar had seen the seven old prune faces looking since their arrival in Rangfara. Skyla held her head up, but she did not smile or glance in the direction of her intended husband, Ofarir.

"But the matter ought to be put to a vote," Eadgils said. "Whether or not the word of Mistislaus and Skjoldur will substitute for the missing scroll is an important point in this issue. It could result in trouble later on if all of you aren't in agreement."

"I say let it stand," a Krypplingur voice rumbled. Herrad waved one hand impatiently, as if all this confabulation about a piece of dead sheep's skin were of no more moment than a fly buzzing around his ears. "A scroll is completely useless without the art of reading. I'm willing to take the word of Skjoldur and Mistislaus."

"Well, some of us are not!" Vigulf declared hotly, leaping to his feet. "There are rules that must be kept! If you start throwing out the scrolls, everyone will start ignoring the rules of gifting and marriage until people everywhere will have no idea of who their ancestors are or what they accomplished. We must have that scroll in order for the wedding to be legal.

We're talking about the chieftaincy of the Skylding clan here, not about the mating of one likely horse to another or some such trivial affair. We must have the scroll or there will be no gifting."

Quite a few of the crowd agreed, and out in the courtyard the opinion was just as divided, as evinced by the start of several pushing matches.

"Then we shall vote on the matter," Hoggvinn said. "All those not in favor of accepting Mistislaus and Skjoldur's word as proof of Skyla's claim, leave the hall to be counted outside."

"No, no, that's not the best way to do it," Eadgils said. "You're dividing people when you need to unify them most. Take a few days to discuss the matter thoroughly. Perhaps by then the scroll will be returned." He gathered up his staff and rose to his feet. "Thank you all for your indulgence. That is all for today."

"Is that all you're going to tell us?" Hoggvinn demanded. "You don't have the name of the thief or the murderer?"

"No, but it will come to light in time," Eadgils said. "I've given you a clear picture of who is most likely to be causing the trouble in Rangfara. Now that you know where to look, you might catch your criminals quite soon. In the meantime, I think I would double the guard around Skyla."

"Skyla is in danger?" Hoggvinn demanded, his fists knotting as he glowered around the hall. "If anyone so much as looks at her with harmful intentions, I'll have him gibbeted! From now on the Hall of Stars is off limits to everyone until further notice. Guards will be posted at the doors, and I will determine who comes in or not."

Jafnar fell into step beside Mistislaus as the hall quickly emptied. A huge debate commenced in the streets of Rangfara as everyone speculated on the words of the wise Eadgils and the banishment of everyone from the Hall of Stars.

"Mistislaus! How does it feel being one of the chief suspects?" Jafnar demanded, simmering with ire.

"At least I'm still alive to be insulted," Mistislaus said. "I've never heard such a lot of useless blather. He comes up with a list of people who are opposed to the gifting and declares that one of us is the killer. For this Hoggvinn will pay him an extravagant price? I could have done as much with half as much thought. Those windbag Skynsamur are a pack of charlatans!"

"Mistislaus, who killed Skriftur?" Jafnar asked in a low

voice as they passed under an archway that offered a brief island in the clamor of the busy street.

"Use your common sense," Mistislaus snorted. "It was Kraftugur. He's the only genuine killer I know of, as I've seen on strand after strand of the Web."

"He's a peacemaker on this strand, though. I doubt if you could convince Hoggvinn."

"Hoggvinn couldn't be convinced of the nose on his own face if he couldn't see it," Mistislaus grunted. "And now his pigheaded stupidity has gotten Skriftur killed."

They returned to Athugashol, where the Skjoldurssons were gloomily picking at the scraps of food remaining in the house.

"I suppose," Modga said in a put-out tone, "this murder means there won't be any more fun in Rangfara for a while. I wonder what a suitable mourning period is for an old dried-up scribe? Do you think we'll be back to normal in a day or two?"

Einka rose up from his sleeping platform, huffing and sputtering, red-eyed with wrath. He gripped Modga by the throat, taking him to the floor in an earnest endeavor to throttle him. The sound he made between his clenched teeth as he pounded Modga's head on the paving stones would have done credit to a berserker attacking fifty enemies. Lofa and Lampi pried him off his intended prey, but not before Modga's eyes had gone back in his head and he was making feeble rattling sounds in his flattened throat.

"I'll kill him! I'll kill him!" Einka raged, surging valiantly against Lofa and Lampi's restraining arms. "Please let me kill him! It will be a favor to all of us!"

Jafnar helped Modga sit up, wheezing. "What did I say?" he whispered painfully.

"You dolt," Jafnar replied. "I probably couldn't explain it to someone like you if I cared to try. It would've served you right if we'd let him strangle you."

"Has everyone gone crazy?" Modga demanded. "Since Hoggvinn claimed Skyla, Rangfara has been turned upside down. This is quite the last straw for me." He waved one hand toward Einka, who bared his teeth at him in reply.

"Let me kill him!" Einka begged.

Mistislaus came stalking down the stairs from his room above. "Yes, please do," he said. "Let's have all of you kill each other and then maybe it will be quiet enough around here so I can think."

"I will kill him if he ever opens his mouth again in disrespect toward Skriftur," Einka answered fiercely.

"Yes, I give you permission to do that," Mistislaus said. "There are others who grieve for Skriftur, too. His death was senseless and useless even to those who are trying to manipulate everything to their own liking around here. He was a gentle soul who cared only to defend the records he held precious."

Mistislaus settled down beside the fire, thrusting his feet out toward the coals and beckoning for a pot of ale to be fetched. He took a long swig and heaved a deep sigh.

"I wish I dared drink myself insensible tonight," he said, "but I'm afraid I'd wake up dead. Rangfara is not a healthy place any longer."

"I'm tired of standing by helplessly and letting it happen," Jafnar said, striding blindly around the room, sending a stool scuttling with one kick. "What can I do, Mistislaus? I have all this knowledge, but my hands are still tied by everybody else around me. Skyla is there, surrounded by black-hearted Krypplingur and conniving Viturkonur. And Hoggvinn like a blundering ox, embracing the ones he ought to drive out at sword's end and driving out the ones who want to protect him."

"And all for a scroll with some hen scratchings on it," Mistislaus said, narrowing his eyes and gazing into the fire, half-hypnotized. "There's a world of trouble in that scroll, my lads."

"Will it stop the gifting?" Jafnar asked, coming to a halt suddenly, knowing how ale always made Mistislaus wax garrulous when he'd had enough.

"Oh, yes, I'm sure it will," Mistislaus said. "Skriftur knew it, too, which is why he is dead, the old fool. Why couldn't he have let them have the scroll? He could have saved himself. He could have hidden himself."

"And die the death of a coward?" Einka rumbled, his eyes turning to nasty slits. "Skriftur may have been a dried-up old scribe, but he died defending his post. How many Skyldings can you say that about these days? Hah?"

"Do you know what's in the scroll?" Jafnar asked.

Mistislaus shut his mouth with a snap and shook his head warningly. "I was there when it was made," he said. "Believe me, there are things in that scroll, if it ever came to light, that would curl your hair and curdle your blood. Stop the gifting? I should say it would. It'll stop a lot of other things, too." He paused to take another long swig from his pot, perhaps realizing he was waxing a little too eloquent.

"If that scroll will stop the gifting," Jafnar said, "then I am going to find it."

"But how do you know," Ordvar spoke up in a cautious tone, "that it won't just clear the way for Ofarir? You can look at it two ways, you know. Perhaps Ofarir won't be allowed to marry her without a scroll. If you bring it back, you may be frustrating your own purpose."

"If I don't like what I find," Jafnar said stubbornly, "then I'll see to it the scroll gets lost again."

"If only it were that simple," Mistislaus said, shaking his head lugubriously. "Remember, Skriftur died because of what's in that scroll. I don't want the same thing happening to you. That scroll should never have been made, should never have been found, should never have been stolen. Mark my words; the next person to die in Rangfara will have something to do with that cursed scroll."

CHAPTER SIXTEEN

"WHAT EXACTLY IS in the birth scroll that is so dreadful?" Jafnar asked delicately, hoping he had judged the amount of ale in Mistislaus' stomach accurately enough to ensure an answer.

But Mistislaus only eyed him owlishly and retorted, "I'll never tell. I swore I wouldn't breathe a word of it to anybody, and so I won't." With that, his head fell back against his chair and his mouth dropped open in a short salvo of snoring that would shortly lead to his usual cavernous reverberations.

"Which means he doesn't know," Modga said.

"You shut up," Einka said, rearing up again, his eyes still screwed up with rage. "I'm bigger than you now, Modga. I'll never be afraid of you again. I'll rub your face on the ground from here to the rear gate of Rangfara, where they dump the midden."

"Mistislaus does know," Jafnar said. "He'll tell us what we need to know one of these days."

"We? What?" Einka sputtered. "You don't think—you're not about to—I'm not going to be dragged into this. I've already lost one friend because of that scroll."

"Precisely why you should be anxious to help me now," Jafnar said. "Don't you want to avenge Skriftur's death, Einka? You don't intend just to let them get away with it, do you? What sort of apprentice turns his back on his master's murdered body?"

Einka turned pale and clenched his fists. "I'm sorry. That was the old Einka talking. You won't be hearing much from him anymore, but if you do, don't listen. He should have died with Skriftur. The new Einka wants very much to find that scroll and murder whoever's got it."

"Count us in," Lofa and Lampi said.

"And me," Ordvar added.

"Not me," Modga said. "I've got better things to do than get myself killed with a pack of fools. I'd hate to disappoint the lovely Borgildr by my untimely demise."

"Faugh," Einka said. "She doesn't even know you're alive."

"She will, one day," Modga retorted. "If I have to kill myself, she will."

"Hush, enough chatter," Jafnar said, steadying Mistislaus as he sagged dangerously in his chair, threatening to fall into the fire. He glanced around for Illmuri, who was apparently upstairs. Lowering his voice, he continued. "I think we have a pretty good idea of where to start looking for the scroll. Eadgils named all the people today who would want to steal it and stop the wedding. I was privileged to be included in that number, and so was Mistislaus. I know I haven't got it, and neither does Mistislaus. Now, then, who was the loudest today to object to the gifting without the scroll?"

"There was a lot of shouting," Einka mused.

"Vigulf," Ordvar said. "From where I stood, I heard him the best. He sounded pretty angry."

Modga hitched up one eyebrow in the most incredulous expression he could manage. "You're going to beard Vigulf in his den and demand to know if he stole the scroll and killed Skriftur, just like that?"

"Not if we expect a truthful answer," Jafnar snapped. "I doubt if he'd come right out and admit it if he were guilty, don't you?"

"Vigulf is as hot-tempered as a sow with new piglets," Modga said. "He'll tear your head off and stuff it down your neck if you cross him."

"We won't cross him," Jafnar said. "We'll just go and look in his windows at him. You can learn a lot by spying on someone."

"Oh, splendid!" Modga snorted. "And if you get caught, what are you going to say? You were looking for birds' eggs on the rooftops, maybe? If anyone asks me, I'll say I had no idea you were going to do something so stupid."

Nevertheless, Modga was in Jafnar's number as they scaled the walls and crept across rooftops to get near Vigulf's windows. Illmuri was asleep upstairs, and Mistislaus was snoring earnestly in an alcoholic stupor.

Haggashol was a run-down and gloomy house that Vigulf

and Mord Fidla shared with various red-haired offspring of different sizes and uniformly surly dispositions. Perhaps with his ambitions lying in the direction of the Hall of Stars, Vigulf never cared much for the idea of setting up an establishment of his own, thinking that one day a chance accident or sudden illness could remove Hoggvinn's obstruction of Asi's succession to the chieftain's seat. Thus far Vigulf and his brood were still waiting, camping out in a smoky old ruin of enormous size where there was plenty of room for his six or eight sons plus the livestock, who all lived in happy camaraderie in the lower rooms, while Vigulf and Mord Fidla occupied the second story.

Even at midnight, fires were burning and voices were upraised in quarrelsome shouts, and the pitiful wails of a young captive incarcerated in the bathhouse for some crime resounded in vigorous protest against the bleak walls of Haggashol. The house and outbuildings were like a small fortress with the gates shut and locked. Jafnar remembered this house from his wild-boy days. A conglomeration of Krypplingur had moved into it, raising such a stench with their garbage and skins and bones that even the wild boys had been repulsed. More than a few human carcasses were found on their midden pile, unfortunate wretches who had dared gamble with the Krypplingur at games whose stakes were higher than they could afford to pay with anything less than their blood.

Jafnar climbed onto Einka's shoulders, secured a rope atop the wall, and scrambled up. In a moment the others had climbed up behind him, including Thogn, who amiably let them push and pull him around as if it were just another lark.

"I don't know why you had to bring him," Modga growled. "He doesn't even know what we're doing."

"Thogn deserves an outing once in a while," Ordvar declared.

Einka had to be hauled up last, with much puffing and cursing, but he was determined not to be left behind.

They crept along the wall and onto the roof of a barn, where Modga promptly stepped on a thin spot in the turf and fell through up to his waist. Below, forty or fifty dogs commenced barking and howling frantically, lunging against their chains with a ferocious clatter. Jafnar and his brothers flattened themselves on the roof as a door was flung open with a crash. The voice of Mord Fidla bellowed through the dark, silencing the dogs except for a chorus of resentful whining and a rebellious bark or two. Growling and snarling, Mord Fidla stalked into the barn and distributed rough justice with his foot, raising some terrified yelps and yips. When discipline had been thoroughly established, he stomped back into the house and shut the door with another crash.

Just as they rose to their feet, a bell clanged at the front gate, where a dark, cloaked figure stood in the light of the guttering lamp over the door.

"Illmuri!" whispered Jafnar. "Traitorous dog! He's hot on the scent of that scroll himself."

"Halloa, who's that?" came a gruff shout from within.

"Illmuri. I'm befogged and I saw your light. Is there a thrall I could borrow to light me home to Athugashol?"

"Come in," growled Mord Fiala, and the door was shut.

Jafnar proceeded from the barn roof to the back of the house, where an addition had burned down long before, with the roof collapsed in a heap of turf. From the top of the wall they were able to climb onto another roof, which gave them access to the windows. A light burned dimly in the far end window, so Jafnar led the way toward it.

"This has been easy so far," he whispered to Ordvar.

They peered into a small barren room under the eaves, where a small fire burned in a makeshift hearth, the smoke trickling out through a convenient hole in the roof. A table sat in the center of the room, and a tall chair was drawn up to it, where a shadowy form sat before a half-eaten meal. Jafnar ducked down involuntarily, not seeing Vigulf at first, then slowly ventured another peek. Nothing in the room had changed a particle.

Suddenly a hand closed over his shoulder, and he nearly yelled with fright. It was only Thogn, his eyes gleaming in the faint light.

Jafnar ventured another peek, with Thogn leaning over his shoulder and breathing loudly. He could see Vigulf just sitting there, staring straight at him, without the faintest twitch of movement. His expression was startled, and his hand looked as if he had been reaching out or pointing when it had sunk to the table. His chest was covered with blackened gore, and his throat had been shredded.

A sickening wave of disorientation struck Jafnar. For an instant he saw the face of Hoggvinn staring vacantly back at him. Then he blinked, and it was Vigulf once more.

"He's dead," Thogn said in a normal tone, as if all pretense of silence were now useless.

"Dead?" Einka gasped.

"The Kellarman," Thogn said. "He'll steal your soul and eat it for his breakfast."

"What about the scroll?" Einka squeaked with a little moan, sounding very much like the old and despised Einka.

"I don't know," Jafnar said grimly. "I think we're too late. Someone else has been here ahead of us. Stay here, all of you; I'm going to do a little searching."

Jafnar climbed through the window, ignoring the hisses and sputters of protest from Modga. In moments he was able to tell that virtually every object in the room had been turned over or pushed around, as if someone had already searched it thoroughly. His neck hair bristled the entire time, with Vigulf sitting there, still startled and still pointing his finger at someone—in an angry remonstrance, no doubt, at being intruded upon. The assailant had struck so fast that Vigulf probably had not known what had killed him.

Without warning, heavy boots clumped up to the door and Mord Fidla strode into the room without so much as a knock or a by your leave. He found Jafnar with one leg out the window and one still inside, a dubious position indeed for any guest, let alone an uninvited one. With a roar, Mord Fidla plunged across the room and dragged Jafnar back inside by one foot, barely snagging him as he was diving out the window.

"Stop, thief!" Mord Fidla bellowed, setting all the dogs barking hysterically once more, or possibly it was the rest of the Skjoldurssons scuttling across the roof again that set them off.

"I'm not a thief!" Jafnar bellowed back. "The thing I came to steal is already gone! Your brother is dead, you great fool!"

Mord stared at Vigulf for an instant.

"Murderer!" he then roared, dragging Jafnar halfway across the room by one leg. "Help, help, help ho! Murder!" There was an axe standing in one corner that he was eager to get his hands upon. Jafnar, divining his intention, struggled and kicked and pulled in the opposite direction.

"Halloo! What's this all about?" a voice demanded suddenly. It was Illmuri standing in the doorway. For the first time, Jafnar was actually happy to see him.

"He's murdered my brother!" Mord Fidla bawled, still in a fury as he struggled toward the axe, keeping a hold on Jafnar's ankle all the while.

"Silence!" Illmuri commanded in a voice that quelled even the wrath of Mord Fidla. "We'll have a look here and determine whether or not Jafnar is our murderer."

Mord Fidla released his hold on Jafnar and stood back to look at Vigulf. Illmuri prodded at him scientifically, lifted his hand and let it fall, and tried to listen for sounds of breathing.

"He was like that when I came," Jafnar said. "If I were to kill anyone, you'd find him with a smashed skull or a knife in him or blood everywhere and signs of a terrible battle. Look at him. He went so suddenly, his face didn't even change expression."

"Yes, I can see that," Illmuri said on an impatient note. "This happened hours ago. The blood is dried."

"Something strange is going on here!" Mord Fidla gasped, backing away and clutching at an amulet hanging around his neck. A sudden sheen of sweat burst out on his beefy red face.

Jafnar continued rapidly. "This is no ordinary murder. Somebody with powers did this. You know I don't have powers. I couldn't possibly have done it. I just came here to spy in the window at him. I thought maybe he might have stolen Skyla's scroll. It looks as if someone else had the same idea sooner."

"And someone else murdered him?" Illmuri replied. "I'm afraid it doesn't look that way to the casual observer."

"What do you suppose he was pointing at?" Jafnar was more than glad to change the topic of conversation.

"People point for many reasons," Illmuri said. "Anger, discovery, throwing someone out, astonishment—where are the rest of your brothers?"

"Halfway home by now, I should think," Jafnar said, waggling one shoulder toward the window.

"All of you will be blamed for the death of Vigulf," Illmuri said. "This is exactly the reason Mistislaus told me to keep you out of trouble. He knew you'd do something stupid like this. Clever of you to have gotten him drunk."

"We didn't murder Vigulf," Jafnar said. "He's our chieftain's brother. It would be suicide. Consider how many sorcerous and wizardous individuals are in Rangfara right now. Any one of them could have done this."

"But I didn't see them," Mord Fidla said in a savage rumbling voice, pointing a huge finger in Jafnar's face. "I came into the room, and there you were, trying to run away. Hoggvinn's going to hear about this, and he's not going to be any more convinced than I am that you didn't kill Vigulf.

Eadgils says you might have killed Skriftur, and a killer usually kills again."

"I'll take charge of him," Illmuri said to Mord Fidla. "Hoggvinn must of course be notified. I don't want anything touched until Mistislaus comes in the morning to look. You stay here tonight and watch in case something more is going to happen in this room."

Mord Fidla clutched his amulet anxiously, peering around uneasily at the dark corners of the room. "It might have been the snow lynx," he whispered.

"Anybody can haggle a throat that way," Jafnar retorted in sudden alarm. Visions of Skyla that didn't bear thinking about popped into his head. "There are plenty of people in Rangfara who would want us to blame the lynxes."

It was a grim party that assembled in Vigulf's house at morning's earliest light. Mistislaus, red-eyed and rumpled, and Hoggvinn, pale as death himself, were accompanied by Skjoldur, whose state was near distraction.

Last to arrive was Eadgils, who serenely studied the stiffening corpse of Vigulf, wandered around the room without touching anything, then strolled to the window where Vigulf was pointing and gazed out of it for a long time while he smoked his pipe. In his most judicial voice he announced, "We shall begin this court of inquiry," and seated himself in a chair across from Vigulf.

"I can't believe it," Skjoldur blustered when Jafnar and his brothers presented themselves haughtily as the falsely accused murderers. "Is this what happens when I leave you without proper supervision?" He fired an accusatory glare at Mistislaus. "I might have known something disastrous was going to happen."

"Don't blame it on me," Mistislaus said. "They got me drunk and stole away. The last thing I remember was sitting down with a pot of ale by the fire."

"I don't believe they could have done it," Illmuri said. "This was done by someone with powers."

"That will be determined by those more knowledgeable than yourself," Mistislaus snapped testily.

"I wonder what it was he was pointing at," Eadgils mused, studying Vigulf across the table from him as if he were a dinner guest. "If he were alone, would he have pointed out something to himself? I don't think so. One doesn't generally point unless another person is present for something to be pointed out to."

"But what about the scroll?" Hoggvinn demanded. "Was it here? Do you think my brother was the one who stole it? He wanted the gifting stopped. He might have done it."

"Someone else evidently thought so, too," Mistislaus said. "Someone besides Jafnar. Someone who acted more swiftly upon his suspicion. I've known this lad all his life. He's not a killer."

"It's true; I wanted the scroll, if Vigulf had it," Jafnar said. "I would have done my best to steal it. But I don't think it's here."

"Very well," Eadgils said. "You may go, Skjolderssons. I wish to speak to Kraftugur next. Notify the lady Logregla that I wish to speak to her, also."

"What about Alvara?" Jafnar demanded. "She could have done this. What about her?"

"Alvara is not opposed to the wedding," Eadgils said. "We are having trouble among those who wish it stopped. You are a nasty and rivalrous group, it seems."

Jafnar turned his back on them a moment to show his utter contempt. Facing the window, he stared out angrily a moment, wondering what awful apparition it must have been that had faded away on Vigulf's dying eyes. Suddenly his own eyes focused on a patch of green moss growing in a velvety tuffet between the stones of the window ledge. Pressed perfectly into the soft green velvet was the track of a large cat—a lynx.

Speechless, he turned and bumbled out of the room quickly, his thoughts whirling. Thought of Skyla seared his brain, refusing to be denied or ignored. Skyla coming to get her scroll, coming to silence the opposition to the gifting. Skyla killing Hoggvinn. His ears roared so that he could scarcely hear the inanities everyone was babbling as he left Vigulf's house and found his way to the street.

If news of Skyla's gifting was cause for excitement and celebration, the murder of Vigulf was even more thrilling. Skriftur's death was interesting, too, but it simply did not merit the attention that the brother of the chieftain demanded. People stayed up late at night, speculating, and they barred their doors more securely than before and started an uneasy search for forgotten lucky amulets to protect them from the dangers of the unseen realm.

"Now we're suspected of being murderers," Modga moaned,

peering around blindly for a wall to pound his head against. "Our real lives are over, you realize. We're going to be outlawed, outcast, and homeless. We're going to be hated, hunted, and despised. We'll die like dogs in the ditch."

"No, we won't," Jafnar snapped fiercely. "This time it's going to be different. We'll survive this time."

While his brothers lamented their fate by eating everything they had bought in the Skurdur, Jafnar watched the Hall of Stars out the little slit window upstairs. The courtyard was jammed with idle gogglers who had come to hang around and gossip, waiting for any more snippets of news to inflate. The Drottningur paraded out to the bathhouse. The Viturkonur were admitted to the hall, and the door was shut fast against the curious and the suspect.

"Jafnar! What have you done?" Modga demanded. "If something happens which comes between me and Borgildr because of your insane visions and prophecies, I'll just kill you, Jafnar."

"I doubt if you'll have that privilege, with so many others vying for the honor," Ordvar said.

Vigulf's body was entombed in the Kjallari with all due honor and solemnity, commemorated by riotous drinking and singing by night. Eadgil's court of inquiry continued. Posted guards kept the curious onlookers at bay, but once anybody came out of the hall and passed into the courtyard, he was considered fair game for questioning.

Jafnar took up lurking around the outer gate to the Hall of Stars, waiting to hear word about the inquiry. According to those privileged few who were allowed to pass the gates, no one who favored the gifting was under question.

Finally Skjoldur emerged at suppertime, bent on some errand in the Skurdur before darkness fell.

"Don't you think it's a bit strange Eadgils isn't questioning Alvara, since everyone else is being questioned?" Jafnar demanded, falling into step beside Skjoldur. "It makes sense that they would want to eliminate anyone who was opposed to the gifting. Neither the Viturkonur nor the Krypplingur have had any great reputation for dealing kindly with their opposition in the past. So why does everyone believe they can restrain themselves now?"

"Because they're both closely allied with Hoggvinn now, you great dolt," Skjoldur explained with his usual patience. "Nobody is going to attack Hoggvinn's allies. To question them is to question Hoggvinn himself. Besides, it's slowly coming to light that our dear lady Logregla was hatching a plan to kill Hoggvinn as well as Skyla. So it appears we're on our way to solving the riddle."

"Logregla a killer?" Jafnar uttered a mirthful bark. "That's ridiculous, and you know it. Can you imagine her plotting a murder? She wouldn't know what to wear."

"She confessed it herself, with a great deal of weeping and repenting. She's so jealous of Skyla, she'd like to kill her. Hoggvinn forgave her, of course."

"He's not out of danger yet," Jafnar said.

Skjoldur sighed and stopped in his tracks. "Was there anything else you wished to quarrel about? Good, I'm on my way, then. I want to get off the streets before it gets dark, now that we have murderers among us." His tone was light, but the glance he cast over his shoulder glittered with alarm.

"You might come by for supper anytime you wished," Jafnar said.

"Not as long as Mistislaus and that Illmuri creature are in my house," Skjoldur replied. "I've got to do my best to protect what little remains of my reputation. It doesn't look at all good for you to be suspected of Vigulf's killing. People might start to think I had something to do with it."

Jafnar fell into step with him, since he seemed bent on hurrying away to the Skurdur. "Anyone who knows you knows your first duty is always to Hoggvinn," he said. "And the ties that bind you are stronger than fealty. There's nothing like secrets to bind a friendship—or lead to murders, like Vigulf and Skriftur. Something in Skyla's scroll killed them, Pabbi, and I think you know what it is."

Skjoldur blanched pale as a fish belly. "Ridiculous. It's just an ordinary birth scroll. I wish you'd stay out of this. Bungling around the way you are is just going to make everything worse."

"Then perhaps you'd better tell me what's in the scroll. You know, don't you?"

"I know nothing. Now, if you're quite finished harassing me—"

"Everyone who seems to know gets murdered. One side wants to kill you because they think you can stop the gifting and won't, and the other side wants to kill you because they're afraid you will. Be careful, Pabbi."

"What rot. No one's going to kill me. Rangfara is a civilized place, and we are civilized people." His snort came off somewhat lacking in conviction.

"Civilized is not a word I'd apply to the Krypplingur and Viturkonur," Jafnar said. "I wouldn't trust them if I were you."

Skjoldur shook his head and swatted imaginary foes from the air with one hand. "Go away. I don't wish to hear such talk, especially from someone who fancies himself a prophet. By saying such things often enough, you make them come true."

"By ignoring them, you don't make them untrue," Jafnar replied. "Why won't you let me help you? Tell me what's in that scroll so I'll know how to defend you, and against which enemy."

Skjoldur halted a moment, clenching his fists. "There's nothing to tell you. Now, if you're done wasting my time, I'll be going. I don't know what Rangfara's coming to. It's become a crazy place since all this gifting business started. Killings, thievings, and people are afraid to walk the streets at night. And worst of all is my own son turning into a prophet. There's nothing you or anyone else can do. Now leave it alone before you get into worse trouble."

CHAPTER
SEVENTEEN

WHEN JAFNAR RETURNED to Athugashol, he shouldered open the door and entered upon a peaceful scene of general dissolution and waste. The other Skjoldurssons were comfortably arranged around the table and on the benches and chairs, eating and drinking as if they planned on dying the next day and were fearful they hadn't met their lifetime food quotas.

"We may be hanged tomorrow as murderers," Modga greeted him with a wave of a gnawed leg bone of some creature, "so we may as well enjoy ourselves while we can. Everyone is saying we look like the most likely suspects."

"We'll be famous killers," Einka said, "without even going to all the trouble of killing somebody."

Ignoring them, Jafnar galloped up the stairs to Mistislaus' quarters in the upper story. He found the wizard glumly contemplating a blackened pot of something hissing and plopping over his little hearth. In a shadowy corner Illmuri sat poring over a large book with a stub of candle in his hand, scarcely glancing up at Jafnar's entrance.

"We're going to be outlawed," Jafnar said. "Like we were on the other strand. Outcast, unwanted, despised wild boys, hunted and killed by their enemies. I can see everything falling into place, going back to the way it was then. You'll kill Kraftugur, Skyla will kill Ofarir, Ofarir will come back as Kraftugur, he'll kill you, and Alvara will kill us. I thought we were going to make it different this time."

"It's like a huge, swift, strong river," Mistislaus said in a leaden tone as he poured out the sinister black concoction. "We can't fight against it. We're swept away helplessly, like little sticks."

"Mistislaus! We can't just let everything run its same course again!" Jafnar protested. "We must do something!"

"When no one will listen to a word of what we say? When they all seem totally bent upon their own destruction? What are we to do, Jafnar?"

"I don't know. There must be something. You're the great wizard. You tell me."

"Alright, I will. I'm going to drink myself senseless and let you all go your merry way to destruction. I certainly don't care. I'll be dead soon and won't have to be around to witness it."

Drinking himself senseless was exactly what he proceeded to do, and with no good humor about it, either. To Jafnar's disgust, his brothers were content to follow Mistislaus' example.

Jafnar turned away, cold with fury. The only one of them who seemed sensible was Thogn, who sat in a corner humming and whispering and making little creatures out of mud balls.

"You fools! You deserve what's coming to you!" he said to no one in particular, and stomped out of the house. Hearing Guthrum in the stable singing Dvergar dirges, he stalked out to the stable and found the dwarf with his feet in the coals and a pot of dark bitter Dvergar ale in his hand.

"We're all doomed," Jafnar said by way of greeting, and sat down in the cold stone horse trough with his chin in his hands.

Guthrum nodded lugubriously and offered him ale. "I've always known that," he grunted in dour reproof.

To his everlasting disgust, Illmuri followed him and sat down beside him in the horse trough.

"You mustn't give up," he said.

"There's no hope," Jafnar retorted bitterly. "We're on a road, and we can't turn around. The destination is death and destruction. I can't make them see anything—not even Mistislaus, and he knows."

"Let me help."

"You? You're a traitor. You sold us out."

"I also lasted longer than you. I've seen the end of the story, which you have not, and neither has Mistislaus."

"Hah. Hum," Jafnar muttered. "That's true."

"You say I was a traitor. How was it that I betrayed you?"

"You sold us to a slave trader. As a result, Otkell the Slaver and all of us were killed. You know all this. You were there, and I'm sure you remember."

"Who was your killer?"

Jafnar's temples stabbed with pain as he struggled with the memories that ought to have been buried on the other strand that had created them.

"I'm not sure," he said through clenched teeth. "There are barriers I can't cross."

"Perhaps time proved me otherwise than a money-grubbing traitor and seller of human flesh," Illmuri said. "It is possible I thought to send you away to a safer place than Rangfara. On some strands our resolutions are stronger, our intentions more capable of becoming reality. On other strands we are more helpless in the stronger flow around us. You must know that we are destined to struggle together with the fate of the Skyldings."

"If I were to trust you and ask your advice . . ." Jafnar's words stumbled to a halt, and he eyed Illmuri sidewise, squinting distrustfully.

"Get the scroll. You've got to go back and search Vigulf's house."

"What? Haven't the killers got it?" Jafnar demanded. "Isn't that what they killed Vigulf for?"

"The only person who truly knows why Vigulf was killed was the person who killed him," Illmuri said.

"The place was torn up by a search," Jafnar said. "I never imagined the killers didn't find what they were looking for. Perhaps we interrupted them before they found it. Perhaps it's still there. But what if we get caught? That would just about put the cap on everyone's suspicions that we murdered Vigulf."

"Then we'd better not get caught, had we?" Illmuri said agreeably.

The ruins of Vigulf's house lowered dark and repellent. Mists were oozing out of the Kjallari vent holes and clinging to the ground like Drottning veils. Jafnar shuddered in the dank atmosphere, brushed with a wave of gooseflesh. Rangfara had a new and ominous feel to it. He no longer felt safe and sequestered here in the arms of his clan and kin.

Illmuri stood up and beckoned to the others, who waited with considerable reluctance on the far side of the wall for further instructions. After a great effort, they boosted Einka up and over with an alarming crash.

"I told you this was insane," Einka hissed after Jafnar had hauled him out of the underbrush. "We could get killed, you know!"

Modga joined the conversation after a graceless descent into the underbrush. "I really don't see why we have to make this dangerous and foolhardy journey in the dead of night among the depraved Krypplingur to search Vigulf's house. With so many people searching for the scroll, I'd say we've lost our chance."

"Perhaps they missed it," Jafnar said. "As long as there's a chance, we've got to search that house. It could be anywhere, not just in the room where Vigulf died. Is everyone here?" He counted swiftly. "Good. Let's go. Modga, keep your eye upon Thogn."

Moaning because he knew it was a lost cause to argue, Modga trailed the others into the house. They started in the scullery, looking in pots and boxes and barrels and chinks in the stones.

"Our father wouldn't approve of this," Modga grumbled. "It makes us look remarkably guilty."

"That's all you're concerned about, the looks of things," Einka answered. "Like your dear Borgildr. Nothing to her but looks. Coldhearted and empty-headed Drottning."

"An excellent match for our little brother Modga," Lofa added with a wicked snicker, giving Modga a friendly wallop that nearly flattened him.

"You might be bigger, but I'm still older than you," Modga snarled. "One day you're going to regret that. The two of you will be my thralls and live in miserable huts while I have a grand hall!"

"You won't live at all unless you find the scroll and stop the gifting," Illmuri said. "I suggest you quit the clowning and get to work."

While the others searched, Thogn obediently followed Modga around and held a light, humming to himself or performing some monotonous repetitive motion until someone became annoyed with him and told him to stop.

"Alvara," Thogn murmured from the vicinity of a window, but no one paid him any heed.

"Look at this!" Modga exclaimed in considerable excitement. "Mord Fidla left half a loaf of stale bread! I can't believe he'd be so wasteful!"

"Alvara," Thogn hummed, nodding his head. "Alvara."

"For leaving in such a hurry, they were remarkably thorough packers," Einka observed.

Jafnar idly turned to the small window where Thogn was digging some dirt out of the turf and spitting on it.

"Someone's coming!" he gasped, and the brothers froze.

"Alvara," Thogn said happily. "I told you."

"We're trapped!" Modga blurted out. "She's going to kill us all, tear our throats out, strew our guts—"

"Shut up, Modga!" Einka flared. "Find a place to hide!"

The interior of the house was completely barren of convenient hiding places, being simply built of plain stone and turf.

Furiously Jafnar turned upon Illmuri. "Once a traitor, always a traitor! Was this your plan?"

"Upstairs! We can get out on the roof!" Illmuri said.

Modga led the rush up the stairway through the hole in the ceiling. Jafnar and Illmuri vied briefly to see who would be last, then Jafnar gave in and let him follow. Instead of scrambling through the window and out onto the roof, Illmuri knelt beside the opening to watch a moment. Not to be outdone, Jafnar took his leg out of the window and returned to kneel beside him.

Alvara entered the room below with a small lamp in her hand, her face hidden in the shadow of her black hood. Jafnar's vision blurred suddenly, and his head reeled as if someone had struck him a blow. He felt as if he had suddenly been torn forcefully from his moorings in the present and thrust back to the green where Otkell the Slaver had tied his horses and pitched his tent. Jafnar felt the cold shackles around his wrists and ankles. He heard Thogn's dismal moaning and the endless slow tattoo as he banged his head against the side of the wagon in his distress.

Out of the darkness came a shadow, gliding to the edge of the firelight where Otkell lay sleeping in a smelly heap, still clutching his leather bottle. In horror the captives saw the shadow overwhelm Otkell, stilling him forever without a sound, leaving him twitching in the long grass, seeking Hakarl dozing on the other side of the fire, unaware of the swift death that would take him before he could even draw breath for a last scream. Not that there was anyone to heed a scream in Rangfara, with so many voices so frequently raised in terror, duress, and final anguish.

Jafnar yearned to close his inner eye to what came next, willing himself away from the black lynx padding swiftly toward him, teeth parted in welcome, still reeking of fresh blood. As he smelled its breath, knowing there was no deliverance, he willed himself to fall back into the tunnel of time with a sickening spinning sensation. For an instant he wondered how he would ever know where to come out again, but suddenly Illmuri's hand and influence shot out to steady him, pulling him in from the vast spinning web. He found himself kneeling unsteadily on the floor in Vigulf's house, looking down again at Alvara. The vision had taken only moments and had left him gasping and weak as a baby.

Then, from outside, came the sound of a clumsy crash, and everyone jumped. Alvara glided to the window and peeped out for a moment, then silently hurried out the door.

Jafnar heard the faint creak of the front door, then someone came into the scullery, breathing noisily. He unwrapped a lantern, casting far too much light, revealing himself and half the scullery to anyone who happened to be passing by the open doorway.

"Pabbi!" Jafnar gasped, his voice obliterated in the racket Skjoldur made when he blundered into a broken bench. Illmuri's hand clamped Jafnar's arm warningly.

Skjoldur headed straight for the stairs, casting fearful glances all around at the swinging shadows. As he came creaking upward, Illmuri pulled Jafnar to the window, where they climbed out onto the roof and waited for Skjoldur to appear. The light blazed as he entered. He made a quick circuit of the room, then stopped by the cupboard bed, where the searchers had worked off a loose board. With haste he shoved something inside that looked remarkably like a scroll.

Illmuri floated over the windowsill like an owl and seized Skjoldur from behind, strangling any startled cries.

"Pabbi!" Jafnar whispered, following Illmuri and shoving his face close for Skjoldur to recognize. "What do you think you're doing here?"

"Be still!" Illmuri hissed. "And close down that lantern. It's making too much light."

Skjoldur's breath rasped in his throat as he flung off Illmuri's restraining arm. "What are you doing here?" he wheezed at Jafnar, with a wild-eyed glare at Illmuri.

"Looking for Skyla's scroll," Jafnar answered. "And I'm not the first. Alvara was here already. What is this thing you put here?"

Illmuri already had it out, unrolling it. "Hah, it's Skyla's birth scroll," he said. "A pity it wasn't here a little sooner, and someone might have found it and revealed it to Rangfara with the proper fanfare, and the gifting could have continued as planned."

Skjoldur's shoulders sagged. "You mean I'm too late? The killer's already been here?"

"Several of them, I'd bet," Jafnar answered. "Not counting you—unless you killed Skriftur and took the scroll, but I hate to believe it of my own parent."

"Of course I didn't, you dolt," Skjoldur snapped. "But what are you doing here? Everyone thinks you did it, and here you are, looking for that scroll."

"It's almost as incriminating as what you're doing," Illmuri said. "Coming here and hiding a false scroll."

"Ah, well, it might still work," Skjoldur muttered, blinking anxiously as something outside rattled in a thicket, "if you'll just oblige me by discovering the scroll and making the proper fuss about it."

"It won't work, Pabbi," Jafnar said. "Not as long as someone's got that real scroll. Unless, of course, this scroll is exactly the same as the old one. And I suspect it's not, is it?"

"There are things you don't need to know," Skjoldur said loftily, snatching the scroll from Illmuri's hands and rolling it up swiftly. "And now, since you've spoiled everything, I suggest we get out of this dreadful place and return to our homes and beds, where we belong, before something worse happens. You never did satisfactorily explain to me what you were doing here, but I don't expect to get any straight answers from you at this point, standing here and looking like you may very possibly incriminate my name in this heinous plot to destroy the peace of Rangfara by obfuscating Skyla's gifting. I bid you good night, and in the future I urge you to exercise the same discretion which I plan to practice when it comes to choosing my whereabouts."

"No, wait—" Jafnar began, but Skjoldur seized the muffled lantern and plunged downstairs into the darkness.

"Quick, after him!" Jafnar commanded, and they flowed down the stairs in a controlled avalanche. They heard Skjoldur making his way toward the front door, kicking things and cursing as he encountered obstructions.

Muttering angrily about a barked shin, Skjoldur jerked open the door, revealing a paler square of darkness. An invisible hand seemed to grip him, jerking him like a hanged man at the end of a rope. His hands flailed, and he uttered a choking rattling sound.

"Fara af stad!" Illmuri thundered, shoving Jafnar aside with a powerful sweep of his arm.

Skjoldur fell to the earth in a heap. Illmuri charged past him, his staff gripped in one hand as he scanned the dark courtyard.

"Pabbi!" Jafnar knelt beside him, ignoring the pool of spilled oil warming one knee. Skjoldur stared skyward, unblinking and pale. Then he gasped for air.

"Great Hod," Skjoldur said, feeling his throat with both hands, patting his face, and feeling his earlobes. "I was dead for an instant. I saw myself standing there, stiff as a stockfish. I was in the realm of shades and shadows. A good thing you came after me," he added in dawning surprise. "Someone wishes me dead. I was nearly murdered just now. Did you see who it was?"

"Any sign of anyone?" Jafnar asked as Illmuri scanned the shadowy courtyard.

"No one but your brothers hiding under a dung cart on the other side of the wall," Illmuri said. "Come along. Let's get out of here before our killer decides to try again."

Taking Skjoldur firmly by the arm, Illmuri piloted him out of Vigulf's courtyard into the cobbled lane beyond and pointed him in the direction of the Hall of Stars.

"We'll see you home safe," he said. "Come along, the rest of you," he added in the direction of the manure cart. Sheepishly, the rest of the Skjolderssons crawled out, brushing off their clothing self-consciously.

"We waited for you," Lofa said with a grin.

"This won't do at all," Skjoldur said, pinching his nose in distaste. "As if your situation weren't messy enough without hiding under a dung wagon."

"Alvara tried to kill Pabbi," Jafnar said.

"Nearly succeeded, too," Skjoldur added importantly.

"Then what are we waiting for?" Modga demanded. "Let's tell Hoggvinn she is the killer and be rid of her."

"It's hardly that simple," Illmuri said. "Did anyone actually see her do it? We can't afford to annoy the Viturkonur with false accusations. Besides, the cloak of darkness could have concealed anyone."

"The rest of you stay here and watch," Jafnar commanded. "See who else feels compelled to search Vigulf's house tonight. Don't let yourselves be seen."

Modga moaned in abject misery. "Back to the manure wagon," he growled, pushing Thogn ahead of him.

Ducking his head and pulling up his hood, Skjoldur scuttled through the shadows, retreating at a fast clip.

"Pabbi, why were you trying to hide a false scroll?" Jafnar demanded, catching up to him and speaking softly.

"I just want an end to this wretched situation. Hoggvinn and I thought this would settle it quickly."

"I don't see how that would have helped. When the bearer of the true scroll came forward, Rangfara would have been split down the middle, trying to decide who was telling the truth. And it appears to me that you and Hoggvinn aren't on the truthful side."

"Nor have we been for quite some time, I'm afraid," Skjoldur muttered, heaving a weary sigh. "I wish you were out of it. I never dreamed the consequences of what we did twenty years ago."

"You know what's in the real scroll," Jafnar whispered. "And there's something in there you and Hoggvinn don't want known. Have you got the true scroll, Pabbi?"

"No. Next you'll be thinking I killed Skriftur for it. But why would I do that when Hoggvinn could have gotten the scroll at any time? If I were the killer, why would someone have just attempted to send me to Niflheim?" He passed a trembling hand over his brow, his breath catching in his throat. "It's been a good many years since someone tried to kill me. I forgot what an unsettling experience it is."

"Pabbi, let me help you," Jafnar implored. "Tell me what you know so I can protect you."

"Then you'd be in as much peril as I am," Skjoldur retorted. "You're my eldest son. I don't want to risk your neck, too. If something should happen to me, at least I'll have the satisfaction of knowing that you'll carry on our fine old name and fine Skylding blood. Now, then, here we are." They halted at the rear gate of the Hall of Stars, where a pair of Krypplingur gripped their axes and commenced eyeing them suspiciously. "You've seen me safely home, and now I insist you return to Athugashol and bar the doors and set Guthrum on the doorstep. I shall be perfectly safe once I'm inside."

Jafnar thought of the Drottningur and Alvara, all sleeping behind the protective walls and guards of the Hall of Stars. He also thought of his vision of Hoggvinn, dead.

"Don't go in, Pabbi," he said. "Come back to Athugashol."

"Not as long as that traitor Mistislaus is there. Get rid of him and I'll come home, but not until. We shouldn't be seen together." Skjoldur showed the Kryppling guards the signet given him by Hoggvinn, and they let him go in.

Guthrum was already posted on the doorstep, and Mistislaus was inside, snoring mightily in his chair before the fire. His slippers had half burned off unnoticed, filling the house with a terrible reek of burning fleece.

"I can't believe I ever asked a boon of this man," Jafnar grunted as he and Illmuri bore Mistislaus to the bed in the storage room and stowed him there, still unconscious.

"A great wizard, except for this curse of ale," Illmuri said bitterly. "How are we ever going to put a stop to this endless destruction if he keeps getting drunk?"

"It's a riddle," Jafnar said. "If the killer is searching for the scroll, he's going to kill everyone else under suspicion."

"Or does the killer already have the scroll, so he has no need to come searching Vigulf's house for it? Perhaps we ought to examine who was not at the house tonight."

"Herrad? Hoggvinn? Logregla? Ofarir? Because we didn't see them doesn't mean they weren't there."

"Mistislaus?" Illmuri added.

"That's ridiculous! And ungrateful!"

"What has gratitude to do with it?"

"He plucked you up out of oblivion and taught you and made you everything you are. Like he did for me when I was a wild boy. I won't hear of anybody suspecting Mistislaus."

"As angry as you are, I'd say I was just speaking the darkest thoughts in your own mind. You know as well as I do that Mistislaus knows what's in Skyla's scroll. Killing everyone else who knows about it is the best way to protect that secret, as well as its maker."

"Hoggvinn. It always comes back to him."

"Yes, of course. Hoggvinn and Thordis." Illmuri glanced down at Mistislaus, who was snoring mightily in his straw bed. He beckoned Jafnar away and whispered, "Perhaps he's not drunk at all. We left him here alone. He might have followed us to the house."

"I refuse to believe it," Jafnar snapped. "I'd be more willing to believe you're the killer."

"I'm not saying I believe it, either," Illmuri said. "But when it comes to the darkest corners of the human heart, none of us knows each other at all. And what about Skyla herself?"

"What about her?" Jafnar demanded.

"Do you think she truly wants to be Hoggvinnsdottir and

marry the Kryppling? Perhaps she wants out. If there's something in the original scroll to disprove her claim, she would like to know about it. Or even if she doesn't want to get out of the gifting, she'd want the scroll to hide the evidence that she is not Hoggvinnsdottir."

"What rot. I know Skyla. She's a gentle, healing sort of person, not a killer."

"She's a snow lynx and a Viturkona, and bound to do what the Viturkonur tell her. You must look around you on all sides, Jafnar, or you'll be the next corpse we find with its throat slashed out."

"It's not just lynxes who slash throats," Jafnar said. "It could be you with a knife. It could be Kraftugur trying to make the Viturkonur look suspicious. It could be Herrad trying to start a battle with the Skyldings. There's no one I dare turn my back on, including you."

"Yes. Some of us are not what we seem."

CHAPTER
EIGHTEEN

JAFNAR RETURNED TO Haggashol and watched for the rest of the night, but no one came near it. At dawn they all gave it up and went home, in a very poor mood and reeking of the dung wagon. Einka detoured through the Skurdur and brought a large basket full of breakfast, which was summarily devoured before they all fell unconscious.

Jafnar slept awhile, then awoke about midday when Mistislaus bestirred him and his sodden brothers.

"We must get ready for an attack," he announced with an offensively cheery hustle-bustle attitude. "Ordvar, I'm putting you in charge. All of you start gathering weapons and supplies and storing them in easily accessible places. Here in Athugashol will be one place. Get Guthrum to help you with the hauling."

"What attack?" Einka mumbled sleepily.

"The Krypplingur, you oaf," Ordvar growled.

"Gather weapons?" Modga repeated. "What are we going to tell people? Turn over your weapons to us just because we want them?"

"I don't know. Tell them anything you want to. We're going to put them in a place of honor, or hide them from our enemies, or dispose of them as a gesture of peace. Just don't alarm the Krypplingur. We'll make Athugashol into a fortress because it's one house that we know will survive."

Jafnar saw them started on their rounds, grumbling, then told Mistislaus about their search of Haggashol and what they had found.

"Whatever are you trying to kill yourselves so soon for?" Mistislaus demanded with a wrathful snort. The benign sparkle in his eye was replaced by an angry glint. "When it's gold in

228

such a quantity as the Skylding treasure, the ones who covet it will stop at nothing. Some people would walk on a path made of the hearts of their loved ones to get it. Mind you, the rules of common decency no longer apply. But if you want to get killed, that's your privilege, I suppose. Just go on doing what you're doing, and pretty soon I'll be alone here."

Mistislaus went on ranting for a while before Jafnar made his escape. He went to the Hall of Stars and loitered around the gate, listening for gossip. He was treated to a view of the Drottningur parading to the bathhouse. Skyla must have been with them, but he couldn't recognize her. With a shudder, he thought of the bloody cloaks stuffed in a barrel at Athugashol and wondered if the lynxes had found prey again the previous night.

Skjoldur came out, pushing his way impatiently past the guards and making long strides down the street toward Athugashol. Jafnar hurried to catch up.

"Where's Mistislaus?" Skjoldur demanded the instant Jafnar made his presence known. "I hope he's sober today. We've got a tremendous problem."

"The last time I saw him, he was alchemizing something upstairs. He seemed sober enough."

"I've told him a thousand times I don't want his experiments in my house. He's going to set it on fire one of these days."

"Don't worry. Athugashol will be standing when the Hall of Stars is nothing but ruins."

"Don't say such things! I don't want to hear it!"

"Whatever is the matter?"

"We are in the middle of a serious predicament. I don't know how we're going to come out of this mess with the Krypplingur."

"I told you that long ago."

"Hush! That's all I'm going to say."

They found Mistislaus puttering over his hearth, humming some iteration over and over in a monotonous drone like a hive of bees on a hot summer afternoon. Illmuri sat at a table near a window, laboriously copying something out of a shabby book.

"Mistislaus, I must talk to you." Skjoldur flung himself down in a chair, then leapt up and stalked around the cramped room rather blindly, peering out the windows suspiciously. Jafnar sat down and waited.

"I was nearly murdered last night because of that scroll."

Mistislaus hitched one eyebrow a notch higher. "So? I should care what happens to you?"

Skjoldur glanced around at Jafnar and Illmuri. "I want to talk to you alone."

"Your son and my apprentice probably know more about this than you do."

Skjoldur glared at them a moment. "Well, then, what passes in this room goes no farther. We shouldn't have done what we did, Mistislaus."

"Tell me something I don't already know."

"We're both in danger. You and I are the only ones who can stop that gifting or vouchsafe for certain that Skyla is the Viturkonur child. Don't you see how that places our gullets on the chopping block?"

"Yes, of course. That's why I'm going to leave Rangfara tomorrow."

"You can't go off and abandon me to deal with this alone! Someone already tried to kill me last night. They'll try again, and they'll try to kill you, too. We must do something, Mistislaus."

"Yes, we must, and you know what it is."

"I do?"

"We must do the right thing. We have to stop the gifting. Your phony scroll will fool no one."

Skjoldur took a double handful of his own hair. "And infuriate the Viturkonur and the Krypplingur? I can't think of a better way to start a clan war. Mistislaus, you can't oppose this gifting and expect Rangfara not to be torn asunder. Help me silence the opposition. Think of something that will render this alliance somehow palatable to most of the Skyldings."

Mistislaus heaved a deep sigh and rolled his eyes in the direction of Jafnar, listening intently from his chair.

"Does this mean we're friends again?" Mistislaus asked.

Skjoldur sputtered furiously, his eyes bulging with choler. "We've always been friends and always will be, you great dolt! Now help me, Mistislaus."

"I shall do all I can," Mistislaus said, but the knots and creases in his brow were deeply troubled.

"And something else," Skjoldur continued. "Herrad's disappeared."

"That's bad news?" Jafnar asked, unable to restrain a sudden surge of irrational hope. "Then the gifting is off. Maybe he's gone home."

"No. He took about six men last night and went down into the Kjallari. It seems he was doing a bit of unauthorized exploring."

"Looking for the treasure he thinks he's going to get his greedy paws on when Ofarir marries Skyla," Mistislaus said.

"Well, some people might think so," Skjoldur said. "I'm personally unwilling to believe the worst about somebody until I have more proof."

"Even a Kryppling?" Jafnar asked.

"Faugh!" Skjoldur said. "If you want to make yourself useful, why don't you join a search party instead of eating me out of house and home like a swarm of pestilential locusts? We've got to find him and hush this up. We've already had one murder down in the Kjallari. Herrad being killed would put Ofarir in the chieftain's seat, and Ofarir's nothing short of a mad dog."

"Herrad will be found, but what you find with him isn't going to make you happy." Jafnar's head was beginning to roar with prophetic flames, and his voice sounded strange to his own ears. "He's been hurt, bitten by one of the creatures of the Kjallari. His leg—the left one—will begin to swell and suppurate while his body is wracked with devouring poison. The day will come when no one dares go down into the Kjallari. Skyldings will throw their abundant dead down the old well, which only gives the Kellarman more fodder to work with."

"You're mad!" Skjoldur sputtered, starting to stalk away. "Stay away from me! And begin to consider changing your name. I don't want a prophet for a son!"

Jafnar caught the tail of his long hood, bringing him up short on a tight rein. "And if I'm right? Will you want a prophet for a son then?"

"I don't know," Skjoldur retorted. "All this gives me a staggering headache. Rangfara is a crazy place, full of crazy people. I don't know what all this is coming to."

"We do," Mistislaus said, pushing his pot a little farther into the fire. "Have you checked your bowstrings lately, Skjoldur? You used to be an expert marksman with a longbow. How long has it been since you've let fly an arrow?"

"Bah on you and your prophecies!" Skjoldur snorted, striding toward the stairs. "Find Herrad for me and then possibly I'll believe."

Mistislaus pulled his pot off the fire and wiped some soot on his sleeve. Illmuri softly shut his book and watched his master.

"Well. That sounds like a challenge, wouldn't you say?" Mistislaus inquired of no one in particular. He strode to the window and looked out, perhaps seeing visions denied to the lucky masses born without the prophetic eye.

"It isn't a good time for Herrad to die now, in the Kjallari," Mistislaus continued. "Ofarir loves nothing better than warfare. A creature such as he is tolerable only when others with more power keep him tightly leashed and muzzled. He would prefer to attack Rangfara and kill all within, then search for the treasure."

"No one will ever find it that way," Jafnar said.

"Find Herrad, then, and save the lives of your clansmen," Mistislaus said. "The longer he's down there with who knows what unnatural creatures, the less likely he is to survive."

"We'll find him," Jafnar said, mentally cursing himself for dispersing his brothers out over Rangfara. "I'll take Illmuri with me if you can spare him."

"Take him, take him." Waving them away, Mistislaus sat down at the table and unwrapped a skrying sphere. "Now scat. I've got important work to do."

"We're going to search the Kjallari?" Illmuri murmured, following Jafnar into the street outside Athugashol. "Won't there be scores of searchers already going over it inch by inch? Searchers who know it far better than we do?"

"Yes, of course," Jafnar said. "But they aren't going to find him in the Kjallari."

Jafnar commenced his search of Rangfara, methodically examining every vent hole or natural fissure that led down into the maze of tunnels below the city, not stopping even when the night fog oozed out of the low places, wreathing the houses and halls with gloom. The stench of the Kjallari was strong around the vent holes that lent light and air to the tunnels below.

"You must know every hole leading into that place," Illmuri said by way of mild protest when they stopped to rest awhile long after everyone else had left the streets.

"It's important survival knowledge," Jafnar said grimly. "The time is near when the Kjallari starts coming up into the streets."

Many times before he had seen the shadowy figures creeping out of the vent holes, crouching to peer and sniff for prey, then slouching away and disappearing into the maze of houses, streets, and alleys that was Rangfara. In the poorest regions there were agonized screams and disappearances, but no one would care much if a ragged wanderer was plucked from his fetid hut or alleyway and seen no more.

Wearily, longingly, he thought of Athugashol with its fires lit and food waiting, a warm and inviting haven from the bleak memories raging inside his skull. Sighing, he resumed his searching and trudging.

At last he found what they were searching for, where the effluvium from the tanner's establishment trickled into the Kjallari through a natural opening. Jafnar knelt and held his lantern over the tunnel. A long figure struggled in the muck, trying weakly for a handhold in the stinking slime.

"Help me!" Herrad's voice gasped.

Jafnar reached out his hand, bracing himself against the other's greater weight. Together, he and Illmuri hauled the Kryppling out of the shaft to the safer ground above. Herrad groaned like a wounded bear, too weak to do more than lie in a heap, shivering and soaked. One shredded leg dragged behind him, already swollen and oozing a trail of putrescence.

"Go fetch a cart from the tanner," Jafnar said, "and a couple of his big lads to lift him into the cart."

Illmuri dashed away to raise a hullabaloo at the tanner's gate. Herrad raised his head, his eyes fixed in horror on the opening into the Kjallari.

"Creatures," he whispered. "Horrible things. Like no man has ever seen before."

"Where are your men?" Jafnar asked.

"Gone. Dead. Eaten." Herrad tried to move his wounded leg, groaning in agony. "I'm going to die."

"Not just yet, you're not," Jafnar said. "You aren't finished with this game yet. You've got to become far more miserable than this before we're done with you."

Jafnar drove the cart up to the gateway of the Hall of Stars, bellowing furiously for assistance. Groaning and threshing about in animal agony, Herrad was bundled up and carried into the hall by two Krypplingur guards. The event immediately summoned forth an outpouring of general shouting and waking up of servants and messengers and the guests in the main hall. A gifting, two murders, and now Herrad's adventuring in the Kjallari were even greater diversion than any of the guests had hoped for. They immediately began giving advice, generally useless, and doing what they could to get in the way. Skjoldur trotted about, giving orders that no one heeded, until Jafnar collared him and pulled him aside.

"I found him," he whispered. "Right where I suspected he'd be. I myself escaped from the Kjallari once through a sewer drain. Now you must believe I truly know the future."

Skjoldur shook his head in distraction. "I've got to get all the physicians. He mustn't die."

"You've got to summon Mistislaus to treat him. Ordinary physicians are no good at what he's got."

"I don't have time to argue," Skjoldur snapped. "Mistislaus is no physician. We have many famous ones in Rangfara who aren't suspected of being traitors—or charlatans, at the very least."

Jafnar was shuffled aside in the general hubbub as half a dozen physicians were summoned forthwith. The main hall was transformed into a hospital, and nearly every servant and thrall was busied running to and fro fetching supplies, removing tables and benches, and relaying misinformation.

"Whatever is that stench?" demanded Hoggvinn, who still lingered on the physicians' turf like a general who refused to leave the battlefield to the true warriors.

"We don't know," the elder physician replied snappishly. "Now we want this room cleared out at once. We don't need an audience. Everyone out, immediately!"

Banished with the rest into the courtyard, Jafnar found Mistislaus trying to thrash his way forward in the protesting throng clustered around the main door.

"Fools! Let me through!" he sputtered as the tide turned against him, shoving him outside once more. "They've got to let me in! Those bumbling physicians will only waste valuable time and make it worse!"

"It's no good," Jafnar said bitterly. "Can't you see we're fighting the inevitable? We can't change anything, Mistislaus. We can't win!"

Mistislaus puffed himself up and thundered at the door, receiving nothing for his troubles but a good jostling from two Kryppling guards.

"Be off, you old fraud, or we'll throw you over the wall!" one of the Krypplingur snarled, menacing the pressing crowd with a fearsome axe.

"Very well," Mistislaus said grimly, dusting off his hands and rearranging his disordered cloak and hood. "On your heads be whatever falls next. Don't say I didn't try to warn you." He turned on his heel and stalked away, radiating self-righteous wrath.

In two days the questioning about Herrad's injury had cooled somewhat, and to Jafnar's surprise, he emerged as a hero. Skjoldur came bursting in without warning as they were sorting out the heaps of old weapons the brothers had assembled.

"You're being summoned to the hall!" he exclaimed, beaming around at them, almost bursting with excitement. "Come along. Leave all this rubbish and put on your best cloaks. We've spent these last two days thinking of a suitable reward for saving Herrad's life, and the Viturkonur have come up with a splendid idea. You're going to be given Drottningur birthrights, free of bride-price! What do you think of that? Imagine, such an honor for unknown young bachelors! I daresay, in all modesty, my name helped you along a bit, but it didn't hurt one bit your rescuing Herrad from the sewer. Hasten along; we're meeting in the great hall."

"Drottningur birthrights?" Modga gasped, turning pale. "Did you say Drottningur birthrights? All of us? We'll just be handed a birthright and not be expected to pay for it?"

"Yes, you ninny. Now quit muddling around with all this old steel and put on something decent to wear to the women's hall," Skjoldur replied, almost hopping up and down in his impatience lest the capricious Drottningur change their minds.

"This is somewhat of a shock," Jafnar said. "One moment we're under suspicion of murdering Vigulf and probably Skriftur, and now we're being handed the most valuable birthrights in Skarpsey?"

"Oh, all that murdering stuff is forgotten," Skjoldur said impatiently. "Skriftur was an old scribe, and Vigulf was nothing but a thorn in Hoggvinn's flesh. Saving Herrad was a master stroke. Now you've got their undying gratitude forever. Will you please hurry and stop asking questions?"

The Drottningur sat along the walls on the sleeping platforms, tricked out in their best finery. Logregla and the Viturkonur, including Skyla, occupied the place of honor on the dais. Hoggvinn and Ofarir and miscellaneous Krypplingur of high rank, who all looked very similar, sat around the table. Herrad on his bed had been trundled in and placed in a prominent position. To Jafnar's critical eye he appeared far worse than he had two days before, when he had been dragged out of the drainage hole. His skin looked yellow and feverish, and his sunken eyes glittered unhealthily in their sockets.

Ofarir rose to his feet and bestowed his wolfish grin upon Jafnar and his brothers once they were all seated.

"We invite you here to do honor to you for your rescue of my father," Ofarir said, sneering slightly on the last word. "Doubtless he would have perished in a most gruesome and unseemly manner if he had been allowed to remain much longer in the Kjallari. We have thought long and hard upon a suitable reward for your excellent service. We think we have settled upon a prize of lasting value, far beyond mere gold or personal possessions. We have decided that the most suitable and solemn of rewards is the awarding of Drottningur giftings to all the Skjoldurssons."

A gasp and a murmur went through the hall at the magnanimity of the reward.

"Thank you—most kindly," Jafnar said when he could find the words to speak. His ears roared as the visions pressed in upon his brain, images of women and fire and bloodstained clothing and the shadowy forms of lynxes leaping, snarling, and clawing. "We are honored to accept," he continued, hoping his voice betrayed none of his inner turmoil.

Afterward there was feasting and dancing and singing and poetry, none of which Jafnar heeded much. People kept congratulating him and professing their admiration and envy. Modga in particular was beside himself with bliss, certain that the beautiful Borgildr was his at last, and at a bargain price to boot.

As he sat contemplating the scene of his triumph, he thought he had a vision of Skyla stopping by his chair to speak to him without the watchful presence of Alvara to interfere.

"Beware, Jafnar," she whispered.

When he looked at her, he saw blood splattered all over her white embroidered gown and white cloak.

"The lynx stalks tonight," she said, then she turned and was gone. Jafnar turned his head and saw her sitting in her chair, gazing serenely straight forward, without a speck of gore marring her white gown.

"What's the matter with you?" Modga demanded, sitting down beside him on the bench and digging his elbow into his brother's ribs. "You're staring like a stockfish, and you don't look at all pleased or grateful. Don't you realize what we've been given? Young bachelors our age don't have the money to buy a Drottningur birthright unless their fathers are chieftains or warlords. Doesn't your gloomy prophetic nature permit a little natural pride and gloating?"

"You've got nothing worth thanking me for," Jafnar said.

"What! Don't be a fool, Jafnar," Modga exclaimed. "Imagine, being given your choice of a Drottning bride! It's a dream come true!"

With everyone beaming and congratulating, Jafnar wondered how it was possible for him to continue feeling so mean and suspicious. Even Alvara offered him her hand.

"I hope now we'll lay to rest your suspicions of us and the poor Drottningur," she said in a low voice, smiling as if she were being friendly.

Jafnar also smiled. "You forget, I have proof."

"Ah, yes, your prophetic vision. And those bloodstained cloaks you stole, I believe?"

Jafnar maintained his aplomb as his thoughts raced. Hoggvinn must have confronted the Viturkonur with mention of Jafnar's suspicions. But no one had said anything about the cloaks, unless it was their owners themselves.

"Well, perhaps it's time we began anew," Alvara continued. "Put the past behind us, where it belongs. It would be a very nice gesture on your part if you returned those cloaks to their rightful owners."

Jafnar respectfully declined to return the cloaks, and Alvara stalked away with an ugly little scowl.

They returned late to Athugashol, where Mistislaus was still grumping over his sooty little hearth, presumably because he had been specifically not invited to the celebration. Not that he would have attended if asked, but he was still sore about the whole affair.

"They've offered us Drottning wives," Jafnar said. "I don't have a good feeling about this. I saw Skyla trying to warn me, her gown covered with blood. What do you think it means?"

"If you can't figure it out for yourself, you're a sorry excuse for a prophet or a human being," Mistislaus snapped at Jafnar. "Now don't bother me again. I'm going out for the night." So saying, he seated himself at the table and closed his eyes, his lips moving in murmured words of power.

"Wait, Mistislaus; don't leave," Jafnar said. "I've got those cloaks yet. Alvara was asking about them. I think she's planned a scheme of quite a different nature. I'm going to need your help. We might all be in danger."

Mistislaus didn't stir an eyelash. The wizard's ruddy skin gradually turned the cold white of marble. When Jafnar ventured to give Mistislaus a shake to revive him, it was like shaking the hollow shell of a dead person.

"You can't call him back," Illmuri said. "He's gone traveling in other realms."

"This isn't a good time for him to be off wandering around," Jafnar said.

He returned downstairs, where his brothers had been reveling. Someone had brought home a large round cake of plumabrot in celebration, and they had devoured it with large quantities of ale. In short order they were all itching and hilarious, too ill to stand up any longer. When the hallucinations wore off, they collapsed where they were, in chairs, stretched out on benches, curled up on the floor, snoring peacefully.

Jafnar alone remained by the fire, staring into its brilliance and shadow. The tantalizing aroma of plumabrot tickled his nostrils and made his mouth water with craving until every nerve and muscle was crying out for the sweet poisonous plumabrot. Unable to stop himself, he finished off a sizable portion left over in someone's trencher. It filled him with a comfortable glow, and he thought perhaps he had left its ill effects behind him on the other strand.

Behind him, Illmuri's soft boots made a whisper on the stairs as he descended and stood still at the edge of the firelight. The only sound was the hiss and crackle of the fire and the deep breathing of Jafnar's brothers.

"This is just like the old days," Jafnar whispered with a ghost of a chuckle. "My brothers asleep, and me standing watch. You don't belong here, though."

"It has always been my intention to help and protect you," Illmuri said.

"Where has Mistislaus gone?" Jafnar demanded sleepily. "How could he just go off and leave us like that?"

"He's on other strands," Illmuri said. "Looking for hope that this one can be salvaged somehow."

"Fighting against fate," Jafnar said. "Trying to swim against the river."

"Perhaps. But we need such swimmers to make us think it might be possible."

Jafnar couldn't keep his eyes open. He rested his head on the table with a clunk, letting himself fall into a deep and welcome cavern of sleep.

* * *

Everyone in the Hall of Stars knew it was Hoggvinn's habit to retreat to the bathhouse early each morning for a rigorous steaming and switching and general scalding, before a breakfast laden with greasy sausages, pickled trotters, and other juicy items. The bathhouse attendants knew to have the rocks heated and the water ready and the sausages sizzling over the fire at the earliest crack of dawn. Usually the sky was pitch black when they started their preparations.

In the predawn dimness Hoggvinn traversed the ground between the hall and the bathhouse, humming with good cheer and a feeling of well-being he hadn't experienced in years. Even the troublesome murders of his brother and Skriftur could not entirely destroy his hopes for the future. Change of any nature required sacrifice, however painful. He glanced up toward the little tower room where Skyla abided and felt a surge of fatherly protection and pride like a fierce ache in his bosom.

A sense of motion caught the tail of his eye, and he turned to peer into the shadows with a ripple of gooseflesh. Belatedly, he thought that perhaps his old early morning routine might not be particularly safe any longer. Six Krypplingur had been slain by the snow lynx, and six more had mysteriously disappeared in the Kjallari. He supposed that the lynxes had acquired a taste for tough Kryppling flesh and would leave Skyldings alone, but something was definitely stalking him.

A catlike crooning came from the darkness, a soothing call from a mother cat to her kittens. Hoggvinn froze, listening, scarcely daring to breathe. His unblinking eyes discerned a dark form crouching atop a wall, gazing straight toward him, long tufted ears pricking and stumpy tail twitching. He plunged toward the bathhouse and its stout plank door and thick turf walls.

"Father! Wait," a dear soft voice called out.

"Skyla!" he gasped, whirling around. "No! Go back!"

"Why ever?" she asked with a laugh, and came skipping up to his side, slipping her hand into his and leading him along toward the bathhouse.

"Skyla, it's not safe," he hissed. "Go back to your room at once. The lynx is on the stable wall! We'll be safe in the bathhouse!"

"There's nothing to be afraid of," she answered with a laugh. She pushed open the door to the bathhouse and peeked inside. "It looks like your bath is all ready. The rocks are hot, and the water is ready. When you are done, we shall have breakfast together. I shall bring it myself from the kitchen."

He reached out and stopped her as she was about to fly away back to the hall. "Skyla, be careful. I thought I saw the snow lynx."

"Perhaps you did," she said. "The lynx has been the protector of Rangfara in years past, Pabbi, not always the destroyer. I'm certain she wouldn't harm you."

Hoggvinn breathed a little easier. "Maybe it's only the warning of my own death. If I die, you shall inherit the chieftain's seat. The burden of Rangfara will be upon your shoulders. I fear for you, my child. Perhaps this Kryppling alliance is wrong. If I were not here to protect you and your Viturkonur relatives did not defend you, then you would be in terrible danger, my love."

Skyla was very still for a moment. "I have other protectors, Father. If this is what we must do to save Rangfara, then we will do it. And I shall protect you, never fear."

When he looked again, the dark form of the lynx was gone from the wall and the gloom was somewhat lighter. Skyla hurried away, a noiseless shadow in the silvery atmosphere of dawn. Silently he made a resolve to change his bathing schedule. Then he would talk to Jafnar Skjoldursson again as soon as possible.

The sound of soft laughter awakened Jafnar from heavy, troubled sleep, and he opened his eyes to the eerie white light of the full moon shining in through the window. Something brushed past him like a breath of cool wind; still he did not move his head from its resting place on the table. As his eyes focused in the strange silvery light, he saw human figures moving about the room where his brothers slept. They were women in long cloaks, bending over the recumbent forms, laughing softly as they looked down at them. Modga, half awakened, was murmuring, "Ah, Borgildr! You've never looked more beautiful!"

The barrel where he had hidden the Drottningur cloaks lay on its side, with the rest of the incriminating evidence spilling out in a trail across the floor. Jafnar stared frozenly as a mist gathered over the clothing, swirling, picking up the cloak, and building a form to fit it. A young Drottning woman stood there, fastening the brooches of her cloak. As she turned and swirled away, Jafnar saw the streaks of blackened blood smearing the soft white fabric. He noticed then that the women were placing marks on the foreheads of his brothers, a spiral made with something black that he suspected was blood. He sat up then and tried to call out a warning, but his throat was paralyzed in the favorite tormenting fashion of all nightmares, and he was unable to voice a single sound.

The Drottningur turned then and saw him, drawing back with a hiss of alarm. For an instant all their dark eyes were turned toward him, dark holes in the white faces of skulls, all spattered with blood.

"We are your brides," said one, stepping forward with a sinister smile, and the others echoed her with a ripple of chilling laughter. "We came to take you to a celebration feast. You will be the guests of honor."

"No," Jafnar whispered with tremendous effort.

"Take them away, Sisters," their leader said. "A pity they will never awaken and never see their gifting days. But we shall feast well tonight."

CHAPTER NINETEEN

WITH A SINISTER churning of mist the Drottningur shifted shapes, turning into seven lynxes before his eyes. Jafnar struggled to rise to his feet, battling waves of weakness and surges of amazing insight. It was a typical example of the vile effects of the plumabrot, and he bitterly swore he would never touch it again Raising his hand, he opened his mouth to speak the words of power that he knew were within him, but his voice was only a croak.

"Fara birtu!" Someone else spoke the words at the same instant in a voice of power and authority. The moment the words were spoken, he felt a force smite the room a resounding blow, and every piece of pottery and crockery scattered about the table exploded into dust. Every metal object resonated and clattered; the heaps of old weapons set up an unnerving clangor against the stone floor. The sleeping Skjoldurssons leapt up, instantly awake and ready for battle, crashing over chairs and drawing their weapons. Einka snatched up a huge axe with a shout, facing the lynxes with his back braced against the wall.

The lynxes curled their lips and hissed, then vanished like smoke, leaving behind their cloaks and finery upon the floor, as if their owners had just stepped out of them.

Jafnar gaped around at his brothers, and they did the same, as if they weren't quite sure whether they were awake or dreaming.

"Brodir!" Thogn gasped, striding across the room and gripping Jafnar by the arm. "Are you alright?"

"You said the words," Jafnar said before the light disappeared from Thogn's eyes. "Stay here with us, Thogn! We need your help!"

"I can't," he whispered urgently. "Jafnar, the stars will rest upon the well and the chieftain's seat. You must take me there. Cleanse the well of its pollution. Get Skyla away—" The strength and power and light of manhood drained away from him, leaving him again the large, passive child they had always known. He turned away with a yawn, looking for a comfortable place to curl up and go to sleep.

"Thogn!" Jafnar groaned in despair. His brothers commenced an indignant nattering to cover their confusion. Hastily they erased the bloody marks on their foreheads.

"Most peculiar!" Illmuri said, advancing from the shadows to poke warily at one of the cloaks with the end of his staff. "The substance of these cloaks was used to summon the essence of their owners. A devious variant of the sending spell."

"And where were you when we needed a wizard?" Einka demanded, propping his axe negligently in the crook of his elbow.

"Cringing in the shadows," Illmuri said. "It happened so fast, I nearly slept through it. I'm only an apprentice. Mistislaus should have been here."

"What made them go away?" Modga asked. "I heard—I thought I felt—something, I don't know what."

"Lynxes! Our Drottning brides are lynxes?" Lofa and Lampi rumbled, scowling and clutching their axes.

"Someone's trying to kill us!" Ordvar decided in an astonished tone.

"I knew it was too good to be true," Modga said. "After all, it was only Jafnar who saved Herrad, so why did they volunteer to give us all birthrights? Not to mention the fact that we're suspected of killing two people. We weren't even there to help," he added accusingly, turning to Jafnar. "This is all your fault. You should have let Herrad stay there and rot."

"These were Drottningur," Ordvar said on a protesting note, poking at the fine cloaks. "Not Viturkonur. Why are they turning into lynxes?"

"Alvara taught them her trade," Jafnar said grimly. "She must think we're causing her a trifle too much trouble. We're lucky to be alive. You can thank Thogn the next time he's allowed to join us, and you can thank the plumabrot someone thoughtfully supplied us. Otherwise our hearts and livers would probably be roasting by now over a fire somewhere."

"They tried to kill us," Ordvar said. "Hoggvinn, our own chieftain."

"I don't think he's in on it," Jafnar said. "This is Alvara's doing."

"I think you'd better dispose of those cloaks in some safe spot," Einka said, keeping well away from them. "They might come back, mightn't they?"

"Almost certainly, until they catch us unprepared," Jafnar said grimly, prodding warily at one of the cloaks with one toe. "Bundle these things up and lock them in a chest with good stout bands and a strong lock."

They ate a huge breakfast to steady their nerves and were scarcely through it when Skjoldur pounded on the gate, rousing the irascible Guthrum.

"Hoggvinn has sent for you," Skjoldur announced with a proud glimmer in his eye. "At last, the honor that my sons are due. I'm really very proud. What luck you pulled Herrad out of the Skurdur."

"What luck, indeed," Jafnar muttered.

With the escort of Skjoldur to get them within the forbidden walls of the Hall of Stars, they went to see Hoggvinn in the privacy of the bathhouse, carrying the chest with them. Mistislaus was still upstairs at Athugashol, planted at the table, immobile as a tree and cold as a stone.

"So, are you pleased with your reward?" Hoggvinn demanded. "Nothing like an honorable first gifting to set a man up in life. Here, you must share my breakfast. I'll have more sent in."

"We're not in much of a humor for breakfast," Jafnar said.

"Nor am I, if the truth were told," Hoggvinn said, shoving away the greasy sausages in revulsion. "This morning I saw the lynx waiting in ambush for me outside the bathhouse. I'd be dead now if Skyla hadn't come along. For some reason she prevented it from killing me. I didn't much believe your story before about the Viturkonur and the Drottningur shape shifting into lynxes, but now I know lynxes are within the walls of the Hall of Stars. I have only one question: Is Skyla a lynx, also?"

Jafnar looked away from his piercing gaze. "Yes, she is. But you have nothing to fear from her. She isn't like Alvara's lynxes."

"Was she brought here for the purpose of killing me?"

"No. She is here for the purpose of saving Rangfara," Jafnar retorted. "If such a thing is any longer possible, thanks to the Krypplingur you've invited right in."

"Use a little respect!" Skjoldur snapped. "This is your chieftain you're speaking to!"

"We were nearly murdered last night," Jafnar went on. "The time for respect is gone. Open the chest, Einka, and show our chieftain what we've got."

"Cloaks? Well!" Hoggvinn murmured, turning pale as the bloody gowns were spread out for display.

"The cloaks of our brides," Jafnar said. "Last night someone breathed life into them, and the women changed into snow lynxes."

"Great Hodur!" Hoggvinn gasped, restoring his courage with a large swig of ale. "This looks like a conspiracy! I'll send those smirking Drottningur packing! And the Viturkonur—" His courage deserted him at the thought of the Viturkonur, and he looked bleakly at Jafnar. "I should have listened to you sooner. Are you certain Skyla is a lynx?" he added woefully.

"Yes, but not as the Viturkonur are," Jafnar said. "You have nothing to fear from her. She was raised by Mistislaus—remember—who is an enlightened creature. So I regret to inform you, my chieftain, that I respectfully decline your offer of Drottningur women for our wives. We wish to preserve our throats and livers and hearts for a great while longer."

Skjoldur groaned and buried his face in his hands. "This will infuriate the Viturkonur. Not to mention insulting the Drottningur. Are you certain it wasn't just a nightmare? Maybe you imagined it. Maybe you ate something that disagreed with you."

"We did eat plumabrot," Modga said, brightening with hope. "And that stuff never sets well with any of us."

"They were lynxes," Jafnar said coldly. "Not exactly the kind of reward we expected for saving Herrad's life. I have come to warn you, my chieftain. There is a spreading rot commencing in Rangfara. It must be stopped before it spreads too far and destroys us all. Gather up your fighting men and your courage and send away the Viturkonur. Kraftugur should be executed. Perhaps the Drottningur can be saved, or at least some of them. Send the Krypplingur packing before Ofarir takes command. He's a doomed and demented creature who will become a monster."

Hoggvinn looked appealingly toward Skjoldur. "What am I to do now? It's far too late for any of that, without causing a clan war. That's the trouble with you prophets; you're good at seeing the problems, but you never offer any real solutions anybody can live with. There is no way we can get rid of the Viturkonur and the Krypplingur without causing a war. If only I had that scroll of Skyla's, I could end this entire mess. Where is Mistislaus? Tell him I wish to see him immediately."

"He's gone wandering on other strands, and we don't know when he'll be back," Einka said.

"What is in that scroll?" Jafnar asked. "It's something dangerous, isn't it? Some curse or geis on whoever marries her?"

"Perhaps the false scroll would work," Skjoldur suggested with the sheen of desperation on his face.

"No, that's absurd," Hoggvinn retorted, glaring at Skjoldur an instant. "Now I think it's time we concluded this visit. It's not good that I be seen with you. You are, after all, under serious suspicion for two recent murders. Take those bloody things with you. I shall relay your rejection of the Drottningur offer to Alvara and the tjaldi. I think I'd be most reluctant to be in your shoes after this. And when Mistislaus returns, tell him I wish to see him immediately regarding the treatment of Herrad's leg wound. It doesn't seem to be responding to ordinary medical procedures."

"Of course it's not," Jafnar retorted. "Nor will it. All you've done is prolong Herrad's agony with this time you've wasted with ordinary physicians. A wound from a Kjallari creature results in death or madness. I bid you farewell, Hoggvinn. Guard yourself from every quarter. Trust no one and you may survive to see Rangfara saved."

"Saved? I think there is no hope," Hoggvinn said.

Skjoldur followed his sons out to the gate, making small fuming, whimpering noises.

"You fools!" he blurted out. "How could you do this to me? You simply don't know the repercussions that are going to follow. The Viturkonur will be angry. The Drottningur will be insulted. Everyone will wonder what insanity runs in our blood."

"Would you rather they killed us to save your pride?" Einka demanded indignantly. "It would be a great tragedy, all the Skjolderssons killed by the snow lynx. But maybe at least we'd be cleared of the murders of Skriftur and Vigulf, once we became victims."

"Pabbi, someone must reveal what's in that scroll or there may be many more murders," Jafnar said.

"No, no, we mustn't stop the gifting," Skjoldur said. "It's our only hope for survival. Once we're allied with the

Krypplingur by a peace bride, no one will dare attack us. The Viturkonur will see their daughter inherit the chieftain's seat, and the Krypplingur will see Ofarir on that seat."

"They don't want the seat; they want the treasure," Jafnar said, "and they're willing to kill every Skylding and destroy Rangfara stone by stone searching for it."

"Not if we have a peace bride," Skjoldur retorted.

"You overestimate their sense of honor and underestimate their greed and ferocity," Jafnar answered.

"Faugh!" Skjoldur snorted, turning on his heel and stalking away. "On your own heads be your own stupidity. You're going to suffer for your delusions!"

"It was no delusion," Jafnar said, watching him go. "And Hoggvinn has the proof of it in that chest."

"What if Eadgils decides that we are guilty?" Ordvar asked. "That Vigulf business made us look about as innocent as a fox with the hen in its jaws."

"We aren't guilty," Jafnar said. "And we won't act guilty, either."

When they returned to Athugashol, they found Mistislaus cheerily rummaging around for breakfast in the scraps remaining from the brothers' last meal.

"So there you are," he greeted them accusingly. "I daresay you were out frolicking around already."

"Hoggvinn wishes to speak to you about Herrad's treatment," Jafnar said. "We took the cloaks to Hoggvinn. He's resigned himself to inevitable doom. He refuses to reveal what's truly in Skyla's scroll. Mistislaus, you could end this entire situation by simply speaking out."

"I'm sworn not to," Mistislaus said. "Besides, it would get me killed, and I hope you don't want that. Now tell me how you're progressing in your preparations for the battle."

"Is there any hope of avoiding a battle?" Jafnar asked. "The Skyldings haven't been ready to fight for twenty years."

Mistislaus pursed his lips. "I'll speak to Guthrum about the forging and grinding. Then I'm off to see Herrad's wound. The longer we can keep him alive, the longer we're spared dealing with Ofarir."

They busied themselves with the gathering of the weapons. Guthrum fired up his forge and commenced grinding and sharpening and repairing the handles of swords. Bundles of rosewood were gathered for making arrow shafts, and feathers for fletching were harvested from local fowl. The old bowmaker of the Skylding clan had continued his craft long ,ast the time when he was in active demand, and Jafnar discovered an arsenal of beautifully crafted bows waiting to be used. Shields and armor were in plentiful supply but in poor repair, thanks to years of complacent neglect and generations of nest-building, leather-chewing mice.

They bumped into Ofarir with an armload of old swords.

"What are you doing with these old relics?" he sneered, exchanging a leer with his hulking Krypplingur companions. "Starting your own junk heap?"

Jafnar stifled his urge to make a fiery retort. He smiled instead and answered, "Old rusty swords hanging on a wall don't look as nice as sharp shiny ones, so we're taking them to be cleaned up a bit. How is Herrad doing, by the way?"

"Pretty bad," Ofarir said, his grin widening. "I don't think he's going to last long enough to see the gifting, unless we hurry it up a bit."

"What a disappointment that would be," Jafnar murmured. "I suppose he's very ill and wasting away in terrible pain all the time."

"Well, Mistislaus has helped him quite a bit," Ofarir replied with a slight darkening of his good spirits. "Has he ever cured anyone of this kind of wound before?"

"Yes, as a matter of fact. I was also bitten in the Kjallari once," Jafnar said. "And I recovered perfectly."

"Bitten? What bit you?" Ofarir asked in a low voice.

"A vile creature possessing the attributes of both human and beast. Utterly savage yet filled with human hatred and cunning. Anyone foolish enough to go into the Kjallari takes his life in his hands."

"A most convenient safeguard," Ofarir added, his insulting smile returning. "If it is to be believed. I never did thank you for finding my father, did I? It was just you and that apprentice of the wizard's, was it not? How convenient that you seemed to know exactly where to find him. How lucky that you knew he'd received a poisonous wound."

"Fate seems to smile upon me at every turn, doesn't it?" Jafnar replied. "Your thanks are unnecessary."

"Is that why you refused the Drottningur brides?" Ofarir demanded. "You're too consumed by modesty?"

"Perhaps I feel a certain unworthiness. I'd much rather see the Krypplingur so gifted than myself."

"And so you shall, one day, if you live long enough," Ofarir said with a nasty laugh, which was echoed by his companions. "When I'm chieftain of two clans, things are going to change around here. You've become slackers, and you need someone to whip you into shape. I'm not the tolerant man my father is." With another guffaw, he and his cohorts shouldered Jafnar and Einka off the path and strode away with a menacing clatter of weapons and armor.

"I hate them," Einka said quietly. "I never wanted to fight before, but now I've changed my mind."

They returned to Athugashol and delivered the swords to Guthrum's forge in the stable. He looked at the pitted, dull weapons and shook his head, muttering dourly under his breath.

"I don't know why I even try," he growled. "These Skyldings are the most hopeless bunch of fools that ever walked the earth."

Skjoldur came bursting out into the courtyard, his beard and hair disheveled from a savage winnowing from both his hands. "Where have you been? Alvara has sent for you! No doubt to explain your irrational and boorish rejection of her generous offer."

The brothers shouldered the trunk and betook themselves to the women's hall, where Alvara and the old tjaldi sat scowling on the dais. For once the place was empty of chattering preening Drottningur. The silence struck an ominous chord in Jafnar's bosom. He darted a glance around, making sure of escape routes. His sword was a comforting weight at his side.

"So you've refused the Drottning giftings," the old tjaldi said. "This is a mysterious thing to us. The Drottningur are our sisters and very dear to us. We sought only to do you honor and bring peace to the clans."

"We would be pleased to be honored and grateful for peace," Jafnar said. "But what we found was anything but peace and honor. The wearers of the cloaks I stole came to kill us, and it was you who sent them."

"We were nearly killed," Einka added a little too loudly.

The old tjaldi narrowed her eyes and tented her fingers, exhaling a long, thoughtful hiss. Alvara made no movement except a quick sharp glance at Thordis.

"It is a most unfortunate misunderstanding," the old tjaldi said after a long pause. "We have no idea who those cloaks belong to. Are you perhaps accusing the Viturkonur of this misconduct?"

"They were Drottningur," Jafnar said. "I saw them before, eating the heart of a Kryppling."

"Indeed! The Krypplingur are our friends and allies," Alvara said. "Are we not intending to wed our sister to Herrad's son? Why should we then wish to damage them?"

"Viturkonur have no friends except Viturkonur," Jafnar replied. "When you're done using the Krypplingur, you'll find some way to get rid of them. Once you've gotten your revenge on the Skyldings, that is."

"Your disrespect is second only to your stupidity," Alvara said. "Fortunately you have the excuse of having had your brains dashed out, so we can find it in our hearts to forgive you. Do you speak for all your brothers?"

The Skjoldurssons all nodded. Modga opened his mouth in a faint croak of desperation but shut it again with an expression as bitter as bile.

"We all saw the same thing," Einka said, trying to keep his voice manly and steady. "Drottningur women transformed into killer lynxes."

"Most regrettable," the old tjaldi murmured. "Most regrettable, indeed. Your intended brides will be most disappointed."

"Let them eat someone else's liver," Einka muttered.

"Disappointed again if you thought we have Skyla's scroll," Jafnar said. "We don't have it. At least, not yet. We will find it, and we will stop this gifting."

"My blessings upon your endeavors," the old tjaldi said.

"We'll take our leave now," Jafnar said. "We'll leave you the cloaks. I'm sure their owners will be glad to have them back."

Pale of features and set around the jaws, they strode out of the hall with an impressive clatter of boots and swords.

"From now on," Jafnar said, "never leave your back unguarded for a moment. We have no friends in Rangfara except ourselves."

Early the next morning Mistislaus returned from Herrad's bedside and shook Jafnar awake.

"Get up; it's nearly dawn, you lazy clot. The gifting is still on, and the dowry ceremony is going to take place at noon today. I don't know what I'm going to do. That ceremony must be stopped. Every step makes this gifting much more likely to happen, and of all the things on earth that mustn't occur, Skyla must not be gifted to that loathsome Kryppling!"

Jafnar leapt up, sick with revulsion at the fresh memory of

Ofarir's evil face and nasty grin shoved into his face, mocking him, threatening him. The thought of such a vile creature possessing Skyla made his head light and his heart pound with demented fury.

"I must do something," Mistislaus said distractedly, pacing up and down in an agony of torn loyalties. "Yet I can't do anything. I swore on one side, yet Skyla is on the other. What am I to do, Jafnar?"

"You must stop it, Mistislaus," Jafnar said hoarsely, clenching his fists. "How can you even think to allow such a terrible event to occur? Are you so afraid you're going to die? Won't life be more intolerable than death if you let this happen?"

"I'm sworn on the sacred bonds of friendship," Mistislaus answered with a moan. "If I break those vows, my life won't be worth two sticks to anyone. I'll be an outcast for the rest of my life, hunted and despised. What then would happen to Skyla? She'd be cast out, too. And I doubt if it would stop these ravening Krypplingur and Viturkonur. Do you think they'll simply go away and forget what they had in mind? Rangfara would still be destroyed."

"At least Skyla won't be part of this great vile plan," Jafnar said. "She's far more likely to be hurt if she stays and marries Ofarir than if you get her out of this. If you don't do something to save her, Mistislaus, I'm going to turn my back on you and never speak to you again."

Mistislaus heaved a sigh. "Well, then, you'd better wangle some invitations for yourself and me to the dowry ceremony. I can't do anything if I'm not there."

"My father will get us in," Jafnar said.

"Yes. This is his fault, anyway."

All ceremonies of importance were held in the Kjallari. Jafnar stifled his raging premonitions of doom as he and his brothers treaded resolutely at Skjoldur's heels, having promised devoutly not to disgrace him in any way. Mistislaus still huffed and glowered, thoroughly insulted by Skjoldur's insistence that he forsake his lucky gown and cloak of many years dirt and duration to don a new and totally unfamiliar habiliment in exchange for permission to attend the dowry ceremony.

"I raised her as my own daughter, after all," he growled. "I have a perfect right to be here."

"Not if you look like a scavenger," Skjoldur retorted, his

eyes still bulging in a choleric manner from their quarrel about the new clothes. "Once in a while a man needs new clothing!"

"The old ones were just getting comfortable."

The party gathered at the genealogy shrine in the large, domed subterranean gallery that whispered with a thousand echoes from the human voices below. Dozens of lamps stood about on ledges, making the cavern almost as bright as day. Skyla and her Viturkonur relatives were placed in the position of honor on a platform surrounded by inscribed pillars. Ranked around them were the Krypplingur, Hoggvinn, and dozens of Skylding friends and relatives. Logregla caught sight of Jafnar and his brothers and scowled mightily first at them, then at her husband. The Viturkonur pretended not to see the Skjoldurssons, except for Skyla, who gazed at Jafnar from the far side of the old tjaldi. Thordis clutched her hand with one skinny claw, like an old raven clutching a dove.

When Herrad was carried in on a litter and positioned in a prominent place, the ceremony was ready to begin. It consisted of a ritual haggling and bargaining over the bride-price and dowry until an agreement was reached or until one party's oratorical skills prevailed and the other side's resistance was simply worn down. Since Herrad was too weak to do such verbal battle, his chief retainer was employed to argue for Ofarir. From Hoggvinn's viewpoint, the basic premise was that Ofarir was totally unfit, and from Ofarir's side, Skyla's bride-price was unreasonably exorbitant. Hoggvinn commenced by offering a negligible dowry, compelling the other side to use every means of elevating the amount the bride would bring to the marriage by means of promises of wartime protection, trade, and travel privileges.

It was almost intolerably boring, except for Mistislaus rocking on his toes and casting worried glances all around at the Skylding guards, the Kryppling guards, Hoggvinn, and Ofarir.

Suddenly it went completely dark. The lamps vanished in a single instant, as if the light had simply been swallowed up by darkness. The crowd gasped and shuffled apprenhensively, and several officious voices commenced shouting. "Light! Someone strike a light!"

Jafnar shuddered and swayed, feeling a dark wave of unknown power pass through the chamber. For an instant he scented a ripple of fetid Kjallari breath.

In a few moments most of the light was restored, and everyone breathed a sigh of relief, whispering and tittering at the brief alarm.

Then Skyla screamed loud and long. Beside her, still holding her hand, the old tjaldi Thordis lolled in her seat, her head hanging at a sickening angle. It looked as if some great force had wrenched her head around, wringing her neck like a chicken's. She wore an expression of polite boredom, as if still listening to the ceremonial bartering. How it had happened with people crowding tightly behind her and before her seat on the dais was impossible to contemplate.

CHAPTER
TWENTY

SKYLA'S SCREAM WAS echoed by shouts, shrieks, and a general trampling confusion as the fact of a murderer's being among them dawned on the spectators. Their only thought was to get away from the central chamber and back to the sunlight and air aboveground. Jafnar felt himself being shoved to and fro in the human riptide as his eyes searched wildly for Mistislaus in the swinging shadows. Keening and wailing with chilling cries, the Viturkonur gathered around their slain tjaldi, refusing to let anyone else near her.

The light, shadow, color, and sound all swam together as Jafnar's skull commenced a deadly pounding. The faces around him melted, shimmering into distorted, leering, grinning skull faces, part human and part animal. Over it all he heard the children's chant endlessly repeating "Kellarman, Kellarman, he'll catch you if he can."

Suddenly a hand clamped onto Jafnar's arm and dragged him back to the ugly reality of the situation.

"Jafnar!" Einka whispered, giving his arm a shake. "Let's get out of here!"

Hoggvinn and Skjoldur were directing the guards to split up into small groups to search the tunnels. Others carried Thordis out on a makeshift litter, with the Viturkonur following behind, still raising an unearthly wailing and lamenting.

Jafnar demanded, "Where's Mistislaus? Did you see him after they got the lights lit again?"

"No, I didn't," Einka said. "I was standing right beside him. What's wrong? Did he do something?"

"I don't know," Jafnar replied. "You don't think he did it, do you?"

"I don't know. He was pretty determined to stop the cere-mony. Cranking the neck of the tjaldi was a good tactic."

"He didn't do it," Jafnar snapped. "He wouldn't do anything that cowardly."

"Come on; let's get out of there before old Eadgils starts looking at us again," Einka pleaded.

"Why are we going this way?" Jafnar smelled the dank, wa-tery air of the ancient well.

"Shortcut."

Jafnar came to a sudden halt. "Do you hear that?" he whis-pered, straining his ears toward a faint, indiscernible sound rus-tling in the old well.

Einka stopped for a moment, but he was breathing like a winded horse, filling the tunnel with his wheezing and gulping sounds. "No, I don't hear anything," he replied shortly. "Let's get out of here."

"I thought you liked the Kjallari."

"I do—or did. But it's different now, especially with Skriftur gone. And now this murder. Did you see the way her head was turned almost clear around? Horrible! Who could have done a thing like that, so fast?"

"Kellarman, Kellarman, he'll catch you if he can," Jafnar chanted softly.

"Stop it!" Einka gave him a shove and a buffet on the back. "By saying a name you call its owner. Now, let's get out of here!"

Supported on both arms by her thralls, Logregla treaded along with as much haste as she could make with her tiny feet and ridiculous dainty shoes. Between sobbing and weeping, she could hardly see where she was going, so her brothers had to maneuver her around corners and pillars and up and down stairs like an incompliant feather bed. A nervous thrall stum-bled along ahead, carrying a wavering horn lamp, jumping and twitching at every moving shadow.

"It was me they wanted!" she panted deliriously. "They know! They know!"

"Don't be ridiculous!" puffed her thrall, Thrand, who had suffered with her all his life. "Can't you at least try to stand up? We can't carry you all the way home!"

"Just leave me here!" she whimpered. "Try to save your-selves! They're following me, they're following me!"

"Nonsense," Thrand said. "There's no one following, and no one seriously wants to kill you. Now try and get your feet under you. You know we'll protect you against anyone who looks suspicious. Aren't we your fierce protectors, all three of us?"

"You thralls wouldn't even slow down this killer." Logregla moaned. "No more than three little old sticks."

"Who, then, is the killer?" whispered Vorsa, on her other side. "You know who it is?"

"I can't tell you or you'll die, too," Logregla said distractedly. "Look what happened to poor Thordis! Oh, if I get out of this alive, I'm going to become a hermit and dedicate myself to thinking kind thoughts!"

Sweating and puffing, the thralls finally reached the surface level and conducted Logregla home, where she collapsed, weeping and fainting.

"Do you think she's really in any danger?" Ozurr whispered after they had left her.

"Only from her own fancies," Thrand replied with a snort. "How could she know anything? She's never cared about anything except food and clothes in her whole life, has she?"

"I've never known her to be afraid of anything or anybody," Vorsa said, tweaking his nether lip. "Do you think we should stand guard outside her chamber?"

"And be killed? Not me!"

The Viturkonur funerary customs were simple, brief, and unsentimental. The body was carried to the top of a hill and placed in a shallow grave, which was covered with a cairn of rocks to discourage digging scavengers. Then the women cleaned out the old tjaldi's tent, gave away all her possessions, and selected another tjaldi by throwing a bundle of sticks. The lot fell to Alvara.

After maintaining a full day's silence in honor of the old tjaldi, Alvara's first proclamation was: "This gifting must proceed at once."

Her second: "The killer of our tjaldi will be found and punished."

Hoggvinn called a convocation of his retainers to the Hall of Stars. As the eldest son of Skjoldur, Jafnar was privileged to attend, but only after some severe warnings to keep his head extremely low and his mouth securely shut. To Jafnar's surprise, Kraftugur presented himself as the chief speaker.

"It has grieved me a great deal to see Rangfara cast into turmoil of late," he began. "I am only a humble man who came here as a peacemaker, and I intend to withdraw into my comfortable obscurity once more as soon as I have accomplished what I have set forth to do. You must wonder at my presumption to offer you any advice, but my regard for the Skylding clan forces me to speak out. Things have not gone well since arrangements were made for this gifting with the Krypplingur. Three hideous murders have been committed in secret, with no confession or explanation or offer of weregild, as if the killer bore a savage and unrelenting hatred for the victims. No ordinary quarrel or feud could spark such bitter rage, almost as if the very elements were in opposition to this gifting. Powerful forces have been unleashed in Rangfara because of this gifting. Perhaps it would behoove this council of wise men to reconsider the wisdom of this alliance between Skylding, Kryppling, and Viturkonur if such natural opposition has been bestirred. We are mere puny mortals, surrounded by a world of forces guiding us toward our inevitable fate. Who are we to resist the might of fate by insisting upon something merely pleasing to ourselves? I verily fear that if you persist in this alliance, worse events are bound to come."

The council members sat riveted, listening, then erupted into vociferous comment. Most agreed with Kraftugur, some thought it was rot, and they all wanted to quarrel about it, almost at daggers' ends.

Hoggvinn silenced the uproar by hammering on the table with the handle of his knife. "It seems we don't completely agree," he said. "Nor am I ready or able to simply call a halt to this gifting. It is a more complicated agreement than the sale of a horse or house. Valuable treaties have already been exchanged that will benefit all three clans."

"But if we're destroyed by our own bad luck, we won't be alive to enjoy all those benefits," someone pointed out. "We can't fight it if fate is against this gifting."

"We make our own fate," someone else rejoined. "We aren't helpless tokens being shoved around on a board."

"Kraftugur is a rejected suitor," another voice chimed in. "He would like to see the gifting called off."

"So would I," Jafnar said, and Skjoldur elbowed him and glowered.

"You're too close to me to take sides," he hissed.

"You mean we're obliged to agree with Hoggvinn no matter how wrong he is?" Jafnar demanded.

"Exactly," Skjoldur said. "If you want to maintain your position."

"Silence!" Hoggvinn commanded. "Kraftugur has made his point—a point well taken, judging from the looks of you. It seems to me we've neglected Kraftugur's valuable wisdom of late. I will take it under consideration, but to me it seems that we have gone too far already to cancel the gifting now. But if the signs become any stronger or more persistent that fate is truly in opposition to this match, then we will have to decide what is best for the Skylding clan. Aggravating the Krypplingur is not in our best interest. So far I've seen no sign that the Krypplingur are worried that fate is against them."

"What about Herrad's misfortune in the Kjallari?" Jafnar called out. "Doesn't that seem like a sign to them?"

"Krypplingur are not superstitious," Hoggvinn said. "And now that Mistislaus is taking care of Herrad, he does truly seem to be somewhat better. Or at least not—er, decaying so quickly." He shuddered slightly.

"You promised to be still!" Skjoldur spit.

"Don't be led over a cliff just because you're loyal to the leader," Jafnar retorted.

Eadgils rose to his feet, immediately commanding a respectful silence. "I have some questions about the murder of Thordis the Viturkona," he said. "From questions, you will learn far more about your situation than from answers. First of all, who was closest to her when she died?"

"Skyla was holding her hand," someone said into the silence. "But a little lass like that isn't strong enough to wring someone's neck."

"Why would someone kill the tjaldi?"

"To stop the gifting, of course."

"Who is closest to Skyla?"

"I am," Hoggvinn said, "as her father."

"No, I disagree," someone said. "Her Viturkonur relatives are closer."

"But she's only known them a little while," Eadgils said. "Likewise Hoggvinn, her father. These people are virtual strangers to the girl. Who raised her from an infant? Who might possibly resent her change in status and her gifting as a peace bride?"

Suddenly, the name Mistislaus was hissing through the hall and everyone was nodding, shocked and knowing.

"Let's go get him," someone suggested eagerly.

"We are not yet ready for a formal accusation of anyone," Eadgils said. "I still have many questions you haven't heard yet. But that will do for today."

Jafnar got himself away from the council chamber as fast as he could. "I want to see Mistislaus!" he commanded, grabbing his father's arm. "Take me to him so these great loud Krypplingur won't throw me out!"

Protesting, Skjoldur took him to the main hall, where Herrad and about twenty Krypplingur had taken up residence. While the warriors ate, drank, guzzled, and belched, Herrad lay fitfully on his bed behind a screen, lashing around in semiconscious agonies as his leg oozed and stank.

Mistislaus sat beside him, eyes closed, fingering the knots of his iteration string and droning on and on in a monotonous rhythm. He opened his eyes owlishly at the interruption of his important work and angrily stuffed the string in his belt pouch.

"Every other moment I'm besieged with interruptions!" he exploded, rolling his eyes in irritation.

"I refuse to speak to you," Skjoldur announced loftily. "Not as long as you persist in your opposition to our chieftain in regard to the Kryppling gifting."

"You pompous ass," Mistislaus replied. "I take pleasure in persisting in opposition to anything you think worthwhile."

"Mistislaus! They suspect you of killing Thordis!" Jafnar whispered. "Be on your guard!"

"Suspect me of wringing old Thordis' neck? That's the most absurd thing I've heard yet!"

"The two of you can stop the gifting," Jafnar said, glaring at his father. "You know you can, and you know you must."

"I won't have anything to do with that murdering vagabond," Skjoldur snarled, turning his back on Mistislaus.

"And you're nothing but a sheep, trotting along at the end of a string while Hoggvinn leads you to the slaughter," Mistislaus spewed.

"I am his friend," Skjoldur snapped. "You, on the other hand, do everything you can to annoy him."

"If he's being stupid, I'm going to annoy him," Mistislaus retorted. "It's a man's duty to relieve the ignorance of his friends whenever he can."

"Then he'll soon find himself without friends, as you have," Skjoldur replied.

A subtle shifting of atmosphere in the hall alerted them to the approach of Hoggvinn. Behind him, Kraftugur kept a desultory distance as Hoggvinn joined the tableau gathered around Herrad's bedside. Kraftugur contemplated Herrad with a pious expression as the hapless sufferer thrashed and groaned.

"Well, this is a strange place for us all to meet," Hoggvinn said with dignity. "How is he doing, Mistislaus?"

"Little change so far," Mistislaus reported. "And that's good news. He can't get better, you know. Only worse. The rate of decline is all we can regulate."

Herrad moaned and struggled against the leather straps that kept him from flinging himself onto the floor. "No! Fools! Attack!" he muttered, rolling his crazed eyes around as if he were on a battlefield.

"How regrettable," Hoggvinn said. "You don't seem to have done him a bit of good. I've decided to try another tack in his treatment. Kraftugur will take your place. Your presence is no longer required in the Hall of Stars. But I insist that you do not leave Rangfara under any circumstances just yet, until certain questions are answered."

"Yes, I believe you're trying to hang some murders on me," Mistislaus said. "I'll be sure to stay around so you can execute me. If I have any say in the matter, I'd prefer hanging to gibbeting, beheading to dismemberment or impaling, and I really can't say I'd care much for being thrown into a bog alive. Torture is always a possibility, but admittedly quite messy, as is being torn apart by wild horses. I do hope you'll consult me further before you proceed with any drastic actions."

"Do you admit to the murder of Thordis?" Hoggvinn gasped, his face suddenly dawning with a hopeful expression, as if he had unexpectedly come to the end of all his troubles.

"No, you dolt," Mistislaus snapped. "I can stop the gifting without murdering old ladies."

"You'd better not even contemplate it," Hoggvinn rumbled, darting venomous glances at Mistislaus and Skjoldur. "Now take yourself out of here. Your name is a blot upon the sacred oaths of brotherhood and loyalty."

"Thank you, I esteem you just as highly." Mistislaus snorted, tucking his ragged satchel under his arm. Skirting Kraftugur as if he disdained to brush so much as the sleeve of his garment, he added, "Herrad will be dead within a week with this hoaxer treating him. I hope you'll enjoy Ofarir's reign of terror, however brief its duration."

Hoggvinn glared at Mistislaus, speechless with rage, while Skjoldur's eyes darted back and forth nervously.

"Jafnar, stay here," he commanded when Jafnar started after Mistislaus. "I won't have my son seen with that charlatan. I want him out of Athugashol."

Jafnar paused a moment, having a brief, dazzling image of

himself giving up the struggle and simply following in Skjoldur's footsteps and letting fate have its way with Rangfara.

"No, I fear not," he said, with the weight of his choice settling heavily upon him like a stone around the neck of a dog doomed to be drowned. "No one can do any more good in the Hall of Stars."

"Hem," Kraftugur coughed as Jafnar stroke after Mistislaus. "A most unfortunate situation, an ungrateful son and a treacherous friend. It doesn't take much prophetic sight to know that the two of them are headed for disaster."

Mistislaus was in no mood for idle chatter. He returned to Athugashol and took himself upstairs to his quarters with strict orders that no one disturb him for several years. When Jafnar ventured to creep up the stairs and glance in on him, he was sitting rigidly at the table, pale as chalk, his eyes glassed over in his traveling state of inanimation.

As darkness descended upon Rangfara, the rest of the Skjoldurssons arrived at Athugashol and the doors were securely barred. Warm summer evenings no longer beckoned people to take a leisurely stroll among the houses and halls and gardens of Rangfara. A pervasive atmosphere of dread haunted the deserted streets, and no one liked to be the last to find home and hearth once it became dark. Once inside, there were noises: calls, wails, sobbing, and scratching at the gates.

"Listen to that," Modga whispered when something sniffed under the crack of the door.

"It's just a dog," Lofa said. "Or a cat," Lampi added, not looking up from the swords they were sharpening.

Jafnar leapt to his feet as the crooning call of a large cat came in through the crack.

"Skyla," Thogn said, looking up from his mud mess briefly, then returning to his mumbling.

"Skyla!" Jafnar exclaimed, and the answer from the other side of the door was a soft meow.

He surged to the door with Ordvar at his heels.

"You can't open that door!" Ordvar gripped the bar, bracing himself in Jafnar's path.

"It's her; she's gotten away!" Jafnar charged at Ordvar, but Lofa picked him off and set him down at a safe distance.

"We shan't fight among ourselves," Lofa said warningly.

"But Skyla!"

"You don't know what's on the other side of that door, nor

its intentions," Lofa said, giving Jafnar a friendly little shove that sent him staggering toward a chair. "Now be a good elder brother and show us what an example of courage and restraint you are."

In the taut silence they all heard a savage lynx call, followed shortly by the sounds of a terrible squalling battle that rapidly diminished down the street.

"I don't like this," Einka said in a firm voice that quavered at the end.

"Never mind, little man," Lampi said, giving him an encouraging swat on the back. "Daylight's not far off, and all the creepy creatures are done with their mischief then."

"Until tomorrow night," Lofa added amiably, sighting along a newly sharpened sword.

Jafnar turned on his heel and strode upstairs to glare at Mistislaus, who was sitting there as helpful as an iceberg. Illmuri rose up from his cot in a corner, making warning gestures for silence.

"Go away and leave him alone," he whispered.

Jafnar scowled at Illmuri and turned to Mistislaus. He was holding a sheepskin vellum under one frozen hand, while several others blew about the room and floor, enlivened by the gusts puffing in through the narrow windows. Illmuri dutifully gathered up the scrolls to anchor them in a safe place. Then he went downstairs to see what there was to eat.

Jafnar sat down on the bench beside Mistislaus, determined to wait out his trance. It was not a comfortable feeling, with Mistislaus' cold and vacant eye sternly fixed upon nothing in particular, reminding him horribly of Vigulf sitting in his chair and pointing out the window. Uneasily Jafnar noted that Mistislaus had the appearance of having departed unexpectedly for his excursion upon the planes of a different strand. He looked as if he had just glanced up momentarily from the scroll he was reading. A cup sat beside his elbow, half-full, and a slab of black bread was threatening to attract mice, creatures against which Mistislaus conducted bitterest war in Athugashol, since he had so many valuable books and vellums to be chewed and spoiled.

Holding his breath, Jafnar leaned over to look at the scroll. It was elaborately illuminated with colors and elegant writing—a birth scroll, he instantly realized. "One female child, born to Reykja Onasdottir of the Viturkonur clan, on the sixth day of the twelfth month of Murari's calendar, sired by Hoggvinn Sverdsson, called Shield-breaker, of the clan Skylding."

Jafnar's head reeled, and he remembered to take a breath before he collapsed from lack of air. The next part of the scroll described the astrological conditions accompanying the birth, along with a few prophecies and promises attached to the circumstances, then the scroll launched forth into a description of the infant.

"The infant is to be named Skylda, to remind her of her duty to her clan and sisters, to always shield them and uphold the dictates of her clanswomen. The child is of healthy appearance with a dark complexion, with the mark of the chosen on her left brow. As a sign of obligation and sorrow, the child has been given a deformed left foot to remind her always to walk with care and pain in the path her tjaldi dictates."

Jafnar sank back on the bench beside Mistislaus' inert form, staring at the far wall just as blankly as if his soul, too, had deserted him. Skyla's left foot was not deformed. Many times—in that other life—he had seen her running barefoot over the flagstone walks of Athugashol or paddling in the carp pool, flying lightly up the stairs, two pink, perfectly healthy, dainty little feet trimmed with tiny half-moon toenails. Nor was there a mark of any sort on her left brow except a pale dusting of golden eyebrow. Nor was she of a dark complexion. She was as pale as thistledown.

The scroll was for a different child. Jafnar ventured to pluck it out from under Mistislaus' rigid hand. The vellum had none of the feel of a fresh new sheepskin; it was soft, and someone had carefully oiled it to keep it from drying and cracking. Even so, it firmly maintained its persistent curl, wanting to roll up in his hands. The ink had a slightly cracked appearance; it was not fresh, as it would have been for a forgery.

At the bottom of the scroll were Hoggvinn's mark and Reykja's mark and those of the clan genealogist and matchmaker. It also listed agreements that stated that the child Skylda had full privileges of inheritance if she proved to be the only legitimate offspring of the union and various other pacts and promises concerning her dowry and gifts and property. At the very bottom he recognized the marks of Mistislaus and Skjoldur as witnesses to the agreement.

Numbly Jafnar replaced the scroll under Mistislaus' hand. Now he understood how Mistislaus and Skjoldur had the power to stop the gifting on their word only. They both knew that the child born to Reykja had a deformed foot. It was obvious to anyone that Skyla had two good feet and no mark on her left brow. Skyla was not Hoggvinn's child.

got it," Mistislaus said, sniffing loudly in a snuff-box. "I think the ... hm ... first took hold, don't you?"

...

CHAPTER
TWENTY-ONE

MISTISLAUS' RETURNS FROM his walkings were abrupt and unpredictable. One moment he was as stiff as a haunch of frozen meat, and the next he awakened with a snort and a cough and a general hullabaloo of ruffling his clothes, clearing his throat, and making a pretense of resuming what he had been doing when he left. He snatched up Skyla's scroll and glared at it, then hastily rolled it up and shoved it into his sleeve, where it had resided since Skriftur had given it to him for safekeeping. Poor fool—he had not thought that someone would consider him as much of a threat.

Looking out an arrow slit, Mistislaus perceived that it was nearly dawn. His stomach reminded him of the cheerful fact that breakfast was due. Heaving a great sigh, Mistislaus ran his fingers through his hair to bring it to order, then went downstairs to deploy the Skjoldurssons on needful and time-consuming occupations. He found Jafnar already dispersing Einka and Thogn after more disused weapons and sending Lofa, Lampi, Modga, and Ordvar to the practice field.

When the others were gone, Jafnar turn to face Mistislaus. Before he heard a word, Mistislaus knew that Jafnar was wise to at least one of his secrets.

"Why didn't you tell me she's not his daughter?" Jafnar demanded. "And why don't you tell Hoggvinn? Who is Skyla?"

"I don't know," Mistislaus replied. "What's to eat, or do we need to make a trip to the Skurdur?"

"Hoggvinn's daughter had a deformed foot," Jafnar said. "I know you've got that scroll. Skriftur died because of it. Do you want to die, too?"

"I'll be alright as long as the Viturkonur don't suspect I've got it," Mistislaus said, sniffing loudly in a small pot. "I think this cabbage has gone bad, don't you?"

"Mistislaus, nearly everyone in Rangfara wants to kill you. I want to help, and you're just ignoring me as if I were a small child."

"Help kill me, you mean? No thanks, I've got plenty of people on that job." Jafnar glared at him in silence until he relented. "Alright, I apologize. But I don't want to get you embroiled with me. You know what happens to people who get in the way of certain other people. The Viturkonur killed Vigulf, you know. Snatched his soul out of him and ripped out his thoat."

"And Skriftur and Thordis?" Jafnar demanded.

"I don't think it was Alvara who killed her own tjaldi woman," Mistislaus said. "I'd like to believe it, but it stretches even my credulity that she would be so treacherous as that."

"Mistislaus, I beg of you, please show that scroll and put an end to this chaos. How do we know who'll be the next one killed? It might be Hoggvinn himself, and you'd be responsible for his death."

Mistislaus winced. "I am sworn to defend him and guard his secrets. Besides, we can let it go on a little longer with no danger to Skyla. We're getting very near the end of this cycle of disaster. Perhaps this time it will be different and we'll escape. But I promise if Skyla is endangered, I will rescue her at whatever the cost."

"Who is she, Mistislaus?"

Mistislaus sighed. "The first infant died very shortly after we stole it. The poor little creature had many more problems than a deformed foot. I think she would have perished anyway. So Skjoldur, ever enterprising, obtained another infant from a tribe of scraelings who had probably raided some isolated settlement and stolen away the little child."

"But Hoggvinn didn't want the child. Couldn't you have left her dead?"

"And enrage the ever-suspicious Viturkonur? They would've flayed us alive. Hoggvinn didn't want a Viturkonur child. It's not true he wanted her exposed to die. Logregla did, and he had to appease her, so we took the new one away to raise her as a foundling, knowing the Viturkonur would be watching."

"Hoggvinn knows it's a different child?"

"Hum—ho—no, he doesn't. He thought the matter ended with the death of the sickly child—until lately." Mistislaus' elusive gaze wandered around to the window and sharpened intently. He slapped his hands on his belly and declared, "Ho, look at that daylight. We've got to get to the Skurdur. Come along; it will be interesting."

Protesting, Jafnar followed him into the street, hurrying to keep up as Mistislaus strode along toward the Hall of Stars. As they approached the gates, Mistislaus halted at the sight of a crowd gathering around the gateposts. Something dangled from the archway. For a moment Jafnar had the impression that someone had butchered a couple of cattle and hung them up to age. His disbelieving eyes did not want to report that it was two human bodies hanging there.

Sputtering curses, Mistislaus parted the crowd on either side of him and plowed forward. The two Kryppling guards had met a hideous end, their throats raggedly slashed, their chests and bellies torn apart to strew their guts around in a huge pool of clotted blood. On their foreheads was the red spiral mark of doom.

Jafnar seized Mistislaus' arm, whispering in his ear, "Look there! The mark of the lynx! And I'll bet you their hearts and livers are gone. Probably eaten by now."

Hoggvinn and Ofarir stood at the gate, gray-faced and staring, frightened men looking for reasons, and excuses, and a scapegoat.

"How many Krypplingur does it take to secure one gate?" Hoggvinn demanded. "Look at these fools, trussed and hung up like a brace of rabbits! We could have all been murdered in our beds!"

"I didn't bring my best men here to be butchered in this insulting manner," Ofarir retorted, hacking at the ropes with his sword. "It seems to me I've led them into a worse trap than I ever dreamed existed here. I thought we were brought here under the terms of friendship, but since we've come to Rangfara, I've had eleven of my men slaughtered, as if some demented animal had attacked them."

"We've violated no treaties of friendship," Hoggvinn growled furiously. "Yet your men have swaggered around terrorizing our gentle citizens and bringing this havoc down upon us all. My own brother was slain by an unknown hand, thanks to this alliance between Skylding and Kryppling."

"Are you hinting that Krypplingur may be to blame? This is perhaps retaliation for Vigulf?"

"Certainly not. If I had the proof that Krypplingur were to

blame, I would come to you and your father straightforwardly and demand an explanation and a suitable amount of weregild. It's not my way to go sneaking about in secret, when no secrecy is required. Had your father, Herrad, mentioned he wanted to explore the Kjallari, we would have provided a suitable escort and six of your men would now be alive and Herrad would not be thrashing about in a delirium."

"There's more hugger-muggery about you Skyldingur than you care to admit." Ofarir snorted. "Who's got Skyla's scroll? Why was it stolen? Why are people being killed because of that scroll? Something is dreadfully wrong here in the fair city of Rangfara. Now, can we get rid of this gawking crowd and fetch a cart for these carcasses?"

The crowd disintegrated at the encouragement of five Krypplingur with axes. Mistislaus grabbed Jafnar and dived out of sight behind a moving cart, which had provided excellent bleacher seating for more than a dozen admirers of guts and gore. Now it was shedding passengers like rats from a burning barn.

"When a ruler is annoyed, it's a good time to keep your head out of sight," Mistislaus said, silencing Jafnar's protests, "unless you want it cut off. Now come along; we're going to be late for the opening of the stalls." He strode along with his eyes fixed ahead, like a cat intent upon its prey.

"How can you think of nothing but eating all the time?" Jafnar demanded.

"There are more curious things in the Skurdur than food," Mistislaus said. "Now hurry!"

They took a back lane of the Skurdur, where the tents and booths were small and ragged and the proprietors were dark and furtive.

Mistislaus shoved Jafnar into a niche between two shabby booths as Kraftugur emerged from a dingy apothecary's tent, still in the act of slipping a small parcel into his sleeve pocket. Glancing right and left, he pulled his hood down and hurried away, disappearing into the stream of merchants and customers.

"Just as I thought," Mistislaus said. "He's going to poison Herrad. This is an apothecary known for dispensing such useful herbs. Come along!"

Mistislaus plunged after Kraftugur, heedless of the opposing traffic, overtaking him just short of the butchers' stalls.

"Why are you following me?" Kraftugur demanded, whirling around suddenly to confront Mistislaus and Jafnar.

"I know what you're doing," Mistislaus said. "And you're not going to get away with it."

"Dear me," Kraftugur said, "is walking down the street such a crime? I never knew it."

"Innocence is a game you'll never play with any success," Mistislaus said. "Mark my words. If you proceed with your plans, you're going to be eternally sorry."

With that he jostled past Kraftugur and strode away, impatiently beckoning Jafnar to follow. Jafnar tore his savage scowl away from Kraftugur and followed, bestowing a few threatening glances over his shoulder. Kraftugur merely stood still and watched them go, his narrow face expressionless.

"I hope I've foxed him," Mistislaus said. "I truly don't wish Herrad to die just yet, not until all those stinking Krypplingur are out of Rangfara."

"Mistislaus, I want Skyla out of this mess immediately," Jafnar said. "The longer you wait, the worse it gets. Something might happen to her. You might get killed. You did before, you know."

"Yes, of course I know," Mistislaus snapped. "Do you think I don't remember? I find it highly encouraging that someone hasn't killed Kraftugur yet. As long as he's alive, he can't occupy Ofarir, which is always disastrous."

"If we could get rid of Ofarir first, that would solve it," Jafnar said.

"And have him come back as a draug? I don't think you'd like that scenario."

"I don't care what happens. I want Skyla out of there. You get her out of the Hall of Stars, Mistislaus, or else I'm going to."

"No one is more concerned about her welfare than I am," Mistislaus retorted testily. "At the moment she's safest right where she is, where Hoggvinn will protect her."

"Hoggvinn! He wants her to marry Ofarir! What does he care for her happiness or safety? He's worried most about his own skin and the safety of Rangfara. He'll sacrifice anything for Rangfara and that cursed treasure!"

In midafternoon three days later Illmuri burst into Mistislaus' chamber in a flying disarray. "Herrad is dying! Come quick! He wants to see you!"

Mistislaus slapped on his hood and gathered up his staff and satchel and cloak, all needful appurtenances for state occasions and public appearances.

"I knew it, I knew it!" he spewed wrathfully, wrapping the tail of his hood around his neck like a noose. "What did I tell you when we saw a certain party coming out of a questionable apothecary's booth? Come along, the two of you! I'm not going in there alone!"

Jafnar strode at Mistislaus' side to the Hall of Stars, casting a contemptuous look back at Illmuri, who stopped diffidently at the door to the hall.

Herrad lay gasping and straining on his cot, with Ofarir and Kraftugur cheering him on from both sides, sitting and staring at him hopefully. The leg did not bear looking at; the straw of the bed was soaked with reeking, blackish fluid that was dripping into a bucket.

Herrad opened one yellow slit of eye at Mistislaus' approach. He bared a couple of teeth in a sneer of greeting. "I thought you were a hoax," he croaked, "until this murderer got his hands on me."

"I knew it." Mistislaus threw a furious glance at Kraftugur, who brushed it off with a small shrug. "I fear it's too late for me to do you any good now. All I can do is teach you an iteration to relieve the pain and ease you into the realm of shadow. Don't be alarmed; someone you know will be waiting to guide you to the waiting place. If a stranger should accost you, or someone you knew here and didn't trust, you must use the rune of Eihwaz to protect yourself. We will meet again, perhaps, at the next turn of the wheel, on the next strand of the Web of Life."

Mistislaus closed his eyes and commenced iterating, and presently Herrad uttered a sigh and his hectic panting and sweating became calm.

"Is he dead yet?" Ofarir whispered, a shade too eagerly.

Herrad's eyes snapped open, blazing with a furious glare. "No, not quite, you slinking, stealing dog," he snarled. "I should have dashed your brains out on the floor the minute you were born. Looking at you now, I wish I had done it then. You're almost drooling with anticipation, aren't you, waiting for me to die and be out of your way."

"Well, then, get on with it, you loathsome lump of carrion," Ofarir retorted. "I've got a hundred things to do. It's going to be a very nice funeral, Pabbi, so why are you delaying my freedom? All my life I've lived for this moment, to see your breath stilled and realize I'll never hear your hateful voice again. Die, you old vulture, and let my life begin!"

"You wretched thief! Murdering scum!" Herrad struggled as if he would sit up, but he fell back coughing, gasping raggedly for each breath.

"Be calm; there's no need for struggling now," Mistislaus said, making the sign of a rune in the air. "This is a time for preparation for a journey of greater importance."

"You wouldn't have wanted to go on living as a one-legged Kryppling, anyway," Kraftugur said. "It would have made no sense to try. The Kjallari poison is throughout your entire body."

"And so is yours," Mistislaus murmured.

Herrad gasped, gurgled, and stopped breathing. Ofarir leaned close, holding his breath, his eyes glittering with triumph. After a long moment Herrad commenced breathing again, dragging each breath out with difficulty, and Ofarir threw himself back in his chair in disgust.

"I can't believe how he's hanging on," he said. "Perhaps he's going to recover."

"No, no, there's no hope of that," Kraftugur said.

"As well you should know," Jafnar said. "You poisoned him. We saw you buy the poison and hide it in your sleeve."

Kraftugur stared at him with no expression on his narrow face, and likewise Ofarir stared at Jafnar, his countenance darkening and curdling in guilty hatred. Ofarir clenched his fist and said, "Mind your tongue. I am chieftain now, not this reeking carcass, and I'll see to it you suffer for your stupidity."

Herrad snorted and sputtered, his eyes opening wide with fury. "Poisoned!" he gasped. "Wasn't it enough that I die the shameful death of the straw bed instead of the battlefield? Not that alone, but I was poisoned like vermin by my own son."

"You weren't going to get better," Ofarir said, rising to his feet. "So look upon it as a mercy killing."

"There's no mercy in poisoning a man," Mistislaus retorted. "Eating his guts away like maggots before he's dead—it's a coward's way of murdering in secret."

"Wizard, your life isn't worth a straw in Rangfara," Ofarir rumbled. "If you value your scrawny neck, you'd better see to it you're a thousand miles from Rangfara when this old dog draws his last breath. Let me know when he's dead," he added to Kraftugur, and with that Ofarir turned and strode from the hall.

Kraftugur pressed his hands thoughtfully together and made a regretful clicking sound with his tongue. "You shouldn't have said that, Mistislaus, but you ever were the heedless sort. Your greatest weakness is your impulsive nature. Thus it is you will always fail to stop the cycle of Rangfara's destruction. It's the will of the Web, you old fool, and you can do nothing about it."

"I can do whatever I wish to do about it," Mistislaus retorted.

"But it's all the same in the end," Kraftugur said. "Even if you draw a sword and kill me now, you still fail."

"I have no intention of killing you," Mistislaus said. "I would like to see you die of extreme old age before you strike up your unholy liaison with Ofarir. You're a mad, insane thing, devoured by vengeance. And what's more, you're a murderer."

Kraftugur shrugged his shoulders and smiled faintly, as if he were enjoying his moment of triumph. "Yes, and so are you. You and I are tied to the wheel together, Mistislaus. Fate will always bring us together, and the result will always be the same. You will murder me, Mistislaus."

"Not this time," Mistislaus said. "I know your plan."

"Go ahead and kill me," Kraftugur said. "Truly you want to, do you not? Your overdeveloped sense of justice cries out that I should perish. Shout for help; let them put a noose around my neck and hang me. After all, you see the evidence here before you. Freely I admit to poisoning this struggling wretch. I should die, should I not?"

"Yes, but I'm not going to do it," Mistislaus said. "It only frees you to do greater mischief."

"Trusting fools," Kraftugur said. "All the while the viper has been in your midst, killing you one by one, but no one suspected the loyal and trustworty Kraftugur. I'll be almost sorry when it's over." He bent down to inspect Herrad a moment, admiring his own handiwork. "He's in terrible pain. His vitals are eaten away by the poison. It's not quite as satisfactory as when I killed Thordis. Her neck was as brittle as a dry reed. I stood there, and no one suspected me. Skriftur was more of a challenge, because he could have defended himself quite well if I hadn't taken him totally by surprise, reaching up to bring down a scroll box I had asked to see."

"And Vigulf? Was that your handiwork, also?" Mistislaus demanded.

"I fear not. Alvara beat me to him."

"You have no reason to do all this killing," Mistislaus said. "Kill them all and you'll still never marry Skyla and have the treasure. You killed them for your own revenge, for your own satisfaction."

"It's the best sort of killing, revenge," Kraftugur said.

"A warrior hates to die alone," Herrad whispered.

"Eleven of your men are waiting for you," Kraftugur answered. "I knew you'd be lonely. My creatures, the ones I created and breathed life into, killed them. Remember the two hung up by their heels at the gate? Everyone thought it was the snow lynx, but it was my handiwork. How frightened you were then, suspecting the Viturkonur had turned on you. You didn't know it, but already the poison in your body was doing its work."

"Clever Kraftugur," Herrad murmured with a weary sigh. "I can scarcely hear your boasting. I think I am going out, like a weak candle."

"Stay a moment and hear the best of all," Kraftugur said, leaning down and putting his mouth close to Herrad's ear. "I sent you and your men into the Kjallari, knowing what was waiting for you. The Kellarman and my little imps were ready for you, weren't they?" He chuckled dryly and shook his head pityingly. "You'll all be dead soon, so it doesn't matter, does it?"

Rallying suddenly, Herrad gasped with a burbling snort, yellowed eyes glaring. "You sent us down there to die, didn't you? Those hideous little creatures, that monstrous horned man—you knew, and you hoped we'd all be killed?"

"Yes, I planned it so carefully, telling you about the treasure until your mouth was watering. It was such a disappointment when this one found you and dragged you out before they finished you off," Kraftugur said with a venomous glance toward Jafnar. "But I think he'll be joining you soon. Your son doesn't like him."

"Tell me—once more before I'm gone—about the treasure. The jewels—the gold—the silver," Herrad whispered. "Come closer. I can't hear you."

"Wouldn't you have liked to see it once before you died?" Kraftugur chuckled mirthlessly and bent closer once again. "There are chests and boxes of gold chains. Great rubies like drops of clotted blood—"

One yellowed claw of a hand shot out, snaring Kraftugur's cloak. With a maniac's grin, Herrad pulled a dagger from beside him in his bed. In a glittering arc it flashed once in the firelight and plunged into Kraftugur's throat. Herrad fell back, laughing and wheezing and sputtering in the gore that spattered over him from Kraftugur's gaping wound.

"Who's laughing now?" he gasped. "Who's laughing now? You've been murdered by a dead man, you fool!"

Kraftugur swayed, his expression mildly astonished as he tried to gasp. Then he collapsed across Herrad's body. The dagger fell from Herrad's nerveless grasp with a sudden musical clatter.

And then Herrad passed out of life with a laugh gurgling in his throat and a wide grin overspreading his wizened countenance. He had died on the battlefield as he had wished, and he had not gone into the shadow realm alone.

Mistislaus leapt up from his stool, suddenly noting the rain of blood staining his beloved old cloak and gown. He gaped a moment at Jafnar, who was likewise paralyzed.

"Oh, dear!" Mistislaus whispered. "I suppose we should tell somebody. Ofarir at least will rejoice."

"We'll tell no one!" Jafnar sputtered. "Anyone who looks at this mess will think we did it! Look at you; you have the evidence all over you!"

"My favorite cloak and gown," Mistislaus murmured distractedly. "How am I going to stroll out of here nonchalantly past twenty suspicious Krypplingur? I don't think they'll believe it's pickled beet juice."

"Halloa!" Jafnar whispered suddenly, listening to the murmur of voices and tramping of feet approaching. "It's Hoggvinn coming!"

The murmur of voices rose to a rumble in the hall beyond the screen. Jafnar peered around the edge of the screen. Hoggvinn and Skjoldur approached with an escort of Krypplingur, moving with the haste of bad news recently received. Following close behind was Illmuri. Jafnar's scalp prickled in sudden suspicion. Once a betrayer, always a betrayer.

"Well, we'll just tell him what happened here," Mistislaus said with a sigh of relief. "Hoggvinn and I have been friends since we were knee-high. He'll believe us, Jafnar. We may have our differences of opinion, but our friendship is rock-solid at bottom."

"Stop! Wait a moment!" Jafnar scuttled out to slow their approach to prepare them for what they would find.

"What are you doing here?" Skjoldur demanded with a scowl. "Is that scoundrel Mistislaus here?"

"Yes, and I've got to tell you something—" Jafnar began.

"No time for talk," Hoggvinn said, threatening to walk right over Jafnar unless he stood aside. "The apprentice said he's dying. We've come to pay our last respects. Are you certain he's truly . . ." Hoggvinn's voice died away to a feeble wheeze, and his eyes widened as he beheld the scene of Herrad's carnage. "Who did this? Herrad and Kraftugur both dead? Two more murders? And you, Mistislaus, standing over them covered in blood?"

The Krypplingur crowding around glowered at Mistislaus and drew their weapons.

"Have you ever known me to murder anyone?" Mistislaus demanded angrily. "Is our friendship of such thin fabric as that to you? You know who I am, Hoggvinn, and knowing me as you do, you know I didn't do this!"

"Strange things have been happening," Hoggvinn said. "Perhaps you're angry at me because I've taken Skyla away from you after nearly twenty years of calling her your daughter. It's enough to make a man crazy for vengeance."

"Hah! Vengeance?" Mistislaus roared with an incredulous scowl. "You think I might have killed these two because I was jealous of you?"

"Someone has been doing a lot of killing lately that hasn't made much sense," Hoggvinn retorted. "Senseless killings have to be revenge killings. You thought that by killing enough people you could frighten off the prospects of Skyla's marriage?"

"Oh, bah! You always were a blind fool!" Mistislaus snapped. "Just look and you can see that it was Herrad who killed Kraftugur, and then he died. You see there the dagger that fell from Herrad's hand."

"It could have been placed there," said the voice of Illmuri.

Mistislaus swung around like a wounded bear, astonished by a rear attack. "What, you're turning against me?"

"I've been suspicious since the death of the old tjaldi," Illmuri said. "I went to Ofarir and Kraftugur and told them what I suspected. Together we discovered the truth of who the killer is. Unfortunately, Kraftugur's voice was stilled before he had a chance to speak."

"You young liar," Mistislaus rumbled. "You brought me here to be trapped by them because I know the real truth.

Kraftugur was the murderer. It was Ofarir's doing to have him poison Herrad. They called me here today intending to blame me for Herrad's death as well as the others so I'd be put out of the way."

"I can't believe it of an old friend," Hoggvinn said.

"And I can't believe my own apprentice would try to destroy me," Mistislaus said.

"But I have no choice," Hoggvinn continued. "You were treating Herrad at your own insistence. You had every opportunity to poison him with some slowly working substance."

"Oh, what rubbish!" Mistislaus declared. "You want me out of the way, do you? Are you afraid I'm going to stop the gifting? I can, you know. I have the scroll, Hoggvinn."

"Then you must surrender it. It belongs to me."

"I have it in a safe place, as insurance," Mistislaus said. "Possibly I won't be killed as long as it's hidden."

"Mistislaus, my oldest and dearest friend, why must we quarrel this way?"

Before Mistislaus could sufficiently contain his temper to form an answer, Ofarir came charging into the midst of them, stopping short at the unexpected sight before him. He reeled back a pace, stunned.

"Kraftugur dead—and my father?" His tone was baffled.

"I'm sorry to say the killer is standing here before us," Hoggvinn said. "One I would never have suspected. But jealousy is a potent poison, as potent as the drug he used upon your luckless father."

Ofarir responded with a faint grunt. "So Mistislaus is the killer? He's the one who has terrorized Rangfara? It doesn't surprise me in the least. His apprentice came to me and told me everything."

"What's to tell, you faithless rogue?" Mistislaus demanded, turning his fiery and rolling eye upon Illmuri. "If I were a murderer, I'd get my hands on your throat next. After all I've done for you, this is the way you repay me? Merely to insinuate yourself into Ofarir's vile plan for taking over Rangfara?"

Illmuri only shrugged, keeping well behind Ofarir.

"And you." Mistislaus swung around on Ofarir. "You're the poisoner just as much as Kraftugur. You wanted Herrad out of your way, and you hired Kraftugur to kill him. Jafnar was here. He heard it all; he'll speak for me."

"That's true," Jafnar said. "It was Kraftugur and Ofarir that killed Herrad. And Herrad killed Kraftugur and died the next moment."

"As if we could believe you." Ofarir sneered. "You'd say anything to try to save this old goat's skin, as well as your own."

Skjoldur ventured a brief foray. "Jafnar has always been truthful. And so has Mistislaus. We've known Mistislaus all our lives, Hoggvinn."

"But poor Kraftugur could not have poisoned Herrad and killed Skriftur and Thordis," Hoggvinn said. "A more gentle and harmless fellow I have never met. He wanted nothing more than peace between Skylding and Krypplingur."

"He wanted nothing more than the treasure," Jafnar said. "He's the one who sent Herrad down into the Kjallari looking for it, hoping he'd be killed by the Kellarman and the creatures he created down there with his evil arts. Remember what he did with the vitlaus ones? My own brother was there. He could tell you."

Skjoldur cringed and winced. "Jafnar, I think you've said enough about this matter."

"Whatever the cause of this murder, I am now the chieftain of the Krypplingur," Ofarir said. "As such, I command that the gates of the fortress be closed until this murderer has been properly punished. For all we know, there may be a rebellious faction opposed to the gifting. Their intention must be to keep killing those who are in favor of it until no one is left, perhaps including Skyla herself. We'll lock up these two and search for others."

"Mistislaus, the scroll," Jafnar sputtered as the Krypplingur guards surged forward to seize their captives. "You've got to tell them about the scroll, or I will."

Skjoldur's eyes took on a sheen of terror. "No, no, you can't! Mistislaus, how does he know?"

"Hush!" Mistislaus said furiously. "I'm sworn not to tell anyone, and I won't let you, either!"

"What about Skyla? Don't you care what happens to her?" Jafnar demanded.

"Of course I do, but this is not the time!"

"It's as good as any I've ever seen!" Jafnar retorted, struggling against the iron grip of the Krypplingur.

"Let him speak, if he thinks we need to hear," Ofarir said.

"If it involves my daughter, I want to hear it," Hoggvinn added.

"Skyla's not your daughter," Jafnar said. "Your daughter's birth scroll describes her as having a deformed left foot and a mark on her left brow. Skyla isn't marked like that. She doesn't have a deformed foot. She isn't your daughter. The Viturkona infant died shortly after it was taken away from its mother. It was sickly to start with. So Mistislaus and my father obtained another orphan from some scraelings, and no one was the wiser until I read the birth scroll."

Hoggvinn reeled back, his face blanched. Ofarir stared at Jafnar a moment, digesting the information. Then his weaselish little eyes flickered over Mistislaus, Skjoldur, and Hoggvinn. "You were trying to pass off a fake daughter on me," he said.

Hoggvinn passed one trembling hand over his brow. "I didn't know," he said. "Believe me, it was no plan of mine. I assumed Mistislaus had been keeping the child well hidden. I never planned to reveal her parentage, thinking I would have sons to inherit my seat, but my children all died. And now Skyla." He shook his head, his fondest hopes all dead.

"We have been tricked, murdered, and lied to," Ofarir said.

"I had nothing to do with the murders," Hoggvinn said. "Besides, I lost my own brother and Skriftur, and an attempt was made upon Skjoldur and upon me, so you can't blame Skyldings for all the murders."

"And you Krypplingur didn't come here with strictly peaceful intentions," Jafnar said. "You came for the treasure, and if you had to marry Hoggvinn's daughter to get it, you'd do it. And then you planned to destroy all the Skyldings to ensure no retaliation. I am a prophet. I have seen other strands on the Web of Life, so I know full well what you intend to do."

"Bah on your prophecies," Ofarir said. "You said that I would be killed by Skyla, and you can see that it hasn't happened. Nor will it happen now that you have told us she isn't Hoggvinn's daughter."

"Then the gifting is off," Jafnar said.

"Not so," Ofarir said with a grin. "We must trap the haughty Viturkonur in their deception. The gifting will take place. Tomorrow, when Fantur and Kanina marry in the sky." He turned away after a last satisfied look at Herrad lying dead. Striding into the main hall as if he owned it already, he commenced giving his men directions for surrounding and securing the Hall of Stars. "If anyone is so bold as to oppose us, kill them. And place these prisoners in confinement," he added, indicating Hoggvinn, Skjoldur, Mistislaus, and Jafnar.

CHAPTER
TWENTY-TWO

"SOMETHING IS WRONG," Skyla said, looking out the arrow slit in her room, which had once been Logregla's. She had a good view of the front gate to the Hall of Stars. It was not a window she liked looking out of anymore, not since the two Kryppling guards had been killed and hung up like trussed chickens.

Logregla and Alvara bracketed her small hearth, drawing a bit of heat from the bed of whitening coals.

"Nothing is wrong," Alvara said.

Skyla watched the increasing numbers of Krypplingur passing to and fro through the courtyard. The gates were closed, but that was usual. It was not so common to see such activity among the Krypplingur during the daylight hours, when they were usually rather like somnambulant buffalo, dozing in the shade and waiting for nightfall. They used to have some good long roistering evenings with Hoggvinn and his retainers, a custom that had fallen off of late because of the rash of murders and the general aura of fear that ruled the night streets.

"She's waiting to see when young Jafnar Skjoldursson is coming out again," Logregla said slyly, holding her favorite white cat in the crook of her arm and caressing it.

"Jafnar is a friend," Skyla said. "But isn't it rather strange to you that he hasn't gone out the gate yet? I saw him with a group of men going around to the back, and they haven't come out yet."

"Don't fret over him," Logregla said. "He's not worth a moment's thought. You should be thinking about your gifting to Ofarir. Aren't you the least bit ... nervous?"

"I don't think about it," Skyla said.

Logregla cackled and threw Alvara a conspiratorial glance.

"I've never seen a Kryppling child. I wonder if they look like their fathers—hump-shouldered, dark, and hairy. I do hope it won't be picked on by the other children in the nursery."

"It may try to kill them," Alvara said. "You might have to keep it chained to a wall somewhere."

"It isn't going to happen," Skyla continued, keeping her eyes upon the courtyard below.

"Why do you say that, my dear?" Alvara questioned with a cold little smile and a slight frown.

"Just a feeling," Skyla said. "A storm cloud is gathering over Rangfara."

The sky, however, was perfectly clear, except for the perennial clouds of mist that hovered on the distant mountaintops.

The heavy tramp of boots signaled the approach of the men. Logregla arose and led the way into the common hall, which was occupied by the Drottningur and a riotous contingent of their children and nannies. At the sight of Ofarir and his attendants, the children ran and hid, with a few muffled shrieks of terror.

"Herrad is dead," Ofarir announced with a grin. "I am now the chieftain of the Krypplingur clan." An excited murmur rippled through the hall. "He was, I am regretful to announce, poisoned to death by a treacherous fiend. Likewise, our beloved Kraftugur has met a horrible death at the hands of this murderer, so our hearts are now twice grieved. But be of good cheer. The killer and his cohorts have been captured and are awaiting judgment. Perhaps now the streets of Rangfara will be safe for our ladies to walk again."

"Who was it? Who was it?"

"It was none other than the wizard Mistislaus, jealous and angry because his daughter was taken away from him. He thought to stop the gifting by these murders."

"Mistislaus!" Skyla murmured.

"You need not be alarmed by the coming events, my dear ladies. Unfortunately, we may have some difficulties with some stubborn Skyldings who are still opposed to the gifting. Until I deem it safe, we require you to stay within the walls of the Hall of Stars, where you will be guarded well against the ill tempers of foolish men."

"I don't like the sound of this," Alvara said. "Is there going to be a battle?"

"There might be, but you are in the safest place possible," Ofarir said.

"And my sister Viturkonur in their tents beyond the walls?"

"They will be taken care of," Ofarir said with an involuntary grimace. "Never fear. Now, then, since we have mourning to attend to, I've called the first of the feasts for tonight, and you are invited to be in attendance. My father would have wanted us to celebrate, and so we shall. A small and modest feast for his grieving friends and relatives."

Alvara threw down the inconsequential bauble she had been pretending to work at. "Herrad and Kraftugur both dead?" she murmured with a frown.

"The last victims of the Rangfara killer, I certainly hope," Ofarir said.

"Fool!" Alvara muttered to herself.

In the Kryppling tradition, the feast commenced at midnight. Skyla was escorted into the hall by Alvara, who always hovered beside her as watchfully as an eagle. It seemed there were more Krypplingur guards each time she came to the main hall. This night she saw no Skyldings except her father and Skjoldur, who sat far away down the line of twenty or so Krypplingur retainers and minor chieftains of diminishing importance. Skyla and Alvara were seated near them—no slight was intended, Skyla told herself, but an uneasy feather of fear was tickling the back of her neck. Ofarir sat at the head of the table in Hoggvinn's customary place, in the great carved chair blackened by age and grease and the polishing of many hands. Skyla frowned; perhaps it was just a gesture of honor or condolence for the death of Herrad, not a permanent arrangement. The sight of Ofarir in that chair was not comforting.

"As you know, I have a certain announcement to make tonight," Ofarir said, standing up and making a sign that somewhat subdued the sound of clashing knives and the massive chomping of jaws and other uncouth accompaniments to the meal. "My father is now dead, so I have become chieftain of the Kryppling clan. He was a good Kryppling, ever fierce in battle and merciless to his enemies. He might have lived longer had he not come to Rangfara to make peace with our old enemies the Skyldings, which only proves that making peace is often as perilous as making war. As a result, my father is now dead at the hand of a foul poisoner, who is captured, I am happy to say, and awaiting our judgment."

"It was not Mistislaus." Skyla's voice rang out clear and sweet in the gloomy hall, silencing the rumble of men's voices.

She rose to her feet, a pale slender flame in a dark place, sending her flashing gaze down the length of the table at Ofarir.

"Hear, hear," Hoggvinn murmured rather faintly. "Sit down, my dear, and hear the rest of his speech."

"Thank you for your loyal defense of your old mentor," Ofarir said, his grin widening a notch. "It seems there is nothing to stand in the way of the gifting now. We regret that so many have died at the hand of this killer, but as our Krypplingur forefathers have taught us, better them than us."

The Krypplingur all chuckled and rapped their knife handles on the table. It was one of the few and ancient Krypplingur jokes, one that never went out of style.

"As I was going to say, nothing now remains in the way of the gifting between the daughter of Hoggvinn and my own worthy self, so we have determined to hasten the marriage. It will take place at once, at the conjoining of Fantur and Kanina. We are indebted to the Viturkonur for arranging such a match, and they will be suitably compensated for all their planning." Ofarir shot Alvara a calculating glance. "We also wish to make note of the death of our friend and benefactor Kraftugur, who labored so long to bring about this union of Kryppling and Skylding, who was also cut down by the fell assassin's ruthless hand, in the very act of offering aid and comfort to my dying father."

At that moment a Kryppling guard strode into the hall with a lumbering clatter of his ponderous armor and weapons.

"Sorry to intrude," he said gruffly, making a brief salute in Ofarir's direction. "Mistislaus and the youth have escaped from the spring house, with the aid of the Skjoldurssons."

Ofarir leaned on his knuckles on the table and scowled portentously.

"They're no sons of mine from henceforth," Skjoldur said hastily. "Bad blood always plays false. I've had nothing but heartache and bad luck with them."

Ofarir waved his hand for silence. "Call out every man we can spare from guard duty and scour Rangfara from end to end. Just when I begin to believe we may be safe again, this foul creature escapes. I have no doubt he's plotting his next murder at this very moment."

Skyla started to get to her feet again, eyes flashing, but Alvara gripped her wrist with one strong hand and whispered, "This is not the time or the place to defend him. Let a bit of time run out and see what happens next."

"I want Mistislaus and the Skjoldurssons captured," Ofarir went on. "Put them in the charnel pit, alive. It will be a suitable recompense for the death of my father and eleven good men."

Ofarir recommenced his fatuous speech, boasting of Kryppling courage, but Skyla did not hear a word. The dangerous roaring sound was in the back of her head, but she struggled to resist it, drawing what comfort she could from the news that Mistislaus and Jafnar had escaped. They would go to a safe place somewhere, she told herself. Mistislaus was not stupid; when the entire Kryppling clan turned against him, he wouldn't dawdle around trying to reason with them. Even now he was probably miles from Rangfara. She uttered a desolate little sigh as her eye traveled hopefully around the table. No, there was no one who dared or cared to get involved in her plight. Logregla sat like a frightened lump; Hoggvinn refused to look at her. Skjoldur never stirred a hair without Hoggvinn's specific approval. She was a doomed sacrifice.

When the Krypplingur had satisfied their hunger and thirst, they got up and wandered away from the table, until only Ofarir, Hoggvinn, Skjoldur, Logregla, Alvara, and Skyla were left.

"Enough of this twaddle," Alvara said suddenly, rising to her feet. "You're prating about the nobility of the Kryppling clan, your kindness and generosity, while outside something peculiar is happening. I've been watching all day. All the Skyldings are being thrown out of the Hall of Stars, and all the Krypplingur are moving in. Are we soon to be in the midst of a battle, Ofarir?"

Ofarir smirked and wiped his greasy fingers on his shirt. "Well spoken, my dear Viturkonur sister. You are clever enough to know what you are seeing. Yes, it appears that relations are deteriorating."

"Through no fault of ours," Hoggvinn retorted.

"And you would have been content to marry this girl off to us on the pretense that she is your daughter. No doubt the Viturkonur gladly went along with your farce, pretending to be friends and allies of the Krypplingur. All the while you knew you were lying, trying to trick the Krypplingur. It would not have worked for long once that cursed scroll reappeared. Using an innocent girl as your pawn was a masterful move, since you truly were risking nothing."

"Pretense? What do you mean?" Alvara demanded.

"This girl is not Hoggvinn's daughter," Ofarir said with a sly grin, "and you know it better than I do. Skjoldur, you can tell her all you know. I urge you not to be stubborn. You are, after all, a prisoner in my hall."

"The true child of Hoggvinn and Reykja is long dead," Skjoldur said reluctantly. "It was a sickly little thing and perished soon after we took it from its mother. We obtained a child stolen by the scraelings, and it luckily prospered and became Skyla."

"Another Viturkonur killed at your hand!" Alvara cried. "I'm glad Thordis isn't here to learn this treachery!"

"How could she not have known?" Skjoldur retorted in a sudden spate of temper. "The Viturkonur child had a deformity of its left foot. How many times have you observed Skyla's feet at the bathhouse? Is there any deformity? Thordis knew, and she said nothing. All she cared about was her revenge and a share of the Skylding treasure!"

Skyla leapt to her feet. "Not one of you cared what happened to me! You were just using me! I'm nothing to any of you here, so why don't you just let me go back into the street, where I belong?"

Alvara swiftly regained her aplomb. "You're safer here, child. Now sit down and be silent. I have a feeling the streets are going to get very dangerous in a short while. Skylding and Kryppling have lost their only chance for peace."

Ofarir grinned, his eyes darting from Hoggvinn to Alvara. "It's ugly enough in here now that we know people are playing a deadly game with false markers."

"I never knew it," Hoggvinn said, looking from Alvara to Ofarir. "I thought she was my daughter. I thought your offers of peace were genuine."

"You are a fool!" Ofarir said. "A worse fool than I thought if you truly didn't know the girl was not your daughter. It's a wretched man whose friends make a fool of him before his enemies do."

"Living or dead, that Viturkonur child has been your ruination, as it was foretold," Logregla said grimly, her eye sparkling with triumph. "You should have listened to those who told you to kill her."

Hoggvinn scowled, laboring under a load of unwelcome truth. "As my luck would have it, she did die, but my friends resurrected her and the promise of the destruction she would bring. Not even my own flesh and blood, yet she will destroy me."

"It's not her fault," Skjoldur said. "It's my fault. I knew, and Mistislaus knew, but we had sworn to each other never to speak. We never dreamed the child would one day assume such importance."

"I am not the child, and I am glad," Skyla said. "I may be homeless and nameless, but at least I'm not going to be a sacrifice. I turn my back on all of you. You're nothing but a pack of wild dogs fighting over a bone, and the bone is that cursed treasure. How I've learned to hate it, seeing it behind everyone's eyes who comes into this hall. Hoggvinn, there are only two men who value you as a friend. All these others want nothing but your gold. Mistislaus and Skjoldur are worth more to you than all the blood-bought treasure you and your ancestors have hoarded up all these years."

Hoggvinn sank into his chair. "I never liked the idea of mixing the blood of Skylding and Kryppling anyplace else but the battlefield. I suppose it's come down to nothing but a fight for the treasure now."

"Correct," Ofarir said. "We've got you and the Hall of Stars and the Drottningur and the tjaldi of the Viturkonur. Considering the state of neglect your fighting men seem to be in, I think we have a pretty good chance of winning. No one can assault the Hall of Stars and expect to get through. We have ample provisions in case of a siege. We have knowledge of the fine arts of torture. I don't see how we can lose, do you? But you could spare the destruction of your clan if you would just hand over the treasure, and we'll be on our way."

"We shall have to talk about it further," Hoggvinn said. "Under different conditions."

"What about the Viturkonur?" Alvara demanded. "You surely don't think you're going to cut us out after we provided the girl, do you?"

"The girl you provided was not Hoggvinn's daughter," Ofarir said, glaring at her with reddening eyes. "You thought you were playing both ends against the middle, the clever Viturkonur deceiving both the Krypplingur and the Skyldingur. You've outwitted yourselves this time. You won't see as much as one gold coin from that treasure. Our truce is at an end."

"Very well," Alvara said coldly. "All this might have come out very differently if your father hadn't murdered Kraftugur. He will not go unavenged, even though his killer is now dead."

"Kraftugur! The unworthy suitor?" Ofarir sneered. "He wasted no love on the Viturkonur after you tossed him away like an old boot."

"So it was meant to seem," Alvara said with a wintery smile. "Kraftugur has been an old friend for many years. Luckily he has left behind his handiwork in the Kjallari. Anyone who goes down there will be killed. See if you dare search for that treasure!"

"You thought to get rid of us?" Ofarir demanded with a short, nasty bark of mirth. "And take all the treasure for yourselves? What ambitious women you are! How did you think you could do it? Now that Kraftugur is dead, you'll never get it, either."

"Never mind," Alvara said. "You may find out for yourselves even yet. I've seen sicker dogs than this get well. Now, what I recommend is that everyone sit down and stop shouting and let's finish our supper. It will be our last meal together under the pretenses of friendship. I suppose tomorrow some of us will be locked up in dark, unhealthy places. Some of us may even be dead."

"Dead, indeed," Ofarir said, lifting his cup. "To all my treacherous friends. May your blood run in the streets before the rise of Fantur."

"The same to you," Alvara said, raising her horn.

It seemed a reasonable suggestion. Skyla could touch nothing, nor could Hoggvinn and Skjoldur find any appetite for anything but copious amounts of ale. Ofarir alone was in high spirits, eating and guzzling with gusto and regaling his reluctant audience with gory tales of Kryppling slaughter.

A cold wind rippled through the hall, flattening the lamps and candle flames. Suddenly it went completely dark in the hall, all light extinguished. Skyla felt something touch her cheek that felt like a cold, dank hand or like the damp nose of a dog. She gasped in fright, and Hoggvinn's hand closed comfortingly over hers. "Don't be afraid," he whispered. "I won't let anything happen to you. You're my daughter still, even though we're not kin."

Darkness was scant inconvenience to Krypplingur, who were long accustomed to nightfaring, but Ofarir grumbled anyway and sent up the call for the firebuilder. Things were knocked off the table, and someone upset a bench. Someone made a retching, choking sound, as if the dinner had taken exception to his constitution.

"Here, I'll start it," Skjoldur's voice said nervously in the dark. "I've got flint and tinder . . ."

In a moment the light returned, and the other lights were relit. Logregla suddenly opened her mouth and screamed, pointing toward Ofarir's end of the table.

He had fallen forward on the table, and a spreading pool of blood polluted his plate and mingled with the spilled ale. One hand clawed in a feeble pretense of escape, and he uttered choking sounds. In a sudden convulsive movement he flung himself back in his chair, mouth agape, eyes fixed wide in an expression of desperate horror. The great wound in his throat spewed a mixture of wind and blood. Logregla screamed piercingly.

"Now who's got the upper hand, Kryppling?" Alvara called.

"He's dying!" Hoggvinn said with a note of elation. "Skjoldur, take the women out of here. It won't take long before he's finished, and then we'll be done with Krypplingur forever!"

Alvara seized Skyla by the arm and dragged her forward. "I don't think you're finished quite yet, my friends. The Krypplingur yet have their main duty to perform, and they must have their chieftain to lead them. Skyla, come with me. Remember what you know about the shadow realm. An exchange must be made if we are to bring something back."

"No, I refuse!" Skyla retorted, trying to break away. "Ofarir deserves to stay dead! I won't do this hideous thing for you!"

"You cannot refuse," Alvara said, "unless you want to see all your friends here die before your eyes. Logregla!" She added the words of a transformation spell.

With a despairing cry, Logregla's form was shifted to that of a lynx. The creature retreated to the shadows, baring its teeth in a vicious snarl.

"She will do what I tell her," Alvara said coldly. "I can't believe that you wish to see Hoggvinn and Skjoldur with their throats torn out. They have been very kind to you for you to repay them with such a fate. Now, come along and use your skill before it is too late."

Skyla approached the struggling form of Ofarir, her slender form rigid, her features pale as cold stone. Chanting softly, she closed the wound with her fingers, not minding the blood smearing her gown and cloak. The gaping wound became a purple scar, and Ofarir's dying sputters became gasps for air.

"Skyla! No!" Hoggvinn exclaimed, springing after her. "Don't bring this creature back!"

The lynx surged forward with an angry yowl, and he retreated, pressing his back to the wall. Alvara called the lynx back.

"I don't think you want to end it this way," she said with an evil little smile. "Be sensible, Hoggvinn."

"Sensible, when you're about to take everything I have from me?" he demanded. "Even the daughter I thought I had?"

"I can see him," Skyla said, as if from a great distance, and her eyes were clear as glass. "He is coming closer."

"You are not one of these witches," Hoggvinn said sharply. "You are clean of their vile magic! It's wrong to call anyone from the realm of Hela once they are dead!"

"I must try," Skyla whispered. "There is no higher calling than to thwart the curse of death!"

Skyla resumed her chanting and crooning. Alvara touched her tentatively on the shoulder and was ignored, so she hovered nearby, listening intently to the words Skyla used.

With a strange whimpering cry, Ofarir slumped forward on the table. The gushing of blood was halted, and his body went slack. Skyla continued her calling, making signs of the runes in the air over him.

Then the body flung itself back in the chair, and the eyes opened slowly, not with the glazed stare of the dead but with calculating life behind them. Slowly Ofarir raised his hands, looked at them a moment, then gingerly felt at his neck, where the wound was now closed and beaded with drying blood.

"Kraftugur, my friend," Alvara said. "Are you back with us? Are you well?"

"I'm as well as can be expected," he croaked with a ghost of a chuckle.

"Kraftugur? He was dead!" Skjoldur whispered. "No man comes back from the shadow realm!"

"Not without help, he doesn't come back," the revenant croaked, his voice strained and hoarse from the recent ravaging of his throat.

"It's only a draug," Hoggvinn retorted. "Don't listen to him! He wants only to destroy us because we're living!"

"Nonsense," Kraftugur's voice said. "I am as alive as you. Watch; this will prove it."

He reached out slowly for a horn of ale and lifted it to his lips. Suddenly something seemed to seize hold of him, shaking him as a dog would shake a rat and sending the ale horn and several trenchers flying in a spray of ale and food.

"Fools! Idiots!" he snarled in a grating voice, his hands clawing the edge of the table. "Why are you sitting here? The killer is in our midst!" Then he went slack again, slumping forward onto the table like a sack of grain and making the groaning noise of a dying man.

"What have you done?" Alvara demanded, pulling Skyla out of the way. "Something isn't right with him! You didn't make a clean exchange! Both of them are in there!"

"Save me!" Ofarir whispered, struggling upright again and looking around the room wildly. "The killer is in the room! I saw the teeth, the claws—a black lynx! These women—" He shook himself convulsively, and his expression changed to one of rage, and he roared in an astonishing bellow, "It's Mistislaus you're after, you goggling idiots! Get into the Kjallari and search for him! He's our killer! He's the snow lynx, death cat, stalker of Krypplingur hearts and livers! Unless you capture him, it's your hearts and livers he'll be eating next! He was the one who put out the lights and tore out my throat in an instant! Then out the window, laughing at the clumsy Krypplingur all the while!"

It was the voice of Kraftugur that spoke, and Kraftugur's cold hatred gleamed in his eyes.

"What is happening?" Hoggvinn demanded, looking toward a window, where a sudden glare of firelight danced in the dark, accompanied by a chorus of shouting and shrieking. "What are you doing to my city?"

"It is yours no longer," Kraftugur's voice grated, his face a snarling mask of hatred. "It belongs to the Krypplingur now, and the Krypplingur belong to me. I think I shall send them into the Kjallari to search for the treasure. That will eliminate a great many of them very quickly when they run into the Kellarman and his legions."

"No! Not my warriors!" the strangled voice of Ofarir answered, suddenly contorting his face with a furious expression. "You sent my father down there to die!"

"Silence!" Kraftugur said.

"Can't we make a bargain?" Ofarir whimpered.

"I've made my last bargain with Krypplingur!" Kraftugur snarled. "Treacherous dogs! Now you are mine! And you," he added, turning to Hoggvinn, "will tell me where the treasure is if you wish to live."

"I demand that you release us, Kraftugur," Hoggvinn said. "I'm willing to forgive this temporary insanity, since you were recently murdered, but we did nothing to wrong you. How can you hold us here as if we were nothing but hostages and prisoners?"

Kraftugur twitched like a fish on a hook a moment, then managed a shrug. "Hostages and prisoners is what you are," he said with an evil laugh. "What we came here for was the treasure and revenge for Reykja."

"Ofarir! Can you hear me? Muster your courage and roust that demon! I was ready to give you all I had: my daughter, the chieftain's seat, and one day the treasure you covet. Why, now, do you want to go to war?"

The voice of Kraftugur replied. "A wife is a nuisance, useless baggage to a warrior clan, and what good is a city to warfaring men? What do they care for streets and markets and little gardens? The whole clan of Skyldings is a pack of useless old men and even more useless young men who scarcely know one end of a sword from the other. The only thing of any use in all of Rangfara is the treasure. Surrender it and you shall have everything else back and we shall leave."

"Prisoners, in my own hall?" Hoggvinn demanded. "Where are my Skyldings? What have you done with them?"

"They've been put out, and the doors locked," Kraftugur said with a grin. "There's no one here but you and us. But you're the one who knows where the treasure is, so we don't really need them, do we? I can see a great battle as the loyal Skyldings come to the rescue of their chieftain and his daughter. But the fearless Krypplingur will destroy them all, to the last man. Rangfara will be a waste place, and no Skylding will survive. Is that what you want? I am prepared to cut your throat if you won't tell me where the treasure is and to spend the rest of my life taking Rangfara apart stone by stone. Besides that, we have all the lovely Drottningur held captive here as well. I'm certain you wouldn't want to see their beauty marred. No one else need know about this shameful debacle, Hoggvinn. You can end it easily and quickly, and the Krypplingur will be swiftly disposed of. Your name and reputation will be saved."

Hoggvinn gripped the edge of the table. His face alternately flamed with humiliation and frozen with white rage.

"I am besieged by enemies within and without," Hoggvinn declared, his shoulders sagging. "There is no deliverance. You shall have the treasure. I must save my clan and the Drottningur from destruction. I am a doomed man."

"You always were," Kraftugur said with a thin smile. "Now, my dear ladies," he continued, "we can sit here and resume our pleasant chatting." His hairy lips parted in an ingratiating smile. He didn't seem to notice or be offended by the congealing blood pooled around his place.

"It's good to have you back, my old friend," Alvara said, settling down in her place with a pleased smile. Negligently she shifted Logregla's shape back to human.

Logregla slowly sank back in her chair, fanning her flaming cheeks as if she would faint. Moaning under her breath, she kept her eyes averted from Ofarir's body. Skyla sat as if frozen, her eyes moving from Kraftugur to Alvara.

"I am a curse!" Skyla said, her eyes dark and unseeing. "I am destruction to everyone who comes near me!"

"Don't take it so much to heart," Alvara said soothingly. "It was the purpose for which you were formed. And you have done very well. Skriftur, Vigulf, Thordis, Herrad, and Ofarir: all have died because of you."

Skyla covered her face with her hands.

Kraftugur suddenly stiffened, gasping and twitching as if he were mortally wounded. Ofarir's voice erupted with terrible effort. "I trusted her! No one else but her! She is not yours!"

"Silence!" Kraftugur roared, clenching his fists and foaming at the jaws like a mad creature. Ofarir's voice uttered a last smothered screech.

"Kraftugur," Alvara said cautiously. "Are you quite alright?"

"Of course I'm alright," the grating voice answered. "But you and your little soul shifter have bollixed up the job, Alvara. You didn't get rid of Ofarir." Throwing himself back in his chair jerkily with a savage grimace of pain, he whimpered in a small voice, "Help me! Get out, get out!"

"Back, you sniveling coward!" the voice of Kraftugur roared. "You had your chance, and you ruined it. Now I'll show you how one wizard and a small band of Viturkonur are going to clear the streets of Krypplingur and Skyldingur once and for all!"

Kraftugur lurched to his feet and stood swaying slightly, listing to port and starboard like a drunken man. With a burst of draug energy he heaved the table over on its side and settled himself proprietarily in the chieftain's seat.

"Now, then, you may all go," Kraftugur's voice said, his eye sliding over to Alvara. "By dawn within a day or two the new chieftain of Rangfara will take possession of the chieftain's seat and the chieftain's daughter."

"What need is there for this travesty of a gifting?" Hoggvinn demanded. "This poor girl has nothing to do with our quarrels. Let her go!"

"The Krypplingur and Skyldingur are expecting a gifting," Alvara said with a smile. "What better way to turn them to fighting than to violate the terms of the treaty?"

"This girl must come to no harm!" Hoggvinn flared, closing his hand over Skyla's.

"She won't if she does what she is told," Alvara said. "Now go to your rooms and stay there until you are wanted. You will be guarded."

Kraftugur looked up at the small patch of dark sky showing through the smoke hole in the roof. "May Fantur and Kanina shine down upon the new chieftain of Rangfara!"

CHAPTER
TWENTY-THREE

HOGGVINN STRODE UP and down in his room, with Skjoldur watching dolefully from the shadows.

"They're just going to take my clan, my city, and my daughter!" he exclaimed.

"Skyla is not your daughter," Skjoldur said.

"It doesn't matter. I've adopted her as my daughter, then, if she's not my own flesh. We can't stand by and let this happen, Skjoldur. They'll kill us like sheep unless we fight them. At least then we could die like warriors."

"What can we do?" Skjoldur turned away from the window with a sick expression.

"Lead Rangfara out to fight," Hoggvinn said. "It will be a grand battle and our last. We can slip out, Skjoldur. They're not expecting it. We'll go to the stable and saddle our horses. Two guards at our door is nothing short of an insult. We'll awaken Rangfara for our last great battle."

Kraftugur loitered over his table once his captive guests were no longer suffering in his company. Alvara remained, undisturbed by the congealing pool of Ofarir's blood. Sipping a horn of ale, she relished her position nearly as much as did Kraftugur, who was lolling in the chieftain's chair and watching the stars through the smoke hole.

"It would be an easy thing to make them think the Krypplingur killed Skyla," Alvara said. "A mutilated body flung out on the paving stones, and the Skyldingur will go wild with rage. And we shall be safe here in the hall until they have annihilated themselves."

"Clever Alvara," Kraftugur murmured. "Are you certain she can find that treasure?"

"She has powers she doesn't dream of. She will find it. Is she not a Viturkona?"

"I do despise being a Kryppling. You'll have to find me something else when the fighting is done."

"Whatever you wish. Perhaps you'd like to be Hoggvinn?"

"Too old. I want to be young again. That arrogant Jafnar Skjoldursson—quiet, you dog!" he added to himself when Ofarir set up a pathetic whimpering.

Suddenly a hullabaloo in the courtyard outside raised a clamor of shouting and the pounding of running feet.

A shout echoed off the walls of the Hall of Stars. "Halloa! Come out and fight, you cowardly heap of carrion!"

Kraftugur leapt to his feet and rushed to a window. With a mighty clashing of hooves and flashing of sparks, a massive war-horse and armored rider came plunging to a halt in the center of the courtyard. Behind him came another rider, holding his chieftain's banner snapping in the wind. Others materialized on the walls, waving weapons and cheering mightily.

"If there's a battle to be fought in Rangfara, then let her chieftain strike the first blow! Awaken, Rangfara, and defend yourselves! The enemy is among us! Death to the Krypplingur!" Hoggvinn's words rang out over the courtyard and echoed off the walls. His horse champed his bit menacingly, snorting great steamy gusts into the chilled air, and raked one iron-shod hoof on the stones with a shower of sparks. Behind him Skjoldur sounded a brave second, and his horse answered with a ringing neigh.

A Kryppling battle cry echoed off the walls like the guttural bellow of a mortally wounded beast, swollen by encouraging grunting and chanting from the watching Krypplingur.

"Perhaps Hoggvinn is starting our battle for us," Alvara said. "Impetuous fool."

Kraftugur chuckled. "He is doomed. He will die."

A pair of Krypplingur came pounding into the hall, breathless and eager to announce the challenge of Hoggvinn in the courtyard.

"Never fear, my comrades, I shall meet with him," he said. He drew Ofarir's sword and swung it around in a flashing arc; it was already blood-red from the glow of the fires outside. Then he exchanged the longsword for a tall halberd, which was more suitable for attacking a rider on horseback, and stepped out of the great doors of the Hall of Stars to meet Hoggvinn.

The Skyldings were rioting around the walls, cheering on their chieftain and lighting the scene with a hundred flaring torches.

"So you've come to meet your doom at last," Hoggvinn greeted him.

"There is no doom in my future except yours and your clan's. Let your carcass rot as a warning to everyone," Kraftugur said, striking a slashing blow calculated to disable the snorting war-horse.

As lightly as a dancer, the big horse feinted to one side, and Hoggvinn struck his first blow, resounding off Kraftugur's armor. The watching Skyldings raised a savage bellow of triumph as Kraftugur reeled back a pace.

They fought, the three of them, two men and an expertly trained horse that reared, lunged, and caracoled to defend his rider. The reek of sweat and blood mingled with the stench of the Kjallari. A wicked feint wounded the horse. Rearing and twisting away with a startled squeal, he unseated his rider. Skjoldur plunged forward to defend Hoggvinn, but Kraftugur retreated to a neutral distance until Hoggvinn rose to his feet and waved Skjoldur back.

"This is my seat I'm fighting for," he said, breathing hard. "Leave this battle to a chieftain!"

"We can rest a moment," Kraftugur said, leaning on his sword. "Fatigue makes a warrior sloppy. I should have finished you long ago."

On foot Hoggvinn fought as well as he had on horseback. Then Kraftugur called for another breather. He was wounded, but his wounds did not seem to cause him any discomfort, and the blood that flowed from them was black and sluggish.

The battle recommenced, ringing grimly within the stone walls, cheered on by Skylding and Kryppling shouts. Kraftugur glanced upward at the sky, which now was showing the two stars creeping closer together and the undeniable taint of dawn approaching. With a curse, he battled with the renewed energy of fury and desperation. Then Hoggvinn's sword sailed away in a twinkling arc and fell with a musical clamor. Relentless, Kraftugur surged forward, felling the chieftain with a cowardly and murderous stroke.

"Well, then, that's done," he panted, raising his eyes to the stars. Dawn was turning the black sky to indigo, and the two stars were not yet merged. "Another day, and then I shall be chieftain of Rangfara."

The Krypplingur raised a roar of victory, drowning out Skjoldur's single note of grief as he leapt forward to kneel beside Hoggvinn. The Skyldings raised a terrible wail of grief and rage as the Krypplingur tramped away with Hoggvinn's body flung across the saddle of his war-horse.

Skjoldur followed, steadying the body with one hand. When a Kryppling moved to turn him back with the others, he said, "I go where my chieftain goes. You can burn our bodies together."

The body was not burned or callously thrown out with the midden; it was put into a metal cage and hung at the main gate, on display to taunt the Skyldings and excite the Krypplingur battle lust.

Alvara accompanied the guards who brought breakfast to Skyla and Logregla and the rest of the Drottningur imprisoned in the women's hall. Logregla leaned heavily upon Skyla, heaving with dry, angry sobs. Skyla stroked her hand and held her arm reassuringly, turning a bright and furious glare upon Alvara.

"I thought I already was forced to share my roof with a poisonous serpent," Logregla declared. "But I discovered too late that the serpent was harmless, and the friend I treasured was far more deadly."

"Logregla, you are a fool," Alvara said. "All you empty-headed, idle Drottningur are fools, nothing but useless encumbrances to all who know you. Nasty, trivial creatures, bought and bartered like nothing more than cattle because you belong to a rich clan. I'll warn you, however, you are going to become truly useful for the first time in your lives, and you'd better obey me to perfection or you shall be punished severely. You don't like pain, do you, my dear?"

Logregla squinted apprehensively. "No, of course not. What are you going to make us do?"

"You're going to help me kill Krypplingur when we're finished with them," Alvara said with a faint twisted thread of a smile. "You enjoyed shedding their blood before, didn't you?"

Logregla looked away guiltily. "Then what is going to become of us? When we have destroyed the Krypplingur?"

"If you behave and serve us well, you may stay here and continue as if nothing had happened," Alvara said, tossing her head impatiently. "Rangfara will be our city, with the Skyldingur destroyed by the Krypplingur. Your wealth and power will belong to the Viturkonur. But those of you who are troublesome and persist in asking questions will be made slaves."

Logregla gasped. "I shall ask no more questions, then. Come along, Skyla; let's sit down and eat."

Skyla planted her feet and stared at Alvara. "I think it was you and Kraftugur who killed the old tjaldi so you could take her place."

"Old age replaces courage and daring with common sense and caution," Alvara said. "Some call it wisdom. Whatever you call it, we had no place for it in our plans. Thordis had come to the end of her usefulness to the clan. I hope you are not arriving at the same place, my child. We have a great deal of work to do. I hope you are equal to the task that is expected of you."

"I do not wish to be anyone's slave," Skyla said.

"Good. Then you will cooperate."

"I don't want to stay here. I don't belong here. I wish to go back to Mistislaus."

Alvara replied with great satisfaction, "My dear, that is impossible. You do belong here. You are Hoggvinnsdottir, and you belong to the Viturkona clan until we decide what to do with you."

"No! That scroll is not my scroll. That child is dead." She started away, but Alvara caught her arm.

Alvara smiled, enjoying digging her fingers into Skyla's arm. "The scroll and the child were false. We traded you at birth for the sickly scraeling child, in case Hoggvinn wanted to kill it. As luck would have it, the poor thing died anyway, and Hoggvinn relented. You owe your existence to us, and you must fulfill your purpose. You were given to Mistislaus to raise in poverty and obscurity, waiting for the day we would need you to humble the haughty Skyldings."

"I am Hoggvinnsdottir? Truly?"

"Yes. Hoggvinn's bane, truly."

"Then I have a birth scroll somewhere."

"Of course. Safe in my tent with our clan genealogist. You are the heir to Rangfara. You will be gifted to Kraftugur—Ofarir to the rest of the world—and he will be the chieftain of Rangfara."

"But Kraftugur on the chieftain's seat—he's nothing but a draug."

"No, he was merely exchanged for Ofarir when Ofarir

died—except that you didn't get rid of Ofarir. But never mind—you and I shall attend to it later."

She turned and was gone with a silken whisper of her garments. The guards posted at the door joked and chuckled unpleasantly about being foxes guarding the geese.

"A prisoner in my own hall!" Logregla whimpered, casting herself down on a sleeping platform to begin sobbing, heedless of the growing murmur of frightened voices around her.

The women gathered at the windows, straining to hear what was happening in the courtyard on the other side of the hall.

"It's a battle of some sort!" called someone.

"We are doomed!" Logregla moaned.

"Hush," Skyla said, standing still to think. "We may be prisoners, but we are not helpless. They need us if they are to defeat the Krypplingur."

"I can't believe a handful of old women and one wizard could destroy two clans," Logregla moaned. "Stupidity is to blame. Hoggvinn is a blind a man as ever I've seen. His life was ruined by his tawdry meddling with a Viturkona. Those were the days he had no regard for consequences. Now we will all die because of his arrogance. It's so unfair!"

"It's over! Hoggvinn is dead!" came the cry from outside the window.

Skyla stood still, not breathing. "Kraftugur has killed my father."

Logregla turned very white, but she did not faint or dissolve into weeping. "Hoggvinn! My husband! What will become of us now?"

"I am enough of the Viturkonur to feel the fires of vengeance," Skyla whispered "Come with me. You are the only mother I have ever known. Wife and daughter, we will avenge him."

Bending down, she breathed words of transformation into the keyhole. The lock opened without a sound, its crude parts simply turned to dust that blew away in a fine cloud in the breeze coming down the corridor.

The three guards gaped in astonishment as the door swung open softly. The light of their torch stuck in the wall gleamed in the multitude of eyes awaiting them. A silvery catform leapt forward in an aggressive pose, fur bristling from ears to short tail as the creature opened its jaws in an eerie wail. Her eyes gleamed like twin points of living fire.

The Krypplingur staggered back, gasping faintly in a desperate attempt to sound a warning as a dozen snow lynxes pressed forward into the corridor, ears twitching, lips drawn back in wary snarls.

"Don't make any sudden moves," one of the Krypplingur panted. "Back away slowly. Maybe they won't attack."

The foremost lynx suddenly sprang forward, spitting and hissing like a house cat. With a wild yell, the three Krypplingur whirled around and took to their heels. Several lynxes bounded after them a few strides, but a sharp yowl brought them back. Then, like shadows, the lynxes melted away into the shadows of the gloomy old Hall of Stars.

Kraftugur returned to the hall, still steaming from his battle, and cast himself down in the chieftain's chair. Outside, the Krypplingur were roistering and brawling and working themselves into the proper berserk fury for attacking the Skyldings. Kraftugur downed a horn of ale, then poured himself another, feeling an intolerable thirst that would not be quenched.

With the great doors closed, the ancient hall was almost silent, except for the distant mutter of Kryppling voices in the courtyard. Kraftugur closed his eyes, relishing the power that lapped around him and would soon be augmented by the stars conjoining overhead. In the silence, he heard the soft padding of paws approaching from the corridor. Instantly his hair bristled in alarm, and he twisted around to see what was approaching. Too many Krypplingur had died lately at the teeth and claws of the lynx.

A lynx crouched in the silvery dawn shadows, its eyes fixed upon him with a fiery gleam of hatred.

Kraftugur took a step backward, his glittering eyes darting around feverishly for a weapon, but he had left his sword and halberd beside the doorway, still running with Hoggvinn's blood.

When he turned his eyes back to the lynx after only an instant, she had vanished and Skyla stood there wrapped in a white cloak blackened with soot and dried blood.

"You killed my father," she whispered. "Remember the prophecy of Jafnar Skjoldursson, Kraftugur. You may marry me today, but one day I will drink your blood."

Kraftugur cast another glance at the sword and halberd beside the door. In that interval, Skyla disappeared. He stared at the spot where she had stood, holding his breath and wondering if it had been his imagination, fired from the battle and the killing of Hoggvinn. Rising resolutely to his feet, he strode down the corridor to the women's hall. Three Krypplingur stood there as he had ordered, so stiffly vigilant that they eyes scarcely blinked. Had he checked more closely, he would have seen that they were merely frozen statues with the life driven out of them.

Shrugging his shoulders, Kraftugur turned, went back to his solitary splendor in the main hall, and commenced drinking until he fell asleep. Tomorrow would be his gifting day and the day the stars affirmed him as chieftain of Rangfara. Then he would begin getting rid of Alvara and her tribe of prune-faced old hags.

Jafnar shuddered in the pervasive chill of the Kjallari. The stench of the old well was almost overpowering, reeking of ancient bones and carcasses beneath the black and scummy surface. At one time it had been a hall or court, with pillars carved from the stone to form a gallery around the well, but rubble and offal had covered the paving stones, rendering the stinking pool a fetid swamp.

"Look, there they are," Mistislaus said, pointing upward to the distant opening of the shaft. "The Rogue and the Rabbit stars. It's nearly dawn again—almost time. This time they will merge."

"And I wonder who will be on the chieftain's seat to receive the blessing," Jafnar said.

"We're going to die down here like cowardly rats," Ordvar growled. "We should be up there, fighting to defend Rangfara, instead of being eaten by foul beasties in this reeking pest hole."

"Why didn't the Krypplingur just kill us and be done with it?" Modga moaned.

"Listen!" Einka hissed suddenly, his ears more acute from a lifetime of fleeing bullies. "They're coming! We can't hold them off this time! We're down to two torches!"

A few rocks rattled down the steep winding path to the well, and they heard a faint scratching of claws on stone.

"Listen to me a moment," Mistislaus said gruffly, still scowling. "The time is almost gone for giving advice, but as long as I'm still alive, I'm going to tell you what I can. We're going to be killed and eaten by these creatures of Kraftugur's, but don't be discouraged by this; there are worse things that can happen to a person."

"Such as?" Modga prompted skeptically.

"Living a long and shameful life," Mistislaus retorted, his eye kindling. "Being a liar, a thief, a coward, a hider of the human light. We will die good men, honorable men, fighting for a just cause. There is no shame in that, and there will be no one left to feel any sorrow. The next lifetime we meet, we will try not to make the same mistakes. I should have guarded Skriftur better. I should never have consented to Hoggvinn's deceptive scheme to start with. And let me tell you this, my lads—I don't regret a single one of those pastries or pickled pigs' trotters. Now I go to my death saying that I have truly lived."

"We can fight them!" Ordvar declared in a fever of desperation. "There are seven of us, after all! At least we can seriously reduce their number before we're cut to pieces!"

"We should have defended Skyla better," Jafnar said. "If only—"

"Tut tut! Those are the most pathetic words in human history," Mistislaus said. "We shan't be using them here. We'll admit our defeats, our mistakes, and say our good-byes. I thought we had a good chance at breaking the cycle this time. Who knows what I'll find next time we meet? Shifting on the Web has such a way of juggling everyone around. Who knows? Perhaps we'll succeed. A thousand failures don't mean that success is impossible."

"And one more failure after a thousand isn't going to matter much," Modga said glumly. "I only wish sometime I'd get a real chance at Borgildr."

"Borgildr! Is that all you ever think about?" Jafnar snapped. "She doesn't even know you're alive, and she wouldn't care if she did. You're not rich enough for her."

"This is all your fault, Jafnar," Modga exclaimed. "I knew we had no business rescuing you and Mistislaus! It was that slimy Illmuri who came to us and told us how we could do it and pleaded with us—"

"Illmuri!" Jafnar groaned. "How could you have believed anything he said?"

"He said it was the only way to help," Modga muttered. "He said something about duplicating the past to preserve the future, and we believed him."

"And we're dead," Ordvar added.

"We're not dead yet," Einka snapped. "And Mistislaus

wasn't killed. Isn't that an important change from the usual pattern?"

Mistislaus snorted into his beard. "Yes, I think it's very important. At least it is to me. What I wouldn't give to make it just until those two stars convene!" He stopped at the sound of a mocking laugh from the shadows of the crumbling gallery. The Skjoldurssons, already weary from battling the Kjallari-folk, froze at the appearance of a new threat.

"Mistislaus!" came a hissing voice. "Mistislaus, you've come to see me at last."

"Who's that?" Einka gasped.

Mistislaus peered into the shadows. "The creature you've always known as the Kellarman. It's me he wants."

"Kellarman?" Modga almost laughed. "Are you joking? The Kellarman is nothing but a childhood myth."

"Myth? Watch this, then." Mistislaus strode forward to the edge of the pool, his staff flaring, his cloak billowing. "Kellarman!" he roared. "I am waiting for you! I challenge you to a duel of honor!"

A hulking, horned form appeared on the other side of the pool, almost human but more beastly in configuration.

"I hear you, and I accept your challenge. You are doomed, Mistislaus. Always you are defeated."

"The hearts of the doomed are lightened of earthly cares," Mistislaus said. "How shall we do it this time? Fire? Ice? Poison gases?"

"No magic. No powers. Only words." The Kellarman chuckled again, sweeping his red gaze over the Skjoldurssons. "It seems you have plenty of bargaining chips here. Seven of these, but I always wanted the girl the most, Hoggvinnsdottir. Hoggvinn is dead, did you know?"

"No, I didn't know," Mistislaus said.

"The game is almost over again. Give it up, Mistislaus. You can't win. This time is even worse for you. I'm going to get your soul. And I'm going to get theirs." He turned suddenly toward the Skjoldurssons, who flinched involuntarily. "Didn't I warn you when you were children? Did you think those were nothing but bad dreams? Your fathers and nannies all told you it was nothing, but they lied, you know. I was really there. Children are easily stolen away unless they are guarded well with noxious herbs and stones."

"I don't believe in you!" Einka spit in a voice that trembled. "You're nothing but a bad dream!"

The Kellarman chuckled. "Yes, I know how frightened you always are, Einka. Remember how you used to hold your eider over your head until you could scarcely breathe, hearing me standing right beside your cot? You believed then, my little friend. If you'd doubted a moment and stuck your head out, I would've had you. And you, Modga. Remember how you used to weep into your pillow? Listen to that! Do you remember that sound? Didn't you always hear it at night when you were children?"

The rock around them hissed with rustling sounds, almost like the sound of a herd of sheep pattering over a rocky fell.

"Lost spirits," the Kellarman whispered. "Always looking for other spirits to steal away, like little boats out of their moorings. They're coming for you again. You'll be their wedding feast while Kraftugur celebrates in the Hall of Stars."

"Get away!" Mistislaus commanded, brandishing his staff with a virulent flare of light and smoke. The Kellarman laughed, but he disappeared.

"We mustn't despair," Mistislaus said, breathing hard in the sudden silence. "I shall nourish my courage upon thoughts of what I'd like to do to Illmuri when I get my hands on him again. He pretended to be a son of my own Galdur clan, the treacherous dog, saying he had heard of my fame, begging me to take him in and teach him from my vast store of wisdom. I should have known he was nothing but a flattering snake. My wisdom is not generally sought out much among my own clan. Not sought out at all, if you must know the truth. In fact, I was officially banished once upon a time." He heaved a sigh, rapped his staff upon the stone, and cast a suspicious stare upward. Already the forest of eyes sparkling on the winding trails above was returning. "Well, we must prepare for a fight with Kraftugur's little monsters."

"What are you going to do, iterate them to death?" Jafnar demanded. "I thought I'd die of iteration, but it was from boredom."

The Kellarman's voice returned with a grisly chuckle. "How long can you keep iterating, Mistislaus? When you stop, I'll still be here, waiting. A pity you're going to fail. You're really so close this time. So close, you could touch it. The demented one knows. Thogn, Thogn! I'm going to have you one day soon!"

Thogn moaned, huddled in a ball with his head tucked under his arms and his eyes tightly closed.

"You're a vile and puny apparition," Einka snarled, "to pick on poor Thogn!"

"True, true, the elemental of childhood nightmares is not as fearsome as a storm giant or a mountain giant, but I'm the best that Kraftugur could do," the Kellarman replied. "Don't be deceived, however. I can be quite nasty, as you have seen from our little creations. Kraftugur brought me the bodies and the vitlaus, and I helped him create the Kjallari-folk. Clever little brutes, aren't they?"

A bestial creature suddenly exploded right in their midst, wild-eyed and blotched with fur, snarling and slashing around with razor claws, until the Kellarman banished it with a flick of one bony finger.

"Crude but effective," he chuckled. "Now, Mistislaus, I realize you are all mine, of course, but I'm a gambling man. What are you willing to wager in a battle of wits? Name all the lesser frost giants? The greater storm giants?"

"Naming all those elementals would summon them and cause the destruction of half the earth," Mistislaus retorted.

"Exactly," the Kellarman crooned. "Name them, or shall I take one of the Skjoldurssons now?"

Far above a voice called down, "Halloa, prisoners! I've brought you something to celebrate the wedding with!" A faint bluish light gleamed on the high rim directly above them. The Kellarman uttered a furious squeak and dived out of sight behind a pillar.

"It's Illmuri!" Jafnar growled.

"Bring it down to us yourself!" Mistislaus bellowed back, setting the echoes thundering. "We'll gladly share it and our delightful company with you!"

Illmuri chuckled, and his dark shadow leaned forward. "No thanks. I fear you have plenty of uninvited guests as it is. Look out below; it's heavy."

With that, he dropped a parcel, and it slithered and bounced down the steep side of the cliff, sending hosts of the Kjallari creatures sputtering and scuttling like rats. It landed before them in a cloud of dust. It was stoutly bound up in a leather bag and seemed none the worse for its descent.

"How thoughtful of him to remember us," Einka said.

"It's probably poisoned," Modga said.

"Don't touch it!" the Kellarman hissed, his eyes blazing in the gloom. "Illmuri's a traitor!"

A familiar sweet smell tickled Jafnar's nostrils. "No, it's

plumabrot," he whispered. His mouth began to water, and he could almost taste the sweet and sour flavors of plumabrot. The smell of it alone was making his head feel light.

Jafnar delved into the pouch, discovering five large cakes of the deadly stuff wrapped in fine cloth bedewed with buttons of mold, which signified very good plumabrot, indeed. He licked his fingers. He hadn't eaten much in the past two days, and he realized he was famished.

"Plumabrot!" Jafnar said, and the Kellarman flinched backward. "Plumabrot! Is anyone hungry?"

"This is no time to be thinking of food," Ordvar said.

"Plumabrot, Kellarman!" Jafnar said, stuffing a gooey handful into his mouth. "Do you want some?"

The Kellarman made a gagging sound and flung up his claws. The Kjallari-folk screeched like a flock of disturbed bats and retreated. "No! Get that stuff away! It's awful!"

Jafnar grinned into the gloom at his brothers, relishing the puzzlement and annoyance on their faces. "Plumabrot. Illmuri brought us plumabrot. Illmuri, our clever friend. Our only ally in the Hall of Stars besides Skyla. He alone knows the drastic effect of plumabrot on Skjoldurssons."

"No, no!" the Kellarman screeched. "Don't eat it, you fools! You know you hate it. Remember how your mothers forced you to eat it as children because it was healthy? It gives you spots and makes you itch. It's poisonous! You'll die if you eat it! It's horrible!"

"I take back everything I said about him," Mistislaus said fervently as he divided up the plumabrot. "Kellarman, I'll make you a bargain. Tell us how to end the Viturkona curse and you'll have Kraftugur before the conjunction of Fantur and Kanina. Otherwise, when these lads are full of plumabrot, I'll have them start in on you. They'll have powers, old boy, of life, death, and transformation."

"Kraftugur is an arrogant pig. I'll take him. Throw in Alvara for good measure and it's a done deal."

"And take any of the Krypplingur you can get your hands on," Jafnar added.

The Kellarman shook hands with Mistislaus, taking care to keep his distance from the plumabrot crumbs and juice, which were being spilled around liberally by the Skjoldurssons. They conferred in low voices for a few moments, then the Kellarman retreated into the darkness.

The strange effects of the plumabrot commenced before it

was completely wolfed down. Lofa and Lampi groaned, and Ordvar wiped beads of sweat from his brow.

"I feel sick," Einka said with a giggle. "And I'm seeing stars swirling around."

"Good, good," Mistislaus said impatiently. "Now I want you to join hands and stand around the spring. In the old days this was a holy place for important rituals to repel characters such as the Kellarman. You must chant and you must dance until the stars are conjoined."

"How can we dance when we can scarcely stand up?" Ordvar demanded, with his mouth stuffed and oozing a small purple stream down his chin.

"I just want to go to sleep," Lofa moaned.

"I want to throw up," Lampi added

Staggering, protesting, they formed a circle around the dark pool, swaying slightly on the precarious footing around the water.

"Now what?" Ordvar grumbled, trying to steady himself and gritting his teeth at the urge to scratch.

"Will you be still?" Modga snapped to Thogn, who not only refused to stop his monotonous mumbledy-jumbledy chanting but got even louder. His voice echoed against the walls above them, and he swung his head back and forth to the rhythm with his eyes shut fast.

His grip on Jafnar's hand was like iron. Jafnar shook his head, trying to stop its mad spinning. As always, he bitterly regretted his decision to introduce plumabrot to his stomach. The cavern walls whirled, and the flitting eyes gleaming in the dark performed wonderous maneuvers. He wished he could stop his ears against Thogn's chanting, which struck on his ears like the hammer strokes of Guthrum in his forge. He squeezed his eyes shut, feeling a desperate scream wrenching itself upward from his vitals. His brothers, likewise, lifted up their voices in a wild, howling shout, like a chorus of wolves on the frozen fell.

"This doesn't seem to be working," Mistislaus said, peering around anxiously. "I should've known better than to make a bargain with an elemental. Now he's going to come back on me for payment." He rubbed industriously at the Kellarman's mark on his palm, but it wouldn't come off.

Dimly, through his misery, Jafnar became aware of a source of light. Opening his eyes, he saw something glowing beneath the sludgy surface of the pool. The surface of the water steamed, the light made it clear, and he saw tangles of bones and skulls beneath the surface. And down below, beneath the bones, a mountain of gold objects gleamed with a red, lustrous light. The corruption and carcasses were dispersing like mud melting in clear water, until nothing remained but water as pure as a mountain spring and the gold blazed away with a light that rose from the surface of the water like steam. In clouds it arose, swallowing the darkness until the cavern was as brilliant as noonday. The Kjallari creatures scuttled and shrieked in consternation, dispersing in puffs of dust as the light reached them.

"Brodir!" Thogn's voice said, and Jafnar turned to look at him. The heavy curtain was gone from Thogn's eyes, and he grinned in pure delight, holding up both hands to the light. To Jafnar's amazement, they were as transparent as new leaves with the sun behind them. He warily inspected his own hands, which he had thought were securely clasped by Thogn and Modga, but he found them floating on the air as light and translucent as sunbeams. A quick inspection proved that the rest of him was just as radiant.

Wonderingly, the brothers examined themselves and their surroundings. Everything bathed by the light lost its accustomed solidity and weighty drossness. Jafnar's hand passed through the solid stone wall with no disturbance at all. Turning around, his mouth agape with his discovery, he saw Einka strolling across the surface of the water, looking down at the treasure beneath his feet. Lofa and Lampi were kneeling, reaching through the water to bring up various pieces: a gold cup, a sword, and a breastplate.

"We've reawakened the well," Modga said softly, his head tipped back to watch the golden light brimming to the top of the great pit, where it would spill out into the tunnels and galleries of the Kjallari.

Mistislaus also stood transfixed, holding his staff away from him as if he mistrusted the sudden searing light of his smoky old orb clasped in its tip.

"Mistislaus! What does it mean?" Jafnar gasped, reaching out for his old mentor's sleeve. To his amazement, the fabric disintegrated in his grasp.

"Don't touch me," Mistislaus said, "unless you want to see me cooked. "I'm not yet changed as you are."

"Does this mean we're dead?" Modga asked in a hushed voice.

"It means we have broken the cycle," Thogn answered. "Nor are we yet quite finished, Brodir. Look up."

Looking upward at the black stones of the charnel pit, Jafnar realized that every particle of them was dancing with the light, solid and weighty no longer. He could see beyond them to the surface above, to the halls and houses and stables and streets. The streets were snarled with carts and people trying desperately to flee the fighting; knots of horsemen clashed and fought, leaving the dead and wounded strewn in the streets. He saw the Hall of Stars as clearly as if he were standing before it or inside it; he saw Kraftugur sitting in Hoggvinn's chair like a heap of pollution, with Krypplingur skulking around him, their weapons still running with blood.

"Follow me, Brodir," Thogn said, beckoning and smiling with such perfect peace and calm that Jafnar had no fear. It was as if he had no capacity for fear, or wrath, or hatred any longer.

They all followed Thogn into a corridor of light that went straight into the solid rock of Rangfara.

CHAPTER
TWENTY-FOUR

ANOTHER DISTANT, STRANGLED scream tore through the shadowed stable yards of Rangfara. The Krypplingur in the Hall of Stars ceased their eating and guzzling and quarreling for a moment, glancing around and taking mental inventory of who was present and who might have become the most recent victim of a snow lynx. A serving girl dropped an empty platter and ran away down the dark corridor leading to the scullery.

Kraftugur twitched involuntarily and shot a vicious look at Alvara, who was standing beside the sullen glow of the hearth.

"Don't blame me," she snapped. "It was your intended bride who let them escape." She darted a spiteful glance toward Skyla, who sat alone on the dais of honor in her wedding finery, beside the empty chieftain's seat. The rich red cloth did not lend any color to her marble features, and she did not seem to hear Alvara speak.

"Those are your lynxes running loose," Kraftugur snarled. "Am I intended to be their next prey?"

Alvara's lips twisted slightly, and she averted her face to glare toward the window. "I told you it was Skyla who freed them. With Logregla leading them, I'd say we'd all better look to our own throats and livers."

"I should be afraid of Logregla?" Kraftugur sneered, lurching backward in his chair in a strange convulsion, twisting his head upward to look at the sky through the smoke hole. He sat at the head of the table with his men, but he did not eat. "It's almost time," he gloated. "Fantur is high and strong in the east, and I can see Kanina approaching. When they merge, that seat will be mine." He grinned wolfishly at the empty chair beside Skyla. "I shall then marry Hoggvinnsdottir, and the stars shall make me doubly the chieftain of the Skyldingur. The first thing I shall do as chieftain is have you beheaded." He laughed unpleasantly and turned toward Skyla, who was sitting stiffly on her straight chair, keeping her face turned away from him. "What a lovely queen she'll make, don't you think, my dear Alvara?"

"She looks a little pale," Alvara said. "But who wouldn't be when your husband is nothing but a corpse? Are you going to do something about that rotting smell?"

"Silence! There is no smell!" Kraftugur hissed with a livid glare around the noisy hall.

"There is indeed a smell. Very shortly you'll cease to be much of a chieftain, I fear, when you start falling apart. Or will you have an attendant go behind you sweeping up the fingers and bones and things you lose?"

"Be silent or I shall have your throat cut here and now," Kraftugur spit, gripping the arms of the chieftain's seat. "This chair has been anointed with blood many times, I'm certain, so it won't mind yet another. Is it time yet?" he demanded of the trembling Eadgils, who was standing at the ready with his scrolls and stylus.

Eadgils cocked one eye skyward. "I believe we can begin the preliminary ceremonies," he said. "The reading of the birth scroll, the listing of the dowry and attending treaties and conditions, the signing of the bride scroll—"

"Faugh on all that!" Kraftugur spewed. "Just get to the wedding part! All I care to make certain is that she is mine and she will bear the race of wizard warriors! One son is all that I demand, and that will start it!"

Skyla blanched even whiter. Her eyes were deep pools of shadow, and her hands were clasped in her lap. Elevating her chin, she answered, "I, too, would welcome the opportunity. I say forget the formalities and let the wedding begin."

"How pleasant that she is so eager," Kraftugur said with a fulsome grin. "A pity Hoggvinn is going to miss the wedding of his only daughter. At least we have Skjoldur to appreciate what follows here."

Skjoldur stepped forward, his lips tightly drawn. "Are you not done with this travesty and humiliation?" he demanded, his voice low and tremulous with fury and grief. From the arrow slit where he had stood, he watched the sporadic fighting in the streets and the cage that swung over the gateway to the Hall of Stars, which contained the body of his friend and chieftain. He far preferred Hoggvinn's position to his own. Even the fate of his sons, thrown down into the Kjallari pit to feed the creatures that dwelt there, was better than this.

"You find my service a travesty and a humiliation?" Kraftugur asked. "Good. It is as it should be, for the years of scorn you haughty Skyldings have heaped upon me. How pleasant to see Rangfara humbled at last—once again. Come here and stand beside the bride. You shall take the position of her father. Read the birth scroll but don't dawdle over it."

Skjoldur took Skyla's true birth scroll into his hands, which trembled slightly. He looked at her and said, "All my fealty is now yours, my lady. You are the daughter of my slain chieftain, and I will be your servant to the end of my days."

"Thank you," was all she said, with a slight nod.

At that moment a commotion arose at the front doors of the hall, fifty paces away. The Kryppling guarding the door dragged forward a ragged scavenger woman in a filthy cloak clutching a bundle of firewood in her arms.

"This creature demands to see Skjoldur," announced the Kryppling who attended the door. "She insists upon selling him her firewood, and none other."

"Is this the important sort of work a chief retainer does?" Kraftugur cackled. "Buying firewood from scavenger women?"

Looking down the length of the hall crowded with the stinking Krypplingur and their weapons, Skjoldur felt a sheen of sweat burst out upon his brow. He had no trouble recognizing Solveig, rigged out in her outlandish scavenger attire and darting him that commanding look from under the ragged beak of her hood. He could scarcely imagine why she wished to heap this further humiliation upon him, unless she had a vengeful streak he'd never suspected before.

"We may need every stick of wood we can get," Skjoldur said, "when the Skyldings lay siege to the Hall of Stars. I daresay all she wants is protection for the night from the chaos of the streets."

As he traversed the length of the hall, the Krypplingur jeered and threw bones at him or contemptuously ignored him, as if he were a toothless old dog that could no longer bite. At least Hoggvinn in his gibbet had a slight degree of honor.

"What is it you want, woman?" he demanded roughly. "Don't you know these are perilous times? Take your bundle of sticks and go around to the scullery. The front door is for chieftains and kings and conquerors."

Solveig clasped her hands. "Oh, aye, well I know about kings and conquerors. They come in by the front gate and leave with the midden."

"You're mad," Skjoldur snapped.

"Yes, and you're a coward," she retorted. "Letting Krypplingur eat your chieftain's food and drink your chieftain's ale. I don't believe he'd be happy to know what you were doing in his absence."

"Will you get out of here?" Skjoldur whispered furiously. "Go around to the scullery. They'll take care of you there." He tried to shove her and her bundle out the door, but she planted her feet stubbornly and decided to truly humiliate him.

"And what about my firewood?" she demanded in a loud voice, casting her eye boldly around the hall. "Trying to cheat me out of a fair price, are you? How is a poor old woman to earn a scrap of bread and maybe a warm place to spend the night? The Krypplingur won't deny a poor lone wanderer a bit of comfort, will they? Oh, isn't this lovely? Is there about to be a wedding? Mightn't a worthless old stick of a wood gatherer offer the bride her congratulations? All I have to offer for a gift is this bundle of sticks. Take them and my blessings with you."

She snatched up her bundle and pressed it into Skjoldur's arms. Only then did she seem willing to be propelled toward the door.

"A good use for an old chief retainer who isn't needed anymore," a Krypplingur sniggered around the leg of a roast goose.

Solveig rested her hand briefly upon one stick of polished wood that had been honed and bent to its purpose. Skjoldur's eyes must have deceived him, he thought swiftly, but no, it was indeed his bow, with a new bowstring twisted from Solveig's golden hair. Two perfect arrows, gray fletched, lay beside it, their fatal iron points sharp and deadly.

"Two? Did you think I might miss?" he whispered .

"I hope this wood will warm the new bride and protect her well," Solveig said. "Good night to you, one and all."

Skjoldur counted on the shadows to mask him for the few vital seconds he needed to grasp the bow, drop the firewood, and nock an arrow. His fingers and arms had not forgotten their old craft. He turned to take aim, drawing the bow back until the fibers of wood and string thrummed with a faint cry.

"This is for Hoggvinn! Now let me die a hero!"

The arrow flew straight down the length of the long table, past the noses of startled Krypplingur, and buried itself in the unbeating heart of Kraftugur and the stout wooden seat he leaned against. The Krypplingur surged to their feet with a bellow of rage, reaching for their weapons. For a moment their attention was divided between the pleasant prospect of tearing Skjoldur from limb to limb and the fascinating spectacle of Kraftugur struggling vainly to pull out the arrow. It was completely buried in the ancient wood of the chieftain's seat and would not come out, nor would it break off.

"The stars!" he raged in a fury. Fantur and Kanina were almost merged, and their light shone down upon the empty chieftain's seat beside Skyla. "Fools! Help me! Take me to the chieftain's seat!"

The attention of the Krypplingur focused completely upon their chieftain as he struggled like a fish on a gaff. There was no blood, only a thick black welling of something that smelled of death and corruption. A living man would have perished by then, but he was still glaring and spewing curses at them in a voice that was not Ofarir's.

"Destroy him! He's a draug!" Alvara's voice rang out. "But let no harm come to the girl!"

Skyla leapt to her feet, her eyes fixed upon Skjoldur, who was standing with his next arrow nocked and held half-ready.

"Don't waste your arrow on a Krypplingur!" Her voice carried like a flute over their uproar. "It is my only salvation!"

Skjoldur uttered a sob and took aim, knowing he had to let fly before the Krypplingur reached him or Skyla.

"Skjoldur!" Skyla implored. "Do what you must! You cannot leave me here! We shall meet my father together!"

The arrow left his fingers with a soft whisper of feather and wind. Alvara screamed with fury, a short, sharp sound suddenly choked into silence as a blinding light sliced through the gloomy old hall as cleanly as the flown arrow cut the air. The slender defiant form of Skyla stood drenched in it in the same instant that the arrow passed through her breast and pierced Alvara to the heart. Gasping, Alvara staggered away from the light, but it overtook her and commenced burning her cloak with an acrid, hissing stench. She shrieked once, trapped against the wall by the light, futilely flinging up her arm across her eyes.

Every Kryppling it touched melted away like a puff of smoke, and the rest of them fled from it in terror. Skjoldur leapt behind a post as it approached, then leapt away again as the post before him turned golden and insubstantial as a beam of sunlight, dancing with a haze of dust motes. It seemed as if a long-forgotten doorway opened up in the Hall of Stars directly under the smoke hole where the two stars now shone down as one brilliant beam, conferring their power directly upon the crown of Skyla's fair head. When the golden light lapped up to Kraftugur's feet, he commenced disintegrating into elemental dust even as he continued to struggle against his impaling arrow, shrieking and cursing until the light had devoured him completely, leaving only the chair he had sat in, blazing like a great red ember. Skjoldur's arrow stood alone, quivering triumphantly.

As if that weren't enough for Skjoldur's poor mortal eyes to disbelieve, he saw his own sons standing in a protective half circle around Skyla and Jafnar. To one side stood Mistislaus, holding his staff out, his hair and beard flaming like a salamander. All nine human figures glowed like hot white fire, as did everything the light touched, quickening but not consuming. He scarcely dared to blink his searing eyes, afraid to miss even the briefest instant of the wonder before him. The light traveled like a sumptuous carpet unrolling straight toward the door, through it, and into the courtyard beyond, finding the gateposts where Hoggvinn's body hung on rude display. The cage was gone, and the figure of Hoggvinn stood there restored, still dressed in the garb of war. After a moment he came striding toward the hall, reaching out to shove the glowing door aside and passing straight through it as if it were nothing more than a curtain of mist. Hoggvinn hesitated a moment, looking at his own hand still outstretched and glowing like flame.

Skjoldur's knees gave way, and he collapsed in a kneeling position, speechless, too startled to think about breathing as his chieftain strode into his own hall and stood a moment contemplating the surviving Krypplingur paralyzed against the walls in the shadows. Hoggvinn glared at them a moment, then pointed sternly toward the open door.

"Depart, every one of you, and never let your treacherous faces be seen again in Rangfara," he commanded. "From now on, clan Kryppling will be outcast and despised."

"You're alive!" Skjoldur croaked from his hiding place.

"Yes, and so are you," Hoggvinn said. "My old friend, don't be afraid of me. It's the power of the well and the holy waters. It's all clean now. Join with us and live, Skjoldur." He reached out his hand into the darkness that surrounded Skjoldur and drew him into the light. Fearful at first, Skjoldur felt no heat, only a vital force that awakened every particle of him and dazzled him with the forgotten wisdom of generations of Alfar.

As the two stars crossed paths in the heavens and went their separate ways, the light diminished swiftly and all the solid, mortal objects that had been so animated resumed their customary dull existence.

"It's gone," Jafnar said, his voice choking. He looked around the hall as if seeing it for the first time. "How dark it is now. Will it be back, Mistislaus?"

Mistislaus glanced up at the dwindling stars and at the chieftain's seat. "When summoned, it will return, if you can bear it."

Hoggvinn held Skyla tenderly, with silent tears coursing down his cheeks and losing themselves in his beard. Logregla materialized from the shadows, casting off her bloodied gown and cloak and standing unadorned in her plain white shift, more dignified than she had ever appeared in her most costly splendor. She touched Skyla's hair with her fingertips and was rewarded with a warm, teary smile.

Logregla's sisters also cast off their bloody gowns, flinging them with no uncertain spite into the smoldering hearth.

"It will be your decision," Mistislaus said gruffly. "From now on you're making the pattern, not me, not fate, not the Web of Life. You've broken the cycle of destruction."

Skjoldur felt a tug on his sleeve. Turning, he looked into the wise gray eyes of his eldest son, Thogn.

"Thogn? I have a feeling you'll be silent no longer," Skjoldur said. "You're back to stay?"

"I'll never be silent again," Thogn said with a smile. "I've been a far traveler, and I have a great deal to tell you. And teach you. For Alfar, your powers are seriously neglected." His expression grew stern and pained. "The sword is no exchange for wisdom, and the Skyldings must be taught this lesson once again. There is only one among you fit to be a true teacher, and none of you have ever given him the slightest credence."

Mistislaus hemmed in pleasure, inflating his chest. "Oh, I wouldn't say that, in so many words—" he began.

"Illmuri of the clan Galdur," Thogn said. "Come forward and take your place."

Illmuri came out of the shadows diffidently. "I am but a student myself," he said. "Now that the well is cleansed, I am the least of all students until I learn its mysteries. Skyla is the one who drew me to the search of a thousand lifetimes. The light of the well was always in her. I was nothing but a gray dusty moth drawn to the candle. Now the flame has been found."

Skyla smiled. "My own darkness has gone away. I have a

name, and I know the duty that I was named after. It is my duty to return the Four Powers of life, healing, substance, and death to the scope of mortal mankind. But these are not powers that all people should possess at once. You saw that too much of the power can destroy as easily as too little leads to ignorance."

"And I and my clan have been among the most ignorant," Logregla said with a heavy sigh. She gave her sisters a stern glare. "We need something to do besides sit around prinking and preening. We want real work to do with our hands, something difficult and important."

"The well must be guarded and attended to," Illmuri said. "Someone needs to make it a clean and pleasant place to come and learn. Someone needs to guard it, because there will be evil ones who come thinking to steal what isn't theirs to take. Whoever wishes to protect the well must be willing to fight to defend it."

"We know how to fight," Logregla said, and her sisters nodded grimly.

"But no more lynxes," Hoggvinn said. "No more shape shifting. No more secret murders. Rangfara must become a place free of evil and fear."

"One of the first things we must do is appoint another chief scribe," Jafnar said, looking at Einka, who turned bright pink with pleasure. "And I know just the man. We must chart our new course with care, and we need a good historian to record our every step. This is the new Rangfara, one which has never existed before today. Each day will be a marvel, to shape our own future with our own hands."

"We need to be proud to be Skyldings once more," Lofa said, and Lampi added, "We need a calling of the clan back to Rangfara. We will never again be incapable of defending our clan and city."

"We are Alfar first and foremost," Ordvar said. "Not warmongers or money grubbers. Alfar protect every dayfaring creature from the powers of darkness and chaos and death. We've become far too lazy and careless. We were about to embrace the dark side with this pact with the Krypplingur. It would have destroyed us utterly. We must be more wise and less lazy and greedy."

"I shall be humble forever," Modga said virtuously. "As long as I can have Borgildr for my wife."

"Anything is possible," Mistislaus said.

About the Author

Elizabeth Boyer began planning her writing career during junior high school in her rural Idaho hometown. She read almost anything the Bookmobile brought and learned a great love for nature and wilderness. Science fiction in large quantities led her to Tolkien's writings, which inspired a great curiosity about Scandinavian folklore. Ms. Boyer is Scandinavian by descent and hopes to visit the homeland of her ancestors. She has a B.A. from Brigham Young University at Provo, Utah, in English literature.

After spending several years in the Rocky Mountain wilderness of central Utah, she and her husband now live in Utah's Oquirrh mountains. Sharing their home are two daughters and an assortment of animals. Ms. Boyer enjoys horseback riding, cross-country skiing, and classical music.